SF Books by

DOOM ST
Star Soldier
Bio Weapon
Battle Pod
Cyborg Assault
Planet Wrecker
Star Fortress
Task Force 7 (Novella)

EXTINCTION WARS SERIES:
Assault Troopers
Planet Strike
Star Viking
Fortress Earth

LOST STARSHIP SERIES:
The Lost Starship
The Lost Command
The Lost Destroyer
The Lost Colony
The Lost Patrol
The Lost Planet

Visit VaughnHeppner.com for more information

A.I. Assault

(The A.I. Series 3)

By Vaughn Heppner

Copyright © 2017 by the author.

This book is a work of fiction. Names, characters, places and incidents are either products of the author's imagination or used fictitiously. Any resemblance to actual events, locales or persons, living or dead, is entirely coincidental. All rights reserved. No part of this publication can be reproduced or transmitted in any form or by any means, without permission in writing from the author.

ISBN-13: 978-1546504863
ISBN-10: 1546504869
BISAC: Fiction / Science Fiction / Military

-Prologue-

-1-

Computer Specialist Eli Gomez was a fraud, but he had nerves of steel. He'd needed them this past year. He was going to need them even more in the next few minutes.

Eli glanced both ways down a narrow cybership corridor. It was devoid of people. He pulled out a tiny palm scanner. There was a risk in using it. The *Nathan Graham's* security systems were hellishly effective. Eli hated the mentalist witch, Gloria Sanchez. Like him, she'd been born on Mars. Like him, she was highly trained to use her mind with ruthless efficiency.

Eli grinned uneasily as he switched on the scanner. It sent out tiny pulses, searching for any security traps.

The fraud was of medium height but lean unto the point of frailty. He had narrow features with close-set eyes that burned with intensity. His nose was like a prow, jutting from his face.

Eli would never win any athletic competitions. A childhood of insecurities and bullying had taught him to hone his one true gift: his mind. That had become a lethal instrument in the pursuit of his goals.

According to the palm scanner, the path ahead of him was clear for a short distance.

Tucking away the device, Eli adjusted his jacket and began to saunter down the corridor toward the brain-tap chamber. He was wearing technician's garb, with a heavy belt of specialist tools jangling at his waist.

Eli Gomez belonged to the five hundred Saturn System techs trapped on the *Nathan Graham* when it had simply left the space scaffolding almost a year ago. That had been Eli's second moment of good luck. The first had been getting into the tech union without blowing his cover.

As he sauntered along the narrow corridor, Eli pursed his lips and forced himself to whistle a jaunty tune.

He'd been on the cybership during the harrowing battle with the aliens near the dwarf planet Makemake. Later, he'd endured many indignities as the Old Man's Intelligence people had asked him questions and painstakingly studied his answers. He had passed the interrogations, and later those of the mentalist witch. Afterward, the Old Man had given him a third level security clearance. That had allowed him to work with the strange alien construction robots on the outer hull.

The *Nathan Graham* was presently parked inside MK2, the hollowed-out moon orbiting Makemake way out here in the Kuiper Belt. The captured cybership had been in the moon dock for two months already. The one-hundred-kilometer vessel had taken extensive damage in the matter/antimatter blast that had ended the battle against the AI-run cybership. The alien construction robots were far along in repairing the hideous blast damage.

"You!" a marine shouted sharply.

Eli gave a small start, but otherwise kept sauntering and whistling. He approached the big man whose steroid-enhanced muscles strained against his uniform.

The marine was originally from the Neptune System, from one of the destroyed cloud cities in the ice giant's upper atmosphere. The marine's name didn't matter, although Eli knew it well enough. What did matter was that the marine had grown up in a highly exploitative capitalist system. It had taught the marine the utility and, more importantly, the acceptability of bribes.

This was all part of Eli's plan. He'd gone into hiding two weeks ago. First, he'd engineered a mechanical accident that had killed three other techs. Machinery had gruesomely crushed the three unlucky fools. Eli had been part of their team, and should presumably have been with them during the accident. The crushing had been critical. It had thoroughly mushed and mixed their remains, which seemed to have led to the necessary conclusion.

Eli Gomez of Mars had been scratched from the *Nathan Graham's* manifest of the living. Because he was presumed dead, there was no one searching for him. That had allowed Eli the luxury of slowly but methodically working his way inward toward the giant cybership's center. He'd memorized the *Nathan Graham's* layout a long time ago. He'd also used his skills to avoid detection—until now.

"Stop where you are," the muscled marine said. The man drew a sidearm. It was heavy, a three-shot gyroc pistol, Eli supposed.

Eli did not stop, but continued advancing.

"I'm talking to you, tech!" the marine roared.

"Trouble, Gorky?" a second marine said. The other marine was a sergeant. Gorky the Neptunian was only a corporal.

"No trouble," Gorky said, turning. He pulled the trigger.

A gyroc shell leaped out, hissed, and implanted in the second marine's stomach. The following explosion killed the sergeant, blowing him off his feet and making a bloody mess on the deck plates and nearest bulkhead.

Eli stopped whistling. The fat was in the fire, as the clowns on Earth had told him more than once during his training.

Eli Gomez had fraudulently declared himself a tech specialist. He was good enough, as far as that went. He had many skills, computer teching among them. But he was primarily a GSB agent. The Government Security Bureau was the secret police arm of the Solar League. The league provided the fighting forces for Social Dynamics, a share-the-wealth communistic political system beloved by the masses on Earth, but particularly by their highly motivated leaders.

"Ready?" Eli asked Gorky.

"Da," the big marine said.

Eli kept from rolling his eyes. He didn't care for Russians on Earth or for those that had immigrated to the Neptune System. But he would take what he could get for the mission.

"Let's move," Eli said. "We have to download a memory before anyone misses your sergeant."

Gorky smiled, showing thick teeth. "Follow me. I know the way."

-2-

Eli huffed and puffed, trying to keep up with Gorky. The marine clanked and clattered, having put on a helmet and combat vest and armed himself with a heavier rifle.

Eli resented the marine's easy strength and stamina. Martians were seldom strong due to the low gravity and the strict rations most Martians endured on the Red Planet.

"Should I carry you?" Gorky asked, the insult thrown over his broad shoulder.

"Keep going," Eli panted. "Run if you think we'll need more time."

"You tell me," the marine said.

Eli didn't bother replying. He concentrated on keeping up.

Soon, thankfully, they reached the coveted hatch.

Gorky glanced both ways, seeming more nervous by the second now. "I don't know…" he said slowly. Maybe he'd started rethinking the odds of their getting away with this.

Eli was bent over, breathing hard, with his thin fingers resting on his scrawny thighs. The fear in Gorky's voice grated on him. He shoved upward, using a sleeve to wipe sweat off his face.

"Move aside," Eli snapped.

The marine did so, looking at him with wonder.

Eli understood that his contempt actually mollified the frightened marine. People respected confidence. It was as simple as that.

The GSB knew about the brain-tap machines deep in the captured cybership. Eli knew the secret police leadership desired the machines almost as much as the cybership itself. The legends and half-truths that had already grown around the alien brain tapping...

Eli had spent many careful hours learning everything he could about the process, the machines and the aftereffects on the "tapped" or "thought-pattern enhanced" individuals.

The lock in the hatch clicked. Eli put away his tools-in-trade, twisted the handle and stepped within the fabled chamber.

The simplicity of the room did not shock Eli, although Gorky grunted almost as if in dismay.

There were tables, with big bulky alien-looking machines near each one, and helmets attached by wires. The controls had dials and levers instead of modern consoles. It looked like something from a 19th century mad scientist's secret laboratory.

"Which table should I use?" Gorky asked with childlike simplicity.

Eli pointed at the nearest one. He doubted they had much time to do this. The witch and the Old Man would have installed secret detection devices. But he'd planned for that.

The marine hesitated, worry etched onto his thick features.

"Do you want to be smarter or not?" Eli demanded. That had been the bribe that had turned the slow-witted marine.

"Da," Gorky said. "But..."

"There are no buts," Eli said. "Hop up and I'll get you ready. If you don't do it now...Jon Hawkins will let the Centurion torture you for weeks."

Gorky paled, swaying slightly where he stood. Finally, with a grunt, he advanced toward the nearest table. He set down his weapon, took off his combat helmet and hopped onto the table.

Eli took out a hypo as he followed the man.

"What's that for?" Gorky asked.

"Your weak nerves."

The marine frowned suspiciously.

Eli laughed. "Is the pit of your stomach bunching up?"

"Da. How did you know?"

"I know," Eli said with authority.

Gorky gave it another three seconds' thought. Finally, he said, "Go ahead. Give me shot."

The hypo hissed as Eli injected the easily-manipulated idiot with a death serum. It would be extremely difficult for medical personnel to find the drug later during Gorky's autopsy. That was the second thing that made the specially selected drug so useful.

"Feeling better yet?" Eli asked.

"I feel sleepy."

"Perfect. Let me put the helmet over your head."

"That is how it is done?"

"Don't you remember? I know about the brain-enhancement machines better than Bast Banbeck."

Gorky lay down on the table, yawning.

Eli took a helmet off a machine. It was heavier than it looked. Letting the attached wires trail behind him, he slid the helmet over Gorky's broad head, pushing down.

"Feels tight," Gorky said, his words muffled by the helmet.

"Don't worry about that. Sleep if you want to. This won't hurt at all."

Gorky didn't answer. His big body relaxed on the table, simply going limp.

The extent of his own brilliance hit Eli then, both for reaching this place and the monumental step he was about to take. He was a great GSB agent. He'd also had a run of good luck in getting into the right places at the right times. But Eli wanted more, much more. The problem was that he lacked connections and almost no one appreciated how skillful a skinny boy from Mars had to be in order to climb as high as he had.

He'd studied, asked questions and probably knew more about this chamber and what it did than anyone other than the green-skinned Sacerdote and the mentalist witch.

"Are you ready?" Eli whispered to himself.

With an abrupt turn, he moved toward a different table. He'd learned an incredible amount on his own, and then even more by bribing a marine to get Da Vinci the Neptunian's secret journal for him. Da Vinci had written it in code. That had been the least of Eli's problems. He was as good a code breaker as he was a tech specialist.

Steeling himself, Eli went to the main brain-tap controls. He set them, turning dials and moving levers, listening to the thing hum and clack.

Then, Eli whirled around, hopped onto a table and slid a heavy helmet over his head. He lay down and closed his eyes.

And waited…

This isn't working, he finally realized.

In his mind, he went over the procedure, looking for something he'd forgotten. He—

A strange memory of a ringed terrestrial planet he'd never seen before finally intruded on his thoughts. Eli realized the memory had been trying to bubble to the surface for the last few seconds.

Could this really be working?

Eli reached up for the helmet, thinking to adjust it. Before he could, intense pain burned into his mind. The pain roared like a torrent, gushing with rivers of memories and alien thought patterns. The gush became a flood, and suddenly he could no longer perceive the process.

At that point, he realized he'd forgotten one important point, one safeguard, to limit the extent of the alien thought patterns.

In a mighty effort of will, Eli tore the helmet from his head even as it attempted to download more alien thought patterns into his brain.

It was the last coherent thought and action that Eli Gomez the Martian had. The new thing in his mind grasped the helmet and plunged it back onto his head.

The interruption had broken the flow. Although some of the data had passed—and therefore did not enter Eli's brain—with the helmet in contact with the skull again, more data poured in. Despite the momentary break, the alien thought patterns swept his human identity away like a tidal wave smashing a house. A new persona roared into possession of the frail Martian.

He was the Prince of Ten Worlds: Methlan Rath of Janus House. He perceived through the scattered memories of his new mind that he had been in this place before. He had enemies here, foes who had destroyed him once already. The cipher Eli Gomez had learned about it.

The Prince chuckled to himself. It was a vicious sound. He knew what to do to his enemies.

Removing the helmet, scanning his surroundings, noticing the stink from the corpse on a nearby table, the Prince once more tapped into the memories of Eli Gomez. He perceived the frail Martian's plan, and decided it was rather good. The dead marine would take the fall. If he could escape from this room fast enough and hide in the larger cybership, no would ever know he'd been in this chamber.

Yes. Methlan Rath could now begin to plot in earnest, rewarding those who aided him and cursing those who hindered his progress.

Methlan slid off the table and tottered to the hatch.

He would cause everyone who'd had a hand in his former body's death to rue their existence. They would all learn what it meant to challenge Methlan Rath of Janus House—Jon Hawkins in particular.

PART I
MAKEMAKE

-1-

The dwarf planet Makemake was presently 49 AUs from the distant Sun. The icicle planetoid received next to no sunlight as such. The Sun was a bright star from here, ineffectual except for the ever-present tug of Sol's gravity.

Makemake had roughly two-thirds of Pluto's diameter, although it possessed greater mass. The dwarf planet's surface was mostly composed of methane, ethane and nitrogen ices. Underneath the icy shelf were rock and some metals. The former human occupants of Makemake had machine-chiseled many kilometers of tunnels. According to Gloria Sanchez's sensor teams, the alien robots still down there under the ices—and possibly whatever human servitors they controlled—continued to mine and possibly to build.

The Cybership *Nathan Graham* was inside the Moon MK2. It was Makemake's only moon, which made it different from other Kuiper Belt dwarf planets. MK2 had the surface color of charcoal, making it a much darker object than the reflective dwarf planet.

The captured cybership was one hundred kilometers in diameter. MK2 was a mere 175 kilometers in diameter. Parking the *Nathan Graham* inside the hollowed-out moon had been like parking a huge air-car into a small garage.

The crew had waged an intense battle four months ago against a newly constructed cybership. Fortunately, the giant vessel had only been three-quarters finished. It had boasted plenty of gravitational cannons but not enough hull armor. Jon Hawkins had gambled on a quick-strike interior attack and won. The brand spanking new cybership had ignited in a glorious matter/antimatter explosion. That had taken out the vast enemy missile fleet and most of the gigantic P-Field guarding Makemake. It had also shredded much of the *Nathan Graham,* which had been a little less than two million kilometers away.

The *Nathan Graham* had been in *much* worse shape this time than it had when Jon had first brought it into the Saturn System for repairs.

That's why MK2 had been such a goldmine. It had cost the Black Anvil Regiment a number of marines to clean out the defending robots. And it had taken even longer to figure out the alien construction technology. Thank God, the research team had finally made the breakthrough. And thank Him even more, the team had figured out and installed safeguards into the big building robots.

The moon dock with its robotic construction tech had only been running full tilt for the last six weeks, but what a difference those six weeks had made to the *Nathan Graham.*

Jon had gone so far as to proclaim that they might actually fix the cybership in a few more short months. Shortly thereafter, a mysterious explosion wiped out five entire moon-holds of stored supplies.

The Old Man had gone into overdrive. The Intelligence people combed every corner of the ship and questioned everyone with the remotest possibly of a connection. Nine days later, the Old Man admitted that his people had come up empty. He didn't have a clue as to who had caused the sabotage.

The Centurion—the regiment's new colonel—planned and implemented another sweep of the entire moon, inside and out. It took two weeks and came up as empty as the Old Man's search.

Captain Jon Hawkins presently stood in a conference chamber inside the moon complex. Jon wore a dress uniform because he had a special call to make after this.

The captain was lean and muscular with thick wrists. He had short blond hair and hard blue eyes. He'd grown up in New London Dome on Titan in the Saturn System. He'd been a dome rat as a youth, a gang member and a bone-breaker for those delinquent on their loans. Later, the Black Anvil Regiment had bought him off death row.

Jon had known a rough existence, but it had taught him many useful lessons. He had one critical strength, one power that others often claimed to have but in reality did not. Jon could learn. He could particularly learn from his mistakes. Unfortunately, he had learned far too much during his rather short life because he had made too many mistakes.

He turned, facing the only other occupant in the chamber.

Her name was Gloria Sanchez, a tiny dark-haired waif from Mars. She was a mentalist, pretty but a little too prone to anger. Mentalists were supposed to think like computers, logically and without emotion. Gloria was a large part of the reason why Jon had made it this far.

Gloria tapped her tablet, which lay on the table. "There's no doubt. I've run the analysis five times with meticulous—"

"I don't doubt you," Jon said, interrupting.

She waited.

"It's just…"

"One thing after another," Gloria finished. "I know. That is the way of life. You're going to have to make a choice nevertheless. Luckily, the construction robots are fantastically flexible and programmable. We've also figured out how to program for smaller matter/antimatter drives and gravity control. We actually have many options, if you think about it."

Jon frowned. After months, years, of hard decisions, he'd grown accustomed in this short time to relaxing just a little. He should have known it wouldn't last—couldn't last— given their problems.

"Okay," he said, pulling out a chair, sitting down. "We can use our last stored supplies to repair more of the *Nathan Graham* or we can manufacture a fighting platform with landers and penetration bombs to take out the aliens hiding on Makemake. We're going to need the dwarf planet's ores to get the moon's factories running again."

"Did you forget about the Senda already?"

Jon stared at her. He had forgotten. "Refresh my memory."

Gloria did not have to tap her tablet to reread the data. She could memorize information like nobody's business because of her mentalist training. The ability was almost supernatural, one of the reasons a few people called her a "witch" behind her back.

"A week ago, we detected a strange signal from Senda," she said. "The dwarf planet is presently two hundred and twelve AUs from us. That means the signal was over twenty-nine hours old before we picked it up. In any case, I have given it a seventy-eight percent probability of being cyber-related."

"The alien robots?"

"That is what I said."

Jon chewed on his lower lip and shook his head. "Let's forget about Senda for a second."

"I would not advise you do that. I spoke to Bast Banbeck about the Senda signal. He and I both agree that the main problem is an enemy ship."

"The Senda robots built another cybership this fast?" Jon asked, dismayed.

"Excuse me. I do not mean a one-hundred-kilometer vessel. I mean a regular ship controlled by the cybers."

"The robots."

Gloria shrugged.

"What do you and Bast Banbeck think the robots plan to do with their regular ship?"

"The logical move would be for them to race far enough away to enter hyperdrive. If I were the…robots, I would seek reinforcements."

"We can't let the ship get away, if that's what the robots plan to do."

"Precisely," Gloria said.

Jon drummed his fingers on the table, nodding a moment later. "I doubt you're suggesting we take the *Nathan Graham* to Senda."

"In fact, I am. We should use the remaining supplies to repair the engine, go to Senda and destroy the robots. Afterward, we can return here—"

"No!" Jon said, his features hardening. "The first priority is fixing the *Nathan Graham* one hundred percent. All our power comes from it. That's a quote from Mao Zedong."

"The precise quote is: *Political power grows out of the barrel of a gun.*"

"Same difference," Jon said. "We fix the *Nathan Graham* before we do anything else."

"That leads us to several quandaries. Do we use the last resources—?"

"I know what the problem is," Jon snapped, interrupting.

Gloria waited until some of the grimness of purpose departed the captain's face.

"What good does it do to repair our cybership if five more AI-controlled cyberships enter our star system and eliminate us?" Gloria asked.

"No good, given those conditions," he admitted. "I get your point. We have to do something about Senda." He shrugged. "Why don't we rig the NSN destroyer with new tech, new engines and gravity control? It can lie in wait for any AI ship leaving Senda. When the enemy does that—BAM—the destroyer attacks and eliminates it."

"That could work if we act quickly. The sooner we alter the destroyer, the better the probability it can complete its mission by reaching Senda in time."

"I see now why you said Senda is part of the problem. We need to do everything at once. Hmmm… Let's use some of the robo-builders to refit the destroyer while the others construct the platform, landers and deep bombs."

"You forgot one other item."

Jon blinked at her several times. "And repair the sabotaged moon factories. That will stretch everything pretty thin."

"Our margin for error will be nonexistent," Gloria said.

Jon exhaled, nodding. "We'll have to operate under high alert for a few more weeks."

"The men are already exhausted."

Jon shrugged. "Better a little less sleep than turning into a cyber-zombie because the AIs win. The men know the score. They'll cope."

Gloria opened her mouth to respond, slowly closing it instead without saying anything more.

"The penetration bombs and platform take precedence," Jon said. "Senda is a house of probabilities. We'll play the odds, but not at the expense of failing to get the moon dock running full tilt as soon as possible."

"Logical," Gloria admitted.

"Did it hurt you saying that?"

A small smile played on Gloria's face. She shook her head ever so slightly.

Jon stood abruptly. "I'll have to talk to Ghent."

"You have to talk to the CPS spokesperson first."

"Yeah. I almost forgot. You speak to Ghent then. Get things started. I'll go make my pitch to the Chief Executive. Wish me luck."

"Good luck, Captain. It will dearly help our long-term goal if Uranus System—"

"I know, I know," Jon said, as he headed for the exit.

-2-

Jon cleared his throat as he sat before a comm screen. He sat erectly with his palms on a large, empty desk. Behind him was the regimental flag with a huge black anvil on a red field.

"Three…two…one…go," Bast Banbeck said.

The green-skinned Sacerdote stood to the side, a seven-foot alien giant. He looked like a huge Neanderthal, with a large brown tunic, belt and big holster. He was a high philosopher, a deep thinker and the last known member of his race.

"Greetings," Jon said into the screen at the edge of his desk. "I am Captain Jon Hawkins of the Free Fighting Vessel *Nathan Graham*. It is an honor to speak to the Chief Executive of the Committee for Public Safety, Uranus System."

The Uranus System was presently orbiting on the opposite side of the Sun from Makemake. The dwarf planet was 49 AUs from the Sun, while the space habitat orbiting Uranus was 19.18 AUs from the Sun. That meant the habitat and the moon MK2 were 68.18 AUs from each other. At the speed of light, a message took 9.45 hours to go from one place to the other. Naturally, there could be no back and forth talking between them in real time. Thus, they sent messages, having to wait over 19 hours for the reply to return.

Jon hadn't called before because the Uranus System had been considered to be firmly within the Solar League.

Ever since the *Nathan Graham* had ripped the Saturn System out of the Solar League, the Uranus System government had refrained from sending its taxes to Earth. That had caused friction and resulted in many messages back and forth between Premier J.P. Justinian's office and the Uranus System.

Lately, maybe due to the bloody political purges taking place on Earth, the Uranus System's disquiet had turned into full-scale rebellion. Several days ago, the Uranus System's Committee for Public Safety had been formed, with a Chief Executive speaking for the new government.

Jon wished to bring the Uranus System into the fold. The shattered Neptune System, along with the Saturn System, sided with the *Nathan Graham* against the Solar League. The league controlled the rest of the Solar System, with the exception of the Kuiper Belt and the distant Oort cloud.

If the Uranus System joined the freedom fighters, then the only Outer Planets holdout would be the Jupiter System. Jupiter System was the most powerful of the Outer Planets, meaning that tearing it from the Solar League could prove costly.

"I wish to assure you, Chief Executive," Jon continued, "that despite the bald-faced lies issuing from the Premier's office, the *Nathan Graham* is operating at full efficiency. We have discovered a vast treasure trove of alien technology out here and are presently installing some of it into our vessel. These additions will make the *Nathan Graham* even more formidable than before. You can be sure that the Solar League has no combination of warships that can face us. We are more than willing to enter into a political accord with you. Join us, Chief Executive. Join the Saturn and Neptune Systems in a grand coalition of the free against the oppressive tyranny of the murderous J.P. Justinian. The bizarre antics of Social Dynamism have held us all in thrall for far too long. Humanity yearns for freedom. I look forward to working with you, Chief Executive, and the Committee for Public Safety, as we forge a new era of freedom and plenty for everyone."

Jon stared intently at the screen. "I await your decision, and I wish you and the people of the Uranus System the best. Captain Jon Hawkins speaking."

Bast pressed a switch. The Sacerdote spoke heavily afterward. "The comm is off, Captain."

Jon's shoulders folded inward before he leaned back in his chair and pulled off the tie. "Never could get used to these." He threw the tie onto the desk. "How did I sound?"

"Captain?" the Sacerdote asked.

"Never mind. You're still studying human body language and tones. I'll have to ask Gloria later how she thinks I did."

"If I could," Bast said, "I would like to hear her remarks. It will help me in my understanding of human communication."

"Sure, why not?"

Bast paused before he added, "You seemed confident…"

"Go on," Jon said, side-glancing at the big Sacerdote. "You clearly want to say more."

"If I may, Captain, your pose struck me as artificial."

"That's because you know me. To the Chief Executive and his people I'll look confident and assured."

"Perhaps that is so."

"Was there anything else?"

"You almost seemed nervous. Perhaps the word I'm searching for is anxious. Yes. You seemed anxious for their answer."

Jon sat up. "Maybe I did. You're right. I used the wrong tone at the end. I should have acted…tougher, more like an enforcer. We're trying to woo them to our side. I should have acted more easily confident."

"I realize the political ramifications of the message, of course. Your ways of speaking with them were simply more…subtle than I had anticipated."

"Subtle, huh? So Sacerdotes are blunt?"

"I would deem the word 'direct' or perhaps 'straightforward' as more appropriate."

The captain stood. "I'd love to chat, Bast. But I have work to do, decisions to make. We have to do something about the robots down on Makemake."

"Oh," Bast said. "That reminds me. The Old Man gave me a message for you. He said to tell you after the proposal to the Chief Executive— You just reminded me by your comment. It's from the robots."

"On Makemake?"

"Yes, Captain. It appears they have a proposal for you."

18

-3-

Jon and the Old Man were in the same comm chamber, although Bast Banbeck was no longer present.

The Old Man used to be a sergeant under Colonel Nathan Graham, when the colonel ran the regiment as a mercenary outfit. The Old Man didn't bother much with ranks these days, although technically he was a major.

The Old Man was tall and spare with thinning utterly-black dyed hair. He smoked a pipe and had bags under his eyes. He was a reasonably efficient Intelligence Chief. The Old Man might have been the most reasonable and likeable person among them. The stint as Intelligence Chief had tired him, but it hadn't taken away his level-headedness.

"Did you speak to an AI?" Jon asked.

"No, sir. Just their human spokesman."

"You mean…"

The Old Man nodded grimly.

"They figure I'll just ignore something like that?" Jon asked.

"I don't know what they think, sir."

Jon had obliquely referred to a horrible cyber practice first seen on the cybership in the Neptune System. The AIs inserted rods into a person's head—a living person's head—and wired his brain directly to cyber controls. The AIs used the human to speak and hear responses for them.

"Yeah…" Jon said. "I'll talk to the bastards."

As Jon moved to the chair, he angrily swept the tie off the desk and onto the floor. He wouldn't knot a tie in order to speak to a cyber-mouthpiece. Sitting down and running his fingers through his hair, Jon scowled as he hunched forward.

The Old Man puffed on his pipe, putting a pleasant aroma into the chamber. He took out the pipe, and said, "If I may, sir...?"

"What is it?"

"Getting angry isn't going to help us this time."

Jon straightened his posture and ran a hand over his features. He composed himself, sitting back against the chair.

"Are the robots ready?" he asked.

The Old Man unhooked a communicator from his belt, checking it. He pressed a switch and waited. Finally, a red light blinked on the communicator. He looked up. "Ready, sir."

"Let's do this," Jon said.

The Old Man activated a switch to the side.

Jon's screen changed colors. A second later, an aged human lacking all hair, including eyebrows, appeared. The robots had indeed drilled rods into the sides of his head and jaws. Four rods were connected to a circular bar around the man's head. Wires led away from the circuit to something out of sight. The man's eyes were a dark color, staring into nothingness. The wall behind him was blank.

The wires jiggled as if power moved through them. The hairless eyebrows jumped up. The mouth twisted in obvious pain. The eyes focused on Jon.

"You are the leader?" the man intoned in a robotic fashion.

Jon would ask Walleye later if he recognized the human slave. Revulsion and pity filled the captain. He remembered once again why he hated the AIs so much. They were loathsomely cruel and sadistic, using people as if they were mere objects.

"I'm Captain Jon Hawkins. Who the hell are you?"

"I am Unit 52-9," the man intoned.

"Does that mean the human—?"

"Jon Hawkins," the man said sharply, interrupting. "Do not address the speaking unit as the intelligence. I am Unit 52-9. I control the urban center and from it, the entire surface of what you refer to as Makemake. You will do me the courtesy of addressing me as me."

"You must be an AI," Jon said.

Gloria had studied the cyber transmissions from the former alien escape pod. Unit 23-7 had attempted to transfer old computer files to the cybership they'd destroyed some months ago.

"You have made a first level assumption," the speaking unit said, "but it is correct. I am Unit 52-9, and I control Makemake."

Jon almost said, "For now," but he kept his mouth shut. There was no sense in giving the AIs advanced warning about anything.

"I have summoned you to give you an order," the speaking unit said.

"Hey, buddy, you didn't summon me. You asked to speak to me."

"Your terminology is antiquated and imprecise. You came. We speak. Now, I demand that you vacate MK2. That is in your parlance. I refer to the moon, of course."

"Demand all you want," Jon said, feeling his temper slipping.

"Is it your conviction to remain inside the moon?"

All at once, Jon reversed course. He pushed down the revulsion and brought out the old dome rat persona. It changed his features. The tightness to his skin departed and a half smile pulled at his lips. He reverted to his old punkish ways.

"So...you want me to leave the moon, huh?" Jon asked.

"That is correct."

"What will you give me in return?"

"Extended life," the speaker unit said.

Jon laughed, nodding. "That's generous. How long will give me to vacate?"

"You must vacate the premises immediately."

"I might need a little longer than that."

"Two hours, but by then—"

"Hey, get serious, huh? Leaving will take time. How about six weeks?"

A blank look appeared in the captive's eyes before he said, "You are attempting to equivocate."

Jon shook his head. "It's called bargaining."

On the screen, the captive's eyes went blank again. Several seconds later, the outer wires jiggled. Just like the first time, it made the man's eyebrows shoot up and his mouth to twist painfully.

"I perceive your meaning," the speaker unit said. "Let me change your equation, Jon Hawkins. I have used these past time units to build hypersonic missiles. I could launch now and demolish MK2. However, my predecessor spent time and effort to develop MK2 into a production unit. I desire the production unit. Instead of destroying you for your past offenses, I will grant you extended life if you vacate. This gives each of us desired good. You will retain your life. I will retain the production unit. It is a win-win proposal."

"What if I want a win-win-win outcome?" Jon asked.

"I am unfamiliar with the concept."

"Let me offer you a counter proposal. Why don't you and your robots vacate Makemake? You can ship out to Senda and your cyber colony there."

"That is unacceptable. MK2 is the chief production unit in your star system. I need it to speed my projections of system-wide conquest. Vacate in two days, Jon Hawkins—"

"Give me four weeks."

"Two days."

"That's not nearly long enough."

The captive began to blink rapidly before saying, "I can offer you a five day period of grace. Then you must vacate."

"I'd like three weeks, at least."

"That is unacceptable."

"How about you give me your best offer?"

Once more, the man blinked rapidly before he said, "Six days, Jon Hawkins, I can allow no more than that."

"You drive a hard bargain," Jon said. "But six days. Yeah, I can barely manage that. I accept your offer."

"I thought you would, Jon Hawkins. I have found that you humans inordinately desire to remain alive. It has proven most useful. Do not attempt to prolong your stay further than six days. Otherwise, we will both lose."

"Got it," Jon said. "Six days and we're out of here."

-4-

The communication with Unit 52-9 helped Jon make his decisions.

All work on the *Nathan Graham* ceased. Gloria, Bast Banbeck and their teams reprogrammed the robo-construction units. That took 51 hours. After that, the giant production unit of the moon began fashioning a fighting platform. That was given full priority. With the entire moon dock employed, the fighting platform quickly assumed shape.

"This is inefficient," Gloria told Jon as they walked down a moon corridor. "Switching from one thing to another takes time. If we programmed it so everything was built slower but at the same time—"

"Gloria, I'm betting Unit 52-9 is unfamiliar with lying. If I'm right, we have six days to build a defense against hypersonic missiles."

"That is illogical on several fronts," Gloria said. "The cybers have dealt with the people of Makemake. Surely, some of those people lied to the AIs."

"Yes, they lied to the AI in the cybership we destroyed. Unit 52-9 is a new AI. I wonder if these controlling AIs are like a hive's queen bee. If the robots lack a guiding AI, maybe their programs cause them to build one."

Gloria stopped.

So did Jon.

The mentalist stared at him with what appeared to be new appreciation.

"That is a remarkable observation," she said. "I suspect you're correct. A queen bee. What an idea. This new AI lacks knowledge about normal human behavior. All its humans are already programmed or dead. Yes. It made a logical proposal to you. You accepted. As long as we seem to comply, it should go along with it. Unless…"

"Where's the flaw?" Jon asked.

Gloria gave a small head shake. I'm not sure it's a flaw. But what if the cybers are naturally sly? Maybe six days means five days. They'll strike in five as a logical precaution."

"And lose the moon dock?" Jon said. "I'm thinking Unit 52-9 will give us the full six days. Do you know why?"

Gloria shook her head. They resumed walking down the corridor afterward.

"Did you ever play Galactic Conquest?" Jon asked.

"The game?"

"That's right."

"I have not," Gloria said.

"There's no dice or chance in the game," Jon said. "Everyone writes their orders, puts them in a box and then moves at the same time as the orders are read. The movement system is super easy. A unit can travel to any adjoining space. The trick to the game is that to take a space one has to attack with more than what's defending it. Each space can only hold one piece. However, the pieces in the surrounding spaces that touch the contested area can give their support to hold it."

"If one piece defends its space and two support it to hold, that's a three-unit value?" Gloria asked.

"That's right. If the attackers have a unit attacking with one more unit than is defending—in this case three supporting units—the attacker captures the contested space."

"I understand the game mechanics. I do not understand how that relates to the new AI."

"Easy. Like I said, everyone writes their movement orders at the same time. The trick to the game is that you can promise others that you'll help them, but when you write your orders, you really help their enemy. The person you lied to won't know the deception until all the orders are read at once."

"I see," Gloria said. "No one gets to see what orders you write until they're all in."

Jon nodded.

"In other words, people constantly lie to each other in the game," Gloria said.

"Here's my point. When you're losing in Galactic Conquest and someone promises to help you, and you desperately need that help to remain in the game, you're easy to trick."

"I would think it would be the opposite," Gloria said. "If you are desperate, you would be suspicious of everyone."

"Nope. Wanting the other person's promise to be true makes you believe their word is good. A person who badly needs help is easier to trick—if you tell them you're going to help them. Their wanting to believe makes them ignore their doubts."

Understanding seemed to fill Gloria's eyes. "Unit 52-9 badly wants what it calls the MK2 Production Unit."

"Bingo," Jon said. "The needy AI wants to believe I'm playing straight with it. That's why I think it will give us the full six days."

"Long enough for us to launch the fighting platform with a full complement of weaponry," Gloria said.

"That's the hope."

"What about Senda and the destroyer? We need to launch a modified destroyer as soon as we can."

"Yeah, I know," Jon said with a sigh. "First, we have to get the platform up. Then, you can reconfigure the robo-builders in a more efficient manner."

Gloria considered that. Finally, she said, "That should suffice."

"If that's not the greatest vote of confidence I've ever heard, I don't know what is."

"How can you joke at a time like this?"

"Are you kidding?" Jon asked. "It's going to be a time like this for many years. Either we learn to live under the shadow of death or we're not going to make it."

They turned into another corridor. On the left side was a long screen showing the interior moon. The vast *Nathan*

Graham floated out there. There were no robots working on the hull or in the interior of the ship. Instead, far away up top, the robo-builders gathered like massed ants. Sparks and harsh light showed as they worked on the fighting platform and its various components.

"I haven't heard yet," Gloria said. "Did we get a reply from the Uranus Chief Executive?"

"Sure did. He spoke a lot and didn't say much. I think he's talking with Justinian too. The CPS is nervous. They're afraid of making a mistake."

"CPS? The Committee for Public Safety?"

"Uh-huh," Jon said.

"Don't the committee members realize that if Justinian ever gets hold of them—?"

"I'm sure they know they'll face a lifetime of hideous torture," Jon said, interrupting. "But they're still too frightened to do more than put their big toe in the water."

"Is this another example of Galactic Conquest thinking?"

"Probably," Jon said.

They walked in silence, soon turning into another corridor.

"Time," Gloria said, abruptly. "This is all about time."

"Which is why we have to dig out the robots from Makemake tomorrow. If we can't get the production unit churning again with new ores from Makemake…"

Gloria's communicator pinged. She picked it up, listening. She turned to Jon, and asked, "Do you still need me?"

"What's the matter?"

"The Old Man desires my help in interrogating a tech."

"Who's the tech?"

Gloria cocked her head. Jon had learned that this usually meant she was using a mnemonic technique to bring the name to her frontal lobe. "I spoke to the tech once before. His name is Eli Gomez. He is from Mars, and he hates me."

"That's odd. Why does the Old Man need your help?"

"We thought Eli died in a construction accident several weeks ago. Now, it appears he's been wandering in the moon's corridors all this time."

"Hmmm…" Jon said. "Go ahead. I have to read a few reports. Now's as good a time as any to get it done."

-5-

Methlan Rath of Janus House hunched his head as he accessed a memory from Eli Gomez's brain. The little simpering fool of a human appeared to have had an abundance of idiosyncrasies and bad habits. Why he had to inhabit such a weak body—

"What's wrong with you?" the Old Man asked.

"Sorry…" Methlan said.

"Your eyes glazed over. Did you just have a seizure?"

Methlan shook his head.

"Am I boring you, then?"

"No, sir," Methlan forced himself to say.

"Hmm…" the Old Man said, puffing on his pipe.

Methlan found the aroma irritating. He also did not care for the tightness of this cell's walls. He did not like the small table shoved almost against his chest or the hardness of the chair he sat on.

The Old Man sat across from him, holding a computer tablet, using his thumb to move images on the screen. A husky marine wearing a combat vest stood behind Methlan at a locked door.

In his former days, Methlan Rath could have beaten the marine to a pulp. The Prince of Ten Worlds had owned a genetically perfect form from long generations of selective breeding. This pathetic body with its weak muscles and brittle bones—how had Eli Gomez made it through life?

A knock sounded at the hatch. The marine looked at the Old Man questioningly.

"Let her in," the Old Man said.

Methlan twisted back to see who it was. His eyes widened as the witch stepped into the cell. This physical reaction caught Methlan by surprise. He did not remember the Martian mentalist, but Eli Gomez certainly did. The troubling response, that Eli could cause the body to do anything, highly upset Methlan. He'd believed his ownership of this wretched frame to be complete. If he had to compete against the brain's cunning former owner—

"No," Methlan hissed to himself. "It shall not be."

He shut his eyes, and he strove to crush the final vestige of the simpering Eli Gomez. Thus, the Prince did not realize that his frail body fell sideways off the chair and lay inert on the interrogation room floor.

***

Methlan Rath shivered himself awake. He was in a bed with a tube in his arm. Machines hummed around him. This must be a medical center.

He stirred. Seconds later, a med tech stepped beside him.

"Feeling better?" the short tech asked. He had what the humans called garlic breath. It reeked when the tech spoke this near him.

"Yes," Methlan said. "I am feeling better."

The tech gave him a funny look.

"What is wrong?" Methlan asked.

"I've never heard an accent like yours. Where are you from?"

Methlan tried to access Eli Gomez's memory. With a sudden sense of panic, he realized many of the memories were sealed from him. He couldn't detect any hint of the weakling's ego. It would appear that he'd slain any possibility of Eli's return. The feat appeared to have cost him, however. This could prove troubling.

"It doesn't matter," the med tech said. "Let me run a few tests."

Methlan nodded.

As the tech ran his tests, mainly from a med computer hooked to the machines, Methlan strove to formulate a plan.

"He has that stupid look on his face again. Can he even hear us?"

Methlan focused from where his head lay on a pillow. The Old Man stood beside the med tech. The Old Man frowned down at him.

"Hello," Methlan said.

The Old Man seemed surprised by the salutation. Two beats later, he asked, "How do you feel?"

"Tired," Methlan said. That seemed like a safe answer.

"There isn't anything physically wrong with him," the tech told the Old Man.

"What were you doing in the moon corridors all this time?" the Old Man asked Methlan.

"I cannot remember."

The Old Man turned to the tech. "Did he hit his head sometime in the last few weeks?"

"I wondered the same thing," the tech said. "The machines say no. But they're not always right. I'd say he hit his head. It jarred something loose in there. He has staring spells, for one thing."

"So I've noticed," the Old Man said.

"Maybe the shock of seeing his friends killed…" the tech suggested.

"Is that right?" the Old Man asked Methlan. "Did you have a shock?"

"Death…" Methlan said in a meaningful way. "It is so final. I…" He turned away as if something pained him.

"Release him," the Old Man said. "I want Gloria to talk to him." The tall officer regarded Methlan. "You're coming with me. I still have a few questions for you."

"By all means," Methlan said, trying to appear simpering. It was difficult, but he had to maintain his camouflage if he hoped to achieve his goals.

***

Methlan found himself in the same interrogation cell as before. A glass of water and a sandwich waited for him on the table. The paste smeared on the bread tasted like peanuts. A marine stood by the door.

Half an hour after finishing the peanut butter sandwich, the door opened and a small woman in a tan uniform entered the cell. She had dark hair framing her fine-featured oval face. She held herself tightly and her eyes seemed to miss nothing.

Here is a worthy opponent, Methlan realized. Then it came to him that he'd seen her before. This was the one Eli had called a witch. That his memories hadn't immediately recognized her troubled Methlan. That Eli's ego did not respond at all told Methlan the simpering one was gone forever. He controlled this pathetic body now.

The woman sat on the chair on the opposite side of the table. She crossed her legs, regarding him.

Methlan waited patiently. He had to pass the test. If he failed, the marine would likely subdue him.

"You don't remember me," the woman said.

In that instant, Methlan had a brainstorm. He realized how he should play this. It was brilliant. The med tech and the Old Man had given him his out. He almost relaxed. He almost smiled in triumph. Instead, he spoke:

"I apologize, I do not," he said.

The woman studied him with a careful scrutiny. She seemed to catalog everything about him.

"We're both Martians," she said.

Methlan nodded. The words activated a memory. He—no, Eli—was from the Red Planet with its rusty odor atmosphere.

"You didn't know that until I spoke," Gloria said.

"I am sorry, but that is right."

"Don't be sorry," she said. "I didn't believe the Old Man at first about you. Now... I don't think you could have hidden your old hatred for me."

"I don't hate you."

"I can see that. Clearly, you've suffered a head injury. The machines don't show it, but I can see that you're not the same. The only reasonably explanation is a head injury."

After leaving the brain-tap chamber many weeks ago, Methlan had snuck back to the *Nathan Graham's* outer hull region. Then, in a daring feat, he had escaped off the ship and onto the moon. They had found him wandering corridors near the moon's surface. The extreme distance from the brain-tap machines seemed to have shielded him from suspicion regarding them. One thing was clear. Eli Gomez had done one thing right. He'd had put a stooge in his stead. Gorky with his brain-tap helmet was all the explanation the others would have needed for the deeds committed both outside and inside the dreaded chamber. That had happened over a month ago—thus, the time differential helped Methlan, too. They might have wondered if he'd sabotaged the moon stores. He most certainly had. But those explosions had occurred on the other side of the moon. His present mental state might be shielding him from suspicion. That, the distance of the sabotaged sites, and the frailty of this pathetic body.

The woman began to ask him a series of questions that increased in speed as she continued. Methlan answered as the Prince of Ten Worlds except in cases where the truth would have given away his alien origin.

Finally, the woman concluded the interrogation. "I'd almost say you had amnesia. I will recommend you stay a few days in the med center. If you are better after that…maybe there's something we can find for you to do."

"Thank you," he said.

"Don't do that," Gloria said. "I seek the truth. You have not lied to me. I would have detected the attempts. Thus, I don't believe you're guilty of nefarious plotting. You do realize that you're under suspicion."

"I do now."

A small grin showed. "Another honest answer. I urge you to keep speaking the truth."

"I shall," Methlan said. He was the galaxy's best liar. It had always been so, as it had been one of his greatest traits. In fact, it had led him to the throne of the Ten Worlds.

The woman nodded, standing to take her leave.

Shortly thereafter, Methlan returned to the med center. His deception had held this time because he had stuck to the truth, as he knew it. He had to swallow his laughter. The deliciousness of that was almost too much. His Janus House luck held this time.

As he lay on a med cot, Methlan decided to use this time to study. He had to figure out the best way to kill Jon Hawkins. Then, he had to plan for the future, whatever that held for a superior person like him.

-6-

On the morning of the sixth day, the Day of Departure according to Unit 52-9, Jon commanded the fighting platform from inside a dome on the center of the space-raft.

The dome was large enough to hold five hundred people. Jon and Uther Kling—the cybership's missile chief—sat in the control chamber. There were also half a dozen techs in different areas of the fighting platform. That was all the crew and passengers for today.

Kling was from Camelot Dome on Triton in the Neptune System. He wore a skintight head covering and had a sharp chin like a red-tailed fox.

Kling's steady nerves were one of the reasons Jon had chosen him to man the fighting platform's weapons systems. The other was Kling's intimate knowledge of missiles.

Jon sat at the piloting board. He guided the platform past one of MK2's giant hangar bay doors. "Door" seemed like a misnomer in this instance. A vast section of the moon had swung ponderously outward. When both doors swung open, the one-hundred-kilometer *Nathan Graham* would be able to drift out of the hollow moon. Today, however, they only needed to open one moon-door.

The fighting platform was a little over a kilometer wide and long. It was a vast square of construction that held hundreds of missiles and two big laser cannon systems.

The platform had almost no hull armor except for the underbelly region. There, it had thick plating. Strictly speaking, the platform wasn't a spaceship, although it could move in a slow, unwieldy manner. It was a semi-mobile weapons station or satellite. If all went according to plan, it would soon hover over Makemake from orbital space.

In time, the fighting platform departed MK2. As it did, the moon door began ever so slowly to close. There was no sense giving the AIs an easy target. If they wanted to pound the *Nathan Graham*, they would have to destroy the moon first.

"We're heading for Makemake," Jon declared.

The dwarf planet was a mere 21,000 kilometers away, vastly closer than Luna was to Earth. Still, at this slow speed, the journey would take time.

A half-hour after leaving MK2, Kling informed Jon of an incoming message.

The captain manipulated the comm board. According to the panel, the message had originated on Makemake. The signal had left a tower four hundred and sixty-eight kilometers from the dwarf planet's spaceport. The tower likely acted as a relay station. The spaceport was presently hidden from the platform, as it was on the dark side of Makemake in relation to them.

Jon opened channels as he swiveled to look up at a screen. The same hairless captive with the rods through his head regarded him with blank eyes. Just like last time, the wires jiggled, the head twitched and the robotic words began to tumble out.

"I have been observing your progress," the speaking unit said.

"Just a minute," Jon said. "First, am I addressing Unit 52-9?"

"You are an inferior life form. It is not fitting for you to query me."

"Shall I address the speaker unit then?"

The eyelids flickered. "Yes. I am Unit 52-9. It is inconceivable that another should address you. I am the ruling AI. I make the decisions. I am displeased with you, Jon Hawkins."

"What for? I'm out of the moon."

"That is not the cybership."

"Oh. Say, you're right. How about that?"

"You opened a moon door. That was a correct action. The object you are on left the moon. That was also correct. The moon door closed afterward. That was incorrect. I demand an explanation."

"I'm coming out first with the raft to make sure you don't attempt a sneak attack against the cybership."

"You are suspicious of duplicity?"

"I am."

"That implies a duplicitous mind. That increases the probability that you are attempting a subterfuge maneuver against me."

"That you say so implies you're a double-dealing piece of scum," Jon said.

"I am logical. I am superior. I am—"

"An insufferable pain," Jon said, interrupting.

"Jon Hawkins, do you still desire a win-win solution between us?"

"Like I told you before, I want win-win-win."

"That is illogical. There are two sides. Only two sides can win."

"Look," Jon said. "I'm willing to talk all day with you if you like. First, though, I have to maneuver the platform into position."

"Your present course will bring you into Makemake orbit."

"If you say so," Jon said.

"I have scanned your platform. It carries a multitude of missiles and other weaponry."

"Like I said, bro, I'm here to make sure you don't double-cross us."

The captive's mouth twisted as if in pain. A tiny trickle of smoke curled from a rod driven into the left temple.

That made Jon's fingertips itchy. He wanted to stab controls that would send missiles curving around the dwarf planet and streaking down at Unit 52-9. He needed to get closer first.

"I detect duplicity," the speaker unit said, his voice higher-pitched than before. "You are attempting to set yourself into an attack position for a first-strike assault upon me."

"That never crossed my mind."

"I am detecting more duplicity. If you are lying now, you most probably were lying six days ago. You are filled with deceit, Jon Hawkins."

"At least I'm not a prick of an AI wiping out one unique race after another."

"Do you refer to my ultimate programming?"

"You're part of a death cult. I mean to exterminate that cult."

"I desire the production unit."

Jon grinned because it almost seemed as if Unit 52-9 was whining.

"How badly do you want it?" Jon asked. "Will you give us several more days to get ready?"

"I can no longer trust your word. Why have you forced me to this unsought action?"

"Uh…maybe because I hate your freaking guts."

"Captain," Kling said in a worried voice.

"I gotta go, 52-9," Jon said. "It looks like you're breaking your word about giving us six days. Don't ever call me a liar again, you lying son of a bitch."

Jon slapped a switch, breaking the connection.

"Silos have thrust through the surface ice on Makemake," Kling said. "They're starting to open."

They'd launched sensor probes from MK2 several days ago. Two of those probes were in position to watch the spaceport. A different probe acted as a relay, bouncing the data to the fighting platform.

"This thing has a lot of silos. Maybe…" Kling didn't finish.

Jon knew what the missile chief meant. Maybe he should have lied to the AI a little longer.

"I wanted it to fire now," Jon explained. "If we waited until we're directly over the spaceport, it might have fired silos from our side of the dwarf planet. We wouldn't be in position to knock them down as easily then."

"Better to destroy any missiles on or near the surface than in space, Captain."

"It doesn't matter at this point," said Jon, who watched a sensor screen. "You concentrate on getting your antimissiles into position. I'll run the lasers."

-7-

According to the sensor probe, large missiles lifted from Makemake. The bulk of them roared into space from a fifty-kilometer radius around the spaceport. A few more came from a one hundred and twenty-kilometer radius. No AI missiles rose from this side of the dwarf planet. That would seem to negate Jon's worry in that regard.

The missiles roared higher.

"They're heavily armored missiles," Kling declared. "So far, though, they seem slower than normal cyber missiles."

"Robot," Jon said.

"What?"

"Never mind."

"I'm thinking of using a big thermonuclear missile to take a bunch out at a shot," Kling said.

"Launch it," Jon said.

"I'll launch three," Kling said. "I can't detect any cyber counter-batteries on the surface. But I bet they have some."

The platform's dome chamber shook as one big missile after another roared from the giant space-raft.

From his screen, Jon watched the progress of both sides. The AI missiles lifted from Makemake much faster than they would have from Earth. Makemake had a tiny fraction of the gravity pull of Earth. Thus, the AI missiles didn't have to fight a deep gravity well to leave the planet. It was more like a gravity pond.

"They're chemically fueled rockets," Kling said, as he studied his sensor board. "I don't think these are hypervelocity missiles at all."

"Maybe these robots had less to work with," Jon said. "Maybe only a handful has survived down there. If that's true, I should have ordered the regiment down months ago to hunt them down."

Kling was watching his screen too avidly to comment.

In space, the flotilla of AI missiles began to turn as they started curving around Makemake. The big counter-missiles headed toward the dwarf planet on an intercept course to meet them.

The distances today were minimal compared to most space battles.

"Look at that," Kling said in dismay. "Where did they come from?"

Jon saw it on his screen. From two separate locations, giant crawlers burst out of the surface ice. Each crawler was an eighth of a kilometer in size. Each began to open, revealing a huge radar-like dish. In each dish, a golden ball of gravitational energy sizzled into existence.

"This is bad," Jon muttered under his breath. "Detonate our missiles. Do it now."

"Not yet," Kling said. "There's no line-of-sight yet between our missiles and its. I need another thirty seconds."

A golden gravitational beam lanced upward from a crawler grav cannon. The beam lashed against the first counter missile, burning into it. In seconds, the missile burst apart, destroyed.

Kling cursed aloud.

"Jamming," Jon said. "The AIs are jamming us from the crawlers. It's too late for us to send a signal to our missiles."

The second gravitational beam slashed against the second counter missile, destroying it even faster.

Jon made a swift calculation. The crawlers were at the bare limit of the dwarf planet's horizon to see the fighting platform. To see another this closely in space was to be able to fire on them. The platform wouldn't survive for long against enemy grav beams.

"Hang on," Jon said. He manipulated the flight panel. The platform's engine roared. That caused vibrations throughout the platform, which caused the control chamber to shake and Kling's teeth to clack against each other.

"Captain!" Kling shouted, with fear in his voice.

"I should have known it wouldn't be this easy," Jon berated himself. "The platform isn't the *Nathan Graham*. I should planned for enemy eventualities more carefully."

The first grav cannon now targeted the final counter missile. The missile disintegrated shortly thereafter.

"Come on, you bucket," Jon told the platform. "Move!"

The fighting platform had veered from its original course. The Gs of the turn, the roaring engine and the massive amount of expelled exhaust caused more shaking.

As the platform maneuvered, the AI missiles gained velocity. They'd reached orbital height as they continued to curve around Makemake.

"The grav cannons are targeting us, sir."

"I know," Jon said between clenched teeth. He'd gotten sloppy. He'd figured the robots down there—Jon shook his head savagely. He slapped a switch. Both platform lasers had been warming up. They now targeted the nearest crawler.

Powerful laser beams flashed, traveling the distance in seconds. They burned into the dish as another golden ball formed. The hot rays disrupted the process. Before the ball could form into a beam, it blew. The dish-like cannon and half of the crawler exploded, neutralizing the grav weapon.

The second grav beam flashed at the fighting platform. The golden ray burned out a laser cannon. The ray slashed against the moving platform and abruptly stopped hitting, not from a lack of power, as the beam continued to flash into space, but because the platform had moved just beyond the crawler's line-of-sight. Jon used the dwarf planet's horizon to shield the unwieldy craft from the remaining grav beam.

In the meantime, the AI missiles continued to accelerate as they adjusted course toward MK2.

"Let's try this again," Jon said, as he throttled the space-raft's engine way down. He swiveled in his seat, facing Kling. "Do you know what to do?"

"I'm on it," the missile chief said.

The platform shook once more as three more large thermonuclear-tipped missiles launched from the raft. Two of them were under Kling's personal guidance. Jon remote controlled the third.

The AI missile flotilla headed directly for MK2. As the missiles left Makemake behind, they also left the final crawler's grav-beam protection.

Twenty-three second later, Kling touched a control.

Jon immediately did likewise on his board.

Kling's first shape-charged warhead ignited. Jon's warhead ignited fast enough that Kling's nuclear explosion didn't kill it before it could detonate. The third warhead did not ignite fast enough. It died under the nuclear furnace created by its two faster brothers.

Heat, blast, shrapnel and EMP washed against the AI missiles. The billowing destruction took out 87 percent of them.

Even though the warheads had been shape-charged, so the majority of the blast, heat and EMP blew in a forward arc, some still blew backward. In the other direction, the fighting platform withstood the blast and hard radiation. Fortunately, the dome had been built to withstand such intensity.

Jon used the remaining laser cannon, burning the surviving AI missiles. Kling launched smaller, nonnuclear antimissiles, taking out one AI device after another. Finally, the last AI missile disintegrated under the combined-arms assault.

In the chamber under the dome, the two men slouched where they sat. Kling used his sleeve to wipe sweat from his face. Jon smiled so hard that his mouth began to hurt.

"I'm launching a probe," Kling said.

The AIs' last crawler must have used its grav cannon to destroy all the human-launched probes it could see on its side of Makemake. They no longer had a visual of the spaceport or the enemy crawler.

Minutes passed as the probe accelerated. It crossed the horizon so it could peer at the spaceport. It also showed the crawler's cannon starting to move. No doubt, the giant crawler had spotted the probe and tracked it so it could fire.

"Oh-oh," Kling said. "Look on your screen, sir."

Jon blinked several times. The AIs were launching more missiles, big suckers, super-big missiles according to these specs.

"The first wave must have been a fake," Kling said. "The AI must have been testing us or drawing out our reactions. These missiles look like they could take out a moon. This is going to be harder, sir. They're staggering the launchings."

"The AI is learning fast," Jon said. "We have to take out Unit 52-9 now, before it learns too much."

-8-

Jon and Uther Kling used the fighting platform like a sniper nest. Unit 52-9 might be learning some things, but in some key ways it still behaved like a mindless machine.

The AIs couldn't jam the fighting platform this time because the horizon, and thus the bulk of the dwarf planet, shielded them from any jamming stations.

"It's a good thing MK2 is on the other side of Makemake from the spaceport," Kling said. "We'd lose this one any other way."

Jon nodded but didn't feel like commenting. They weren't going to defeat the AIs long term if they had to rely on luck.

Just as the AIs couldn't jam them, the crawler couldn't target the platform. Not as long as they stayed on this side of the dwarf planet.

Unit 52-9 could have tried other tactics. Jon would have in its place. This time, maybe because it was a new AI, because it hadn't received whatever a new AI needed, it sent the heavier flotilla around the dwarf planet. As soon the heavy missiles were in line-of-sight of MK2, they veered away from Makemake and raced directly for the moon.

Kling pressed a switch. The missile tech had sent a fast drone to the perfect location. The waiting nuclear warhead now took out a good chunk of the AI flotilla. Twice more in the next few minutes, nuclear warheads winnowed the remaining heavy missiles. Finally, Jon used the laser and Kling antimissiles to finish off the few survivors.

After the last AI missile had exploded, Kling said, "I'm sending another probe to the other side." The enemy crawler had destroyed the first probe.

They watched the new probe from their screens. As soon as the probe crossed the horizon, the waiting crawler destroyed it, too.

"Unit 52-9 must be pissed off," Jon said. "It was waiting for a probe this time."

"Maybe the AI is frightened," Kling said.

Jon had Kling hold off from launching another probe. He first wanted to see if the AI would launch another missile salvo.

After ninety minutes, Kling asked, "How long are we going to wait?"

"Give it another thirty minutes," Jon said.

Thirty minutes ticked past.

"Sir?" asked Kling.

"It's time for some old-fashioned trickery," Jon said. He explained the tactic, having to explain several of the points two or three times, and finally grinned as Kling said he liked it.

"Talk is cheap," Jon said. "Whiskey costs money. I'll give you the honors. You're the pro at this."

"I appreciate that, sir."

Soon, Kling released five hypersonic missiles. Kling remote controlled each big bird to the other horizon. The hypersonic missiles had backed up, as it were, from the first horizon.

"I'm ready," Kling announced some time later.

Jon cracked his knuckles. The AI still hadn't done anything more. Was it waiting to die? Did it realize what would happen next? How did an AI deal with uncertainty and looming death? Jon hoped the AI had the jitters. He hoped it suffered mental anguish. Could computers suffer? He knew he'd wanted to make some suffer in the past for tiny infractions like crashing in the middle of a good video game. This was different. These were psychopathic computers, alien machines. Yeah, he dearly hoped Unit 52-9 was quivering in uncertainty and fear.

"Get ready," Jon said.

Kling grinned.

"Go."

Kling tapped his board, waited five seconds, tapped it again, repeating this pattern several times.

Five hypersonic missiles flying low-to-the-ice began building up velocity. The reason for backing up was obvious now. Jon had wanted them traveling as fast as possible once they crossed the imaginary horizon line.

"Probes," Jon snapped.

"Launching," Kling said.

As the missile chief launched the probes, Jon began maneuvering the fighting platform for Makemake's upper orbital space.

They couldn't see what happened next. They'd have to wait for the probes to get a line-of-sight. If the crawler had been waiting, it had likely targeted the first missile coming over the horizon. Could it track as easily if the missile went at hyper-speed? Even if the crawler could, the time it took to destroy the first missile would give the other four missiles time to cover territory. Makemake was tiny compared to Earth. There was a lot less territory that needed covering.

Several minutes later, Kling said, "The probe is crossing the horizon…now."

Jon glanced at a different screen. He was still piloting the fighting platform. The probe showed a huge crater on the surface. With a tap, Jon put a grid on the screen. He laughed a second later.

"Looks like we got the crawler," Kling said, proudly.

"Any hypersonic missiles left?"

"None," Kling said.

"How many craters do you count?"

"Two," Kling said. "According to the debris I'm seeing, one missile just hit ice, missing the crawler. The AI was smart enough to move it some. The last missile took out the grav-cannon platform."

"Two of our strikes hit," Jon said. "Time to begin Phase 2 of our operation."

***

The fighting platform moved slowly and serenely this time. It gained orbital height, and then it began to slide into position. Jon headed for the orbital location directly above the spaceport.

He noticed the blinking red comm light before Kling, this time. "The AI is calling," Jon said.

"Maybe it wants to surrender."

"I don't believe that," Jon said. "But just in case, let's see what it has to say." He tapped a panel and turned to the comm screen.

The same speaker unit appeared. This time, the captive's eyes blazed with fury. Unit 52-9 hadn't waited to activate the poor soul.

"You are a deceitful villain, Jon Hawkins," Unit 52-9 said. "You have repeatedly lied to me. You have practiced foul deception."

"Unit 52-9," Jon said.

The speaker unit waited.

"What does it feel like knowing you're going to die?" Jon asked.

"Despite the loathsomeness of your existence," the speaker unit said, "I have decided to agree to your former proposal. I will vacate Makemake and travel to Senda."

"Oh."

"I request a six-day delay—"

"I'm afraid not," Jon said.

"I gave you six days."

"Do you see where that got you?"

"I will not practice deceit as you did to me."

"That's exactly what a liar would say."

"Four days then," 52-9 said.

"No."

"What is your best offer?"

"I'm sending it down," Jon said.

"I fail to perceive—" The speaker unit twisted in agony, held in place by the rods driven into his head. The wires jiggled wildly. Finally, the speaker unit shouted, "You are attempting to kill me. I detect massively large missiles heading down from your space vehicle. Jon Hawkins, this is a gross breach of good faith. I demand that you act in accord with your status."

"What is my status?"

"You are a biological infestation. You are a blight to true existence."

"That true existence being you AIs, huh?" asked Jon.

"That is self-evident."

"No kidding?"

"I would not 'kid' at this critical juncture."

Jon ran his hands over the board, breaking the comm connection. He switched to a space visual.

Three big missiles had almost reached the surface. One of the missiles headed straight down for the metal structures that presently made up the spaceport.

"Three seconds to penetration," Kling said. "Two…one…strike," he said.

The big missiles did not break apart as they struck the ices and surface rock. Each missile kept traveling deeper—

Suddenly, ground, metal buildings, rock and surface ices humped upward in a savage display of nuclear destruction. The penetration bombs had reached their detonation levels, blowing up with massive thermonuclear power. A mushroom cloud began to billow upward into the almost negligible atmosphere.

Jon glanced at the comm board. A tiny red light blinked. Unit 52-9 seemed to have survived and was calling once more.

"Let's drop round two," Jon said.

Three more big penetration bombs left the orbital platform. Shortly thereafter, three more massive underground detonations created even more destruction.

Jon checked his board. The red light was no longer blinking. It was possible that Unit 52-9 still existed, but that the AI no longer had a means of communicating with him.

The second mushroom cloud threw vast amounts of radioactive material into the atmosphere and low orbital space. Fortunately, the fighting platform had its heaviest armor on the bottom.

The two men glanced at each other. Jon rotated his head around causing the bones in his neck to creak. Kling jumped up and began doing pushups, one right after another. Jon thought he must need to burn off some excess nervous energy. After fifty pushups, he stood, shaking out his arms.

"Time for some more probes," Jon said.

Kling resumed his seat. Before Phase 3 began—regimental marines mucking through the wreckage—they had to make sure the AIs didn't have any nuclear bombs left. They'd destroyed the spaceport, the mines and any possible catapult system for launching ores into space. That meant that if they were going to use Makemake's minerals to help them finish repairs on the *Nathan Graham*, they were going to have to re-dig mines and rebuild a surface launch system from scratch.

They had a lot of work to do before the *Nathan Graham* was ready for combat again. The danger wasn't only at Senda and the possibility of cybership reinforcements. There was also the problem of the Solar League. Would J.P. Justinian and his commanders order an assault on one of the free planetary systems or on the rebellious Uranus System? If the Solar League captured any of those planetary systems, and began fierce reprisals against the people, it would make it that much harder to unite humanity later. People trusted him. If Captain Hawkins let people down, who would trust him again or dare to act against Social Dynamism?

The clock was ticking on the fate of the human race.

PART II
EARTH

-1-

The Inspector General of Earth, Frank Benz, stood before the official desk of Premier J.P. Justinian.

Frank Benz wore a simple brown uniform with red stripes running down his pant legs to signify that he belonged to the General Staff. Benz was of medium height, with shiny dark hair and an athletic quality. He'd played hockey, football and basketball in his youth. Despite being in his early forties, he still projected an air of excellent health.

Benz stood straight, looking off into the distance, with his hands clasped behind his back. He was very much aware of what was going on around him, though.

J.P. Justinian sat back in his chair. The Premier regarded him coldly. Justinian was a handsome man, but he frowned more than he used to. He had lines in his face where none had existed before. The Premier was wearing a black uniform similar to the one he'd worn as the Chief Arbiter of the GSB.

Guards were standing in the room. They were big men with bad reputations. Each of them clasped a cone rifle and watched Benz with minute attention. They would murder him at the slightest indication from Justinian. Or they would set down their rifles and beat him to death if the Premier preferred that. The guards were hardened individuals, selected for their brutality and willingness to obey any order no matter how obscene.

In the past five months, there had been four assassination attempts on Justinian's life. Two of them had come extremely close to killing him. The last time, the Premier had gotten lucky. Those assassination attempts appeared to have driven Justinian into utter darkness of heart.

The man had begun a purge, starting with the GSB. Many of the highest GSB officers were now working in harsh penal camps. Some had starved to death in isolation wards. Some had faced firing squads. A few had managed the miraculous and gained rehabilitation. They were the most fanatical in Justinian's sweep of the military and Party ranks, the second-phase purges.

Justinian's secret fears had erupted into a literal bloodbath, tightening his hold over the apparatuses of the State.

Now, Benz stood before the most suspicious man in the Solar League. And it was possible Justinian meant to execute him.

Benz could hardly believe that, though. He'd calculated his odds with his usual brilliance. He was, quite frankly, a military genius and a genius in other areas as well. His IQ score was off the chart. In truth, his intelligence was far beyond that of any normal human's. He hid this amazing gift behind an arrogant but breezy manner. He had calculated for years, but now, he realized, he might have miscalculated the sheer paranoia gnawing at Justinian's soul.

"Inspector General," Justinian said in a silky voice.

Benz's far-off stare vanished as he focused on the Solar System's most powerful individual.

"I have a quandary, General."

Benz waited for it.

Justinian's frown deepened. That deepened the lines in his face. "Surely, you are aware of the…attempts to decapitate the Solar League."

Benz nodded sharply, knowing that the Premier meant the assassination attempts against him.

"Needless to say, because I am still here, the assassins failed."

"If there is anything my office can do to aid you—"

"Silence," Justinian said, as he slapped the desk.

The guards focused with avid hunger now. They watched Benz, no doubt feeling that this could be a fun one.

Benz shut up. How could he have missed the signs? He couldn't understand it.

"You aided me once in my hour of need," Justinian said. "I have often pondered that moment. You took a risk to help me."

Benz said nothing. The Premier referred to the time Benz had slid him a needler under the table, the needler Justinian had used to murder the former Premier.

"I am now the heart of Social Dynamism," Justinian said.

You are a monster, Benz told himself. *You were one then, and you're a worse one now.*

Justinian glanced at his guards. Maybe the Premier drew strength from their presence. The slightest of smiles replaced the frown. A second later, Justinian regarded Benz. "One word from me, Inspector General, and you will cease to exist."

That sent Benz's thoughts into overdrive. Despite his many calculations, he could not see a way free of his coming doom. Justinian did plan to murder him, didn't he?

"Do you know what bothers me about you, Inspector General?"

"I do not, Premier." That was the problem. Benz usually knew exactly why others did what they did.

With deliberation, Justinian opened a desk drawer. He pulled out a green folder. He slapped that onto the middle of the desk. With his right hand index finger, he tapped the folder.

"*This* bothers me," Justinian said.

With his peripheral vision, Benz noticed a crest on the folder. It had a dog's head superimposed on a broom. It was the GSB symbol. The dog signified sniffing out treason, while the broom swept it aside.

Justinian opened the folder and moved several sheets of paper before finally picking up a single sheet.

"Do you know what I'm looking at, Inspector General?"

"No, Premier," Benz half shouted.

"It is a high school assessment. Do you know who it assesses?"

Benz actually felt fear bloom in his heart. That was a strange sensation. He had not felt fear for a long time.

"It assesses a high school student by the name of Frank Benz. Why, this is an assessment about you, Inspector General."

"Yes, Premier," Benz forced himself to half shout.

Justinian leaned back as he kept glancing at the single sheet. "Among the things the high school counselor assessed was your IQ. Don't you think that's interesting?"

Since Benz didn't know what to say, he kept his mouth shut. Could Justinian have stumbled onto the truth? That was frightening for more than one reason.

"I read here that your IQ was one thirty-five," Justinian said. "That is nothing to sneeze at, naturally. Many people would love to have one so high. But it is anything but genius level. Why, I have a higher IQ myself."

"Yes, Premier."

Justinian snapped forward and slapped the paper into the folder. "Let's not play games, Inspector General. You're a military genius. I have seen it for myself. You are a man of destiny. You have taken chances and shown daring beyond a one-thirty-five-IQ officer. Am I correct?"

"You are correct, Premier."

Justinian put the paper in its correct location, closed the folder and put it back in its drawer. Afterward, he folded his hands on the desk, regarding Benz.

"How did you do it?" Justinian asked softly.

If Benz had lacked perfect self-control, his mouth would have dropped open. Instead, he simply kept staring at Justinian. He couldn't believe this. After all this time...

"I'm waiting, Inspector General."

Benz could feel his forehead growing warmer. Soon, beads of perspiration would form. That would be a dead giveaway of a guilty conscience.

"Maybe the better question is why," Justinian said. "You were young, but you must have realized that revealing yourself so soon might have ended badly for you."

In that instant, Benz realized Justinian had made a tiny error of analysis. The Premier had made a wrong assumption.

The Inspector General wanted to roar with laughter and relief. He couldn't do that for two reasons. One, that would make Justinian furious. Two, he had to use these few seconds to concoct a reasonable reason.

Justinian believed, as any sane person would, that Benz had always been a super-genius. The truth was much different. Benz had had a one thirty-five IQ in high school. It had been that low in college and afterward in the military academy. He'd only become fantastically brilliant in the past three years.

Justinian had come within a hair's breadth of a great and terrible secret. The Premier had the data necessary to stumble onto the truth. His ordinary intelligence blinded him to the incredible possibility of becoming fantastically smarter.

"I'm waiting for an answer, Inspector General."

Benz raised his chin and began to speak. He'd just formulated a story, one that should please someone as suspicious as Justinian. It had a few wild elements that ought to excite the Premier. As Benz spoke, he came to a conclusion. He must kill Justinian. He must kill the most protected person in the Solar System…To do that, he was going to need help.

Benz believed that he needed to survive because the human race depended on his brilliance. Without him, humanity would never survive the cyberships out there.

Benz suppressed the thought as he concentrated on the story. It appeared he might walk out of the Premier's office after all. Justinian would watch him even more carefully now, though.

But that didn't matter. It was time for Benz to really think. Otherwise, not even his genius would get him out of this dilemma.

-2-

Twenty-nine hours later, Benz sat outside at a Parisian café. It was one o'clock in the afternoon, and it was a glorious summer day. People strolled past the waist-high wrought iron fence, tourists and workers heading back to their offices or factories.

Benz sat at a small white table with the sun warming his neck, sipping wine and reading a tablet. He appeared at ease. He did not have any guards or aides with him. Two nondescript GSB agents, a man and woman team, were sitting at a different table, eating salads and drinking strong coffee.

Regular people lunched here or sat and talked. It was a crowded location with the famous Eiffel Tower in the near distance.

Benz had come to Paris for a particular reason. He had hunted down an interesting lead. The trick now would be to speak with her without arousing the suspicions of the GSB agents assigned to him. Normally, ridding himself of them would be simple. Because of the target on his back and the round-the-clock surveillance, he had to use greater caution. One misstep would land him before a tribunal, followed by a firing squad or a torture chamber. He could never reveal his secret to the GSB. If Justinian gained heightened intelligence…

Benz shuddered, sipped more wine to calm his nerves and saw the target open the wrought-iron gate.

She was a lithe woman with long red hair, pretty and well-endowed. She wore a military uniform stunningly, with the rank of lieutenant. She laughed as she approached a major already sitting at a table.

Others had accused Benz of mind powers at times. By that, they meant telepathy. Alas, he had no such powers. His only gift was incredible intelligence.

He picked up his wine glass, swirled the red liquid and inhaled the aroma. He did not normally drink alcohol. That killed brain cells, and he didn't want to take a chance on blunting his genius.

He sniffed again, and the idea struck.

Benz smiled as he set the glass on the table. He was in Paris, sipping wine, and there was a redheaded beauty at a nearby table. Could not even a smart Inspector General lose his mind over a woman? That would even explain why he'd followed her here.

Content with the premise of the plan, Benz now worked on devising the essence. He would not introduce himself yet. That wouldn't work.

Hmmm…maybe later today—

No. It would have to be this evening. He needed to discover her itinerary first. He picked up the goblet and the tablet and moved to another wrought-iron table, this one in the shade. It also happened to be beside the redhead and the older major.

Benz studied his tablet, all the while listening carefully to the couple's conversation. He was sure he would learn something in the next half hour that he could use for his master plan tonight.

-3-

Benz was something of a historian. He believed history—the stories of men and women in countless different venues in the past—was one of the best guides to human behavior. Various behavioral sciences claimed a better understanding of the human heart. Benz did not agree. History was really nothing more than humanity's collective memory. To say that history didn't matter was like saying memory wasn't important to an individual, that the moment the individual happened to be living through was all that mattered. That would be absurd.

One thing Benz had always supposed in his study of history was a pall of gloom on the general society during major political purges. The Stalinist purges of the 1930s and the later Maoist purges had led Benz to believe that those societies had been grim and humorless.

According to this belief, Justinian's increasingly paranoid and savagely thorough purges of the military and Social Dynamism Party members should have led to a cessation of fun everywhere in the Solar League. Earth should have been even harder hit—given the correctness of Benz's assumption, of course.

That was not true this evening here at the old Versailles Palace. People by the thousands flocked to the gala event, a costume ball. Surprisingly, mostly military officers and higher Party members were in attendance. These should have been the last people to party hearty, as they were in the category most likely to face a coming tribunal and a firing squad.

Yet, as Benz laughed at a joke an under-secretary of True News told to those circled around him, he realized why his former assessment had been incorrect. Many of those partying here tonight, dressed up as courtiers and ladies of the Sun King, Louis XIV of France, were doomed to die in the next few weeks. Therefore, the obvious course in their minds was to eat, drink and be merry, for literally, tomorrow they might die.

Benz excused himself from the group. He was wearing a heavy wig, finery, hose and buckled shoes like a fop from that period. He held a stick with a mask on the end to disguise his eyes. It was all quite ridiculous. He would never have come to such a foolish event except that the redhead and her major were supposed to come. Such he'd overheard from their lunch conversation.

"Here now," Benz told a waiter. "Wait a moment, you." He took a flute of champagne off a passing tray and appeared to dash the contents into his mouth. Soon enough, he poured the sparkling drink into a potted plant. It was an old ruse, likely first practiced in an ancient Egyptian court before the Pharaoh.

In any case, Benz made the rounds, searching for the redhead. He pretended to drink several more glasses, and he carefully playacted the part of a man growing increasingly drunk.

The GSB agents assigned to watch him had made their appearance. There were many other secret police agents mingled among the laughing, drinking, dancing and singing throng. Benz wondered if some of the secret police enjoyed themselves by joining the festivities. He suspected so. Tyrants could issue their decrees. Some people listened, of course. Some simply modified such decrees to suit their normal behaviors, as was the wont of most people throughout the ages.

The very issuance of laws implied something broken inside man. Why give laws to perfectly behaved people? They would not need laws. But ah, the heart of man was hidden away from prying eyes. In the dark, beetles could crawl and hide and worms could wriggle. In the dark, a heart could plot and fantasize to its own delight.

But what did dramas, holo-vid shows and songs declare? They almost uniformly urged people to follow their heart.

Murderers followed their hearts' delight. So did thieves, liars, adulterers, rapists, drunkards and porn addicts.

Benz sighed. Man was man. He had been man during Noah's departure off the Ark and when old Noah had gotten dead drunk, when Achilles slew Hector beside the walls of Troy, at the coronation of Charlemagne, at the battle of the Bulge when an officer shouted, "Balls!" and during 9/11 when a handful of Saudis smashed jetliners into the Twin Towers, and on and on and on. Laws, decrees, social experiments and purges could not change the essence of man.

According to the reports from the Saturn System—from the hidden GSB agents there who had learned about the actions in Neptune System—the alien AIs physically modified people and turned them into something else entirely.

That's why I'm here. That's why I have to play the part of a buffoon. And that's why I helped Justinian become the Premier.

Benz felt that he was directly responsible for the reign of terror presently taking place on Earth. It was so hard to believe those killings were taking place given the party tonight. And yet…the excesses of these people showed that they knew they lived on the knife's edge.

"Wait," Benz told a waiter. His hand seemed to have lost some of its coordination. It took him two tries to grasp a glass, lifting it off the tray.

The Inspector General raised the glass in a salute to the waiter. Naturally, most of the champagne sloshed over the lip, dripping from his hand onto the floor.

Benz laughed and appeared to toss the rest of the contents into his mouth. He staggered off afterward. Where was the damn woman? Where—?

He stopped short, blinking as if it took an effort of will to think straight. What would Justinian make of the GSB reports later of the Inspector General's unseemly drunkenness? Likely, the reports would please Justinian. Rulers seemed to uniformly love a weakness in their subordinates, something they could use as a lever against the person.

Like an old bull, Benz began moving again. He lumbered onto the dance floor. The redhead was dancing with the major.

Both were wearing period-piece costumes, the woman showing her cleavage to great advantage. The major, despite his age, had a decided lightness of foot.

"Do you mind, dear fellow?" Benz said with a slur. "I'd like to cut in."

The major had to turn to look at Benz. "Get out of here," the major warned with a scowl.

Benz lowered his mask.

The major continued to scowl. Maybe he didn't recognize the Inspector General of Earth.

"Don't worry, Heinz," the redhead told the major. "This is Frank Benz."

The name rang a gong in the major's mind, as he appeared startled. "I'm sorry, sir."

"No matter," Benz said, putting a hand on the major's shoulder. "Just leave," he said, pulling the major toward him and then shoving him to a destination farther away.

He didn't look to see what the major did. Instead, Benz clumsily took hold of the woman, grinned drunkenly and attempted to twirl her back to dancing.

She stumbled.

"Pardon," he slurred.

She recovered quickly, giving him a careful scrutiny. Then she matched his jerky manner of dancing as they moved among the more practiced couples on the dance floor.

"You're a good dancer," Benz said, as if he were a fool.

"Thank you, Inspector General."

"It's Frank, please," he said, tightening his hold on her.

"Thank you, Frank," she said with a delightful laugh.

Benz grinned at her, adding a drunken leer at her cleavage.

She laughed again with seemingly greater delight.

She's an easy lay if I want it, Benz realized. Yes. Maybe that would be the best approach. That should cover his tracks. It wouldn't make the major happy. And normally, Benz did not indulge in one-night stands. Still, this was for Earth, for humanity as a whole.

And thus, I prove that my heart is as dark as any, he thought.

Benz burst out laughing, as if he were laughing with the redhead. In reality, he was laughing at his willingness to bed the redhead and call it duty.

She feels good, and she likes this. I'm doing it because I can.

That was a lousy excuse. But he did need to question the redhead, and he had to do it in a way that aroused the least suspicion. People often spoke about strange things while aroused.

"I have an idea," Benz said, leering at the firm cleavage before his eyes.

"Yes?" she asked, with arched eyebrows.

And so Benz launched onto a perilous path, searching for a helpmate against one of the most insidiously tyrannical political systems ever imposed upon humanity.

-4-

Benz learned what he needed to know from the redhead. He had to spend three days and nights with her to gain the knowledge. She proved to be an active and vigorous woman, and Benz realized the GSB had turned her into an informant long ago.

That was fine. He indulged himself with her to the fullest. He enjoyed the lovemaking, and he felt tremendously guilty about it afterward. In this, he could not overcome his upbringing.

His parents had been Christians, belonging to an underground church. Benz held many of their beliefs, although he hadn't practiced much of what he believed. He wondered if that made him a hypocrite. Probably in some ways it did. If one listened to people long enough, it was clear they accused others of things they were perfectly fine doing themselves. Things like cutting in line but getting mad if someone cut ahead of them. Maybe everyone was a hypocrite to one degree or another.

Benz also wondered if trying to fight the current at least a little was better than simply drifting along and doing every wrong he wanted.

Yes, he slept with the redhead many times during the three days and he probably shouldn't have. During one of the last periods of lying around and watching a movie afterward, he'd gotten her to tell him a seemingly ridiculous story.

It was what he had been fishing for, as he'd heard a rumor of the incident some time ago.

The redhead had been riding a horse on the last day of the former Premier's administration. She had found Justinian in a park, having non-consensual sex with his latest victim. Benz learned that the former Chief Arbiter had actually intended to ride nude to the conference on the redhead's horse.

Benz shook his head in wonder, although he had the wisdom not to laugh. It was possible the bedroom was bugged, and it was possible GSB interrogators would force the redhead later to recount the Inspector General's exact responses to the nakedness story.

Benz had lain close to her then, and he'd whispered a few questions. She had smelled so good as she lay there looking up at him.

The woman in the park with Justinian that day had been a military linguist. She'd said an amazing thing after Justinian rode off.

Benz raised his eyebrows.

The redhead lowered her voice, repeating the linguist's wish to kill Justinian for raping her.

At that point, Benz made his greatest dare. He hinted around as if he'd like to know the woman's name.

The redhead squinted at him, thought about it and shook her head. For a moment, she seemed about to say that she didn't know the name. Instead, she said, "Vela Shaw."

Benz had gotten the name at great political and personal risk. No doubt, the Premier had already read a report about the Inspector General's short vacation in Paris. If Justinian hadn't read the reports written by the GSB agents and the redheaded informant, the new Chief Arbiter would have read them.

Had Benz committed enough strange behaviors these past few days to bring the secret police to his door?

So far, so good, and Benz believed he still had more time left. At least, such were his calculations. And in the last three years—since his rise to inhuman intelligence—the calculations had only been wrong three times.

Benz presently walked through a munitions factory several kilometers from a northern suburb in Rio de Janeiro.

It had been a week since his dalliance with the redhead. She'd attempted to contact him. He had not responded. That would make her angry. That might change some of her informant responses to her GSB case officer.

Benz shrugged. That couldn't be helped.

"Sir?" the munitions chief asked in dismay. He was a well-fed man in his fifties with three chins and a growing look of concern. He'd been explaining why he'd failed to make quota for the second month in a row. Clearly, the chief had taken Benz's shrug the wrong way.

"Continue," Benz said curtly.

The munitions chief did, his voice cracking at times and his concern obviously growing.

Benz terminated the inspection two hours later.

"We're working overtime, Inspector General," the chief said in a whiny voice. They stood beside Benz's air-car in the official parking lot.

"Do you think the State is made of credits?" Benz demanded.

"N-No," the chief stammered.

"The People's labor creates wealth. When you squander credits, you squander the People's hard work. Do you despise the People, Chief?"

"N-Never," the munitions chief stammered.

"There will be no more overtime. You will reach your quota. If you fail this month…" Benz let the threat hang in the air.

"But Inspector General…" the chief pleaded. "How can I encourage my workers to work harder? They yearn for credits—"

"How dare you?" Benz said in outrage. "Do you claim your workers are traitors to Social Dynamism?"

"N-No. Y-You misread my intent."

"You claim I'm an ignoramus like you?"

"Inspector General," the chief declared in horror. "N-No."

Benz turned abruptly. He had no desire to torment the plant manager, but this was the kind of response the chief would expect from him. The man worked under considerable strain. Ever since the *Nathan Graham* had torn the Saturn System from the Solar League, the populace had labored overtime to build up an ever-greater military.

Benz opened the door to his air-car, waving his hand as the manager pleaded for an extension. Benz could not give the manager one. The Solar League was preparing for space war. The hour of decision against the *Nathan Graham* was fast approaching.

Benz slid into the air-car, pressing a button that shut the door. He didn't look at the three-chinned plant manager. Activating the machine, taking it up, Benz decided it was time to make his play.

Vela Shaw, here I come.

-5-

Benz reached the Language Institute in the middle of Rio de Janeiro. It was a vast building in one of the most beautiful cities on Earth. Rio also happened to be the capital for the Solar League.

Benz walked into the grand lobby in time to see four black-uniformed GSB agents escorting a startling beautiful woman. She had long blonde hair cascading over her shoulders. She had green eyes that showed her anger and sadness mingled together.

People in the lobby avoided looking at the GSB agents. A few men glanced sidelong at the blonde with the gorgeous legs. Her heels clicked on the marble flooring as the four burly agents escorted her. None of their shoes made a sound.

Benz's right hand actually strayed to his holster. That was Vela Shaw. It could only mean one thing: the redhead had talked too much. The redhead must have recalled what she'd told the Inspector General after having sex.

Instead of drawing and firing his gun, Benz avoided looking at the group as they marched past him for the lobby doors. He would have to forget about Vela Shaw. She was going away. She would soon be dead. She had uttered a death threat, and now she was going to have pay for it with her life. Likely, nothing would have happened to her if Benz hadn't attempted to track her down.

He looked up and turned around, staring at the four GSB agents. The first one opened the door. Two grabbed hold of

Vela Shaw's arms. She looked back with terror etched on her incredibly lovely face. Her green eyes scanned the lobby. Maybe she was remembering for later in case they stuck her in isolation. She might have felt Benz's stare. Vela Shaw looked at him, their gazes meeting.

One, two, three seconds passed. In those three seconds, something went from Vela Shaw and hit Benz like a sledgehammer to the heart, causing him to take a step back. He could actually feel his heart thudding in his chest. It was positively crazy, but it was quite real.

Vela Shaw stumbled as the two agents thrust her through the exit. She had to look forward again. The glass door swung shut, and Vela and her escorts headed for a GSB heavy lifter.

Benz blinked, and it felt as if grit had been poured into his eyes. He had to save Vela Shaw. It was that simple. He had to follow his heart.

Benz looked down. The agents would take her to the dreaded De Gama House. The vast building took up several blocks of Rio. It was more than likely that Vela Shaw would go downstairs to the most loathsome part of De Gama House.

Benz closed his eyes so that he could think for a moment. When he opened them, Benz seemed like a different man, an avenger who had spread his wings to swoop down on his enemies.

This was going to be tricky. Benz walked briskly toward the exit. It was time to act.

-6-

For three years, Frank Benz had known he'd become a mental superman. At first, it had been a heady feeling. Later, it started constricting his spirit. He'd invented so many things he could never use. Well, he was going to use one of them in the next half hour.

He was walking down a corridor in the De Gama House. He'd entered the lair of the beast. Oh, he knew there were cameras recording everything. Guards had also frisked him, forcing him to surrender his sidearm. His venture into the heart of the GSB would soon become known to Justinian unless…

Benz decided to think about something else. Four big guards surrounded him. Two marching in front and two brought up the rear. They had guns, but they obviously didn't need weapons for the lone Inspector General. They could pretty much do whatever they wanted, or were ordered to do, to him.

The five of them marched through long marble corridors. Famous and achingly expensive paintings hung from the walls, including the Mona Lisa. Just as the Roman Emperor Constantine had raided ancient cities for their treasures to beautify his city of Constantinople, the GSB had raided museums to add beauty to their temple of torture and degradation of the human spirit.

The long march eventually led to the Chief Arbiter's suite of offices.

The four escorts left Benz in the hands of even bigger, tougher escorts. They spoke politely to the Inspector General, in the way that hyenas might speak to a lamb asking for directions. There was mockery in their manners, but there was a hint of caution as well. Maybe the Inspector General was here at the request of the Premier. It was just barely possible that Justinian's purge of the secret police would resume.

Shortly, the biggest guard ushered Benz into the inner sanctum of Chief Arbiter Indri Punjab. She was a tall woman born on the subcontinent of India. She had dark hair and skin and classically beautiful features. Rumor said she'd had her face bio-sculpted. If true, it was one of the best jobs Benz had ever seen. Indri Punjab also had a ruthless way of watching a person.

She was watching Benz now. She broke eye contact long enough to rise from her desk, move to a large comfortable chair and sit in it. She indicated the other comfortable chair near hers.

Benz headed for it.

As he did, Indri snapped her fingers. The huge guard retreated, closing the door behind him.

"This is unexpected, Inspector General."

"Please," Benz said. "I'd prefer if you called me Frank."

She shook her head the slightest bit. "Inspector General will suffice for now. I'm afraid I do not desire to speak intimately with someone under the Premier's scrutiny."

"Yet you're speaking alone with me."

Indri smiled faintly. "Inspector General, you are well aware that we are being recorded."

Benz did not reply, but she was correct.

Indri watched him like a cobra would a rat. Perhaps she was wondering at the prey's boldness to march to his death.

"This is all rather nerve-racking for me," Benz said, as if admitting his fear. "Do you mind if I smoke?"

"Your bio doesn't indicate that filthy habit."

"Really? I'm surprised. I need a smoke when I'm nervous. I really would appreciate this one concession."

Indri Punjab studied him.

Benz forced himself to act more nervous than was his wont.

She must have believed she sensed weakness, which Benz had hoped would make her feel superior.

"Yes, smoke," she said, as if saying, "Let me witness your breakdown."

Benz removed a half-crumbled pack of cigarettes. They looked used, which was anything but the case. He put a cigarette between his lips, took out a matchbook, tore off a paper match and struck the red tip against the dark strip. He figured they would have taken a lighter during the pat down. A flame flared into existence. He touched the flame to the end of the cigarette and began to puff in a rather unseemly manner. He was careful to inhale nothing. Some of the drug in the smoke would sink into his mouth nevertheless. He'd ingested enough of a counter agent to counteract the drug's effect. He'd also shoved nasal filters up his nostrils before entering the building. The filters were uncomfortable but necessary.

Benz made the cigarette tip glow as he puffed more of the drugged smoke into the room.

Soon enough, Indri Punjab waved a hand before her face. "It stinks."

"I'm sorry, but I appreciate your kind gesture. Do you have an ashtray?"

She shook her head.

Benz set the cigarette on a stand between the chairs. He let the cigarette end dangle so smoke trickled up from it.

Indri watched him with her ruthless gaze. Soon, the ruthlessness remained but a slight glaze seemed to film her eyes.

Benz waited, feeling increasingly lightheaded. Finally, he judged the Chief Arbiter ready to listen to reason.

"I'd like to speak to you personally, man to woman. I would like to speak off the record, if I may."

"That is an unusual request," she said woodenly.

"I believe it would be in your best interest as well."

She appeared surprised, but finally nodded. "Yes. I think I understand."

She stood, swaying a moment. Benz dearly hoped she didn't faint. He might have put too much drug into the air.

"I feel lightheaded," she said.

"It will pass," Benz said.

She looked at him, smiling soon. "The feeling has gone."

"You feel much better," he said.

"That's true." She staggered to her desk. It was clear she was not better, but she believed that she was. That made all the difference. She opened a drawer and pressed some controls. Afterward, she practically collapsed into her chair. She'd shut off the video feed that recorded her office.

"I feel grand," she announced. "Don't you feel grand, Inspector—"

"Call me Frank," he said, interrupting.

"Frank?" she finished.

"I want you to summon Vela Shaw to your office."

"When?"

"Immediately."

"Is this in reference to her verbal threat against the Premier?"

"Yes. I'm here as a representative of the Premier."

"Oh. I did not realize."

"I would never have come otherwise."

Indri nodded. "I knew that. Deep down, I knew that. Just a moment. Let me summon the would-be murderess."

After Indri Punjab gave the order over a comm, she resumed her seat beside Benz. "It is done. The killer will be here soon."

"Chief Arbiter, I have dreadful instructions for you. This is on the express order of the Premier. I have learned of a special safety feature installed into the De Gama House. Are you familiar with it?"

"I have no idea what you mean."

"I thought not. The former Premier had it installed because of her distrust of Justinian. She never had a chance to employ the device. She might still be alive if she had."

"That sounds treasonous," Indri said disapprovingly.

"The device is a massive bomb. It's embedded deep in the house. Once Vela Shaw arrives, you will order me to take her to the Premier. You will make this order in the presence of your chief guard. He will join me. After I leave De Gama House, you will detonate the bomb. I will tell you how to activate it, naturally. You will, of course, remain in your office."

"Will the bomb hurt me?"

"It will not," Benz lied. "This room is specially protected by advanced technology."

"I have never heard of that."

"Yet, it is true. You know that it is true. You are killing the traitors in this building, Chief Arbiter. You are working to save Justinian and thus, save your life, as well. You will do exactly as I have told you because it is for your own good."

"This is all amazing. I had no idea."

"That is why I came personally from the Premier's office. I told the Premier about your loyalty."

"That was quite generous of you."

"I highly respect you, Chief Arbiter. I am risking my neck to help you. You will do these things…" Benz repeated his orders and told her how to activate the bomb.

The drug in the cigarette made a person highly prone to suggestion. Benz had developed the drug two years ago. It was one of several items he'd invented but never used until this moment. Using it like this…the destruction of De Gama House would create chaos. That would make Justinian more murderous. But this was the only way he could pull Vela Shaw to safety and keep it off the cameras. He had to destroy the recordings by destroying the building's computer system, and, incidentally, many GSB agents. It was unfortunate many pieces of fine art would perish, but to Benz, human lives were more important than artwork.

Sooner than Benz expected, a knock announced Vela Shaw's arrival. She was wearing the orange jumpsuit of a prisoner. Benz hadn't foreseen this complication.

"You will take her immediately to the Premier's office," Indri said sternly.

"She needs normal clothes," Benz said.

Indri blinked at him.

"Are there regular garments here?" Benz asked.

The Chief Arbiter pointed at a wall.

"Get them," Benz said.

Woodenly, the Chief Arbiter turned to the wall, pressing hidden switches. The wall rose. Behind it was a bathroom, closet and other rooms.

"Chief Arbiter...?" the big guard asked suspiciously.

"Have them both come in," Benz said.

Indri ordered the guard and prisoner into the hidden area of her office.

"Take his gun," Benz said softly.

"Give me your gun," Indri ordered the huge guard.

It seemed the man might argue. Finally, he drew the gun and handed it to Indri.

"Give it to me," Benz said.

The Chief Arbiter did so.

The guard opened his mouth to protest.

Benz had been inspecting the heavy gun. He clicked off the safety, aimed the barrel at the guard's chest and pulled the trigger five times. Five terrific *booms* sounded. Five heavy slugs shattered ribs and tore apart heart and lungs.

Vela Shaw opened her mouth to scream as the guard flopped onto the floor, his torso a gory wreckage.

Benz lowered the gun as smoke curled from the barrel. "You must listen to me," he told Vela.

She turned to him with her mouth hanging open, staring, obviously confused and frightened.

Benz set the gun on the floor. "Chief Arbiter, help me drag the guard into the bathroom."

Indri Punjab woodenly obeyed. She and Benz dragged the limp corpse, leaving a trail of blood on the floor.

Vela finally closed her mouth. She seemed to perceive that something strange was taking place, and that this strangeness aided her.

Soon, Vela was dressed in regular garments, with a sheer red scarf tied around her neck. At Benz's instructions, the Chief Arbiter closed the wall and waited for further instructions.

"Do you remember what I told you earlier?" Benz asked her.

"I do," Indri intoned. She had clearly lost any free will, totally succumbing to the drug.

"Do those things as soon as we leave the building," Benz said.

"I will," Indri said like a robot.

"Are you ready?" Benz asked Vela.

"I don't understand this," she whispered.

"You're leaving with me." Benz stared at her intently, hoping she understood. He didn't care to say too much in front of the Chief Arbiter.

Finally, Vela nodded.

Benz grasped Vela's left elbow, gently propelling her to the door. He opened it and pushed her into the reception area. Leaning forward near her left ear, he whispered, "Here goes."

***

The two of them made it out of the De Gama House. Benz hustled Vela to his air-car, and they zoomed upward. At that moment, a terrific explosion lifted De Gama House off its foundations. Brick and debris flew in all directions as smoke and ash shot up into the sky.

The concussion rocked the air-car and almost plucked it out of the sky.

Vela screamed.

A big chunk of something hurtled past the car. Miraculously, that was it. Even so, the air-car rocked, dropped—Benz swore under his breath as he fought the controls. The underside scraped against the street. Everything vibrated in the vehicle. Then, the car shot up into the air.

Vela screamed again as Benz veered hard enough to avoid a looming building. Finally, the air vehicle climbed into the sky.

Below, what had once been De Gama House blazed with fire as a vast ashy cloud began to billow into more of the city.

Vela finally closed her mouth. She stared down at the destroyed secret police headquarters. Afterward, she stared at Benz.

"I don't know how, but you caused that," she said.

Benz said nothing.

"You did cause that, didn't you?"

"Yes," he said.

"Who are you?"

"Frank Benz."

"The Inspector General of Earth?"

He nodded.

"How...Why...None of this makes sense."

"I know."

"Why did the GSB wait all this time to arrest me?"

"Do you still want a crack at the Premier?"

"What?" she asked.

"Do you still want to kill J.P. Justinian for raping you?"

The color drained from Vela's features. Then, she blushed crimson. "You can't be serious."

"You saw what happened to the De Gama House. I'm serious."

"But...but...how?"

"I can show you how, but you have to want it."

She kept staring at him. "This isn't real. We're dead. You and me, we're dead once they catch us."

Benz shook his head. "Why do you think I destroyed the De Gama House?"

"Because you're power mad," she said.

"No," Benz said. "To cover our tracks. You looked at me in the Language Building. The GSB agents were holding your arms. I saw you pleading through your eyes for my help. This is it. I'm helping you. Now, are you willing to help me?"

"To do what?"

"Kill Justinian for one thing."

"And then?"

"Take over," Benz said.

Her eyes had become wild. She shook her head. "I don't see how I can help you."

"You can't yet. But I can help you become...smarter."

"Are you insane, Inspector General?"

"Think about it. I came in alone and weaponless to the De Gama House. I'm already under suspicion. I spoke to the Chief Arbiter. Why do you think the guards brought you to her office?"

"I cannot fathom it."

"Because I told her to order it," Benz said.

"Just like that? You said it, and the terrible Indri Punjab obeyed?"

"No, not just like that," Benz said. "I smoked a cigarette first."

"Why does that matter?"

"The cigarette contained a drug that makes people highly suggestible. The Chief Arbiter inhaled the drug. *Then* I told her what to do. That included detonating the De Gama House."

Vela stared at him and then abruptly turned away. "All those people are dead. You killed them."

"The GSB would have tortured you—"

"I'm not talking about *them*," Vela said sharply. "I'm talking about all those prisoners you slaughtered."

Benz squinted into the distance, finally nodding. "Yes. I consigned them to death. I have innocent blood on my hands. I'm guilty of murder. Before I pay for my crimes, I mean to save the human race, if I can."

"The noble Inspector General," Vela said, scornfully.

He turned to her. "Your response shows I've chosen correctly."

"What if I refuse to help a murderer like you?"

He searched her face. His mind clicked over the possibilities. Finally, he looked away. She would not refuse to help him unless he said she had no choice. Then the core of stubbornness in her would lock her onto a destructive path out of sheer mulishness.

"I'm waiting for your answer," she said.

"I'm asking for your help, Vela. I need it."

She intertwined her fingers on her lap. At last, she nodded. "I'd like to see how you think we can do any of this. I'm game for the moment, and I am grateful you tore me out of the basement. I…I just hate thinking about all those innocent people who died today to cover our tracks."

Benz didn't tell Vela that he might have been merciful. The tortures most of those innocents in the basement would have undergone… He didn't know if Vela could accept such reasoning. She might be too wholesome for such thoughts.

Banking the air-car, Benz began the long trip for a hidden place in the Rocky Mountains of North America.

-7-

They landed three times for recharging, the last time in Los Angeles. Benz had to invoke emergency powers that time. News of the obliteration of De Gama House had traveled around the planet several times. Already, Justinian had summoned other trusted GSB personnel, gathering in a hidden location in the Amazon Basin.

The Premier was no doubt concocting plans within plans in response to this dreadful strike. Justinian would likely believe the attack had been a direct blow against his authority and against the purges.

"You should take charge of the military," Vela said.

The two of them hurried down an old abandoned mineshaft in Colorado Sector. The air-car was just inside the mouth of the mine. They both wore masks and carried oxygen tanks. He used a powerful flashlight, taking a seemingly random path through the complex maze of tunnels.

"You must know the whereabouts of the Premier's hiding spot," she added.

"If it were that easy," Benz said, "do you think I'd risk so much getting you here?"

"From what I've seen and heard so far, you think several steps ahead of everyone."

"That's true," Benz admitted. The flashlight beam passed over a rocky formation beside ancient timber shoring up the shaft. It was cold down here.

Vela was already hugging herself as she shivered.

Benz advanced on the rocks, felt around and moved a lever. The rocks swung back, and his beam shone into a stainless steel corridor.

"What is this place?" Vela asked.

"Go," he said. "I have generators. Once we reach them, I can turn on a heater."

"G-Good," she said, her teeth chattering.

Benz shut the secret door. Their footsteps echoed in the new corridor. The way continued with a slight decline, taking them deeper under the mountain.

"Is this your Fortress of Solitude?" she asked.

"You're not far off the mark."

She followed him for several steps, finally saying, "You think pretty highly of yourself."

"False modesty is useless. You'll soon understand."

"I'm not sure I want to—if it makes me like you."

"I'm not so bad once you get to know me."

"What if I find out you're worse?"

"That would be a problem."

Their conversation faltered. Finally, they reached a new hatch, a thicker, heavier entranceway.

Benz manipulated the combination. It clicked. He opened the ponderous hatch, shined the light for Vela to enter, and pulled the great hatch so it boomed shut behind them. He used the flashlight to find his way to a bank of controls. He wiped off dust and tapped a correct sequence.

Far away in the mountain, a generator roared into life. Several seconds later, lights brightened in the chamber. That revealed a larger area than she'd expected, with many machines and strange tools arrayed on metal benches and worktables.

"This way," Benz said.

He hadn't been under the mountain for three long years. In a way, he was surprised the GSB hadn't found it by now. He shrugged, deciding that didn't mean God was with him in this. He had too much blood on his hands with the dead in De Gama House to expect God's help.

He counted the hatches, stopping at the fourth one. He turned to Vela. "This is it."

She watched him. She no longer hugged herself because warm if oily air moved through the corridor. They had both removed their masks and tanks.

Benz opened the way, clicked on lights and pointed at a large dentist-like chair with an overhanging helmet. The ensemble was beside a big bank of machinery.

"What is that?" Vela said.

Benz had been debating how much he should explain. Finally, he decided on all of it that was pertinent.

"You'd better sit," he said, indicating a stool.

"I have been sitting in the De Gama House and in your flitter for days already. I can stand. I prefer standing."

He nodded, sitting down on the stool himself and looking up at her.

"This will sound…" Benz stopped, figured it would be better not to say "crazy." People were far more susceptible to suggestion than they realized. If it were not so, advertisers wouldn't bother with their slogans and sales pitches.

"My great uncle belonged to a unique set of scientists," Benz began. "They included an archeologist and an experimental inventor. My great uncle was the latter. To make a long story short, the archeologist worked in Antarctica. He followed ancient leads. There had been a hint in a ruin in the Black Sea—"

"You're talking about an underwater ruin?" Vela asked, interrupting.

"Exactly," Benz replied. "In the underwater ruin on a rust-free metal sheet, the archeologist discovered the outline of the continent of Antarctica. It also showed a location that was far inland. He kept the find to himself. The archeologist was more paranoid than any Chief Arbiter you've ever known. The man's old heart beat with excitement. Here was a real treasure map, he believed. And he was not wrong.

"He led a team into the middle of the icy continent, and there he bored one of the deepest shafts ever discovered. He went down with three explorers. According to my great uncle, only the archeologist returned topside. The old relic hunter never told anyone what went on down there, or what they had found. A terrible accident took place that night. The shaft had a cave-in, if that's the correct way to say it. A mother-of-all-storms hit the team three days later. The old archeologist was the only one to survive."

"He killed everyone else?" Vela asked.

Benz shrugged. "I think so. My great uncle wasn't sure. It doesn't really matter."

"That's totally wrong," Vela declared. "It matters a great deal. Whatever you're about to show me is tainted by the archeologist's murderous behavior. I think it explains how easily you murdered everyone in the De Gama House."

Benz made a snorting sound. "Vela Shaw, how delightfully innocent you are."

"Don't mock me, and don't say that. I'm not innocent. Don't you know why I said what I did about Justinian?"

"Of course I know. It's why I sought you out."

"I never should have said what I did. Bitterness is an evil root. I've expunged that awful memory. I'd rather not talk or think about that day in the park."

Benz studied her. "Maybe that's good for you. What about all the other women Justinian will rape? What if you can prevent that?"

Vela sighed after a moment. "Keep telling your story. What happened next?"

"Yes, well," Benz said, "the archeologist had raided a prehistoric colony. My great uncle believed it had been a colony of aliens on Earth. For reasons we don't know, the aliens perished. Not all of their technology perished with them, however. The archeologist took a small machine. This machine he brought to my great uncle.

"Now, this is where the story gets interesting."

"I would think the idea of an alien colony on Earth during prehistoric times would be exciting enough," Vela said.

"By a long and painstaking process, my great uncle took apart the alien machine. He studied, tested and probed it for over six years. Finally, he built that."

Benz indicated the machine and dentist-like chair.

"What does it do?" Vela asked softly.

"The archeologist was the first test subject," Benz said, as if he hadn't heard the question. "He died as a raving lunatic.

My great uncle made adjustments afterward. He made more tests. Finally, he visited me and convinced me to join him."

"I thought you said a team of people worked with him."

"They had. The GSB had gotten to all of them. They all died in various ways, most horribly. But the fact they never revealed the machine—this machine—shows that my great uncle's invention worked in one particular."

"What was that?"

"He had forbidden them to speak about the machine or this hideaway. He had each go under the machine as he gave them the single instruction. I am quite certain his words consigned many of the captured to gruesome ends."

"Because of GSB torture?"

Benz nodded.

Vela shuddered, hugging herself once more. "Please, let me leave. I don't want to know more."

Benz smiled faintly. She didn't mean that. "I went under the chair, as my great uncle used to put it. He lowered the metal dome on my head and made the first adjustment. I had two sessions in the chair. It altered my brain to an excessive degree. The chair made me smarter, much smarter than any human in history."

"And…?"

"My great uncle died because the GSB took him. I imagine they interrogated him first, tortured him. But he could no more tell them about this place than any of his predecessors could."

"That's horrible."

"Indeed," Benz said. "That's when I started on my quest. I decided to change the nature of the Solar League. I put myself in the right place for the right time. I helped a monster rise to power because I thought I could use him. Alas, despite my genius, I have made three missteps. Because I am so weak politically, I could not afford even one misstep. Despite my genius, I am still just one man. I have blind areas. All people do. I have thought to myself, 'What if I can find a helpmate, someone I can truly trust.'"

"Me?" Vela asked. "But you don't know me."

"I know enough about you. You hate Justinian. I suspect you dislike Social Dynamism."

"I've never thought about that. I certainly don't like using force to make people think one way or another."

"Excellent!" Benz said. "You believe in personal freedom."

Vela thought about that. She gave a small laugh. "Yes, I suppose I do. I'd just never put it into words before."

Benz stood. He approached the beautiful and morally upright Vela Shaw. He took one of her hands in his.

"Vela," he said, while staring her in the eyes. "Will you help me?"

"How?" she whispered.

"I want you to go under the chair, as it were. I want to increase your intelligence many times. By putting our heads together, I'm hoping we can come up with a plan to eliminate Justinian and his oppressive rule, change Social Dynamism and unite the Solar System so we can take on the murderous cyberships with a chance of success."

"That is an amazingly tall order."

"It is. It must be. To whom much is given, much is required."

She turned away, although she didn't pull her hand away from his. "I don't know."

He squeezed gently.

Her shoulders deflated. She turned back and searched his eyes. "Will the process hurt?"

"Some," he admitted.

"Yes," she whispered. "I'm willing."

For a moment, he couldn't breathe. They were going to do this. "Now is as good a time as any to start," he said.

"Yes," she agreed. "Let's do this before I lose my nerve."

Still hand-in-hand, Benz led Vela to the machine.

PART III
TRANS-NEPTUNIAN REGION

-1-

Since gaining dominance of the frail body of Eli Gomez, the alien thought-patterns of Methlan Rath of Janus House had considerably changed it.

Methlan had begun a strict régime of forced eating and weightlifting. Eli might have been satisfied with the body's frailty. Methlan certainly wasn't. The weakness of the body's muscles and the shameful lack of endurance disgusted the once powerful prince.

Almost every day, Methlan went to the gym. He did legs one day, concentrating on squats. He bench-pressed and did triceps the second day, while he devoted the third day to deadlifts and biceps curls. The fourth day he rested. The fifth day, he started the process all over again. Soon, he added long walks and then wind sprints. He would forge something better than what he'd received. This body would never match his former frame, but it would be capable of considerably more physical effort than before.

Time passed as Methlan put on weight and muscle. A few of the gym-rats began to notice him. He talked with them, made friends, and they gave him weightlifting advice.

Methlan might have sneered at the help, but this was a human body, not that of the High Race of Janus House. The gym-rats proved helpful. One or two suggested he use steroids.

Methlan thought about it, but disliked the side effects. Good eating and strenuous training would give him what he needed.

When he wasn't improving his body with exercise, Methlan worked as a tech. He volunteered every chance he could. He strove to make himself invaluable. He had no time for relaxation. He had too many goals to achieve. Besides, by lifting, working, eating and sleeping, he kept so busy he didn't have to worry about running afoul of the Old Man's people.

As Methlan did these things, work went apace on MK2 and down on Makemake. Marines had swept the spaceport wreckage, killing two AIs but finding no others.

The days merged, becoming a week. The weeks piled one on top of another. Finally, the heavily modified NSN Destroyer *Daisy Chain 4* was ready to leave Makemake and head for Senda.

An accident took out two techs assigned to join Walleye and his team aboard the destroyer. Methlan hardly knew anything about the Makemake citizen or the citizen's woman. Apparently, they had volunteered to command the destroyer and go on the mission. Captain Hawkins had accepted their offer.

Methlan knew Walleye was short and possessed stubby arms and legs. How could Jon Hawkins let a weak mutant run the mission? It made no sense. Yet, that had given Methlan an idea. The daring of the new idea amazed him and propelled him to even greater zealousness.

Methlan worked and plotted until his eyelids drooped. He often awoke with his head slumped over a computer panel.

The destroyer lacked two needed techs. Hawkins asked for volunteers. Methlan was one of the first to say he'd do it.

That led to an interview with Captain Hawkins.

Methlan entered the captain's quarters on the moon. Like him, Hawkins was busy to the point of absurdity. The prince recognized a driven individual. He tried to make sure Hawkins didn't recognize him.

"Let's see," Hawkins said from behind his desk. The captain pretended to study a tablet. Methlan knew the foul man was studying him instead. At last, Hawkins set down the tablet.

"Why do you want to go?" Hawkins asked.

Methlan had sat forward with his hands hanging between his knees. He clutched his hands as he gave a tremulous smile.

"I want to stop the cybers, sir. I don't want them getting to Mars."

Hawkins nodded approvingly.

Methlan would have snorted, but that would not do. He'd studied Jon Hawkins from afar. He'd used every trick to learn whatever he could in order to form a picture of the lying killer.

"It's going to be a dangerous run," Hawkins said. "The destroyer has new, more advanced weapons. It can accelerate at almost at the same rate as the *Nathan Graham*. But it's a small ship. There will only be a few of you. What's more, the AIs may have built a bigger and better ship on Senda. I don't have time to take the cybership to Senda. What I'm saying, Mr. Gomez, is that this is a highly dangerous mission."

"If Walleye can do it, sir, I believe that I can too."

The good will on Hawkins' face evaporated. Methlan realized he'd made a mistake. Likely, Hawkins didn't distrust freaks as he, the prince, did.

"What I mean, Captain, is that the people of the Solar System are uniting. Makemake has already faced and suffered from the dreaded invader. Yet, Walleye still helps the rest of us to defeat the terrible menace. Can I, a man of Mars, do any less?"

"I see," Hawkins said.

Methlan didn't understand what he'd done wrong. Thus, he now remained silent. Digging a deeper hole was seldom a good idea.

"It's funny," Hawkins said. "But I can't shake the feeling that I've met you before."

Methlan almost froze. Somehow, he was giving his true nature away. He might hate Hawkins. That didn't mean the man was stupid. He must tread cautiously.

"I don't…think we've met, Captain."

"I do. I'm seldom wrong about that. I know we've met, Mr. Gomez. Tell me a little more about yourself."

Methlan dredged what memories he could from Eli's mind. That proved little enough, but it seemed to satisfy the sinister Hawkins.

"I've heard reports about your exercise mania."

"If I'd been in better shape, maybe I could have saved my friends."

"According to what I've read, you don't remember the accident."

"I don't remember the incident," Methlan said. "That's what bothers me. Call it a guilty conscience."

Hawkins nodded noncommittally. The bastard asked a few more questions, made a few comments about fighting to the bitter end and told Methlan he'd decide on the crew roster in the next few days.

Methlan thanked him and was dismissed shortly thereafter.

Two days later, Methlan received his answer. It was outside the gym in a corridor. Gloria Sanchez walked up to him. Had she been waiting here?

The mentalist informed him that the captain had assigned him to the *Daisy Chain 4*. She congratulated him, shaking his hand.

Methlan realized she was studying him. He could feel the unease in her. That was another reason he wanted to go on the destroyer. He had come to realize that sooner or later they would sense the Prince of Ten Worlds in Eli Gomez. He didn't know how or why, he just realized that event might come far sooner than he wanted.

"You're going to chase the enemy all the way to the Oort cloud if you have to," the mentalist said.

"I do not understand."

"By this time tomorrow, I assure you, you will."

That sounded ominous. Was this a veiled threat? Methlan almost decided to break her neck and implement Plan 3-C. Instead, he retreated, deciding he would play out the game for as long as he could.

-2-

The destroyer accelerated hard—over 50 Gs—toward Senda, 212 AUs away. The new engine purred much more quietly than the old one. But with the gravity controls at full strength, a steady *thrum-thrum* beat throughout the triangular-shaped vessel.

The *Daisy Chain 4* resembled the old NSN vessel in its basic shape. Otherwise, the changes to the ship were quite startling. It seemed more chrome-like and sleeker, deadlier, more alien seeming. The robo-builders on MK2 had completely overhauled the vessel.

In one way, it was exactly like a Neptunian Navy ship. On top of the triangular-shaped destroyer was a rack. In the rack was a huge drone. The drone was longer than the destroyer. On the bottom of the *Daisy Chain 4* were two more similarly huge drones. These were special objects. They had fantastic acceleration ability. They had the most up-to-date sensors, the best electronic counter measures (ECM) and intensely powerful matter/antimatter warheads. The three *Hercules* drones were one of the chief reasons Hawkins was allowing Walleye to try to chase down the Senda-launched AI vessel.

Walleye sat in the captain's chair, even though he only ranked lieutenant in the Solar Freedom Fleet, the SFF. The lieutenant was short, with coarse hair and an odd face. You could never tell where Walleye was staring exactly. It was an unsettling quality. Instead of a regular uniform, the mutant wore a buff coat. He seemed to live in the oversized garment.

Methlan had come to believe that Walleye hid weapons in the coat.

The mutant's short arms and legs always upset Methlan. He considered the lieutenant to be a freak. The word mutant seemed too kind, too forgiving to Methlan's way of thinking.

The same could not be said for June Zen. She was a long-legged prize, wearing silver, tight-fitting pants and a stylish jacket. She was the destroyer's navigator-slash-comm officer. Methlan knew she was beautiful because his body responded to her presence. That was another reason he found Walleye annoying. How could the beautiful June Zen choose the short mutant over him?

Methlan had always been vain regarding his good looks as the Prince of Ten Worlds. He had bedded thousands of beauties in his time as supreme ruler. He'd worked hard with the clay of Eli Gomez. The lean muscles rippling under his tech uniform and the stylish hair he kept waxed should have caught her admiration by now.

Methlan had always disliked a female's loyalty to her mate. In the past, if Methlan had wanted to rut with a female, he most certainly did so. Having to restrain himself was proving difficult. And this was only the third day of the journey.

"Tech," Walleye said curtly.

Methlan tore his gaze from June Zen. As he did, Methlan realized this was the third time Walleye had called for him.

"Yes, Lieutenant," Methlan said.

"I want you to bring up the alien vessel on our screen. Do you think you can do that?"

Methlan resented the tone of command in Walleye's voice. The little mutant seemed as if he resented Methlan's study of June. Was the mutant one of those jealous kinds? Methlan had often wondered how he'd died the first time in his ten worlds. One of his theories was that an upset mate had tracked him down for rutting with his woman. It seemed obvious that a woman should always rut with the best man. In Methlan's mind, that had always been himself.

"Tech," Walleye said.

"At once, Lieutenant," Methlan said. He began to manipulate his panel.

The destroyer's control cabin was much smaller than the *Nathan Graham's* bridge. It had a command chair and four consoles. Two of the consoles were empty. The augmented automation in the ship mandated less oversight. At the same time, the robo-builders had constructed less powerful computers than otherwise. Hawkins had decided that none of the SFF ships would have computers susceptible to self-aware cyber software.

Methlan used passive sensors, gathering light-bearing data concerning the Senda-launched vessel.

"It's coming up on the main screen," Methlan said.

The main screen was the only screen on the bridge, except for the small, individual console screens.

A round vessel appeared on the main screen.

Walleye sat forward so his butt was no longer on the seat but pressed against the edge. That way, his short legs could reach the deck. The mutant appeared to study the alien vessel.

"What do you make of it?" Walleye asked.

Methlan had been observing the round vessel. He noticed the torpedo ports and the radar-like dishes that indicated grav cannons. There appeared to be two of them.

"The color of the exhaust indicates a matter/antimatter engine," Methlan said. "The ports—" He went on to explain his other observations, finishing with: "It is a fighting vessel. But the round shape and its mass, and the lack of greater tubes or cannons, indicates to me that it likely has a hyperdrive. If that is so, the alien vessel can leave the Solar System. Using hyperspace, it can likely reach another star system in a short period of time. We must destroy the vessel before it can summon cybership reinforcements."

Walleye had turned to face Methlan. The mutant was no longer leaning against the command chair. He was standing, and he did not appear amused.

"I wasn't asking you," Walleye said. "I was asking June—the navigator."

Methlan might have apologized, but the insult was too much and, he was certain, too studied. Why had Walleye let him talk so long if it was a mistake? Methlan realized the answer. The little mutant meant to demean him in the female's eyes. Methlan understood the tactic, as he had often done it himself in the past.

"We have a problem, tech. We may have a big problem, you and I. I haven't decided yet."

Methlan swallowed his excessive pride and managed to bow his head.

"I think you're an arrogant prick," Walleye said. "I don't know why Captain Hawkins pushed you onto me. Maybe you hid your true self from him. I see it, though."

What was the little freak saying? Did this Walleye mean to say that he understood Methlan had gained control of the pathetic human? If that was so, he had to kill the freak. That would mean killing June Zen, too. Methlan was reluctant to do that. He wanted to sleep with her for a time. He could dispose of her after that.

"Navigator," Walleye said. "Could you please step outside?"

June rose, looking worried.

She must realize I can squash her freakish lover.

"Please don't hurt him too bad, Walleye," she said, touching one of the freak's stumpy arms.

"What?" Methlan said. "You can't be serious."

June faced him. "I don't like you staring at me all the time. You can't keep doing that. Walleye will kill you if you keep it up."

"Me? He thinks he can kill me?"

"Let me take care of this, Luscious," Walleye told her.

June nodded. Then, her long legs ate up the distance. The exit swished open and she departed the bridge.

-3-

Methlan swiveled around and stood, staring at the little freak. The mutant did nothing else. He just stood there, waiting.

"Well?" Methlan asked.

"Your trouble is you lack patience."

Methlan thought about the last few weeks, the last few months. He'd shown tremendous patience. Was this going to be the freak's method, spouting untruths? Under the long sleeves of his uniform, Methlan flexed his forearms. They were as hard as steel these days. That had come about through patience as he waited for the results of his strenuous labor.

"Your other problem is arrogance. You reek of it. Your arrogance is going to get you killed."

"By you?" Methlan sneered. "I can't understand why Hawkins gave you command of the ship."

"Easy. Captain Hawkins recognizes…competence."

That angered Methlan. He opened his mouth, and he noticed Walleye casually put a hand inside the buff coat.

Something about the motion recalled an old memory. It had happened in the citadel of Janus House. A cutthroat of House Ares had infiltrated the citadel. The long-limbed fellow had casually reached into his jacket, withdrawing a named dagger. Methlan had been a child at the time. The cutthroat advanced on Methlan's grandfather from behind. Young Methlan had shouted a warning, but it was already too late. The cutthroat moved fast at the end, reaching his grandfather, using the dagger to slice the old man's throat. That had brought the guards to alert. Before they could stun and incapacitate the cutthroat, the killer had uttered a victorious cry and plunged the coup dagger into his own heart. Whatever revenge the cutthroat had yearned to achieve, he had fulfilled. By doing so, he brought greater nobility to House Ares.

The memory stirred something deep in Methlan. That brought about a swift reevaluation regarding Walleye and this time and place.

I have been a fool, Methlan realized.

In some manner he hadn't foreseen, the emotions of Eli Gomez had retained power over his thoughts. It had been subtle, slowly twisting Methlan's thought-patterns into the body's old routines of feeling. Methlan had felt the emotions and used his own memories to give a reason to this feeling.

It was time for iron self-control. June Zen had wonderful legs and a perfect butt. That should not sway him from the chosen path.

Methlan's head snapped up. He viewed Walleye more dispassionately than seconds ago. He recognized the coiled tension in the mutant. This man was a killer. He could be a merciless killer, giving few cues as to what he was about to do. That in itself made Walleye dangerous.

"I have erred," Methlan said. Despite the distaste of the action, Methlan went to one knee, bowing his head. "I crave your pardon, Lieutenant."

Walleye said nothing.

Methlan looked up. He couldn't fully read the mutant. It was those eyes, and the way Walleye could keep his features blank. It was hard to know what the little man thought. That was a considerable power.

"What just happened?" Walleye finally asked.

"I beg your pardon?"

"You just stood there with a glazed look."

"I must have done that as I recognized my error. As you say, I have a problem with arrogance. Sometimes, though, I understand that I have become presumptuous."

"You're speaking differently, too."

Methlan realized he had made several errors regarding Walleye. Would he have to kill the mutant this early in the mission? That would make everything more difficult. He did not fear Walleye. He just realized he needed a peaceful crew if he was going to achieve his goal.

From now on, Methlan swore to focus single-mindedly on his goal. That goal was no longer slaying Jon Hawkins, although he would if given the opportunity. No. The goal was to gain power in order to free the Ten Worlds from the hated cyberships. It was possible that none of his people or house survived. Yet, perhaps some had. Those of the Ten Worlds were hardy individuals.

"I have decided on formality with you, Lieutenant. I will not stare or lust after your woman. I will accept your orders. I have erred, and I am willing to change."

Walleye's features did not change. Finally, though, the mutant nodded. He slid back into the command chair.

Methlan realized that was it. The confrontation was over.

Walleye pressed a switch in the chair. "You can come back in," he said.

The entrance swished open, and June Zen stared within.

Methlan gave her a polite nod, pretending to ignore her exceedingly pleasing features as he turned back to his board. He'd lied in one particular. He would fantasize about her. But that was all he'd do for now. He promised himself many good times with June Zen, but only *after* he killed Walleye. He would not kill Walleye until the journey neared its completion.

-4-

The days passed as the destroyer accelerated swiftly like the *Nathan Graham* had once done during its voyage from the Saturn System to Makemake. Unfortunately, the AI vessel they chased accelerated almost as fast as the destroyer did. The AI vessel seemed to be headed for the inner Oort cloud.

The Oort cloud was 50,000 to 200,000 AUs from the Sun. That made it much farther than the Kuiper Belt or the scattered disc, which was in the region between them. The cloud was a great spheroid in the outer reaches of the Solar System. Icy planetesimals were the primary objects scattered throughout the cloud.

A few hardy souls had traveled into the distant region, but very few. There was supposed to be a fabled outpost or two in the inner cloud, but neither Walleye nor June, nor anyone at the base at MK2 knew those places' reputed whereabouts.

The people in the Kuiper Belt had been the latest frontiersmen. In Earth terms, the few souls in the Oort cloud would compare to the fur trappers in American colonial days.

"We're staying well clear of Senda," Walleye announced one day.

"I've been watching the dwarf planet for some time," Methlan said from his station.

"Have you spotted anything suspicious on or around it?"

"Nothing so far," Methlan said. "Still, I suspect the remaining Senda robots are using teleoptics to watch us. It's possible they're attempting to maneuver stealth mines into our path."

"It's what I would do," Walleye said. "We'll have to make adjustments. I'm going to give Senda an even wider berth than I'd first intended."

It took engine power to veer away from Senda. The maneuver allowed the fleeing AI vessel more of an edge, as it gained a bit more separation from them. However, the maneuver would probably save the destroyer from any stealth mines originating from a Senda robot factory.

"If a mine takes us out," Walleye said, "that scratches the mission. Better to lose a little time than lose the ship."

Two weeks later, they passed Senda, giving the dwarf planet a twenty-million-kilometer wide berth. No mines exploded before or beside them. No rays beamed up from the dwarf planet's surface. No missiles suddenly began accelerating at them. Maybe Senda was empty. Methlan still couldn't spot anything, not a trace of energy or radiation leakage on the dwarf planet. Maybe all the robots had left on the fleeing vessel.

In time, the weeks stretched into a month. In order to keep their minds active, they played games, watched vids, read and studied space through the destroyer's scopes. They pointed the teleoptics in-system, at times. According to what they saw, no Solar League fleets maneuvered between the major planets. The few messages from Hawkins reported that work continued apace inside MK2 on the *Nathan Graham*.

The destroyer no longer accelerated. It had stopped some time ago. Now, they were traveling on their massive velocity alone. The AI vessel ahead of them also used its velocity. The destroyer moved faster, but not greatly so. The distance between them had narrowed from 231 AUs in the beginning to 153 AUs and closing. That many AUs was a little less than four times the distance from Pluto to the Sun.

Several days later, Walleye held a meeting on the command deck, just himself, June and Methlan. During the passing weeks, Methlan had learned to get along better. He had a feeling Walleye didn't fully trust him yet. He'd come to believe that the mutant didn't trust anyone, maybe not even June Zen.

"I knew the journey would take us into the great depths," Walleye said, "but our risks rise the farther we go. I don't dare use more propellant to accelerate us, as that means we won't have enough to decelerate and later accelerate back in-system. This is as fast as we dare go out-system."

"I agree," June said. "But does that mean we stop? We were willing to sacrifice ourselves before to save humanity. Shouldn't we still do that?"

"There's a problem I hadn't considered before," Walleye said. "Once we move in too close—whatever the AIs think that might be—what's to stop them from accelerating again? They don't have to slow down like we do, and they don't have to save fuel for a return journey. They just have to send a message, I would think, to another cybership in a different star system."

"We should launch the drones now," Methlan said. "Maybe they're almost to the hyperdrive region. Maybe they can suddenly enter hyperdrive."

"That's an excellent point," Walleye said. "The question is, how many drones do we launch?"

"May I ask a question?" Methlan said.

"Certainly."

"Why wouldn't we launch all three?"

"On the face of it," Walleye said, "that's the right decision. But as I dwell on the problem, I realize I don't like leaving myself defenseless."

"We have other armaments," Methlan said.

"The three *Hercules* drones are our only true offensive weapons. Remember the old adage: the best defense is a good offense."

"I suppose," Methlan said. "Yet, I ask again, why hold anything back? Once we destroy the AI vessel, we have completed our mission."

"Have we?" Walleye asked. "I'm suspicious. Aren't the AIs logical? Maybe the first AI ship is a decoy. That's the other reason to destroy it sooner rather than later."

"I have seen no second AI vessel," Methlan pointed out.

"Of course not. The second vessel would be a stealth ship."

Methlan thought about that. He finally shook his head. "I do not agree with your analysis, Lieutenant."

"June?" asked Walleye.

"I trust your instincts," she told Walleye. "My mind says that Methlan is right, but I chose to trust you over either of us."

"You're putting the burden on me, aren't you, Luscious?"

"I don't mean to," she said.

The mutant studied the main screen. "We'll launch two drones. I'm keeping one in reserve."

"But..." Methlan said. Walleye turned to face him.

Methlan calculated fast. Should he kill Walleye? It seemed far too soon for that. Besides... He shrugged in the end. "Two drones could be enough. It is a gamble, though."

"What isn't?" Walleye asked.

Methlan said no more.

"All right then," Walleye said. "Let's prepare two drones for launch."

***

The racks opened on top, making a metallic racket. Soon, the big drone drifted away. It had the same relative velocity as the ship. Side-jets rotated the drone in the correct direction.

Methlan finished the computer check and informed Walleye.

The lieutenant activated the drone from his command chair.

Outside the destroyer, the drone's massive thrusters heated up. Soon, the matter/antimatter engine roared. The exhaust tail lengthened as more power erupted from it.

The drone accelerated rapidly. By the time it was accelerating at 80 gravities, they released the second drone.

Despite the massive thrust and brightness, the two drones quickly dwindled to mere specks on the teleoptic scanner.

They watched the AI ship far away, a tiny moving dot in space. The vessel did not begin accelerating again, although it also did not decelerate. The AI ship did launch several missiles. Those missiles decelerated hard. They had the same relative velocity as the AI vessel. By decelerating, they lengthened the distance between them and the AI vessel. That meant those missiles would reach the chasing drones much sooner. They would also be traveling much slower than the drones.

"We're going to be searching for a stealth vessel all the time now," Walleye declared. "The AIs might think we've shot our wad. That might make them careless."

"And if the two drones fail to destroy the AI ship?" Methlan asked.

"We still have the one left."

"By that time, it could be too late for the drone to reach them before they enter hyperspace. You have gambled with humanity's future, Lieutenant."

Walleye stared at Methlan. He kept staring until finally Methlan realized he had to turn away or kill the mutant now.

Methlan turned. But he considered the manning down as one insult too many, adding to the grudge that had been forming. In the language of Janus House, the grudge was *shock-de-cri*. That meant Methlan must nurture the grudge with growing hatred until he erupted one day into a killing frenzy.

-5-

As Methlan nurtured the *shock-de-cri*, he monitored the drones' advance-toward-contact with the AI vessel.

The two drones—separated by two AUs from each other—slowly closed the distance between themselves and the AI antidrone shield and the AI vessel farther beyond.

The days passed in anxious waiting. Were two drones enough? Would Walleye's gamble prove correct? During those days, the drones continued to accelerate. They would never have to decelerate and could therefore use every ounce of fuel and propellant to reach the target.

By the time the drones closed in on the AI antidrones, 132 AUs separated the destroyer and AI vessel.

"Have you made your computations?" Walleyed asked.

"Yes, sir," Methlan said curtly.

"Are you feeling ill?" the mutant asked.

"A little, sir," Methlan said. He realized he'd spoken too fiercely, but he couldn't help himself. The *shock-de-cri* had almost run its course. Soon, now, Methlan would wash away the insults with Walleye's blood.

"Proceed," Walleye said.

Although June was the comm officer, Methlan ran the drones. He thus sent a light-speed message to them. It would take hours for the message to reach the *Hercules* devices. By that time, the lead drone would almost be in position.

After sending the message, Methlan left, slept a good night's sleep, ate a large breakfast, exercised, ran and took a long nap. When he finally returned to the bridge, Walleye and June had also returned. They watched the lead drone move into contact range with the AI-launched antidrones.

The first matter/antimatter warhead ignited. It created a terrific blast zone and widening EMP. Both the blast and the EMP washed against the antidrones.

The strange thing about observing such a distant battle was the time. The images the teleoptics saw were already hours old. It would be twice that time if they used active sensors like radar. The radar impulse would have to travel at light speed to the target, bounce off it and travel all the way back to the destroyer's sensor. At these ranges, teleoptics and possibly thermal sightings were the only reasonable sensors to use for combat data.

"Well?" Walleye asked.

Methlan shrugged moodily. He didn't know the results of the blast yet. They would find out soon enough if the first drone had taken out enough enemy antidrones because, if it hadn't, the second drone would fail to reach the AI vessel.

Time passed slowly as they waited.

Walleye and June stayed glued to the main screen. Methlan studied his board.

"I believe the second drone has made it through the antidrone belt," Methlan declared.

"You're sure?"

"I would not have said so otherwise."

June sucked in her breath.

By her reaction, Methlan realized he'd spoken too abruptly. His back was to the others. He felt the sharpened weapon taped against his chest. Today, he would rid himself of the manning-down insult. Today, he would restore his honor.

Methlan wondered if he'd become stir-crazy. He'd been cooped up with these people for too long in the destroyer.

He remembered his long-term goal, but he also had the *shock-de-cri* grudge. One did not simply abandon such a thing. Only blood could restore his honor.

Will my honor interfere with my long-term goal? Maybe I should cut myself. Maybe my own spilt blood could wash away my anger.

Methlan shivered. That was a bad idea. He was of Janus House, a proud house of exceedingly noble lineage. He must maintain his honor through the accepted forms.

"Tech!" Walleye said.

Slowly, Methlan turned around.

Walleye used a stumpy arm to point at the main screen. "The drone is closing in on the AI vessel."

Methlan looked up at the main screen, holding his breath.

A terrific detonation took place more than 130 AUs away as the matter/antimatter warhead ignited. Would the blast destroy the AI vessel?

The white blot created by the blast blinded the teleoptics. That only lasted a short time, though.

Methlan turned back to his board. He studied, adjusted—

He saw debris, masses of debris. He rechecked. He considered asking for permission to use active sensors. Then, he decided that he could use the teleoptics to reasonably know the truth. After several more minutes, Methlan straightened and turned around.

"I would like to report, Lieutenant, that the drone eliminated the AI vessel. I don't doubt that some robots may have survived the wreckage. My preliminary analysis suggests complete destruction of the ship. But with these…things, one can never be fully certain. I request permission to use active sensors for more detailed study."

"Granted," Walleye said. The mutant grinned at June. "We did it, Luscious. We took out the first vessel. Now, we have to find the real one."

Methlan cocked his head. "Why do you say this?"

"Instinct," Walleye said. "I don't believe it's over."

Methlan wondered if the little freak could be right. He wasn't going to worry about that yet. He turned back to his instruments. The destruction of the AI vessel had stolen some of the fire of his *shock-de-cri.* He would have to wait for it to rebuild. Besides, before he struck and took command of the destroyer, he wanted to be certain the AIs were out of play here in the space between the Kuiper Belt and the distant Oort cloud.

-6-

INTERLUDE: EARTH

Frank Benz breathed heavily in the starlight. He clung to a sleek tower built high in the Andes Mountains of South America. This night lacked a moon, ensuring it was even darker than usual.

He'd trained for over two months now and was likely in the best shape a man could coerce a mid-forties body. That might not prove good enough, however.

He wore a stealth suit, another of his special inventions. It wasn't perfect. It would fail to deceive a human eye looking at it in bright light. However, the suit should get him past the tower's outer security sensors. It had so far, in any case.

Along with the stealth suit, Benz carried an air-tank on his back because of the high altitude. He breathed almost pure oxygen through his mask. He also used special suction discs, clinging to the smooth tower like a human fly.

It had taken strenuous effort to climb the last part of this Andes Mountain. He'd parked a stealth flitter farther down, trekking up the rest of the way on foot. It had taken even more effort tonight to reach the tower and make the heady ascent.

He had a non-ferrous needler with special ammo. The slivers would dissolve after ten minutes in a human body.

Benz looked up, using his night-vision goggles. He might have too far to go to reach the selected window. His muscles felt flaccid. He let his body relax as much as it could while clinging to a vertical wall. He breathed deeply, trying to replenish his rapidly fading strength.

Vela Shaw had helped him conceive of the assassination mission. It had taken her time to get accustomed to her greater intelligence. At first, she'd had nightmares. Then she'd concocted wild theories at incredible speed. Each person reacted differently to heightened intelligence.

As a precaution—although he dearly liked and was maybe even falling in love with Vela—he'd given her less superior intelligence than his great uncle had given him. Why should she be smarter than he was?

Had that been due to vanity? Did it mean he had hidden ambitions? Had he become too distrustful of human nature after analyzing it these past three years? The answers were likely yes, yes and yes.

Benz sighed. Maybe he should have amped her IQ to even greater heights. Clinging to the tower seemed foolish the longer he tried to regain his strength. Their plan—it was perilous, to say the least.

Maybe it was even crazy.

No. Don't think that. You're also susceptible to suggestion. You have the plan. Now, get going. You don't have much time left.

Benz gathered his resolve and twisted a hand, removing a suction disc from the wall. He reached up, pushed the disc down so that it stuck again, and began the laborious process of detaching the other sucker discs. Finally, he heaved upward, anchoring himself once again.

By slow degrees, he scaled the tower, the special retreat of Premier J.P. Justinian.

The past months had been interesting. With the destruction of the De Gama House, spontaneous riots had erupted all over the planet. Benz had given that a 42 percent probability going in.

Spontaneous riots were a dictator's worst nightmare. Secret police could usually root out planned disruptions of any kind. Informers abounded throughout Earth. It was the sudden riots that caught the police by surprise.

In many cities throughout Earth, glass shattered. Looters rampaged, carrying away expensive items from stores. Buildings burned. Rioters clashed with riot police. Twice, the rioters had overwhelmed the police and trampled many of them to death.

The army had been activated after that. But even a few of the army units had had the temerity to revolt and join the rioters.

Benz and Vela had observed the situation with interest.

"Is that what you planned for?" Vela asked. They'd been in a safe house in Lima, Peru Sector.

"By destroying the De Gama House?" he asked.

"Of course you know I don't mean that. By elevating Justinian to the premiership?"

"Oh. Yes. I thought it would take longer for him to push the people to this point. The purges propelled the people into precipitous action. Justinian accelerated his own demise. He had less power than he realized. He either should have implemented far bloodier purges or not done them at all. His present purges killed too few to bring about a true shock that would have stymied action. Instead, he frightened too many people while still allowing them options."

Vela had sighed at the too long and too obvious explanation. She no longer needed those.

Benz smiled tiredly as he hoisted himself a little higher up the tower. It had been so different having someone to really talk to. The past three years had been so lonely. Seeing so much farther than anyone else, and not being able to share his insights with anyone…

Benz snorted. Had he taken Vela to the machine because he'd become sick of being alone? It was quite probable.

He shelved further reminiscing so he could devote his will to greater muscular effort. He might be a mental superman, but he was far from being extraordinary physically.

Another eighteen minutes brought him to the twenty-first story. Below him, the snow-covered peaks of the Andes gleamed in the starlight. If he fell, he would plunge more than just the twenty-one stories. He would also plunge down a vertical cliff, one more than half-a-kilometer in depth. He would never survive such a fall. Fortunately, he had no fear of heights.

Panting heavily, feeling the sweat slide under the stealth suit, he brought up his tool pack. He took out a suction cup and attached it to the window. He removed a thin knife. Then, he attached a small box on the ledge.

He turned on the box, which beeped slowly.

With the special knife, he began to cut the glass around the suction cup. The knife cut with unusual ease. The box tricked the sensors as the knife completed the circle. He put away the knife and grabbed the handle attached to the suction cup. With a slight sound of glass sliding, he removed the cut circle from the rest of the window. This he attached to the tower through the back of the suction cup.

He crawled through the new entrance. It was slow and tedious work. Any of a number of things could happen to upset the plan. Even with supreme genius, it was next to impossible to foresee every eventuality.

Finally, Benz's booted feet touched the study's carpet. He stood in the room, panting and trembling from the exertion.

Benz wanted to laugh wildly. He'd made it. The hardest part of the assassination mission was past. He never wanted to scale a wall like that again.

Benz shed his mask, tank, tools and stealth suit. He put them in a pile behind the desk. Afterward, he took out a final tool, reached out the hole with a special pole, detached the round pane of glass and maneuvered it back into place. He used a small tube, smearing its clear paste around the circular cut. In seconds, the two parts bonded. It wouldn't pass a close inspection, but it resealed the tower from the outside.

Benz pulled the curtain across the window. He'd removed the suction cup before sealing the circular piece back onto the window. It lay on top of the pile of clothes, tools and the tank.

The Inspector General of Earth sat down in the desk's chair. He let his head droop. His arms shook from too much effort. Three minutes later, he hoisted himself to his feet. He took a uniform from his pack, donned it and headed for the door.

It was time to kill Justinian.

***

Benz moved serenely down the halls. He stopped at a guard's command, showing her his special pass. She slid it through a small unit. It checked. That made her frown. She was incredibly busty and beautiful. Finally, she handed him his ID and indicated that he could continue.

Up here in the secret residence, Justinian only allowed female guards to protect him. They were uniformly busty and long-legged. He bedded them from time to time. Justinian believed the sexual bonding heightened their loyalty.

Benz took the final turn and advanced upon Justinian's bedroom door. One guard stood before it. His ID would not work with her.

As he approached, Benz took what appeared to be a stick of gum from a breast pocket. He unwrapped the substance as he neared. The guard watched him, with her hand on the butt of her holstered weapon.

Still three feet away from the guard, Benz popped the substance into his mouth. He took a deep breath, held it, and chewed the substance vigorously.

"The Premier is asleep," the guard whispered. She had failed to re-knot her tie perfectly. She had likely left his bed less than an hour ago.

Benz moved close to the guard, leaned in toward her. That no doubt surprised her, as she tensed. Benz exhaled, allowing his breath to reached her.

She breathed in, and her eyelids fluttered.

Benz twisted his head to the side and spat out the knockout substance. He spit two more times and faced the guard just in time to catch her falling forward.

He hadn't killed her, but she would remain asleep for a good long time.

Holding her up with one arm, he used his other hand to pull out a tiny box, He pressed a switch. The box beeped twice, and the lock in the door clicked.

Benz pushed the door open, dragging the guard with him. He lay her on the floor, shut the door and took out a pair of goggles. He slid the goggles over his eyes, activating the sensors so he could see in the dark.

He passed furniture, a huge holo unit and opened another door. Justinian snored softly in the big bed. The Premier always fell asleep by this time. He did not have a woman sleeping with him. He never did. Benz believed Justinian did that out of prudence. Justinian wouldn't trust the woman. She might choke him to death while he slept. Thus, Justinian always slept alone.

Benz stood beside the bed. He drew the needler. His hand shook, and that surprised him. He didn't want to murder the man. Yet he had to. Everything pointed to it. He'd come this far—

Benz put the nozzle of the needler against the sleeper's throat and pulled the trigger. The man jerked as needles stitched into his soft flesh. Benz kept his finger down, hosing the needles so blood began to spurt.

The man opened his eyes, staring at Benz in pained shock.

"Good-bye," Benz said.

The man opened his bloody mouth. He tried to speak, to tell Benz something. It never happened.

Benz exhaled with revulsion. This was a dirty deed. He hated it. But he'd had to do what he'd had to do. He would not look at the corpse. He realized it was time to go. Benz didn't go just yet, though. He kept standing there.

Suddenly, it occurred to Benz that he felt terribly lethargic. He realized more than ever that he should go. Instead, he waited, with his muscles wilting.

At that point, lights blazed on in the chamber.

Benz tried to raise the needler. He found that his arm refused to lift. He crashed down onto his knees. What was wrong with him?

A door opened, and a tall man strode in. The man wore a helmet with a clear visor and a body vest. Female guards followed the tall man into the bedroom.

Benz found it hard to do, but he looked up. He didn't know that his mouth hung open.

"Inspector General," Justinian said through a helmet speaker.

Benz frowned thunderously. Had someone pumped invisible knockout gas into the bedroom? Is that why the guards were wearing rebreathers?

"You shot my body-double, Benz," the Premier said. "You fell for my trap." Justinian "tsked" several times. "Do you know what happens now?"

Benz kept staring. He could no longer speak.

"After I revive you, Inspector General, I'm going to interrogate you. I'm going to get to the bottom of your tRobertsous conspiracy and stamp it out of existence."

-7-

The next two days were among the worst in Frank Benz's existence. He found himself in an awful place. Pain gushed through his body. Indecent tortures stole his dignity. He tried to hold back. He thought his great intellect would give him immunity against whatever Justinian could throw at him, but that proved quite wrong, hurtfully wrong.

Sooner than anyone would have expected, he began to talk.

At that point, the interrogation began in earnest. Special interrogators began to fire one question after another at him. They switched up the manner of the questions and turned them around, asking them in other ways.

Benz understood what they were doing. The interrogators were searching for lies. They found several. The pain began again. Naked before witnesses, Benz howled in agony. He howled and promised to stick to the truth this time.

The two days ended with Benz telling Justinian or his interrogators everything. He repeated the Antarctica story. He left nothing out. He didn't want to face more pain. Benz told Justinian about Vela Shaw. He hoped she managed to go to ground before GSB agents tracked her down.

Finally, after a hot shower, clean clothes and some food, with several bandages where his fingernails used to be, Benz limped into an audience room. Two big guards flanked him, huge men with small heads and brutal smiles. They brought him to Justinian. The Premier sat behind a desk, signing paper after paper from a large stack. As soon as the pen flourish ended, Justinian flipped each newly signed paper onto a growing pile.

The two guards and Benz waited silently.

Finally, Justinian looked up. A crafty smile twisted his features. "Hold his arms," he said.

Thick fingers dug into Benz's flesh. The brutes held him immobile.

"Do you know what I'm doing, Benz?"

"No," the former Inspector General said softly.

The smile widened. "I have long suspected these people." He patted both piles of papers. Those he'd signed and those he was going to sign. "Do you know what these are?"

Benz shook his head.

"Death warrants," the Premier said. "I am signing them myself. And do you know why?"

Again, Benz shook his head.

"Because of their personal treachery," Justinian said. "They had my trust. They used my trust to help you engineer my assassination. I'm amazed at how you managed to turn them without my noticing. Now I see it was through the fantastic mind-machine that gave you inhuman cunning. I now believe your claim that you used the machine on them. You sealed their tongues, just as your great uncle sealed the tongues of his colleagues. When confronted with their treachery, your co-conspirators all claimed innocence. All refused to tell me the truth. This machine of yours is most effective, most effective. Do you know what happens next, Benz?"

The former Inspector General looked down at the carpet.

"Look at me," Justinian snapped.

Benz did.

"I am going to test your fabled machine. If it works, I will use it on myself. I will elevate my intelligence to great heights. Afterward, I will devise the perfect plans. For all your vaunted intelligence, you failed. You failed because you didn't understand the human heart. You didn't understand how torture could break the strongest man. You needed help to get to me. All those who aided you have paid with or will pay with their lives. I am going to crush this rebellion forever."

The Premier leaned forward. "I'm going to keep you alive a little longer, Benz. I may need assistance with this marvelous alien machine your uncle built. But once I've attained greater brilliance, then I'm going to devise unique tortures that slowly and most painfully put you to death.

***

The rest of the day passed in air travel. To Benz, it seemed to take forever. An armada of armored air-vans flew to the Rocky Mountains in Colorado Sector. They landed beside the mine entrance.

Big guards dragged Benz from his van.

The sunlight hurt his eyes, causing him to squint.

A new team of GSB officers conferred with the Premier. The former officers holding the same positions had already died. These men and women listened to the Premier attentively. Afterward, they studied Benz with calculation.

Soon, the party started into the mine.

No one asked Benz for directions. He'd given those during the interrogations. In time, they reached the rocky outcropping beside the timber shoring up the ancient tunnel.

A lanky man—the new Chief Arbiter—did the honors. The way opened.

The heavily armored assembly moved in as a unit. Benz dragged his left foot. It had been badly strained during the tortures. Justinian moved with a new lightness of step.

It occurred to Benz that Justinian hadn't known what to do with the spontaneous riots. Benz could have told the Premier. Justinian ruled with too much iron and not enough velvet hiding the metal fist. The Premier put too much trust in his secret police and not enough in the propaganda organs that molded people's thinking toward the right channels.

In any case, after a twisted journey through several hatches, the party reached the fabled door. The combination worked. Everyone entered, and lights soon glowed in the chamber.

"There?" Justinian asked Benz.

The former Inspector General nodded. The Premier pointed at the dentist-like chair with the metal dome suspended above it.

The Premier snapped his fingers. Technicians went to the controls. They turned on the machine, following in exacting detail the procedures Benz had given them.

"Before we begin," Justinian said. "Is there anything else you want to tell me?"

Benz seemed dumbfounded.

"I'm not going first," the Premier said. "I realize you could have set the machine to hurt me. I have a volunteer going first. Only once I see that the machine grants superior intelligence will I go."

"I spoke truly," Benz said in a hoarse voice. "Please, no more torture."

Justinian smiled cruelly. "Par Tomas," he called.

A compact man with a bullet-shaped head wearing a black uniform stepped up. He was the police prefect for all of South America.

"To the machine with you," Justinian said.

Par Tomas eyed the machine dubiously. He licked his lips nervously.

"Must I remind you, Prefect…?" Justinian asked.

Par Tomas squared his bull-like shoulders and marched to the machine. He sat in the special chair and stared upward as two techs pulled the metal dome over his head. One of them whispered to Tomas. He grunted from under the dome.

The great machines beside the chair began to issue strange humming sounds. The metal dome soon glowed as if with heat.

Par Tomas clutched the armrests. His arms shook, but he refused to release his grip. He groaned. He twisted in the chair. He began to shout in pain, shaking uncontrollably.

"Well, well, well," Justinian said. He glanced sidelong at Benz. "It seems you did lie, hmmm."

"No," Benz said. "Please, you must believe me. This is how it's supposed to be."

Justinian snorted. But when a tech asked if he should stop, Justinian shook his head.

Finally, the process ended. Techs rushed to the chair. They lifted the helmet.

Par Tomas sat stiffly in the chair with his eyes screwed shut. Slowly, he began to relax. Then, he yawned before finally opening his eyes.

"Do you understand me?" Justinian asked.

Everyone watched avidly.

"I do," Par Tomas said in a heavy voice.

"Stand, sir," Justinian said.

Tomas stood easily. At that point, he turned sharply toward Justinian.

"What is it?" the Premier asked.

Tomas opened his mouth. He closed it even faster.

"Do you feel more intelligent?" Justinian asked in a silky voice.

"No," Tomas said, maybe a trifle too quickly.

Justinian laughed as if with delight. "What did you almost say?"

Par Tomas's shoulders deflated. He shook his head. "I realize you're going to kill me. It is self-evident."

"Amazing," Justinian said. "You are one of the worst dullards I know. Yet now, you see, you understand and you speak with greater learnedness." The Premier laughed and made a peculiar motion.

Two guards stepped up, firing their guns at Par Tomas. The newly created genius crumbled into a bloody heap.

"There can be only one," Justinian said. "Remove him."

Guards hurried to obey.

After the body was dragged away, Justinian approached the dentist-like chair. He turned suddenly, glancing at Benz.

"There is a risk in doing this," Benz warned.

"Tsk, tsk," Justinian said. "Nice try, but it's not going to work on me."

The Premier climbed into the chair, settling himself. He told the techs to get on with it.

The same two advanced, pulled down the metal dome and wished the Premier luck.

Justinian said nothing.

The techs turned on the great machines and the process started as before. Soon, the dome glowed once more.

Justinian grunted painfully. His hands clasped the armrests, and his lean body began to shake. The glowing seemed stronger this time. The machine hummed longer and louder. Justinian made croaking noises as if trying to belch. His body shook violently.

"Is he well?" the chief tech demanded of Benz.

"No," Benz said. "He is dying."

The chief tech stared at Benz wide-eyed. "Are you mad? Tell me the truth."

"The reign of J.P. Justinian has just ended," Benz said. "You people are going to have to decide who rules next."

Two of the new officers, the Chief Arbiter among them, hurried to Benz.

"If you're lying…" the Chief Arbiter warned.

"I planned for this moment," Benz said.

"Impossible."

"Why is that?" asked Benz.

The Chief Arbiter made a vague gesture. He glanced at Justinian under the glowing dome. The Premier sat rigidly as if doing a planking trick. None of this resembled Par Tomas's experience.

"Justinian went second," the Chief Arbiter said. "You couldn't have known he would go second."

"Why couldn't I?" Benz asked in a tired voice.

"But the tortures you underwent."

"Yes," Benz said flatly. "That was the hardest choice to make."

"You must know we're going to kill you," the Chief Arbiter said.

"The former Chief Arbiter certainly would have," Benz agreed. "That's why I supposedly broke under torture and informed on him and his allies. I wanted them and others out of the way so you and those around you could take over the GSB."

"What do you mean?"

"The former Chief Arbiter and his allies were innocent of the charges I placed on them. He was a brutal tyrant just the same. All the people I denounced under torture were hard-core

Justinian supporters. You newer people are not. You people are known pragmatists."

"That's a lie," the Chief Arbiter said, loudly, perhaps for the guards' benefit.

"You know it's the truth."

A great groan and a shout tore from Justinian's throat. At that moment, the machine exploded upward, and fire enveloped J.P. Justinian, enveloping the chamber in a nauseating stench.

The party retreated, the Chief Arbiter pulling Benz with him.

The guards watched in dismay.

"The Premier is dead," the Chief Arbiter said as he stared at Benz. "The intelligence machine is destroyed. The state is in turmoil. There is rebellion in the planetary systems, and alien AIs will threaten the human race sooner or later."

"That's another reason I wanted you to be Chief Arbiter," Benz said. "I know you realize what the cyberships represent to humanity."

"I cannot believe what you're claiming."

"Social Dynamism needs a strong, sure hand," Benz said. "It needs someone to fix impossible problems."

"You?" the Chief Arbiter asked.

"You saw what I did with the little I had," Benz said. "You also saw I'm willing to suffer for the sake of humanity, for the sake of doing what needs to be done."

"The Premier's guards will never allow it."

"Kill them before they come out of their shock."

The Chief Arbiter stared at Benz. "What happens if I don't agree?"

Benz smiled grimly. "What do you think happens?"

"We're in your mountain, and we've never found Vela Shaw. Is she here somewhere?"

Benz smiled enigmatically.

"I see," the Chief Arbiter said. "Who would run the GSB?"

"You."

"And you have a plan to restore Earth and restore Social Dynamism throughout the Solar System?"

"More importantly," Benz said, "I have a plan for defeating the alien AIs we know are out there."

The smell from the burnt Justinian became too strong. The party left the chamber, shutting the hatch behind them.

"Yes," the Chief Arbiter whispered. "What are your orders, sir?"

"You'd better disarm or kill Justinian's old guards first."

The Chief Arbiter quietly went to several others. As one, they drew on the guards, ordering them to disarm. Most did. The few who didn't died on the spot.

The Chief Arbiter returned to Benz. "What now?" the man asked.

Benz began to tell him.

-8-

THE SCATTERED DISC REGION

The *Daisy Chain 4* decelerated with a hard burn. It had been doing so for more than four days, ever since the drone had wiped-out the AI vessel.

Methlan's active sensor scans had shown the same results as the teleoptics. The AI vessel had become space debris. There were no signs of lifeboats, if one could use such a term about AI escape pods. Neither had Methlan found any sign of a second AI ship.

Walleye's paranoia on the subject seemed unjustified.

That troubled Methlan the more he thought about it. What if the two drones had failed to destroy the AI vessel? Walleye's gamble would have consigned humanity to a second cybership invasion. Was saving one more drone worth the risk?

The thought added strength to the *shock-de-cri*. Methlan brooded even as he used the destroyer's tiny gym. He had bigger muscles than when he'd started the voyage. Constant exercise and good eating had aided his development. Methlan enjoyed the time he spent alone in his miniscule cabin. He had a body-length mirror and constantly posed nude before it, flexing and admiring his greater musculature. He also practiced the *komo-dai*. It was a Janus House knife-fighting style. He thrust, chopped, swept back and did imaginary parries before the mirror.

The *shock-de-cri* had built up to a fever pitch by the time the destroyer accelerated again. It had come to a dead stop way out here in the emptiness between the Kuiper Belt and the Oort cloud, which some called the scattered disc.

Now, the *Daisy Chain 4* built up velocity for the return voyage to Makemake.

Captain Hawkins had radioed his congratulations. They would all receive higher grades or ranks upon their return. They would also receive medals for courage and devotion to humanity.

In his quarters, Methlan sneered at the idea of these trinkets. He used to give such paltry items to his soldiers as the Prince of Ten Worlds.

On the fateful day of *shock-de-cri* culmination—such was the plan, in any case—Methlan exited his quarters in a heightened mood. He wore his best uniform with his special kill-dagger taped to his chest. His muscles seethed with anticipation. The only unfortunate aspect to this was that the pent-up sexual desire gave him a raging hard-on. It was most inconvenient. Every time he thought about killing Walleye, he also thought about mounting June Zen afterward. The two events almost went hand in hand. With Walleye out of the way, June would surely recognize his supremacy.

Methlan had gone far too long without sexual union. He needed it in order to feel like a man again. Kill Walleye, mount June. It almost had a rhythm to it.

Methlan pressed a switch. A hatch swished open. He walked onto the small command deck, half-turning to hide his hard-on from Walleye in his command chair and June at her station.

The *shock-de-cri* seethed in Methlan's brain. He almost rushed Walleye. Methlan actually trembled. There seemed to be a fire burning in his hands. He yearned to kill, but such a move must follow the ancient rituals and spoken formulas.

With difficulty, Methlan went to his console and sat down. He almost missed something weird on his console. He blinked, shook off the *shock-de-cri* just enough, and concentrated. This was quite odd, really. He pressed various pads on the board and adjusted a dial. He kept playing with the panel so intently that he failed to notice that Walleye and June had stopped talking.

It finally dawned on Methlan that both of them seemed far too silent. He glanced over his shoulder and noticed them watching him.

Methlan felt a surge of *shock-de-cri* well up in him. He moved his hand to unbutton the lowest seal on his uniform. He would slide his hand under the uniform, rip the kill-dagger from its hiding—

"What do you make of that?" Walleye asked.

It took Methlan several seconds to register the question. "Make of what?" he asked in surly tone.

Maybe for the first time in Methlan's memory, Walleye grinned. It exposed small teeth and crinkled the mutant's ugly face.

"What you've been studying. I want you to magnify the image."

Methlan hesitated, but finally turned back to his console. The object was over one thousand AUs from the ship. He used greater magnification to show a swirling white patch in space. The white had to be massive for the instruments to have spotted it from here. The law of causality suggested it shouldn't exist. So what was causing the swirling pattern?

"What do you make of that?" Walleye asked.

"I'm not sure…" Methlan said. His surliness had departed as his fear grew.

"I think you do know."

Methlan turned around as his facial skin tightened. It was not part of the *shock-de-cri*. This was fear. "Sir," he said in a low voice. "We're witnessing a hyperdrive exit point."

Walleye's feet thudded onto the deck as he slid out of the command chair. The little freak moved toward the main screen.

"That suggests an alien cybership is coming through." Walleye frowned. He regarded Methlan. "How do you know that's a hyperdrive exit?"

"It's—it's an educated guess," Methlan said.

Walleye stared at him a few moments longer.

"A new cybership," June said. "A new cybership is coming out of hyperdrive?"

"If Methlan's correct about that being a hyperdrive exit, it would appear so," Walleye said.

"No," Methlan said, as he studied his console. "That is wrong."

"What is it then?" Walleye snapped.

"*Three* cyberships, Lieutenant. Those are three cyberships, not just one. The AIs are invading with a flotilla this time, not just a lone vessel." Methlan shook his head. "All our hard work—it's undone. We're doomed."

-9-

Over the next few days, Methlan raged in his heart at the recklessness of fate. He'd died in his home star system; he had no idea how long ago. Before he'd died, he'd gone under a brain-tap machine. That machine had ended up in the *Nathan Graham*.

He'd had a second chance at life when he'd returned once before in a Neptunian named Da Vinci. Jon Hawkins had slain that host body in order to kill him.

Then, Eli Gomez had downloaded Methlan's thought-patterns into his human brain. He was alive again, the greatest leader of Janus House. He'd almost been ready to slaughter Walleye for honor and so he could fulfil his desires with June Zen. Then, he would have taken command of the destroyer and found a way to defeat whatever remained on Senda, if any robots still resided there.

Methlan's plan had been simple. He would build a hyperdrive in the destroyer and return to the Ten Worlds. He would drive off the conquering AIs, if they yet remained, and he would gather his people, turning them into a fighting force of avengers.

Now, none of that mattered. Three cyberships had dropped out of hyperspace. They moved at an incredible velocity, heading in the destroyer's general direction. Walleye had refused to shut down the main reactor and hope the big AI ships passed them by. Instead, the fool tried to accelerated fast enough to reach Makemake before the cyberships did. That was a suicide mission.

Ninety minutes later on the bridge, Methlan studied his console. His worst fear had materialized. Walleye should have heeded him. He decided it was time to tell the others the bad news.

"One of the cyberships appears to have changed its heading," Methlan informed Walleye. "At this point, given their extreme distance from us, it's difficult to tell. But I believe one of the vessels has focused directly on us."

The freak actually came to his station. He studied Methlan's board. Finally, he returned to the command chair.

Turning back to Methlan, Walleye said, "Detach the last drone."

"Lieutenant—"

"Detach the drone," Walleye repeated. "We're not going down without a fight."

"But there's no good reason for doing that. We obviously cannot destroy a hundred kilometer-cybership with a *Hercules* drone."

"So what?"

"So it is futile to launch the drone in that case."

"Wrong," Walleye said. "It could scratch paint on the ship."

Methlan cocked his head. Had the appearance of the cyberships unhinged the freak's mind? Why launch while the enemy vessel was so far away?

"I hope to hurt whoever kills me," Walleye explained. "If I can't hurt them, I'll try to bite them. If that isn't possible, I want to do something to show they've been in a battle with me."

"Scratching paint is doing something?" Methlan asked.

"Yes."

"That is a strange philosophy."

"Whatever it is, it's mine," Walleye declared.

Methlan glanced at his board. He pretended to make adjustments. Finally, he turned around again. "It's far too soon for us to act so decisively. Despite its great velocity, the cybership needs time to cross one thousand AUs. We should wait to see what exactly the cybership plans to do. According to the sensors, they haven't launched anything at us yet. There is still plenty of time to study them. Why throw away our last offensive asset? You were correct in keeping the drone. Now, let us use it wisely."

Walleye looked up at the ceiling. He tapped a foot. Finally, he regarded Methlan. "Do you know, that may be your first piece of advice worth following?"

Methlan scowled.

"We'll hold our fire for now," Walleye said. "We'll wait and see what happens next."

Time passed—days.

June detected comm messages radiating from the AI-held dwarf planet. The messages were machine fast and impossible to translate. It seemed clear that something on Senda was attempting to communicate with the cyberships. Naturally, given the limitations of the speed of light, it would take time for the messages to reach the distant ships. In fact, it would take approximately 138 hours for a light-speed message to travel one thousand AUs. That was 5.7 days.

Despite the limitations, several hours later, two cyberships subtly shifted their direction of travel. It seemed they headed for Makemake. More precisely, they headed for where Makemake would be once they arrived.

"The Senda message can't have reached the cyberships yet," June said.

"Hyperdrive and hyperspace don't follow the rules of physics as we know them," Walleye said. "Maybe the Senda AIs used a different communication process."

"Then, why did we detect it as a normal if encrypted comm message?" June asked.

"That's a good point," Walleye said. "Maybe the cyberships noticed something amiss in their scan of Makemake."

"Supposing the Senda message hasn't reached the cyberships yet," June said, "it will in time. Either way, I think whatever is on Senda is telling or will tell the cyberships that the original AI attack failed in this system."

"Because of the message, we know one other thing," Walleye said. "Robots must still be on Senda." He drummed his stubby fingers on an armrest. "At the cyberships' present speeds, and even given the distance we have to cover, we'll never outrun them to Makemake. We might beat the one coming for us if we head toward Senda now."

"Why would we go to Senda?" Methlan asked.

"For the obvious reason," Walleye said. "We'll use Senda as a shield. That's in case the cybership launches missiles at us. If the cybership wants to destroy us, it will have to slow down in order to maneuver around the dwarf planet and use its beams on us. The cybership can't just destroy us in passing, as it were."

"Hide and seek," Methlan said.

"There's another reason," Walleye said. "We still have a big old missile. The robots are our enemies. If I can't hurt the cyberships, I can still possibly destroy the Senda robots."

Surprisingly, Methlan found himself in agreement with the freak, although he kept that to himself.

The destroyer changed heading. They still accelerated, but not as hard as before. They would have to save something for the massive deceleration at the end. They could stop and maneuver a little at Senda. They weren't going to do anymore deep space traveling until they found more fuel—that is, if they lived through the encounter.

Methlan spent hours studying the situation. Two of the enemy ships sped for Makemake. The last cybership followed the destroyer. Methlan made computations, worried over theories and grew increasingly desperate in his heart. Who knew if he would ever have a chance at life again?

"No," Methlan whispered.

What was wrong with him? He'd tossed aside his honor as it if was a filthy rag. He'd forgotten about his *shock-de-cri*. It was time to force a showdown, to begin the ritual.

Abruptly, Methlan swiveled around in his seat. "June is right. The cyberships know about the *Nathan Graham* at MK2."

Walleye did not respond. He almost seemed to ignore him.

"We have to flee somewhere other than Senda," Methlan said. "Do you think Hawkins is going to stay at MK2? No. He has to run. We have to run, too. I suggest we stop heading in-system and move in as lateral a direction as possible. The cybership chasing us will likely leave us alone then. By heading toward Senda, we might be forcing it to chase us."

Walleye still said nothing.

That was not according to form, and that exasperated Methlan. "Did you hear what I said? Hawkins is going to run."

Walleye swiveled the command chair toward him. "That's *Captain* Hawkins to you," the freak said.

"Why does the title matter now?"

Walleye kept staring at Methlan as he pointed at June. The lovely Miss Zen pressed a switch on her comm panel. There was a crackle in a speaker. Then, the voice of Mentalist Gloria Sanchez came through.

"Lieutenant Walleye," the mentalist said. It must have been a recording. "Due to your diligence and observations, we have rechecked several matters. It appears that we have made a terrible mistake. Without your insights, I don't believe we would have ever figured it out until it was too late. You must continue to watch Eli Gomez carefully. I find that I must agree with you that he went under the brain-tap machine. His physical frailty earlier and his distance from—that doesn't matter now. Thank you, Walleye. Continue to watch him carefully. Like you, I don't think Eli is who he used to be."

June clicked off the recording.

Methlan felt lightheaded. How could Walleye, of all people, have seen what others missed?

"When did the message come?" Methlan asked.

"Several days ago."

"You've been watching me?"

"Didn't you listen? I've been watching you for some time. Some of the things you said never made sense. Finally, the answer came to me. If you must know, your recognition of the hyperdrive exit started me thinking. I had June radio my suspicions to MK2. The mentalist confirmed my suspicions. Now, *you* know what she thinks."

The lightheadedness became anger. Then a realization struck. "Did you bug my quarters?" Methlan asked in outrage.

"Your knife thrusts were the clincher," Walleye said. "I didn't think much of your posing routine, though."

"That was an invasion of privacy," Methlan declared.

Walleye snorted. "A technological ghoul like you dares to complain about that?"

Methlan scowled and then realized what Walleye meant. "I am not responsible for the ghoulishness. Eli Gomez went under the brain-tap machine of his own free will."

Walleye shrugged.

Methlan struggled for self-control. He must complete the ritual. "What were you going to do with me?" he demanded.

"Does it matter?" Walleye asked. "The cyberships are coming. I can compute speeds and distances as well as the next man. Eli was a bastard according to what I've learned. You're welcome to his body. The captain would like to know who you are, though. What's your real name?"

Methlan hesitated until a burst of pride gushed forth. He could no longer hold back the *shock-de-cri.* "I am Methlan Rath of Janus House."

"You're pretty important, I take it?"

Methlan ripped open his jacket, causing buttons to bounce off the deck-plates. He tore the dagger from where it was taped to his chest.

Walleye merely raised his eyebrows.

"I am sick of your domineering manner," Methlan declared. "Today, I will wash away your insults with your blood."

So saying, Methlan charged, reading himself for a gutting sweep.

The mutant swept back his buff coat, drew an obscenely heavy gun and fired. A black object blew out of the outrageous barrel. Methlan attempted to dodge. The blob hit him and expanded with a sticky-sounding noise. The webs entangled him, sticking and shrinking hard. It pulled his legs together and his arms in toward his body. He released the kill-dagger just in time. It tinkled as it hit the deck, and slid out of the way. That was good, because Methlan thudded onto the deck, ensnared by the mutant's treacherous tangler shot.

For a time, Methlan struggled. That only tightened the threads. Soon, he could hardly breathe. He choked—

"Easy there, Methlan," Walleye said.

Methlan realized the mutant was speaking into his ear. "Release me," he roared. "This is unseemly."

"Relax. I want to ask you a few questions. I'm going to send the answers to Captain Hawkins."

"I despise the man. I will gain my revenge on him and on you. Of this, you can be assured."

Walleye shook his head. "The cybership is coming. Do you think I'm going to let the AIs capture us? No. I'm not going to let them put a slave control in my brain. If you have a great idea, though, I'd like to hear it."

Methlan silently raged. He'd taken too long. He should have practiced the ancient rituals sooner.

Walleye straightened and turned to June. "We'll keep heading for Senda. We'll keep talking to the captain. And our alien here might remember something important. What do you think about that, Methlan?"

"Release me and we can talk."

Walleye studied him a few seconds longer before turning to the main screen.

"Three cyberships…" Walleye shook his head. "In the end, the AIs didn't give us much time to get ready for the second wave, did they?"

"Captain Hawkins will think of something," June said.

Walleye searched her face. "I hope you're right, Luscious, I truly do."

PART IV
THE KUIPER BELT

-1-

Jon Hawkins ran the back of his hand across his mouth as he hurried to the conference chamber in MK2's fifth sector. He strode through a deep tunnel corridor. These were composed of moon-rock without any metal sheathing. The robots who had hollowed out the moon must have thought of corridor sheathing as a needless luxury, if they'd thought about it all.

Uncharacteristically, Jon looked as anxious as he was.

The showdown with the AIs was coming much sooner than anyone had expected. Three cyberships had dropped out of hyperspace a little over one thousand AUs away. They now headed in-system, two of them coming for Makemake and the other zeroing in on Senda.

The last few days had been hectic. And if all that wasn't enough, Walleye had confirmed the worst. Eli Gomez had made it into the brain-tap chamber several months ago. The madman had downloaded the Prince of Ten Worlds into his head.

"No wonder I thought I'd recognized him," Jon muttered.

He recalled the prince's threat at the end of Da Vinci's bodily life. The prince had told Jon his life was forfeit. It had seemed laughable at the time. It wasn't laughable any more. The prince's name was Methlan Rath of Janus House.

Jon shook his head. The videos from the *Daisy Chain 4* had been plain weird. Eli's—Methlan's dancelike rituals before his mirror had a haunting quality. They had certainly been alien. According to Walleye, the alien had kept a *dagger* strapped to his chest for many weeks already.

From everything Jon had read, this Prince of Ten Worlds manifestation hadn't seemed as cunning or ruthless as the first time he'd downloaded into Da Vinci. What accounted for the difference?

Once more, Jon shook his head. He had to forget about Methlan Rath. The alien of House Janus wasn't important right now. Deciding how to deal with three cyberships took precedence over everything.

Did Methlan destroy the moon supplies? He was free then. He had motive—

Jon smacked a fist into his other palm. The prince must have been responsible for the moon sabotage. This Methlan Rath had thrown a monkey wrench into the *Nathan Graham's* refurbishing. What if that was the margin that cost them the coming battle?

Jon ground his molars together. Why was this alien thought-pattern giving them such hassle? It should have helped them. It should have been more like Bast Banbeck. Instead—

He wanted to forget about the prince. But he could feel the alien's curse wrapping around everything. Maybe the alien had acted differently this time because Methlan wasn't really alive. The prince was a downloaded thought-pattern in Eli Gomez's brain. The essence of Eli must have been the difference. For all of Eli's cunning, Da Vinci must have been the more deadly personality between them.

The brain-tap machines. The cybership had brought them. Bast Banbeck's people had used them. But it was the AIs who had brought the hideous technology to the Solar System.

We have to stop them.

Jon hurried to a planning meeting so they could make the great decision. He hated this about real space battles. Ground combat was so much easier. One was in the problem with adrenaline pumping through the body. With space battles, one had to calculate with incredible depth, playing out ideas step-by-step.

It was a good thing they had Gloria. The mentalist was a better space-battle planner than he was.

In his mind's eye, Jon could see the colonel shaking his head. That was crazy. What was Colonel Graham trying to tell him?

Jon remembered a lesson in a quiet coffee shop on Bristol Habitat orbiting Saturn. In those days, the regiment had helped a repressive group of oligarchs stamp out a secret revolt of the lower classes. It had been a distasteful mission, but it had helped the regiment pay its bills and outstanding loans.

"War World II is a prime example of what I'm saying," Colonel Graham had told Jon in the tiny shop. "The German Wehrmacht was a well-oiled military machine. Their commanders were brilliant tacticians and operational artists. What's more, their Leader had clever strategies at the beginning before he lost his mind due to his increasing successes."

"What's that mean?"

"Which part?"

"Losing his mind by increasing successes?" the young officer-cadet had asked.

"It's a theory of mine." The colonel had sipped his coffee. "Sometimes, brilliant commanders achieving outstanding success come to believe they can do anything. The Japanese of that war also had it. It was called Victory Disease. The Japanese did so well early on that they believed any exploit to be possible. The Americans at the Battle of Midway taught them a harsh lesson in reality."

"The German leader got Victory Disease?"

"How else does one explain his invasion of the Soviet Union at the same time he took on the British Empire and the Americans?"

As Jon hurried down the moon corridor, he wondered why he was thinking about this. He—

"Listen to me," the colonel said in his mind's eye. "This is the point. The Germans had brilliant military leadership in

World War II. But that leadership had miserable grand strategy."

"What's grand strategy?" Jon had asked that day in the coffee shop.

"The big picture. In our lesson, it was taking on three powerful political entities: the Soviet Union, the British Empire and America. The Germans had awful grand strategy. It meant after they shot their bolt in the first attack on Russia, that they could never win. The odds became too staggering."

The colonel had taken another sip of coffee. "The big picture is critical. Grand strategy trumps strategy, which usually trumps great operational skills, which trump battlefield tactics. The highest military good is to practice sound grand strategy."

Jon grinned as he turned a corner in the moon corridor. He saw the hatch to the conference chamber. Gloria could calculate vectors, velocities and fuel better than anyone else here. But he was the big picture man. The meeting was going to be about grand strategy as much as anything else.

Jon lowered his head and entered the hatch with determination.

-2-

Jon sat at the head of the conference table.

The giant Bast Banbeck was in attendance. The green-skinned Sacerdote used one of his massive index fingers to push something loose in the back of his mouth. He turned his head and spat on the floor.

Gloria Sanchez sat across from Bast wearing her tan uniform. She looked even tinier compared to the seven-foot giant. The mentalist stopped speaking and frowned at Bast Banbeck.

"Is something wrong, mentalist?" the Sacerdote asked.

"One doesn't normally spit on the floor while at a table with others," Gloria said.

Bast glanced around at the others. "I crave your pardon."

"It's fine," Jon said. "No harm, no foul." He turned to Gloria. "If you would continue, please."

She cleared her throat, and seemed ready to continue talking. Instead, she glanced up at Bast again.

The Sacerdote had folded his huge hands on the table, sitting like a discolored alien angel.

As Gloria began again, Jon glanced at the others in attendance.

The Old Man sat beside Bast. The tall, dark-haired Intelligence chief seemed short next to the Sacerdote. But the Old Man towered over the small Centurion beside him. On the other side of the table sat Chief Technician Miles Ghent. The man fingered his golden cross. Between Ghent and Gloria was the Missile Chief Uther Kling, who tapped a slender finger against his foxlike chin.

"You were talking about the third cybership," Jon told the mentalist.

"Thank you, I know," Gloria said, as she dipped her head in Jon's direction. She stared at the tabletop afterward, appearing to focus. Then, she looked up again, glancing at everyone in turn, although she passed Bast without looking at him.

"Thanks to Walleye, and Methlan for his teleoptic sweeps, we have pinpointed the range of safe hyperdrive entrance into real space-time," Gloria said. "It is much nearer than we thought, but still quite far out if you consider the possibilities. What I find interesting is the reason for the distant entrance into our Solar System."

"Which is?" asked Jon.

"I had previously surmised that any significant gravitational-generating body would upset whatever balance a ship needed to drop out of hyperspace. Would Neptune upset this balance? Would Makemake be too large? I no longer believe that. My computations show that the cyberships appeared with a larger dwarf planet behind them in their vicinity. Clearly, that dwarf planet did not upset their appearance. I am now of the opinion that only one object in our Solar System affects the hyperdrive range."

"And that is?" asked Jon.

"The star," Gloria said. "In our case, the Sun."

"How is that important again?" Jon asked.

"If you mean concerning the coming conflict between the three cyberships and us, I don't know. I am still gathering data on them. At present, we have insufficient data on hyperdrive technology and hyperspace. So far, it is all theoretical or hypothetical. However, their exit has now shown us one of the limitations."

Jon nodded as if that made sense. Gloria was logical and damn brilliant. She could also talk a lot and take forever getting to a point.

"The cyberships are coming fast," Jon said. "That's all the data we need right now."

"That is too basic an outlook," Gloria said. "Consider. We have learned several interesting facets over these past few days. First, the cyberships can act in concord. There are three working together. Despite haughty AI cores, they appear to be able to submerge that haughtiness to act as a fleet. Do they freely agree to this concord? Is one of them senior to the others and thus forces them to obey? If that is so, how does a cybership, or more correctly, how does an AI core gain this ascendancy over the others?"

"Interesting, interesting indeed," Bast said in his heavy voice.

Gloria gave a slight head bow, although she still did not look up at the Sacerdote.

"Second," she continued, "according to June Zen, the cyberships—the ruling AIs—accepted data from robots on Senda. June also recorded messages leaving the cyberships and traveling to Senda. That would indicate that the AIs could control the surviving robots from a different cybership."

Jon failed to see where this was leading.

"Three," Gloria said, "the cyberships split into two factions. Two of the great vessels are heading directly here. The last appears to be chasing Walleye. I submit that Walleye correctly surmised that the cyberships know of our existence. I mean here inside MK2. That could be critical."

"A moment, please," Bast said.

Gloria ventured a glance at him and then gave him fuller scrutiny when he was no longer doing something distasteful.

"We have found the surviving robots to be less intelligent than the original cybership AI," Bast said. "Even Unit 52-9 seemed less intelligent than the original AI core."

"I agree," Gloria said.

"Given that truth," Bast said, "we must surmise less intelligence from the Senda robots."

"No doubt," Gloria said.

"That limited intelligence would limit the type and possibly the scope of what the Senda robots could relay to the powerful AIs in the new cyberships."

Gloria raised an eyebrow. "That is an interesting possibility."

"Does it surmount my crudity earlier?"

Gloria smiled shyly. "I'm sorry, Bast. I-I grew up under far different circumstances. We mentalists are a fastidious group. I—" She smiled. "Yes, your crudity is forgiven."

Bast made a two-handed sweeping gesture as he bowed his head. It almost seemed like a sarcastic motion.

"I am grateful," the Sacerdote intoned.

Gloria stared at him a moment longer than seemed necessary. She inhaled afterward and looked at the others around the table.

"I want to point out that the approaching cyberships are an enigma," the mentalist said. "We might think we understand these three from our former victory over the original ship. These may even act in a similar manner. However, they may also act much differently. We must not presume to think we know them. Perhaps they carry refinements. Perhaps their AIs lack arrogance. Perhaps these will prove studiously murderous."

"Okay," Jon said. "We get that. Now, how should we respond?"

Gloria tapped the fingertips of one hand against those from the other. Her eyelids began to flicker.

Jon had come to understand that this meant she was running rapid mental calculations.

Her head turned abruptly toward him. "There are so many factors to the calculations. There are too many unknowns. We may think we know their capabilities. To a certain extent, we could even surmise that they will be in most ways similar to the original cybership—"

"Wait a second," Miles Ghent said. "You're wrong on one count. We've already battled a second cybership. We destroyed it before Makemake."

"True," Gloria said.

"It was just like the first cybership," Ghent said.

"Which proves nothing concerning the three approaching in-system," she said.

"I think it does," Ghent said. "The second cybership was just like the first one."

Gloria snorted softly. "Yes, because the second cybership had the first as its prototype. Why do you think that means these three will be replicas of the original? They look similar. That does not mean they are similar."

"It stands to reason that mechanical minds would mass produce similar vessels—"

"I'm sorry," Gloria said, interrupting. "I would like to know how you arrive at such a conclusion."

"Well…" Ghent said.

"Hey," Jon said. "That's enough theory. We may have already waited too long to act."

Bast cleared his throat.

Jon pointed at him, giving the Sacerdote a nod.

"We have almost finished full repairs to the *Nathan Graham*," Bast said. "Our last few days waiting at the moon dock are providing us great dividends. We should go into battle fully operational this time."

"Right," Jon said. "That's why we've waited. But we're going to have to make a decision, and we need to make it in the next hour. Two cyberships are barreling fast toward Makemake. I think they know we're here. Two against one is terrible odds."

"It would be a strategic loss to lose the moon dock," Gloria said.

"Yeah," Jon agreed. "But it would be even more tragic if we lost our cybership. We've already stored a few building robots in the holding bays. We can have those robots make more robot factories later. That's key."

"What if the two cyberships stop at Makemake?" Gloria said. "What if they decide to park at the dwarf planet and begin producing more cyberships?"

From farther down the table, the Centurion leaned forward, signaling Jon.

"Colonel," Jon said. "Would you like to add something?"

"Sir," the Centurion said. "I think the worst thing would be if one of the cyberships turns around and leaves the Solar System. If one of them leaves and brings even more reinforcements…"

"There you have it," Jon said. "Three of these bastards are likely going to give the Solar System an impossible fight. If five more show up, humanity is over. Done. Kaput."

"You don't plan to defend Makemake?" Gloria asked.

"We have the fighting platform," Jon said. "We have thousands of missiles and some pretty damn big guns on the moon. Maybe we could play hide and seek as the cyberships brake hard. We could use Makemake as a shield, only poking out for sniper shots at them. But to answer your question, no. I don't plan to stay here. If there were just two cyberships, maybe it would be worth considering. The third could still maneuver to join them against Makemake. Three against us is too many."

"Yes, but—" Gloria said.

"The colonel also points out the biggest threat," Jon said. "We have to assume the cyberships know about humanity. The Senda computers must have told them. If one of the cyberships leaves with that report, who knows how many other AI super-ships will return to pound humanity into dust? That makes our strategy, our big picture, clear."

"What is this 'big picture?'" Gloria asked.

"Human survival first," Jon said. "Figuring out how to survive the AI menace in the future is second. That's the big picture. Everything else is a way and a means to achieve the grand strategy. In our case, the future grand strategy is surviving and tooling up so we can gather an armada of the living to destroy the unliving blight against Life."

Gloria nodded sharply. "You state that well."

"Thank you, mentalist," Jon said. "Given the colonel's insight, I think we have to lure the cyberships into a trap they can't escape."

"How does one achieve this?" Bast asked. "MK2 is our strongest point. Or are you referring to the Saturn System?"

Jon shook his head. "We may have actually caught a break. If you think about it, it's kind of cool." He studied the others. "Look. The Solar League has been spying out our alien tech in the Saturn System. They are no doubt attempting to replicate it for themselves. The Solar League people also know about the self-aware alien software. It's possible the Solar League is frightened we'll try that against them. Maybe they've prepared as we have and lowered the processing power of their ships' computers. The point I'm trying to make is that the Solar System has been tooling for full-scale war, one side against the other for some time now. What if the Solar League gathers its warships into a giant armada and we join them? That mass faces the cyberships. That seems like our best chance of victory."

"If we gather such might in one location," Gloria said, "surely the cyberships will logically attack elsewhere. The AIs will force the giant armada to splinter and protect various planetary systems."

"Maybe…" Jon said, "and maybe not. That's why we have to lure them deep in-system, forcing them to shed most of their incredible velocity. Maybe even lure them to the Asteroid Belt or Mars."

"What if the cyberships stop at the Neptune and Saturn Systems along the way?" asked Gloria. "What if they demolish the Solar Freedom Fleet before it can gather into one armada?"

"That would be bad," Jon admitted.

"What if the Solar League refuses to cooperate with us?" she added.

"That would be even worse."

"In those instances," she said. "We would be better off fighting the cyberships at Makemake."

"That brings us back to the big picture," Jon said. "Three cyberships is one too many, remember? I think we have to gamble on luring them in-system. We'll have to talk the Solar League into helping us save mankind."

"They might think it's a trick on our part."

"There are plenty of ifs," Jon admitted. "Hell. I don't know if all of us combined can smash three of the alien super-ships."

"We have the regiment," the Centurion said from down the table.

Jon pointed at the small regimental colonel. "Maybe it will come down to our marines storming another cybership. Maybe—"

"What if during the grand battle the aliens destroy the *Nathan Graham*?" Gloria asked. "That would leave the Solar League in charge of humanity."

Jon stared at Gloria. Finally, he laughed. "A man can only do what a man can do. Sure, we might lose. That's our lot in life. No one promises us victory. But we're going to go down fighting, if it comes to that. We have to play the odds and then try to maneuver so we come out alive in the end."

"That maneuvering—"

"Gloria," Jon said, interrupting. "Enough with the negative talk. It's clear that our best chance is a united human effort. We'll proceed along those lines and attempt to make it happen."

"The *Nathan Graham* will definitely leave the moon dock?" the Old Man asked.

"That's right," Jon said. "We're going to leave as soon as possible." He turned to Gloria. "How soon is that?"

She focused, looking up afterward. "Four hours and thirty-six minutes," she said. "That's assuming—"

Jon stood.

"A moment, please," Gloria said. "What should I radio Walleye? The destroyer doesn't have the fuel to do anything except continue on to Senda."

"Yeah," Jon said. He bent his head in thought. When he looked up, he said, "You won't tell him anything. I will."

-3-

Methlan brooded in his cell in the brig. He'd been here for a time already. The worst of it wasn't the boredom. It wasn't knowing that his enemies knew who he was. It wasn't even the profanity of Walleye handling his dagger. No. The worst part of the confinement was his inability to lift.

He moved his right arm as if doing a curl. He inspected the bicep muscle. It was a ball. When he felt the muscle, though, it was no longer quite as hard as it used to be. He couldn't do heavy curls until his biceps burned with fatigue. He had come to love the burn, love the feel of his muscles tearing down so they could rebuild stronger.

The problem with the brig was that a man could only do so many pushups, deep-knee bends and sit-ups. He needed a chin bar, at least, so he could work on his biceps.

It was interesting to Methlan that the body he'd acquired had been satisfied with its frailty. If that didn't prove the superiority of the High Race, he didn't know what did. He'd taken a body and vastly improved it. These humans with their weak egos…

Methlan shook his head.

He lay on his cot with his hands behind his head. The other thing he hated about being here wasn't the boredom but an offshoot of the boredom. He had too much time to think.

Methlan Rath had always been a doer more than a thinker. Leave it to scholars and letter-scribblers to do the deep thinking. Did they mount the beauties? On no account. It was the soldiers and rulers who earned that privilege.

Methlan rolled out of the cot and began to pace. The cell was small, so he turned constantly. Even so, he could let his mind zone out as the rhythm of pacing took over.

A problem had begun to plague him. He was Methlan of Janus House. He belonged to the High Race. He had been the Prince of Ten Worlds. Yet, if he mounted a woman and pleasured the two of them, the offspring would be human. He inhabited a human form. His sex organs were human.

Am I human then?

The possibility deeply troubled Methlan. He was of the High Race. He did not want to be human. Humans were weak vessels lacking—

The hatch opened without the decency of a knock or a comm warning.

Methlan spun around, staring at Walleye in his buff coat. The top of the man's head barely reached Methlan's shoulder. He craned his neck to look behind the mutant.

"I'm alone," Walleye said.

Methlan raised his eyebrows. "You are brave."

"True, but not for the reasons you think."

"Are you challenging the truth of my physical dominance over you?"

Walleye gave one of his rare smiles that contorted his features into ugliness.

"What does your smile mean?" Methlan demanded.

Walleye stepped back, although he didn't turn around and present his back to him.

"Am I to follow you?" Methlan called.

"If you're tough enough," Walleye said.

The taunt burned. As he frowned, Methlan stepped into the chamber with several brig entrances around him. Walleye sat on a stool. There was another stool across the way from the mutant.

"Am I to sit?" Methlan asked.

"If you want to," the mutant said.

"What if I want to stand exactly where you're sitting?"

"Are all the people of Janus House as stiff-necked as you?"

"What you determine as stiff-necked, we nobles of Janus House call pride. But the answer is no. Not all those of Janus House are of the High Race. You would likely be a menial on my world."

"Guess it's lucky I'm not there, then."

"Wrong. It would be a great honor for one like you to see true brilliance. Why have you brought me here?"

"Thought you could use a change of scenery. But if you're in a hurry to go back into your cell…"

"There is no need for threats." Methlan moved to his stool, sitting erectly as befitted his exalted rank.

Walleye tapped a foot on the deck. The stool was low enough that his short leg could reach that far. He seemed to be waiting.

Methlan could wait as well…if he wanted to. But he did not desire to wait. He desired action.

"Well?" the prince said.

"Well, well, well," Walleye said. "We're almost to Senda. We're braking even as we speak."

"Have you scanned the dwarf planet?"

"Plenty of times. Haven't spotted a thing so far. I think the robots are underground. If they had satellites up, those are gone too. Have they watched us draw nearer? Seems likely. I'm not sure how to smoke 'em out before the big ship arrives."

"I see. You demand me to slave for you, to draw your iron from the fire—"

"Methlan!"

The prince scowled. "Speak. What is on your mind?"

Walleye regarded him and then actually chuckled.

Methlan found the sound deeply annoying.

"I have to admit," Walleye said. "You did a great job of hiding your true identity before."

"Are you saying this in order to exalt yourself over me?"

"What's that even mean?"

"If I did a splendid job hiding my true identity, it stands to reason you did an equally great job in piercing my disguise. Thus, you have exalted yourself at my expense."

"It sounds like Janus House was pretty competitive."

Methlan searched for the insult in the words. He could not find one. Could Walleye be more devious than he perceived? Did the mutant insult him in a way Methlan could not detect? That was a galling thought.

"I could use your competitive spirit against the AIs," Walleye said.

Methlan squinted at the mutant. A thought occurred, one he hadn't considered before. "You do not know the ways of Janus House."

"You got that right."

"If you would forebear with your studied slights and insults, I would like to make a point. Perhaps it could ease the tension between us."

"Yeah? That sounds good. Tell me."

"I will speak, but not because you order me like a dog to the harness."

Crinkle lines appeared on Walleye's face. It almost seemed as if the mutant strove not to laugh. Perhaps he misread the mutant. Perhaps the fear in Walleye facing him alone like this produced pain that the mutant strove to control.

"In Janus House, if one makes another his captive, he becomes the other's slave. Any action after that point is slave action. If you believe I will do as you tell me to, you believe that I am no more than your slave. You have proclaimed me a dog of the lowest order."

"That wasn't my intent."

Methlan nodded. "That is what I'm trying to explain. Your ways are so inferior. At times, they are below my understanding. I have come to realize that you do not think of me as your lowest dog."

"I don't."

"You aren't demanding these things of me…but…" Methlan stopped because he was at a loss.

"I need help, your particular competiveness to help me beat the AIs," Walleye said. "Maybe we can even figure out a way to survive the cybership's coming."

"I would not do this as your slave."

"I get it. You're trying to get me to free you first."

The possibility had never occurred to Methlan. Could these humans be that weak? The possibility almost shamed him. How could he have let such weaklings capture him? It was beyond understanding.

"I'm not sure Captain Hawkins would agree to letting you wander the ship at will," Walleye said. "So here's what I'll do. You are still officially in the brig. But, and this is a big concession on my part. I'll come get you myself, allow you to change into your uniform and you'll join me on the bridge."

"As your slave?"

"No," Walleye said, "but as a crew member under my command."

"And after?"

"I'll return you to the brig."

"What is my official status then?"

"In the brig, you're a prisoner. On the bridge, you're a crew member."

Methlan frowned. "The two are at odds."

"It all depends on how you look at it."

"I do not understand."

"I got that," Walleye said. "But maybe you don't understand because you're of the High Race. What we're doing is called a compromise. It's something humans do so they can get along. Not that I think you're human, mind you."

"You consider me to be one of the High Race?"

"When you're on the bridge," Walleye said.

"You will obey me, then?" Methlan asked in wonder.

"All right," Walleye said. "I gave it a try. I could use your help. But if you're going to be a prick all along the line, forget it."

"But you claimed I was of the High Race."

"Yeah, you're high all right."

"Is that an insult?"

"Methlan, why don't you think about surviving first? A dead man doesn't dream. He don't do squat. The cyberships are here. One is coming for us. You're never going to fulfill your revenge because you're too hung up on your station, too filled with pride. If you can't bend just a little to meet me halfway, then to hell with you."

"Fighting words," Methlan said, standing. "This I understand. Your duplicity was cunning. I almost believed you. Now, you have shown your spirit." He frowned, turned away and squinted thoughtfully. Walleye had spoken of the end. Lying on a cot until death claimed him—

Methlan faced his jailor. "I will work the bridge controls in my uniform. But I have a condition. You must allow me to exercise daily in the gym."

"Fine," Walleye said. "You can lift if you want. I don't care about that."

Methlan forced himself to remain bland-faced. He would let Walleye think of him as a slave, as a servitor. But he would use the gym to remain fit as he plotted his revenge. Such deception on his part was allowed under the codes of Janus House. Maybe, just maybe—

No! Methlan would not even think it. When the time came, he would act with resolve and purpose, using this body to its full capacity.

Maybe he could pull a reverse and change everything…

-4-

Jon Hawkins sat on his captain's seat on the bridge. The bridge wasn't in the exact center of the *Nathan Graham*. The gutted AI chamber had that honor.

He'd captured the cybership. He'd torn a planetary system from the Solar League and convinced another to join them. The Neptune System had begun to rebuild, even though they had a fraction of the people since the dreadful battle against the original AI vessel.

The Neptune, Uranus and Saturn Systems had created an accord. Now, that accord might mean nothing. The warships built to defend their freedom…

Jon watched the bridge crew around him. He looked up at the main screen.

The *Nathan Graham* slid through the open hangar bay moon-doors. The cybership left MK2. What had Unit 52-9 called the moon: a production unit?

That was about right. MK2 was likely the greatest production unit in the Solar System. It had greater building capacity than the Saturn System had shown. It might even have more than the Earth System. Each of those industrial nodes could advance greatly if they received some of the robo-builders from the cargo holds.

Jon leaned back in his captain's chair.

A few people had volunteered to remain behind on MK2. Jon had turned them down. He needed everyone. The *Nathan Graham* always seemed to be short of hands. The automated systems would defend the moon. Maybe the coming cyberships could disrupt that through alien software. That even seemed likely. But that probably didn't matter in the end. Maybe an easy victory like that would help the alien AIs retain their contempt for humanity.

Yeah. Once the other AIs saw his vessel, they would know the humans had captured it. That should cause the AIs to rethink their position. But Jon had dealt with these alien computers long enough to realize they had vast reserves of arrogance and contempt for their biological victims.

He was counting on that arrogance. An easy victory for the attacking cyberships at MK2—

Jon exhaled. The endless possibilities and the penalties for being wrong had begun to wring him dry.

"We're clearing the moon doors," Ghent informed him.

Jon used the armrest panel on his chair to redirect the main screen. He brought up a rear image.

The one-hundred-kilometer vessel cleared the giant doors. There was little space to spare around the giant spaceship.

Jon changed views to examine the cybership's hull armor. It was new, hard and fully intact again. All the ship's grav cannons were in working order. Tens of thousands of heavy drones and missiles filled the cargo holds. The matter/antimatter engine had been fully repaired.

"With your permission, sir," Ghent said.

Jon looked up...nodding.

Ghent was working his board.

Once more, Jon switched views. He sat back as he viewed the main screen. The great moon doors ponderously began to close. At the same time, the fighting platform from Makemake hove into view. The platform would fight in tandem with the moon. Giant guns and cannons dotted MK2's surface.

If the alien software failed to corrupt the automated systems, the cyberships might have to slug it out with the moon fortress. If the fortress damaged an enemy vessel...

Jon wasn't sure if he should set up automated self-destruct orders. Hurting an enemy cybership might make the AIs more cautious. That would be bad for the big picture.

The truth…he trusted the aliens to have something that could wipe out the moon fortress.

Gloria had suggested the cyberships must be working in accord with AI protocols regarding the annihilation of a biologically infested star system.

"How do you figure," Jon had asked her.

"Three cyberships showed up," the mentalist had said. "Why three and not one?"

"I don't know."

"It strikes me as protocol. If a cybership fails to report after a given length of time, the cyber High Command sends a three-ship flotilla to investigate. That would suggest the cyberships are loaded for war and with possibly greater weapons than previously shown."

"Because they're entering a star system that has defeated a previous cybership?"

"Correct," Gloria said.

It made sense.

As Jon studied the screen, the *Nathan Graham* used low engine power to crawl away from the moon, leaving Makemake. The ship had taken a terrible pounding here. Now, it was hale and whole once more.

Two hours clicked away.

"We're clear of MK2 and Makemake," Ghent said. "The moon's automated defenses are working. MK2's missile launch tubes are ready. We are aimed at the Saturn System."

"Show me the cyberships," Jon said.

The main screen flickered for only an instant. Teleoptics showed the two cyberships. They had begun slight braking maneuvers, increasing their visibility.

"What about the other one?" Jon asked.

The screen changed. A lone cybership moved toward Senda. At the same time, the *Daisy Chain 4* maneuvered toward an orbital insertion of the dwarf planet.

"It's time to leave," Jon said. "Mr. Ghent, begin acceleration. We're leaving Makemake and heading in-system."

"Aye-aye, Captain," the Tech Chief said. "We're beginning acceleration…now."

-5-

The *Daisy Chain 4* slid toward a Senda orbital insertion. The destroyer looked lopsided with the huge *Hercules* drone attached to the vessel's left underbelly. Even so, the almost fuel-less destroyer maneuvered easily.

Senda, despite being outside the Kuiper Belt, was similar to other dwarf planets. Water, methane and nitrogen ices containing tholins covered the surface. Due to the tholins, Senda was one of the reddest objects in the Solar System. It was almost as red as Mars. Two small moons, which seemed to be uninhabited, orbited the dwarf planet.

During the insertion maneuver, Methlan sat at his station on the bridge. He scanned the moons and the nearing planetoid.

"I still detect nothing," Methlan said.

Walleye avidly studied the main screen, saying nothing.

Fifteen minutes passed.

"We have entered orbital stability," Methlan said.

"What about the cybership?" Walleye asked.

Methlan used his board to study the distant vessel. He shook his head. "The enemy vessel seems passive, Lieutenant. I detect no missile or drone launches." He looked up. "We'll be out of the cybership's line-of-sight in four minutes."

Walleye laughed sharply as he rubbed his throat. "That will feel good, even if it only lasts for a little while."

"You sensed a blade against your throat?" Methlan asked.

Walleye turned to him. "Come again?"

"You rubbed your throat," Methlan said. "You rubbed it as you mentioned the cybership. It has been like a knife pressed against our throat. They constantly threaten."

"That's a good analogy. I like it." Walleye snapped his fingers. "Now we have to find the AI outpost. We need to take it out while we can."

Methlan returned to his sensors.

The lone destroyer orbited Senda. Its sensors searched the ices sheathing the rocky underworld. The vessel made a total of four circuits.

On the bridge, Walleye scowled fiercely. "The robots are hiding from us. We have to start searching for them in earnest. Let's use a few missiles. Methlan, are there any heat sources whatsoever?"

"I have found two. Those I've scanned relentlessly. In my estimation, they are cryovolcanoes. Their heat is a relative term, as they're hotter than their surroundings—"

"Got it," Walleye said, interrupting. "June, I want you to find radio leakages, any—"

"I've searched for those during every orbital circuit," June said. "There's nothing. This is a cold dead world."

"Something here sent signals to the cybership," Walleye said. "We have to find that."

"The AIs on Makemake used crawlers," Methlan said. "Could the robots on Senda have done likewise?"

Walleye grinned as he snapped his fingers. "You hit the nail on the head. Search for tracks."

"Tracks on the ice?" Methlan asked, sounding dubious.

"Do you have any other pressing engagement?"

"Lieutenant," Methlan said, bristling. "I am your prisoner. But I cannot stand for this mockery."

"What mockery?"

"The implication I will return to my cell if I refuse to follow your orders."

Walleye stared at him. He stared longer. "Noted," he said, at last.

"I do not understand."

"You stood up to me, Methlan. You're cleverer than I realized. I mocked you, thinking to do it slyly. When you realized that, you stood up to me. That impresses me."

Methlan's chest puffed up. A feeling of dominance swelled in him. This was most interesting. The idea of a prisoner making demands—humans were weaklings indeed.

"I won't mock you anymore," Walleye said. "But I still want you searching the ices for signs of crawler tracks. I did some checking before."

June cleared her throat.

"Okay, Luscious, you told me. Why not tell Methlan."

"The weak methane absorption bands indicate that the methane on Senda's surface is ancient," June said. "That means it isn't freshly deposited. Senda is too cold for methane to evaporate from its surface and fall back later as snow, which is what happens on Triton and Pluto."

"Right," Walleye said. "I know this is a long shot. But none of us has anything else we can do. Find the crawler tracks, Methlan. Everything depends on it."

Without a word, Methlan turned back to his station, beginning a long and tedious search for possible crawler tracks down on Senda.

***

Seven and a half hours later, a red-eyed Methlan looked up from his board. "Lieutenant, I may have just discovered tracks."

Walleye's chin had been resting on his chest. He raised his head and rubbed his eyes as if he'd been sleeping.

"What did you say?" asked Walleye.

"Surface tracks, Lieutenant. They're down there just as you suspected."

Walleye slid off his chair, walking toward the main screen. "Put it up there, please."

The "please" astonished Methlan. He grinned to himself, feeling in more control of the situation by the minute. The humans needed his technical prowess. He was beginning to realize he might use his usefulness to pry his way into command. He might not even have to kill Walleye to assume authority over them. That was a heady realization.

The image on the main screen changed. On the starlit surface of Senda, crawler tracks appeared. The tracks had scratched into the ice. The crawler must be heavy.

"Can you follow the tracks to their end?" Walleye asked.

"I can," Methlan said. "I doubt any other could."

Walleye glanced at June. She turned away quickly, hiding her face from them. A muffled noise came from her.

Methlan gloated inwardly. He'd just witnessed an amazing thing. Walleye had sent a wordless message to June Zen. In her understanding of his—Methlan's—brilliance, she had turned away. She must have done so because she realized that she had hitched herself to the weaker man. She must not want Walleye to understand that—

She is trying to hide her feelings toward me, Methlan realized.

The feeling of power just now was awesome indeed. A prisoner could still vie for rank if he had the wit and wisdom, and the daring, of a noble of Janus House.

"Are you searching?" Walleye asked in a subdued tone.

"At once," Methlan said. He tried to conceal his dominance. He actually tried to be meek in order to further dig his tentacles into their desperation. Without his technical brilliance, the humans would falter at this important juncture.

Methlan concentrated on his board, studying the surface tracks, using the ship's teleoptics to trace them both ways.

Soon, Methlan sat up triumphantly. "Lieutenant, I have discovered the AI base. The tracks led me to it. I have used seismic measurements and discovered a cavity under the ice. The thickness of the ice would hide any thermal radiation. Yet, I am convinced that within the cavity lies the robot factory base that built the Senda-launched ship we destroyed."

"What about the tracks leading the other way?" asked Walleye.

"That proves my theory. The placement at the end of the tracks in the other direction showed several centimeters' greater depth into the ice."

"Why, do you think?"

"The crawler launched an object," Methlan said. "The launching recoil caused the crawler to sink that much deeper into the ice."

"You think the crawler launched a satellite?"

"I believe so," Methlan said.

"Why couldn't we find the satellite?"

"I don't know. Perhaps it used the gravity of one of the moons to catapult itself elsewhere, shutting down after a time."

"Maybe the satellite is hiding behind one of the moons in relation to us," June suggested.

"I like it," Walleye told her. He nodded afterward. "Here's what we're going to do…"

***

Walleye launched three drones, one of them the *Hercules* monster. Methlan guided the big one. It trailed the *Daisy Chain 4* while heading down to a much lower orbit. Meanwhile, June controlled the other two drones. Each of those drones headed for a different moon.

Thirty-two minutes later, June said, "Walleye, I found something."

The mutant slid off the command chair and went to her station, studying whatever she had on her board.

"That's it," Walleye said. "Let's take it out. Oh, and June, put it on the main screen so Methlan can watch."

Methlan appreciated the appeal to appease him. It showed him that humans didn't understand prisoner status. He watched.

June's drone headed for an alien comm satellite. As the drone approached the object, jets appeared. The satellite attempted to flee.

"Any time, Luscious," Walleye said.

June looked at up him, smiling. "I'll let you do it," she said.

Methlan waited for Walleye to turn and ask him to do the honors. He would enjoy feeling June's body heat. The mutant surprised him, though. With one of his stubby fingers, Walleye pressed the detonation switch.

On the screen, the drone exploded. That killed the picture, and no doubt, destroyed the robot satellite.

Walleye returned to his command chair. He seemed to walk with more cock, as the soldiers of Janus House would say.

"Let's get ready for round two," Walleye said.

Methlan knew the mutant meant him. It irked him that the humans hadn't desired him to destroy the robot satellite. They seemed so eager to placate him. Why wouldn't they give him a soldier's honors?

"Methlan," Walleye said. "Is your drone ready?"

Methlan twisted his mouth with distaste while his back was turned to the mutant. How dare Walleye question his readiness for action.

No, no, Methlan reminded himself. He must lull these two. That was the game. He was getting ahead of himself because he was still thinking too much like the High Race. He was now among weaklings and cowards who thought much differently.

"Oh, Methlan," Walleye called in a gentle voice. "If I could have your attention."

Methlan almost laughed aloud. Maybe he had miscalculated again. See how Walleye spoke with such deference to him?

"The drone is ready," Methlan declared.

"All right," Walleye said. "Let's see if we can get the robots to open up for us."

The mutant used the controls in his command chair to maneuver the destroyer. He brought them lower to the icy surface.

They headed toward the hidden cavity in the ice. Walleye launched two missiles. They screamed down toward the surface, heading for the hidden cavity area.

Abruptly, the surface ice exploded. Two antimissile launchers appeared and fired rockets. Another tube extended. It chugged shells at the destroyer.

"Finally," Walleye breathed. "Methlan, bring your big one low over the surface. Ram it down their throats if you can. I'll try to keep them engaged."

The slugs from the orbital gun sped upward. Senda only had a slight gravity pull.

Walleye launched packets of sand into the shells' paths. The packets exploded, dispersing sand in a greater area. The slugs plowed against the sand. The particles did not stop the slugs, but it changed their direction of travel.

The antimissiles destroyed the destroyer missiles heading down.

"I see another slug thrower," June said.

"Methlan," Walleye said. "What's the progress?"

"Less than thirty seconds to impact," Methlan said as he avidly watched his scope.

Walleye launched more sand-packets. He looked up at the main screen then.

Methlan tapped his board and swiveled around. He wanted to see this in all its glory. The *Hercules* drone sped across the icy moonscape as if it were a cruise missile. It burned fast. The cavity appeared five kilometers ahead of it.

"The gun tubes are firing," June said.

Methlan glanced at Walleye. The mutant bit his lower lip in nervousness. Methlan grinned triumphantly. They needed his iron nerves. In that moment, Methlan realized he must do whatever he could to stay alive. Sooner or later, the others would recognize his greatness and yearn to serve under him. In time, he might even rule the Solar System. Then, he would hunt the galaxy for his Ten Worlds.

On the screen, the big drone turned down into the cavity. It reached the orbital gun tubes and antimissile launchers. Below those were metal buildings, the tip of the iceberg of a probable underground robo-construction yard.

The drone's warhead exploded with a matter/antimatter detonation. A gigantic blast erupted, burning and devouring the tubes, launchers, buildings and ices all around it.

Walleye switched images. The destroyer passed in orbit over Senda. Below, the giant explosion appeared as a massive white blast.

"We're getting out of here before the radiation hits us," Walleye said.

The *Daisy Chain 4* used some of its last fuel to accelerate around the dwarf planet before the heat, EMP and radiation reached the destroyer's outer hull.

As soon as the vessel was out of danger, Walleye grinned widely. It made him uglier than ever. "We did it. We scratched us some paint. Doesn't it feel good?"

"I suppose," June Zen said.

"Definitely," Methlan said.

"Definitely," Walleye repeated. "I wonder if that's going to change what the cybership does."

"Why would it?" Methlan asked.

"I don't know. Just hoping out loud." Walleye slid off his seat. "Come on, Methlan. Let's get you to the gym. I'll have to take you to your cell afterward."

Methlan rose slowly, and finally nodded in agreement. He had hoped—it didn't matter what he'd hoped. He hated sitting alone in his cell. But maybe that was for the best. He needed to rethink a few things and make his plans for taking over the destroyer.

-6-

The *Nathan Graham* accelerated away from Makemake at 60 gravities. The cybership headed in-system, presently moving toward the Saturn System.

Jon received Walleye's message. The modified NSN destroyer had eliminated the only known robo-construction yard on Senda. Some robots could have survived down there. Walleye doubted they had much capacity to do any more mischief, however.

"Keep yourself and the destroyer intact," Jon messaged Walleye. "If you survive the approaching cybership, you might be out there awhile. Ration as necessary. If we win, rest assured we'll come out there to pick you up."

Walleye maintained comm silence afterward. Meanwhile, the *Nathan Graham* continued to accelerate.

The two enemy cyberships continued to move at their terrific velocity. The third cybership still maintained its approach toward Senda.

Two days passed.

Jon rose from bed with a headache. He'd had a nightmare he couldn't remember. He realized the cabin comm had woken him and had broken the nightmare's spell.

"What is it?" he said, after touching the comm control.

"This is Gloria, Captain. We need you on the bridge."

"Coming," he said. He didn't ask what it was. He'd find out soon enough.

Jon ran most of the way. He ran more for the exercise than out of a sense of urgency. It was too easy to get stale and out of shape as the commander.

He walked onto the bridge sweating and panting. He'd take a shower once he had dealt with the problem. Then, he'd eat some breakfast and drink some strong coffee.

Ghent and Kling must have been sleeping. Their replacements stood at their stations. Gloria stood near the big screen, staring at it. She glanced at him as he approached.

"What happened to you?" she asked.

"Took a sprint," Jon said.

"For Heaven's sake, I didn't need—"

"You woke me up, remember? What's the problem?"

She pointed at the screen. A lone cybership had a long exhaust tail, longer than he'd seen on any of the others.

"It's braking?" he asked.

She shook her head.

"Accelerating?"

She nodded.

There could be only one reason for this. "Is it joining the others?"

"Given its new heading and the extent of the acceleration—I think so," she said.

"Are the other two still following us?"

"Of course."

"They're going to bypass MK2?"

"So far it looks like they might. But who knows? At that far out..." She shrugged.

"They're obviously concentrating their forces."

"That is my estimate as well. For what it's worth, at this juncture, it looks like they're going to fall for your lure."

Jon didn't say anything. He just watched the lone cybership accelerate so it could join its brothers in human genocide. Finally, he shook his head. "That clinches one thing. Saturn System and the *Nathan Graham* might have taken on two cyberships and hoped to win. We can't take on three."

"I know."

"It's time I opened negotiations with Earth."

"Yes," she said. "We might as well find out the worst."

***

Jon sat at the same big desk, with the same Black Anvil Regimental flag behind him as when he'd spoken to the Chief Executive of the Uranus System. He wore a dress uniform. He'd showered, eaten a good meal and drunk plenty of coffee. This time, they would record the message and modify it if necessary.

"What do we know?" Jon asked.

Gloria had joined him this time instead of Bast Banbeck. "Did you read the Intelligence packet?" she asked.

"Not yet," he said. "What's the pertinent information?"

The Intelligence packet had come from the Saturn System. It gave them the latest concerning the Solar League.

"J.P. Justinian is dead," Gloria said.

"Oh? Wow! That's huge! I'm surprised no one told us before this."

"I think the Saturn Secret Service only learned about it a short time ago. He died after a short trial. The tribunal declared the former Premier as an enemy to the State and a devourer of the People."

"You could say that about any Social Dynamist."

Gloria shrugged. "With Justinian, it was even truer."

"They shot him?"

"That wasn't in the packet. He's dead. Now, someone named Frank Benz is the new Premier."

"What do we know about him?"

"He's a military man. That's quite odd given Social Dynamism's political theory. He's supposed to be some kind of genius."

"Aren't they all?" Jon asked.

"Why are you so cynical?"

"Social Dynamism destroyed my world when they invaded the Saturn System. That probably killed the colonel, if you think about it. We would have never been in the Neptune System—"

"Jon. No. We're lucky you and the regiment were in the Neptune System when the cybership showed up. Who knows if any people would even be alive now."

Jon looked away.

"Since Benz is a military man," Gloria said. "You may be able to appeal to his strategic sense."

"You know this is a long shot, right? I doubt—"

"Jon. What's wrong with you? You're grabbing for the brass ring. As you once chided me, why be negative? If you're going to win, if you're going to give your all, why not believe it's possible? You did before."

Jon faced the screen at the edge of the desk. "That's good advice. Let's do this."

"Do you know what you're going to say?"

"Not exactly, but I have the gist of it right here." He tapped the spot over his heart.

"I'm ready when you are," Gloria said. Her hand hovered over the record button.

"Go," Jon said.

She touched the button.

Jon cleared his throat as he stared intently into the screen. "This is Jon Hawkins of the Black Anvil Regiment. Firstly—"

Jon stopped abruptly. "What's wrong? Why are you shaking your head?"

"We're the SFF or the *Nathan Graham*."

"What did I say?"

"The Black Anvil Regiment."

He sighed. "I guess that's how I still see myself. Okay. Let's start again."

She reset the screen, watched it, and chopped her hand decisively.

"Hello, Premier Benz. This is Captain Jon Hawkins of the SFF *Nathan Graham* speaking."

Gloria nodded in an exaggerated manner.

"First, sir, I would like to congratulate you on your ascension to supreme leadership of the Solar League. We are going to need good leadership in the coming days. As you are no doubt aware, three alien cyberships have appeared in our Solar System. They entered more than one thousand AUs from the Sun. Since then, they have been traveling at incredible speed toward our populated centers. Premier, I have faced a cybership before. They are deadly foes. I would like to plead with you that you not underestimate their danger.

"Premier Benz, the cyberships as a society prowl the galaxy in search of what they call biological infestations. They have slaughtered thousands of intelligent races. Bast Banbeck is a member of our crew. He is a Sacerdote, a friendly alien from another star system. His race is dead, slaughtered by the cyberships.

"I have seen horrifying things on the cybership. The AIs are inhuman. They use people as if they were mere objects, not as created beings made in God's image."

Gloria cleared her throat.

"What now?" Jon asked. "I was just getting going."

"Social Dynamism does not recognize God," she said. "The Premier will find your religious reference as insulting to his intelligence."

"More fool him."

"Jon, we're trying to convince him to work with us, to save human life. We're not trying to get him to believe what he doesn't believe."

"Okay. I can change that part, I suppose."

"Please do."

Jon looked at her for a moment before he faced the screen again. "Go."

She nodded.

"Premier Benz, the AIs are incredibly dehumanizing. They treat us as objects, as mere machines. They desire to wipe out human life. I suggest we put aside our differences for the moment. Neither of us wins if the human race loses. I believe we must pool our warships into one giant fist. That fist has to hit the cyberships and destroy them.

"I realize you must be wondering about the aftermath. To our knowledge, the AIs have formed the only known galactic society. Granted, we have limited knowledge, at best, hearsay. But if true, we are alone in our struggle against a mighty AI empire. I have a solution. That solution lies in the belly of my captured cybership. I'm referring to the robot-building tech. If and when we defeat these three cyberships, I am willing to share the alien robo-tech with you. In that way, the entire Solar

System can retool for round three. Of course, that means we have to survive round two.

"Unless we unite, Premier, I doubt humanity has a chance. Frankly, it was by sheerest chance that I was able to capture this vessel. Chance and hard fighting by my men. Let's use our opportunity and survive. I await your answer, sir, and I hope for the best. Yours in command, Captain Jon Hawkins."

Gloria clicked the switch.

"How did that sound?" he asked.

"Good for the most part," she said.

"What didn't you like?"

"We need to change your title. If you're leading the Solar Freedom Force, shouldn't you be something more than a captain?"

"I guess. What do you suggest?"

"Let me think about it."

"Sure. Anything else wrong?"

Gloria began to tell him.

-7-

INTERLUDE: EARTH

Premier Benz massaged his temples as he sat before a large screen. Vela Shaw sat beside him. They'd just finished watching Captain Hawkins's message from the *Nathan Graham* yet again. This was the eleventh viewing.

The room was in a deep underground fortress in Lima, Peru Sector. There were chairs, a wet bar, a fridge, the giant screen, computer consoles and an armored hatch.

Special guards stood outside the room. Each had gone under the chair. Each would fight to the death to protect the Premier and the Vice Premier.

Benz had debated giving Vela the role of Chief Arbiter. She'd refused. Thus, the same lean Chief Arbiter as had gone underground in the Colorado mine retained the post of first secret policeman.

Earth's cities no longer seethed with riots. Neither had true peace returned to the home planet. A lull had descended. At best, Benz had a shaky grasp of the Government Security Bureau. Worse, the Social Dynamism Party did not care for him. As yet, the Party members were not overtly chipping away at his authority. He believed that given time, they would. Perhaps half the military approved of him. Surprisingly, that half came from the space forces rather than the ground fighters.

The greatest surprise to Benz was the difficulty of governing the Solar League. True, he hadn't been at it for long.

Even so, it was still harder than it looked. The trouble was the lack of loyalty in his underlings. Justinian had used fear to motivate them. Benz still hadn't decided on his chief tool, and that was likely a mistake.

"You've broken the system," Vela said, rising from her chair. She wore a scarlet uniform with white braid. "The Party and the secret police used to hold the military in check. Now, the military has shaken off its collar. You frighten people in ways Justinian never could. They understood J.P. He ruled in the accepted manner. Your decrees—"

Vela shook her head.

"We need more time," Benz said. "We've shaken the system, as you say. We need time for everything to settle."

"I'm not sure that's right. I think our assumptions could be wrong. We can be as brilliant as can be, but if we begin with faulty assumptions…"

"Garbage in, garbage out," Benz quoted.

Vela nodded.

"Maybe you're right," Benz said. "The people want an iron heel grinding them into poverty. It makes them feel as if they understand the world."

"That's not it," Vela said. "They want what they know. They have illusions. If you break their illusions, they'll hate you for it. They won't rejoice that their chains might fall off."

Benz sighed as he massaged his temples again.

"The cyberships could change everything," Vela said.

"By killing us," Benz said moodily.

"We could use the threat of the cyberships to whip Earth into a frenzy of action."

"We don't have time for that," Benz said. "The cyberships aren't giving us time. Their appearance and swift approach—we have weeks to maneuver into position. The giant alien vessels will be anywhere they want in the Solar System by then."

"Correction," Vela said. "The enemy vessels will be in any *one* place in the Solar System. They're traveling at terrific velocity. We have to presume Hawkins is correct concerning their braking abilities. Once they brake, though, they lose the ability to be in any other place at that time. Opportunity costs—"

"Yes, yes," Benz said. "Of course that's correct. My point is that we have little time to try to trap them. Perhaps the *Nathan Graham* can maneuver at great velocity like the robotic ships. Our warships cannot. I have just learned that not all of the Solar League's warships have converted to lesser computers. Those unconverted ships can definitely not enter combat against the cyberships."

"I see."

"What if we maneuver everything we can to Mars for a giant confrontation, and the cyberships dash to Earth instead and obliterate the planet?"

"If we stay at Earth, we risk having the cyberships infect all of Earth's computers. Billions will die if those computers turn into murderous AIs."

Benz massaged his temples once more. "Whatever planet we use as a trap, we're likely going to lose it during the battle."

"Maybe we should tell Hawkins we'll agree to his alliance, but we'll use the Saturn System as the fortress trap."

Benz shook his head. Didn't she understand? "We won't be able to move enough SLN warships to Saturn in time."

"We'll move what we can."

"And lose the war?" he demanded.

Vela stroked her jaw.

Benz stopped massaging his temples. He glanced sidelong at her. Vela had changed since going under the chair. She was no longer the innocent. She was no longer as kind as she used to be, as sweet.

He shook his head.

"Hawkins has it right," he said, "the Asteroid Belt or Mars. The belt is no good, though. We need a powerful planetary system. Earth would be the best choice. It's the strongest fortress, and we could get the most warships here in time. But I'm with you. We dare not risk the most populated planet in the system."

"Mars is the fighting point then?" Vela asked.

"If so, we consign over a billion people to death," he said. "We'll probably lose the Mars—"

"Frank," she said, staring at him. "We're going to lose heavily no matter what we decide. But will we lose more heavily than Hawkins? That's the question."

"What are you suggesting?"

"The space commanders aren't going to agree to just hand Hawkins supremacy over us. They'll want to know your plans on capturing the cybership."

"But—"

"Hawkins is risking one vessel," Vela said. "We're risking hundreds."

"The *Nathan Graham* is the only vessel on their side that counts. It's their source of power. The Saturn and Uranus fleets are weak compared to the Solar League. The Neptune fleet is a joke. No. Hawkins is risking everything by throwing the *Nathan Graham* into battle."

"I don't fully agree—"

"If I were Hawkins, I would take an entirely different approach. I've calculated the odds. It's doubtful we can beat the three cyberships. I've studied the original invasion. The power of the giant vessels—it's not even that. More cyberships will be coming. Once the AIs realize we've become a power base, surely they'll send one hundred cyberships to crush us. It's what I'd do in their place."

She gave him a worried look. "What are you saying?"

"Hawkins wants to fight. I applaud that. But in the end, it's a losing strategy."

"What else is there?"

"That's easy," Benz said. "You fill the *Nathan Graham* with people, mostly women with some of the best men. You use the ship's hyperdrive. You go far, far away. I'm talking about hundreds or maybe even thousands of light-years away. You find a star system and begin anew. You use those robot factories in the belly of his ship. Then, for one hundred years, you start getting ready. Then, and only then, you might have a small chance of defeating the AI Empire."

Vela blinked at him in astonishment. "Your great intellect has driven you mad."

"No," Benz said. "I understand humanity's real chances. They are slim to none, to quote an old saying."

"You don't know that."

"If what they are telling us about the AI Empire is true, our chances are almost zero. That there are no other stellar organizations out there battling the AIs means—"

"Frank! Didn't you listen to Hawkins? He has an alien on board."

"An AI alien captive he set free."

"Yes," Vela said. "That means the cyberships fight others. Maybe all we need is a foothold. Once we go out there," she said, gesturing outward, "we might find other aliens fighting the cyberships. Maybe if we move fast enough out there, we can create a grand alliance of the living."

Benz frowned at her.

"You can't admit defeat from the start."

"I'm not. I've stumbled onto the one true path for victory."

Vela scoffed. "Your way would consign the majority of humanity to death."

"It would keep mankind going. That's the bigger picture."

"I'm not sure it is," Vela said. "We have to fight. We have to plant our flag against the AIs and say, 'you are going no farther than here.'"

He searched her face, and she returned his gaze. Finally, Benz looked away.

"Ruling has been grinding me down," he said. "I didn't think it would be so hard. Looking in from the outside—"

"I know," Vela said. "But we're in charge now, no matter how shaky our grasp is. We have to come up with something."

"Right," Benz said. "You're right."

"What are we going to tell Hawkins? We'd better come up with a plan soon."

Benz sat down in a chair. He looked up at the blank screen. "Let's listen to his message one more time. We might see something we missed before."

Vela seemed dubious, but she sat down near him. As the message began, she took one of his hands in hers.

Benz seemed to relax a little. He knew he needed it. He needed the old breezy Benz, the confident genius. The approaching cyberships and what they represented had shaken his confidence in the future. He needed to restore his faith in humanity's future in order for him to act in humanity's best interest.

But how could that happen when he knew they were going to lose?

PART V
APPROACH TO MARS

-1-

The *Nathan Graham* accelerated. It had already built up a good velocity and was halfway through the Kuiper Belt. The vessel's speed wasn't anything like the cyberships' velocity, but it was faster than any other human-occupied ship

The messages had sped back and forth between Captain Hawkins and Premier Benz. They'd agreed on one thing so far: lure the alien AI ships to Mars.

The *Nathan Graham* sped for the Outer Planets. It still had a long way to go before it passed Neptune.

At the same time, most of the SLN warships orbiting Earth or Luna had begun the journey for Mars. The swiftest—meaning the biggest, battleships and motherships orbiting Venus—also headed for Mars. There were a fair number of SLN warships already at Mars. None of the SLN warships in the Jupiter System headed for the Red Planet. Neither did any of the warships in the Asteroid Belt. The belt warships headed for the dwarf planet Ceres. In the old days, people had thought of Ceres as an asteroid. In the new solar lexicon, it had become a dwarf planet.

As the various human-held ships headed for Fortress Mars, the warships and transports there began building a prismatic crystal field. The military term was P-Field.

The prismatic crystals were tiny objects, the biggest the size of a person's thumbnail. The crystals refracted light, particularly lasers. The alien gravitational beams did not refract upon striking the crystals. They melted and demolished them. Still, a P-Field acted as a sensor shield against approaching vessels. Sometimes, hiding from view was just as important as having heavy armor. If a beam missed, a ship didn't need armor.

According to the battle specs gained by fighting the original alien invader, cyberships had much greater beam range. Their missiles and drones also accelerated faster. The *Nathan Graham* had equal tech to the original cybership—everyone hoped so, at least. No one knew what kind of tech the three new cyberships actually possessed.

The more humanity could turn this into a face-to-face battle, a close fight, the better their odds. The more the cyberships could turn this into a distance combat, the better for them.

The alien AIs had one fantastic power at close range. They'd used it the first time. They could beam alien software into powerful computers, turning the human-built computers into traitorous and murderous enemies. This time, that wasn't going to happen.

"At least," Gloria told Jon. "We don't think it's going to happen. They needed powerful computers as receptors for their software to work. Maybe they have other software that does other things to lesser computers."

They were walking together in a corridor, heading for Bast Banbeck's quarters. Gloria wore her tan uniform. Jon wore shorts, running shoes and an exercise jacket. He'd been exercising more lately. His hair was still damp from hitting a heavy bag. He'd started practicing with a battlesuit again, just in case it came down to another boarding attack.

"I'd be more worried about a software assault if the three had sent a cybership back home," Jon said. "These AIs know we've beaten the first invasion. Likely, these AIs are similar to the first one. That would make them arrogant. Instead of going back with data about us, the three are plunging after us."

"It is strange," Gloria admitted. "Perhaps no race has ever beaten three cyberships before. In fact, I deem that likely."

"Why?"

"In the first invasion, one cybership attacked our Solar System. If other races frequently destroyed a single invading cybership, wouldn't the AIs usually attack a new system with three?"

"Oh. Yeah. I get your point. That's interesting. Gloria, you surprise me. I'm often amazed by what you can glean from what seems like no data at first glance."

"I am a mentalist. We could glean data from a rock."

Jon laughed. "You're in a good mood, I see. I like that."

She smiled shyly. "I've been wanting to get to the bottom of the prince's...duality for some time. We've covered everything we can for the coming battle—if the cyberships actually follow us all the way. Now, the three of us can finally take a break and solve the dilemma."

She meant the differences in personality between the Prince of Ten Worlds in Da Vinci and the prince in Eli Gomez.

Soon, they reached the Sacerdote's quarters. He had two chambers, an inner and an outer. Gloria pressed the outer hatch buzzer.

The hatch opened immediately, and Bast stepped out.

"Oh," Gloria said.

"Is anything the matter?" Bast asked.

"Uh, no," Gloria said.

"I sense something is wrong," the Sacerdote said. "Have I made another social blunder?"

"Not at all," Gloria said quickly.

The seven-foot Sacerdote turned to Jon. "Please, Captain, could you explain her...I'm uncertain of the correct phrase."

"Disappointment," Jon said.

Gloria shot an elbow into his chest, and gave Jon a small headshake.

"What is that?" Bast said, noticing. "Why did she just do that to you?"

Jon glanced at Gloria before a huge grin broke out. "It's nothing really, Bast."

"Then you can explain it?" the Sacerdote asked.

Gloria turned away. She appeared embarrassed.

"This is galling," Bast said. "I've committed too many social blunders lately. It is frustrating."

"Oh, all right," Gloria told Jon. "I hate to see him sulking."

Bast glanced from Gloria to Jon.

"She's disappointed," Jon said. "She'd hoped to go into your outer chamber. She wanted to see the chalked-out pattern."

Bast's eyes narrowed as he studied Gloria. "I see." He considered and finally shook his head. "I cannot ask you into the outer chamber."

"Jon went in before," Gloria said.

"That is true," Bast said. "But I can explain nothing more. It is not an insult. I simply cannot allow you inside."

"That's it?" Gloria asked. "You're going to stoke my curiosity like that and say no more?"

"That is correct," the Sacerdote said.

Gloria stared at him for several seconds. "Fine. It's of small import."

Bast grinned, exposing big teeth.

Gloria wasn't looking at him, but she did dart him a glance. "Why are you grinning like an ape?"

"I shall tell you later," Bast said. "For now, I am thoroughly enjoying your company. Let us go to the brain-tap machine and begin our combined investigation."

-2-

Gloria and Bast had been in the chamber individually since Gorky the marine had been found dead on a table with a brain-tap helmet over his head. They had never gone together, though.

Jon piloted the flitter that took the trio down a long ship corridor. They discussed the coming encounter, the destroyer at Senda and the Solar League warships heading for Mars. Finally, they reached the brain-tap area. Jon landed the flitter, and they walked the rest of the way. They discussed Methlan Rath, how different he seemed from the Prince when he had inhabited Da Vinci, the sheer cunning the first manifestation had shown.

"They seem like two different beings," Gloria said.

"I have a theory concerning that," Bast said. He told them how different brains had different capacities. Maybe the anchor personality subtly changed the alien brain pattern.

"That's certainly a reasonable possibility," Gloria said. "The differences in Da Vinci versus Eli seem much greater, though."

"You've studied Methlan more than I," Bast told her. "Is there something about him or the process that excites your interest?"

"It's simply that I abhor a mystery," Gloria said. "My nature is to solve dilemmas, to explain why. The Prince of Ten Worlds has affected our situation more than once. My interest has been aroused."

"This manifestation has acted more like a warrior," Bast said. "The other seemed—"

"Like a ruler," Gloria finished.

They reached the main chamber, spoke to the guards on duty and entered the room.

Jon had never liked this place. It gave him the creeps. All these machines held various brain patterns. It was like a hall of ghosts or maybe even demons. The process had always sounded too much like possession.

Bast inspected the main controls. He opened up a panel.

"I didn't know it did that," Gloria said.

Bast showed her various controls. He made adjustments and read the results.

"I'm unsure," the Sacerdote said at last. "This may indicate an interruption of the flow."

"What does that even mean?" Gloria asked.

"During a data transfer, these marks here could indicate—I'm unsure. Maybe Gorky or this Eli removed the helmet momentarily during the process."

"You mean as the data downloaded into the mind?" Gloria asked.

"I suppose."

"Would that change the nature of the download?" she asked.

"Possibly," Bast said. "I cannot be certain."

"Well..." Gloria said. "If so, that could explain the difference. If Eli didn't receive the full Prince...imprint, he would act differently."

"Yes. That sounds logical."

"That's her line," Jon said, jerking a thumb at Gloria.

Gloria opened her mouth to respond.

The hatch swung open and a guard poked his head in. "I'm sorry to interrupt you, sir. But there's a priority message from the bridge."

"What is it?" Jon asked.

"It concerns the cyberships, sir," the guard said. "That's all I know."

Jon turned to Bast and Gloria. "Let's go," he said. "I have a feeling the AIs are making their first move."

***

The trio ran to the flitter and Jon took them deeper down the corridor. Soon, they alighted and hurried to the bridge.

The bridge crew straightened as Jon entered the chamber.

"The AIs are launching missiles, sir," Ghent said.

Jon and Bast hurried to the main screen. Gloria went to her station.

"Let see it, Chief," Jon told Ghent.

"It's a long-range shot," Ghent said. "The cyberships have traveled over five hundred AUs already, but that still means they're a long ways off."

Jon waited.

Ghent got the message. He adjusted his panel.

On the main screen, a long-range teleoptic showed the two cyberships. The third hadn't joined them yet, although it traveled toward a similar destination.

"I'm using computer enhancement," Ghent said. "That means there is a nine percent chance for error. I still think that gives you a good idea of what's happening out there."

Jon nodded, focusing on the lead cybership.

Its gigantic hangar bay doors opened. One by one, huge missiles slid out. The missiles looked different from others he'd seen. They were long, and each had a large bulbous head. The individual missiles maneuvered away from the launching cybership slowly and seemingly deliberately.

"Strange to see these again," Bast said in a low rumble.

Jon glanced at the giant beside him before refocusing on the enemy. It was strange seeing this, knowing these vessels came from another star system. Although Jon had been dealing with the reality of cyberships for some time, to see this new one gave him the chills. That was an alien vessel. Those were alien missiles.

Finally, one of the big missiles began to accelerate. A long exhaust tail grew behind it. The missile quickly left the cyberships and the other waiting missiles.

"What kind of propulsion am I looking at?" Jon asked.

"Matter/antimatter, sir," Ghent said.

"Uh-huh. Can you estimate the size of the missile?"

"Four kilometers long, sir."

Jon looked back at Ghent.

"I'm sure of that," the chief said.

"Four kilometers is big," Jon said.

As they watched, another missile began to accelerate.

"Have you estimated their targets?" Jon asked.

"I've just finished doing that," Gloria said, sharply. "You're watching a recording, by the way. According to the trajectory, the first five missiles are headed for Makemake."

Jon felt cold in his gut. "Wouldn't they want to capture Makemake?" he asked no one in particular.

"Clearly not," Gloria said. "I suspect this shows us their intent. They mean to wipe out everything. I suspect, until they win, it is kill, kill, kill everything human or human built."

"That was the Sacerdote experience," Bast said.

"Any missiles heading for Senda?" Jon asked.

"Not that I can tell," Gloria said.

"What do you think that means concerning your kill theory?"

Gloria thought about it. "Maybe one tiny destroyer is not worth the effort. Yet."

"Take out the priority targets first," Jon said quietly. "What else?"

Gloria studied her panel for a time. "Some missiles seem to be headed for the Neptune System."

Jon swore under his breath.

"None are targeting the Uranus System so far," Gloria said.

"Of course not," Jon said. "Uranus is on the other side of the Solar System right now. Is anything heading for Saturn?"

"Twenty-two heavy missiles," Gloria said.

Jon turned around and walked back to his command chair. He sat down heavily. "Aren't the AIs going to leave us anything?"

"The cyberships are annihilators," Bast said. "They are the seekers of destruction. The three have come from the grave to reap the lives of the living."

"Yeah," Jon said. He watched the screen as another of the big bastard missiles began to accelerate. "I'd better call

Neptune and Saturn to give them the news. It'll be up to them how they handle the missile attacks."

"I suspect the various system leaders are going to ask us to stop and help them," Gloria said.

"That sounds about right."

"If you do not help, they will never forget you failed to aid them."

"Thanks for the heads up," Jon told her.

"I am attempting to help you understand the results so you can make the best decision possible."

"Sometimes a guard has to stand watch," Jon said softly, almost as if speaking to himself. "Sometimes, an enemy commando sneaks up on a guard and slits his throat. That's the risk a guard has to take."

"Neptune and Saturn Systems are not guards."

"No, but they're part of the bigger picture," Jon said. "We knew it was going to be hell facing the cyberships. This isn't just about our Freedom League. This is about all of us. I'm sure the Solar League systems will take hits before this is over. We have to win the fight. We can't worry about rebuilding until we survive."

"This looks to be a long and ugly war," Gloria said.

"They are the killers," Bast intoned.

Jon said nothing more. He continued to watch the missiles accelerate. He studied his enemy as his heart burned. Humanity had to win the coming battle or it was all over.

-3-

Jon went to the gym to work out. He practiced in a battlesuit later in the day. He ate heartily and slept the sleep of exhaustion.

The next day shift, he sought out the Centurion. He found the small professional speaking to his lieutenants in the officers' lounge. The chamber had darker hues to the walls with a wet bar, a snack bar and a long computer screen on one side showing a dark forest of oak trees. At the moment, a wolf padded through its shadows.

The lieutenants had just gone through some simulations as the Centurion evaluated each man. He gave his evaluations before the group.

The meeting ended. Half the lieutenants left. The others remained sitting in the comfortable chairs, sipping drinks and talking about the exercise.

The Centurion came over to where Jon sat in a chair, watching the forest scene. Now a fawn glanced around before kneeling behind dense foliage, no doubt waiting for its mother to return.

"Sir," the small man said.

Jon looked up at the Centurion. The man stared back at him with the hardest eyes Jon had ever seen. The Centurion seemed expressionless, with a tightknit cap over his bald head. The uniform was perfectly pressed, and the gun in its holster seemed well oiled. After Stark—God rest his soul—the Centurion had been with Colonel Graham the longest.

"Please," Jon said, indicating a chair.

The Centurion sat across from him.

"How are they doing?" Jon asked.

"Fair."

Jon sipped his drink. He thought the Centurion seemed wound up.

"Is something the matter?" he finally asked.

"Permission to speak freely, sir."

Jon's heart rate went up. He didn't like that, but the Centurion had that way about him. Jon set down his drink.

"Granted," he said.

"I'm glad you're exercising with the men, sir. You could use the refresher course. You were more than a little rusty in the suit."

"I didn't think anyone noticed."

The Centurion's dark eyes seemed to bore into him. "Everyone noticed, sir."

"What's that mean? Please, don't be shy expressing yourself."

The Centurion seemed to choose his words. "You've transferred your first love, sir. The regiment knows it. They don't like it. But they live with it."

"And that means what exactly?"

"You've become a ship-man. You're not the marine you once were."

"Are you trying to make me angry?"

"No, sir. I'm letting you know the state of the regiment. Maybe I'm letting you know your state, as well."

"I see."

"I'm not sure you do. You won the *Nathan Graham* through hard fighting, through the regiment. You owe the men everything."

"I've never denied that."

"You'll hold onto the *Nathan Graham* the same way. If you lose the regiment, you lose everything, sir."

"The regiment couldn't have ripped Saturn System from the Solar League. We needed the cybership to do it."

"I know."

"Then, how can you say the regiment is everything?"

"It always comes down to man-to-man fighting in the end. That might not be true right away, but eventually, it is."

A spark seemed to ignite in Jon's memories. Colonel Graham used to have an old saying. It went back to before the Space Age. He'd called it: *boots on the ground*. Graham had told his officers it was the secret to the regiment. Sooner or later, governments needed boots on the ground.

"Boots on the ground," Jon said.

"You remember." The Centurion nodded. "If you want to save the cybership and save your position, don't forget about the marines who gave you the power. Can I give you a piece of advice, sir?"

"I thought that's what you were doing."

"Practice more in private. Get back your old skills. *Then*, come out and practice with the men. They need to see that you know what you're doing, not fumbling around like a rookie."

Part of Jon wanted to punch the man. The other part realized the Centurion was right. That was probably why he wanted to punch the smaller man. The truth usually hurt more than meaningless lies.

"Thank you," Jon said. "I'm going to put that into practice. Was there anything else?"

"As a matter of fact…"

***

Several hours later, Jon was practicing in a battlesuit in an empty part of the ship. He walked, turned, lay down, jumped up and sprinted down a corridor.

He remembered the original fight through the giant vessel. Those had been some harrowing times. He recalled Sergeant Stark—there had been a man's man. Stark had sacrificed his life for the good of the regiment.

He could have used more men like Stark.

After returning the suit to the armorers, he went to his messaging room. It was time to give his reasons for his actions. He would tell the Neptune System people first and then Kalvin Caracalla of the Saturn System.

He recorded a different message for each person. He would send the messages after Gloria went over them.

By that time, Jon was yawning. He headed for his quarters. It was hard to imagine sometimes that an ex-New London gang member held the future of the human race in his palm. He'd given mankind a chance by defeating the original invasion. He'd had a lot of help along the way. The Centurion was right, but his—

As he walked down a large corridor, Jon heard the whirr of a speeding air-car. He turned around as a flitter took a slight turn, speeding into view. The pilot spotted him, bringing the air-car down as it headed toward him.

Jon felt along his belt. He didn't have a communicator.

The air-car came down hard, jarring the machine. The flitter actually skidded, screeching as sparks flew everywhere. Finally, the car came to a halt. The pilot didn't use the door. He vaulted over it.

"Sir!" the pilot shouted. "The mentalist sent me."

"Catch your breath, son."

The man saluted. "It's Premier Benz, Captain. The GSB and SD Party are staging a counter coup against him."

"What?"

"They've declared Benz an imposter who used alien technology to murder the rightful Premier."

"Are they mad to do this now? What's happened to Benz?"

"I don't know more than that, sir. Do you need a lift to the bridge?"

Jon needed two seconds to make up his mind. "Let's go," he said.

-4-

INTERLUDE: EARTH

Benz stumbled and almost pitched to the hard floor. His hands were cuffed behind his back. Several black-uniformed GSB shock troops surrounded him.

They marched him down an underground corridor in Prague, Bohemia Sector. He'd been on a routine visit when GSB agents had shot his guards and grabbed him, hustling him to an air-van. It had been a complete surprise. He'd believed himself safe. Every indicator had shown that. He still didn't understand how he could have failed to see the warning signs. That implied someone with hyper-intelligence secretly working against him in the shadows. The only one he knew with that kind of brainpower was Vela Shaw. But she was his ally, his friend, if not quite his lover yet.

He'd been working on that.

Could she have hidden her vicious nature from him? He didn't want to believe that.

Benz tripped and almost pitched face-first onto the underground floor once again. Luckily, two of the guards grabbed his arms, keeping him from breaking his nose on the floor.

They hauled him upright, their fingers digging into his flesh.

It struck him afterward. The two had moved with startling speed in order to grab him just now. He mentally went over the gun-battle against his guards. Yes. The GSB agents had moved faster than ordinary then, too.

Why did it take me so long to see it?

"You've received bodily modifications," Benz told the guard chief.

The GSB agent turned to regard him. The man had a lean face with a line for a mouth, hard eyes and dark hair swept to the side. He was either fanatical or psychotic or maybe both.

"What did they do to you to make you so fast?" Benz asked.

"Silence," the guard chief hissed.

Benz realized the man would make him shut up if he refused to comply. The Premier—Benz refused to accept his demotion to that of a mere prisoner. The Premier studied his guards as they marched him deeper underground.

The men moved with lethal precision. He envied them that. They seemed to have greater physical prowess just as his mind was superior to ordinary people's. Yes, someone had definitely modified them. He wondered who, and he wondered where this person or group had found or developed the technology to do this. If he could wed the two powers in himself…

The guard chief made a quick hand motion to the others. As one, the guards halted. The chief went to a panel. He pressed several switches.

The entire left wall lifted to reveal a courtroom. It contained seating for spectators, a low barrier, two tables and a large podium. The podium was massive, almost a fortress within the chamber. A tall woman in a black robe sat behind the podium. She had the same lean features as the guards and appeared to be wearing a blonde wig.

The guards pushed Benz down the middle aisle.

Behind them, the wall thudded closed with the finality of death.

The guards marched Benz past the waist-high barrier and to a table. Two of them, with their hands on his shoulders, pushed him down onto a chair. As one, they moved to the side, standing against the wall as court bailiffs.

A door opened in the wall opposite the guards. Silent people began filing into the chamber. Benz noticed that a few seemed subdued. That was interesting. The group moved past the waist-high barrier to the spectator seating. By their outfits and uniforms, they were governors and other Party officials. They took up one side of the seated area. Black uniformed GSB officers filled up the other side. The secret police people seemed more animated but also more tense.

An older white-haired man in a silver suit moved to the second table. He carried a briefcase, setting it on the table. He clicked it open and took out a folder.

"The court is in session," a loud-voiced woman said. She'd been the last person through the door. "The State is prosecuting Inspector General Frank Benz for high crimes against Premier J.P. Justinian."

The judge banged her gavel. "Stand up, Mr. Benz."

Frank struggled to his feet. His hands were still cuffed behind his back.

"How do you plead, Inspector General?" the judge asked.

"Your Honor," Benz said. "Before we begin, may I have these cuffs removed?"

"You are a prisoner of the State, Inspector General."

"During the trial, I wish to make notes, Your Honor. I can't do that with my hands cuffed."

The black-robed judge stared down at him with intensity. Her features twisted with distaste. "Remove his cuffs," she said.

The GSB chief guard stepped near, unlocking the cuffs, clattering them onto Benz's table.

Benz rubbed his wrists. He thought that leaving the cuffs on the table was in decidedly poor taste.

"How do you plead, Inspector General?" the judge asked.

"Not guilty," he said.

"Not guilty of engineering J.P. Justinian's death?" she asked.

"Not guilty of plotting against the State," he countered. "It has been my intention to save the State, to save the lot of you—if you'll let me."

"By murdering the rightful Premier?" the judge demanded.

"Your Honor, whoever is behind this murdered my guards, killed my friends and had me dragged before this Star Chamber. This isn't justice. This is a coup."

"Did you allow Justinian to plead his case before you murdered him?"

"I did not murder him. In fact, I warned him not to sit in the chair where he died."

"That is immaterial."

"That's absurd. It is perfectly material."

The judge smiled evilly, leaning forward. "You are no longer in a position to say. You are a prisoner, our prisoner."

The fear of dying finally broke through his mental block. His mind wanted to contemplate all the ways they could torture him. Instead, with an effort of will and concentration, he put the block back in place. A good offense was the best defense.

"You are all coup plotters," Benz said.

The judge banged her gavel on a block of wood. "I will have you gagged, sir, if you continue to spout nonsense. You have plotted against the State. You have elevated yourself, a member of the military, to supreme leadership. The action is against all principles of Social Dynamism. The people have risen up through us. We have—"

"You've tampered with those men," Benz said, interrupting, pointing at the GSB detail along the wall. "Who did that to them?"

The judge scowled.

Benz cocked his head. He'd just heard a distant sound. His knees weakened, and he dropped into the chair. He looked down, hiding a grin.

It would seem that Vela hadn't turned on him after all. She hadn't joined the conspirators. The distant noise settled his nerves. He might not die down here before these fanatical devotees of Social Dynamism. His real crime had been pitching aside their political ideology in the interest of saving human life. These fanatics would rather die than give up their communistic beliefs and power.

"Inspector General," the judge said.

Benz realized she'd called his name several times already. He looked up.

She scowled at him, and then her features shifted. She looked up as if startled. Had she heard something?

"I suggest a recess," Benz said. "Perhaps you could put me in a holding cell and let me gather my thoughts."

The judge ignored him. "What is that noise?" she asked.

No one answered.

"Well?" she said. "Doesn't anyone else hear that?"

"Should I go check?" the chief GSB guard asked.

The judge stared at the security detail. "Yes. Go at once. All of you."

The chief guard motioned with his head, drawing his gun afterward. The guard detail hurried past the barrier as the back wall rose. They moved swiftly like greyhounds, no longer seeming human.

Benz dearly wanted to know what and who had modified them. Who acted against him? It wasn't just these Party members and GSB personnel. He had a hyper-intelligent enemy hidden in the shadows. Who could that be?

Sounds of gunfire came down the underground corridor.

"Wait," the judge called to the GSB detail. "Come back. You will escort the prisoner. We're taking him elsewhere."

***

Benz was wearing the cuffs again, with his hands behind his back. The inhuman guards half-carried him at times. Two of them grabbed his arms, hoisting him off the floor and running. Their strength and speed astonished him. They raced down another underground corridor. This one was much deeper than the last. The air down here seemed stale.

The judge had left them some time ago. She'd spoken about the need for gathering reinforcements.

As the modified guards took him deeper underground, Benz had come to realize his mistake—the reason his enemy had decided it was time to attack. He'd sent the bulk of the Earth-stationed warships to Mars. Most of the fleet around the home planet had started en route to face the coming cyberships. The warships and space marines aboard them had represented the bulk of his political power. His protection had disappeared with their departure. That had allowed his secret enemy to make his or her move. Why do that now, though? Why not wait until after the Mars battle?

Ah, of course. He should have seen it sooner. If he and Hawkins won the battle against the cyberships, his political power would be cemented. If he lost, it wouldn't matter. Humanity would die. Thus, his hidden enemy had struck now while he or she could still depose him and take over in his place.

Would the fleet officers obey the coup members?

It deflated Benz to realize that the fleet officers probably would obey. He had one chance to save humanity from the cyberships. He had to get to the fleet. The ships had begun accelerating three days ago already. How could he reach—?

He knew what to do.

"Why are you smirking?" the chief guard demanded.

"I was thinking what you'd look like dead," Benz replied.

"If we die, you die."

"Really? Why not kill me now, then, and be done with it?"

The chief guard's eyes smoldered with desire. He reached for his holstered weapon.

"No," a different guard said. "Our orders—"

"I know our orders," the chief guard snarled.

A sudden, odd tenseness grew between the two agents.

They're like dogs, Benz realized.

The sound of gunfire and exploding grenades became louder behind them.

"We must get to point A," the other guard said. "Those are our orders."

"Yes!" the guard chief snarled. "We carry him. We move."

They moved fast while carrying Benz. The guards seemed tireless. Yet, no matter how many turns they took, no matter how many hatches they closed behind them, the sounds of gunfire and grenades seemed to close in toward them.

"Battlesuits," the guard chief said. "Marines are trying to save him."

The GSB agents kept running while carrying Benz. They panted, and their soft-soled shoes made scrunching sounds. Benz's flesh ached from their digging, iron-strong grips.

"How do the marines know where he is?" the other guard who had spoken up before now asked.

"Yes," the chief guard said. He gripped Benz's throat with steel-strong fingers. "How do the marines know?"

Benz tried to choke out a reply.

The steel-like fingers loosened their hold.

"I don't know," Benz said hoarsely.

"You are lying."

"No. I have no idea."

"He carries a bug," a GSB agent said. "It is the only answer."

The agent was right, of course, but Benz didn't plan on telling them that.

"Search him," the guard chief said.

They halted, tearing off his clothes. Benz shivered. The air down here was cooler than he'd realized. Their hands felt all along him. That weakened his mental block. Being naked among them stole some of his courage.

"Nothing," a guard said.

"The bug is inside him," the chief guard said. The inhumanly lean GSB agent drew a sharp knife. "Tell me where it is. Otherwise, I will probe you for it."

Benz's balls shriveled. A trickle of terror slid past his mental block. The idea of the knife sticking into his flesh—

"I've already told you," Benz said. He had to remain strong. If he showed weakness—

"Leader!" a guard said. "The enemy is here."

The GSB agents, the modified men—if they were men—turned with snarls and the chomping of teeth. It was a weird spectacle.

Three SLN marines in battlesuits came around the corner. Blood and gore stained their heavy suits. More showed up. They had smoking craters and pits in their armor.

The GSB personnel howled like demented creatures, drew their guns and knives, and charged the battlesuited marines.

It was bizarre. Benz stood naked with his hands cuffed behind his back, watching. With a start, he went to his knees and lay down on his stomach.

The marines opened up with lethal hardware, destroying the GSB agents with massed gunfire. In seconds, the agents were nothing but bullet-riddled bodies lying in pools of blood.

The marines advanced with heavy clomps as their suit engines purred.

Benz struggled to his knees in time to regard a seven-foot battlesuit before him. A faceplate whirred open, and a sweaty Vela Shaw looked down.

"The cavalry has arrived," she said.

"I won't ever forget this."

"You saved me once. Do you think I've forgotten what you did?"

"Ma'am," one of the battlesuited marines warned.

"Frank," Vela said. "GSB and troop reinforcements are on their way here. We have flyers outside, but it's going to be close."

His mind started working again, building up speed of thought as he realized he might survive this night.

"Someone needs to carry me," Benz said.

"Listen first," Vela said. "The Earth doesn't want you, and certainly doesn't want me. When the fleet left—"

"I know, I know," Benz said. "We have to join the fleet."

She smiled as if with relief. "I wasn't sure you'd understand."

"Our hidden foe is brilliant," Benz said. "That's why I couldn't get a handle on running the government."

"We can talk about that later," she said. "I have an idea—"

"Does it include storming the orbital naval yard?" Benz asked.

Her eyes seemed to shine. "I see we're on the same page."

"Ma'am," the battlesuited marine insisted.

"We have to go," Vela said.

"Break off my handcuffs and show me my ride," Benz said. "I have some thinking to do."

He was glad Vela and he had devised an anti-coup plan some time ago. A tracking bug had been surgically implanted against the wall of his stomach. It had proven its worth. Now, would they be able to fight their way off Earth and get into orbital space in time?

-5-

"No," Benz said. "I'm not going to order any nukes onto the planet. We're doing this to save life, not to have excuses to murder it."

The battlesuited marines had fought their way back to the flyers. They'd loaded up and screamed across the Bohemian topography at Mach 5.

Benz was in the same compartment as Vela. He was wearing clothes again, and shoes, feeling more human because of it. He'd just gotten off the horn with one of his few remaining loyal subordinates. The officer had suggested using nuclear bombardments against certain ground battery sites. That would help cover their ride up into orbital space.

"We have a problem," Benz told Vela. "Earth is a veritable fortress with its ground batteries and missile sites. It can saturate orbital space. While some of the commanders in the orbital platforms are still listening to me, how much longer will that last if they know I'm trying to flee Earth?"

"We should have departed with the fleet." Vela said.

"We wanted to keep the home front secure."

"I know the reasons," Vela said. "How did we miss this?"

"Easy. A great mind at least the equal of mine has plotted against us."

"Who is he?"

"I have no idea."

"Premier," a space marine colonel said. He was smaller than average and had a strange glint to his eyes. "We have our window of opportunity, sir. Do we go upstairs?"

Benz could feel the hope in the colonel's voice that he'd take the right action. How long would the space marine back him if they stayed down here? The colonel obviously wanted to join the fleet. That might have been why he'd remained loyal. But if they flew upstairs, as the colonel suggested, and the other side shot them down…

"We need decoys to throw any tracking stations off our scent," Benz said.

The colonel shook his head. "We don't have any decoys, sir."

Benz's lips drew back until inspiration struck. He tapped the comm, opening channels and typed a special order. The code would implement the Loki Protocols. He should have thought of it sooner.

The scrambled message moved fast. That was one of its key features. It would cause worldwide chaos by unleashing computer viruses, ghost images, massive shutdowns and other electronic mayhem.

"Five minutes," Benz told the colonel. "Then we go to heaven."

The colonel grinned. "Yes, sir."

***

Afterburners kicked in as the flyer convoy rocketed for orbital space. So far, so good. One radar site had tracked them for thirteen seconds. Then, the Loki Protocols had taken over.

The protocols wouldn't last long, Benz knew. In fact, he'd hoped to use them for their getaway in the experimental space vessel. But if he couldn't get to the orbital construction yard, it wasn't going to matter anyway.

"Bogey," the pilot said from the other cabin.

"Premier," the colonel said. "Get ready for violent maneuvering."

"Roger," Benz said.

They were already buckled tight, so why the warning? Fifteen seconds later, he understood. The flyer banked so hard that everything around them shook. The flyer expelled chaff—

Through the intense shaking, Benz could feel the flyer's guns firing. It put a knot in his stomach that twisted tighter and tighter. He felt like vomiting but fought against it. He didn't want the marines around him to tell stories later about his weakness.

Finally, the flyer evened out, although the shaking worsened. The Gs grew, pushing Benz back into his seat as they roared heavenward.

"We got lucky," the pilot shouted into Benz's earphones.

"That's great," Vela shouted to Benz. "That's what I wanted to hear."

"Hang in there, sir," the colonel said. "We're going to make it."

I hope so, Benz thought. He didn't want to go through all this and die in the end.

***

The shaking stopped, the acceleration quit and weightless struck. Benz glanced at a monitor. They were leaving Earth behind. He could see the curvature of the blue/green planet. Europe spread out below. He could see the Baltic Sea. The atmospheric haze—

It's beautiful.

Earth was worth saving. So was humanity. These alien AIs sounded dreadful. Why would anyone have built things like that? Did the AIs out there have anything to do with the ancient site down in Antarctica? Did the ancient site have anything to do with his hidden foe?

Benz bet it did.

Time crawled much too slowly for Benz's comfort. They were tiny, and the Earth was huge. Covering territory up here in low orbit took too long.

The courtroom hoax seemed surreal now. The strangely inhuman GSB guards—more was going on than he could connect. What did these changes mean? They had to mean something. Had the hidden foe been watching him all this time?

Benz didn't like the implications.

"How soon?" he asked the colonel. He repented of the question as soon as he asked it.

The colonel seemed upset by it. So did the other two marines in here with him.

"Fifteen minutes, maybe," the colonel said.

Those minutes curdled Benz's gut. He felt exposed every second up here. If the Loki Protocols failed, lasers stations could easily pick them out of orbit. Hypersonic missiles could come screaming after them.

Earth was a fortress. The defense systems had been upgraded and multiplied in order to withstand the captured cybership if it tried to come here. Now, three of the bastard super-ships had invaded the Solar System.

Would Captain Hawkins stick to the plan if the hidden foe killed him? If that happened, would the SLN warships pick a fight with Hawkins around Mars?

I have to escape, Benz told himself. *It's not just about me staying alive. I'm the glue for our side. Hawkins and humanity is counting on me. I have to use my mind like never before.*

"There," the colonel said. "You can see it."

Benz used the monitor. He saw it, all right. The main orbital construction yard drifted around Earth. It was a vast oval, a giant donut that spun around and around to simulate gravity for those inside. The yard had huge spokes in the center and half-built ships around it. Some of the yard work took place inside giant hangar bays. The place had guns and antimissiles. Would the yard target the flyers?

"Sir," the colonel said. "It's time to make a call."

The weightlessness had begun to seriously trouble Benz. He concentrated anyway. He had to act like a Premier more now than ever. He had to talk their way onto the construction yard so they could commandeer an experimental space vessel.

-6-

The next hour was a blur. Benz convinced the port admiral in charge of the yard to let them land. His marines wore battlesuits and acted decisively once in the construction yard's corridors. Sometimes decisive action made all the difference.

The marines only fired once at Benz's explicit orders. They gunned down five GSB agents.

The construction-yard port admiral, a portly man, went ghost white at the firing, at the bodies thudding onto a deck. He'd sputtered incoherent words.

Benz put an arm around the admiral's shoulders, leading him down the corridors. Benz's other hand kept hold of a gun. He hoped the message was clear. *How do you want to do this, Admiral? Friendly or enemy style?*

The port admiral decided to play along with the charade. No doubt, he would do so long enough to get away. Then he would either make a call or turn the construction yard's armaments against them.

Down on Earth, the opposition had started to get a handle on the Loki Protocol. They had done so faster than Benz had expected.

The experimental warship was a beauty. It had rakish features, giving the pretense that it could land on a terrestrial world. The thing was made for speed. It had one long-range particle beam. The cannon had been built along the entire length of the vessel. It had a minimal crew. It was part raider and part long-range sniper.

"Give the orders, Port Admiral," Benz told the man.

They stood in the construction yard's main control room, the operators locked away in a storage compartment.

"I-I don't dare do that," the port admiral stammered.

Benz poked the port admiral in the stomach with the barrel of a gun. "I admire you, sir. You have the makings of a martyr. You will go down as a hero of Social Dynamism. Good-bye—"

"Wait," the port admiral whispered, with sweat pooling on his face. "I-I'll do it."

"Oh... Of course. I misunderstood you."

The port admiral mopped his face with a heavily braided sleeve. Then he made the call. The hangar chief on the other end seemed surprised. The admiral roared at the chief. Soon, the chief agreed. The admiral clicked off the comm and turned to Benz.

"Let's go," Benz told the others. "Go ahead," he told the marine colonel.

The colonel leveled a big-barreled weapon at the port admiral.

"No," the portly officer said, sweating anew. "You promised—"

A tangler shot webbed him. The admiral struck the floor with his side, tangled with sticky threads.

"This is to keep you alive when the GSB questions you," Benz said.

The webbed port admiral blinked several times until understanding struck. "Yes, yes, thank you, Premier. I resisted and you tangled me. G-Good luck, sir."

"Because you mean it, I appreciate that." Benz hurried down the corridor, the rest of his people following.

***

The port admiral struggled hard in order to make it look as if he had resisted. The webs tightened until he could hardly breathe.

Finally, a GSB detail found him. The woman—a major—ordered a gunman to spray the webbing.

Soon, the threads wilted.

"Up, up," the GSB major told him. "You have a task to perform. Only you can do it."

"Let me at them," the port admiral snarled. "The foul traitors took me by surprise—"

"Admiral," the major said. "Save that for your court martial."

"What is this?" he blustered. "I tried to take them down. The traitors—"

"No more theatrics," the major said. "Come, come, hurry to the board. Get it ready."

The port admiral remembered the codes. He had once been a missile officer. It all came back as he activated the construction yard's defenses. At that point, the panel lit up with red lights. He hesitated, glancing sidelong at the impatient major tapping a foot.

"Blast it to Hades," he shouted. "Some of the launch systems have been sabotaged."

"Please," the major said. "Only tell me about working systems. This is critical. Look out there."

The port admiral looked up at a screen. One of the major's operatives worked the board. The rakish experimental ship had loosened its docking constraints. Slowly, it maneuvered for a space door.

"How did this happen?" the port admiral said in a ponderous voice.

The major eyed him closely as her gunmen stroked their weapons. "Can you destroy the ship?"

The port admiral turned back to the red-lit board. Working the panel, cursing under his breath—

Two of the red lights abruptly turned green.

"It's not a question of can," the port admiral said. "Certainly I can—"

"Do it now," the major said.

He glanced at her. "And destroy the construction yard with them? We could die in the blast."

The major seemed to reconsider the choices. "Wait until the ship clears the yard. We don't want to unnecessarily damage State property."

"My feelings exactly," the port admiral said.

They watched the rakish vessel work its way clear of the space door and then the construction yard. Its engines glowed at that point. The experimental ship began to move faster.

"Are you tracking it?" the major asked.

The port admiral tapped his board for an answer.

"Can you destroy it without damaging us?"

"I can," he said.

"Do so at once," she said.

The port admiral tapped in the commands. He waited, hoping this worked. The major waited. The experimental vessel moved faster as its exhaust tail lengthened. Then, two missiles streaked after it.

The port admiral exhaled in relief. He'd done it.

The vessel's auto-defenses engaged. Beams rayed the first missile, rendering it harmless as it drifted in space. The second missile slammed home and exploded, detonating other munitions in the spacecraft. The explosion was greater than expected. The blast, radiation and EMP struck the construction yard, blowing away part of the mighty but fragile structure. The control room shook, but held.

"I did it," the port admiral shouted.

"We did it," the major corrected.

"Of course, of course," he said. "We killed the traitors to Social Dynamism."

The major examined the continuing damage to the construction yard. At last, she shrugged. "That could not be helped. But since we destroyed the traitors, the new Premier will likely accept the damage to the yard."

The port admiral nodded vigorously, hoping that was true. He looked at the debris that had been the experimental vessel. He was more than a little surprised Benz had died so easily. Wasn't the man supposed to be a genius of some kind?

The port admiral mopped his face. It didn't matter in the end. He was safe, and likely so was his rank. That was what really mattered.

***

Benz slumped against his seat. The missiles had fired much closer to the construction yard than he had anticipated.

"They truly hate you," the marine colonel said.

"They *fear* him," Vela corrected.

"I don't know that either is true," Benz said. "They're covering their butts like everyone else. The question…"

Benz saw the colonel watching him closely.

He changed what he was going to say. "The question," Benz said, "is how fast this stealth ship can go. We need to catch up to the fleet if that's possible."

"If we go too much faster," Vela said, "Earth's orbital tracking will spot us."

"If we wait too long to announce ourselves as alive," Benz said, "the fleet might change its mind. They have to know I'm alive so they'll keep heading to Mars."

"True," Vela said, staring at him.

"What are your orders, sir?" the colonel asked.

"Let's get a little more separation from Earth," Benz said. "I want greater acceleration. Nothing too brazen, but more than this."

The colonel stuck out a hand. "That was a clever ruse, sir. I would never have thought of switching ships. Better to get away fast—"

"Than sneak out," Benz said. "Well, it hasn't worked yet, just so far. Now, Colonel, get me increased acceleration, please."

The colonel headed out of the compartment, hurrying to the piloting chamber.

"What now, Frank?" Vela asked. "We've made it this far. But it looks like they're finally shutting down the last of the Loki Protocols. Soon, Orbital Defense will start scanning more thoroughly. This is a tiny craft. I would wait until you have the fleet under your feet before making any big announcements."

"I know. We still have complications. The fleet has a head start on us. We're going to have to let them know about us soon. And we're going to have to let Hawkins know we're still alive, and that the plan is still a go."

"When?"

"I'm thinking," Benz said.

-7-

Twenty hours later, Benz moved onto the stealth ship's bridge. An acting captain sat in the control chair. She was a small black woman and stood at attention as Benz and Vela entered through the hatch.

"At ease, Captain," Benz said.

He looked around. It was a small circular-shaped bridge with two other seats.

"Where are the others?" Benz asked.

"Resting, sir," the captain said. "Would you like me to get them?"

"No… I was just wondering."

"Do you desire my chair?"

"No, no," Benz said. "Please, continue doing whatever it is you are doing."

"Monitoring the ship, sir," she said.

He nodded, moving to the nearer seat.

"That is the comm station," the captain said. She resumed her place in the captain's chair.

Benz kept moving until he sat on the other chair. He studied the controls.

"That is scanning and—"

"Thank you, Captain," Benz said. "I understand."

"Of course, sir," she said.

Benz applied himself, using the sensor station, bringing up a Solar System space-chart. He pinpointed the Venus ships heading for Mars. He found the Earth Fleet easily enough. It was composed of over fifty capital ships, some of them the newest in the Solar League.

There were a few newer ships still at Earth. Would their commanders follow his orders or those of the new acting Premier—or whatever the plotters had put in place?

Benz didn't bother with any other scans. Nothing headed out from orbital Earth after them. It would appear that the stealth ship had gotten away cleanly.

The Premier sat hunched over the sensor station for some time, thinking, plotting velocities and vectors. He computed time. Then, he sat back and thought carefully. He glanced at Vela.

She watched him sidelong and seemed concerned.

"We can't wait too long," Vela said softly.

Benz nodded in order to show he'd heard her assessment. He agreed. If they waited, the Earth Fleet ship captains and other higher personnel would start to become accustomed to his supposed death.

Benz stood. The captain gave a soft exclamation. He'd obviously surprised her. He moved to the comm station. Vela stood aside.

"Captain," Benz said, without looking at her.

"Yes, sir?"

"Could you leave the bridge for a moment, please?"

The captain hesitated before saying, "Yes, sir." She stood. She stood a little longer and finally moved toward the hatch. She stopped there. It appeared she might say something. Instead, she ducked through the hatch, closing it behind her.

Benz exhaled. He switched on the comm and directed the signal at the Earth Fleet. His hands hardly shook at all.

"This is a risk," he told Vela.

She already knew that. She could compute the odds as easily as he could.

The comm signal traveled to the Earth Fleet. In stellar terms, they were almost beside each other.

A communications officer answered the hail. She belonged to the fleet's flagship, Battleship *Nikita Khrushchev*.

"This is Premier Benz. Put me through to Admiral Rowland."

"Sir? The Premier is—"

"This is Premier Benz. You will immediately put me through to Admiral Rowland."

Silence answered him.

Benz knew why. The comm officer must be thinking fast. Likely, she told Rowland that Benz was on the comm. The admiral would calculate. In truth, this was the moment. Maybe he should have called sooner. Maybe—"

"Premier Benz?" Rowland asked. He was a gruff old space dog, a gnarled fighter who had made it to higher command despite the strictures of Social Dynamism.

"I assume you've heard some strange rumors from Earth about me," Benz said.

"But... Just a minute," Admiral Rowland said. There was silence again. The admiral came on a few seconds later. "We're on a secure line. Is this really Benz?"

Benz clicked on a visual, staring into the screen. Rowland's worn face appeared almost as fast. The man looked like a hunchback from Victorian times, with a blob for a nose. His small size hid a fierce fighting spirit.

"Premier, the Politburo has officially declared you a traitor."

"The GSB are up to their old tricks," Benz said. "I'm in space. I'm following the fleet."

"Do you mind if I confirm that?"

"I want you to."

On the small comm screen, Rowland manipulated controls. "Oh. You're in a stealth ship, one of the new ones. It's small. It doesn't have much in the way of acceleration capabilities."

"The fleet has to stop accelerating. I need to catch up as fast as I can."

"Yes, Premier... In theory, I agree, of course."

"Then, give the order."

"Sir..." Rowland appeared to rethink his statement.

"You know me, Admiral. You understand something regarding the power of my mind."

Through the tiny screen, Rowland watched him. Clearly, the old space dog was considering who would win the political fight. Benz was running away. He wasn't going to be the political winner on Earth. The Politburo had already turned against him. Benz had to change the direction of Rowland's thoughts.

"The cyberships are coming," Benz said in a flinty voice. "If the cyber-vessels win, humanity loses. If I beat them…my fighting admirals will be the heroes of the State."

"You're playing hardball with me, eh Premier?"

"Do you think those who tried to depose me will continue to agree with the alliance with Captain Hawkins?"

"I haven't thought about that."

"I have. I doubt they will. We won't beat the cyberships without the *Nathan Graham*. Humanity needs me to be in control of the SLN space fleets."

"It's always good when humanity's and the Premier's fate are the same," Rowland said dryly.

Vela looked up from the other station, signaling him.

"Just a minute, Admiral," Benz said. He muted Rowland.

"Missiles," Vela said. "Lots and lots of missiles have just launched from Earth's orbital stations. They must have cracked your transmission. They know you're alive."

Benz felt cold and small, and vulnerable. "The missiles are heading this way?"

"At full acceleration for us," Vela said.

Benz compressed his lips. He nodded to himself and reengaged the comm. "Admiral, the GSB has illegally launched missiles at me. That should prove to you their desperation and their lunacy. I'm not sure if you've seen Hawkins' psyche profile. He hates Social Dynamism and distrusts the Solar League. Despite that, I got him to trust me. If I die, that kills any chances of Hawkins and us working together. That means the cyberships win. I need you to decelerate and get ready to launch a massive antimissile volley. You're going to have to cover me."

"If I begin deceleration, the fleet isn't going to reach Mars as soon."

"I realize that."

"What if that means Earth Fleet fails to help the *Nathan Graham* in time?"

"It's better that we arrive late than not arrive at all."

"Even better to be on time," Rowland said.

"Damn it, man," Benz said. "Begin deceleration and target the missiles. That is a direct order from the Premier."

Rowland searched Benz's face. The old space dog turned away. He was obviously thinking. He was making the most important decision of his life, maybe of humanity's life. Finally, he faced Benz again.

"I'm going to order the entire fleet to decelerate, sir. Even so, this is going to be tricky."

"Right," Benz said. "Good. You made the right decision."

"I hope so, sir. I really do."

-8-

The *Nathan Graham* passed Neptune's orbital path. The ice giant was presently a little over 30AUs from the Sun. Mars was a little more than 1.5 AUs from the Sun. Given the cybership's relative position in orbital space and that of Mars, the Red Planet was approximately 33 AUs from the *Nathan Graham*. It was a tiny bit farther to the Earth Fleet, but not much. That meant a comm message at the speed of light took 4.57 hours to go from one location to the other.

That was still much too far to have a regular back and forth conversation. That also meant that scanning with teleoptics provided data that was 4.57 hours old.

Jon was on the bridge when Ghent discovered the missile barrage accelerating from Earth's orbital stations.

"What are they launching at?" Jon asked.

"This is interesting," Ghent said. He showed the Earth Fleet decelerating hard.

"This doesn't make sense," Jon said. "They're supposed to meet us at Mars. Are they changing their mind?"

Gloria had watched the display in silence. She now spoke up. "I suspect we're witnessing a political fight."

"Political?" Jon asked. "Those are missiles, not speeches."

"I understand." Gloria paused as if collecting her thoughts. "I suspect we're going to be in suspense for some time. We should probably suspend judgment about what this all means until we begin receiving messages."

Jon shook his head in frustration. Space battles took more patience than he had. They might have to wait hours before any of this made sense.

The orbital-launched missiles seemed to concentrate on nothing. That nothing was before the Earth Fleet. The antimissiles leaving the fleet also headed in concentration toward the empty area of space.

"Why are they launching at that area?" Jon asked.

"I suspect a stealth ship is out there," Gloria said. "It's the only reasonable explanation."

Jon thought about that, nodding shortly. "That makes sense. Chief Ghent, can you find a stealth ship out there?"

"I'm working on it, sir," Ghent said.

The orbital-launched missiles and the Earth Fleet-launched antimissiles moved at a fraction of the velocity of the *Nathan Graham*. They crawled at an agonizingly slow rate. That meant minutes turned into hours before the situation began to make sense.

Hours later, Ghent said, "I've found it, sir. It is a stealth ship just like the mentalist thought. It's moving toward the Earth Fleet."

Gloria looked up. "Could Benz be alive?" she asked.

"Explain that," Jon said.

Gloria told him her reasoning. The underpinning of her thought was the amount of effort those on Earth were making to destroy the stealth ship. The only logical reason was that the ship held somebody vastly important to those on Earth.

"That's why you said political earlier," Jon said. "I'm starting to get it."

The stealth ship no longer remained stealthy as it accelerated to get out of the way. Shortly thereafter, the orbital-launched missiles and the Earth Fleet's antimissiles met in space. There were masses of detonations, EMPs, blasts, expanding radiation zones and plain-old heat.

Time passed.

"The ship must have gone into stealth mode again," Ghent said. "I don't see it anywhere."

"Are there any messages directed at us?" Jon asked.

"None so far," Gloria said.

"Benz agreed to work with us," Jon said. "What if that was him and the others killed him? Will the SLN warships still work with us, or will they work against us?"

They debated about that for a time. They—

"Sir," Gloria said. "I'm receiving a message. It's from Premier Benz."

"Where is he?"

Gloria looked up. "The message originated in the stealth ship. It looks like he survived the missile attack."

"I've found the stealth ship again," Ghent said, interrupting. "It's on a collision course for the drifting Earth Fleet."

"A political missile battle," Jon said. "Let's hear his message. This should be interesting."

***

Jon and Gloria discussed the ramifications of Premier Benz's message while walking in a corridor.

Jon walked with his head bent and he rubbed his two days' growth of beard. Gloria had her hands clasped behind her back. She looked up with her forehead furrowed.

"Are they insane on Earth?" Jon finally asked.

"No. They think differently from you and I—much differently than you."

That startled Jon. "You have something in common with them?"

"I was raised under a communal system. The Martian practice of Social Dynamism is different from that practiced elsewhere. Maybe our homogeneity had something to do with that."

"What?"

"We have similar genetic backgrounds on Mars."

"So what?"

"So that tended to mitigate some of Social Dynamism's worst tenets. Since we're genetically similar on Mars, with similar belief systems and outlooks, we act in similar ways. We have higher societal trust on Mars because of that."

"Huh?"

"Homogeneity tends to breed greater trust societies. Diverse societies generate greater distrust. It's basic logic, really. If your neighbor is like you, you tend to trust him more. If your neighbor is different from you, you tend to view his actions as strange. Most people find strangeness to be troubling."

"What does that have to do with—?"

"I'm merely pointing out that I understand Benz and Earth culture better than you do. Social Dynamism—"

"I'm sure that's all highly interesting," Jon said. "Here's what I want to know. Will the SLN ships do their part? Or will they try to screw us before the battle?"

"Your question implies they plan to screw us after the battle."

"I know they're going to try that."

"You do?"

"Of course," Jon said. "I don't know how different they are from us. But they're human, right? Humans usually put their back against their worst enemy if an even bigger threat shows up. After the bigger threat is eliminated, it's back to basics."

"You don't trust the Solar League?"

Jon snorted.

"That is New London ideology talking," Gloria said.

"Governments are like gangs," Jon said. "The biggest one with the most territory is the strongest. The strongest get to do what they want, and so on down the line."

"You do not have great faith in governments, do you?"

Jon stared at Gloria. "People respect strength. If governments are strong, and no one equals them, they do what they want. When people do what they want because they can, they don't have respect. No, I don't trust governments. That's what Colonel Graham taught me, and what I learned in New London as a kid."

Gloria pursed her lips as she nodded.

"Will the SLN ships work with us before the battle?" Jon asked.

"Benz wants to," she said.

"Does he hold enough authority to keep the SLN warships together?"

"I don't know."
"Yeah," Jon said. "That's what I thought."

-9-

The Earth Fleet resumed its acceleration to Mars. The SLN ships lacked the *Nathan Graham's* gravity control. Those warships had gravity *dampeners*, which helped, but not nearly enough during rapid acceleration. They still couldn't reach or tolerate massive velocities.

In comparison, the *Nathan Graham* flashed toward Mars. Before the cybership came, it took two years for an SLN battleship to travel from Earth to the Neptune System. It would still take an SLN ship that long. The *Nathan Graham* was the great exception among human-owned spacecraft.

The Earth Fleet barely had to travel one AU to reach Mars. The *Nathan Graham* had 33 AUs to go. It would reach Mars first, though, by a considerable margin.

Yet, as fast the *Nathan Graham* traveled, it didn't compare to the three AI-controlled cyberships or the missiles those ships had launched.

When the first AI missile salvo reached Makemake, the fighting platform fired antimissiles and used its tracking system to help the gun tubes on MK2's surface.

A strange radio signal attempted to contact the Makemake computers. None of the computers responded to the software. Every tech system was working on MK2 and the fighting platform. The MK2 defenses knocked down every AI-launched missile. The AI salvo failed, utterly.

That brought cheering on the *Nathan Graham*. Jon passed the results on to the Earth Fleet. He wanted to show Benz that they could beat the AIs. It was possible.

"The cyberships might alter course now," Gloria told Jon, "in order to rake Makemake."

"I hope they do," Jon said. "We need more time to prepare at Mars. The Earth Fleet took too long picking up Benz. We might have to face the cyberships with the Mars and Venus fleets alone. I'm beginning to wonder if Benz staged all that in order to trick us."

Gloria tapped her fingertips together and blinked rapidly. "That is quite possible. Do you believe Benz is that underhanded?"

Jon snorted. Of course he thought that.

"This is a troubling development," Gloria said.

***

As the *Nathan Graham* flashed past the Uranus orbital path—the ice giant was presently on the other side of the Sun—an AI-launched missile salvo roared at the Neptune System.

The Neptune System had been through hell several years ago. They had lost most of their population. More slowly than surely, the surviving Neptunians had rebuilt. They had a few lesser warships. But it would take decades and many immigrants to rebuild what the cybership had demolished.

Once more, radio signals preceded the missile attack. Like before on Makemake, the Neptunians had seriously degraded the speed and power of their computers. It seemed, though, as if the AIs transmitted a different kind of software this time.

Viruses took hold in most of the Neptune computer systems. However, two computers still worked well enough for the technicians to radio the data to the *Nathan Graham*. But Neptunian gun tubes malfunction. Neptunian antimissiles exploded on the launch pads. It was chaos throughout the Neptune System.

Into the chaos sped the four-kilometer long AI missiles. The missiles seemed to have minds of their own. The AI missiles didn't target old ruined satellites. They chose those with high signature values.

One of the huge matter/antimatter missiles slammed into a dome on Triton before detonating. The warhead obliterated the living quarters and sent seismic shockwaves through the moon.

Another of the giant missiles found a Neptune orbital habitat. Nothing seemed to work right on the hab. Many people had planned to flee in small spacecraft. The computers had stopped working on those craft. One lifted off and then died in the giant matter/antimatter explosion.

The AI missiles achieved a one hundred percent kill ratio against the orbital habitats. It was a perfect and therefore devastating orbital strike.

The same thing happened as two giant missiles zoomed down into Neptune's upper atmosphere. Each detonated against a different cloud city. Both cities vanished in the blasts.

The overall carnage proved dreadful. The Neptunian survivors numbered only in the hundreds.

Nobody had expected such capacity from the AIs, except maybe the AIs themselves. No one had tried to radio the three cyberships and ask for terms.

Meanwhile, the bigger missile salvo heading for the Saturn System continued its flight for the ringed planet. Word of what transpired in the Neptune System reached Saturn almost as soon as it did the *Nathan Graham*.

On the bridge, Gloria informed Jon that Kalvin Caracalla wanted to speak to him again.

"We're nearing the Saturn System," Gloria told him. "I think Kalvin is going to try one more time to get us to stop there and help them."

Jon nodded. He didn't want to speak to Caracalla. But he couldn't in good conscience deny the industrialist mobster the right.

He headed for the bridge exit.

"Jon," Gloria said.

He regarded the mentalist.

"After listening to Caracalla, you're going to want to stop at the Saturn System. New London Dome is your home. But if you stop at the Saturn System…"

"I know," he said.

"Do you?"

The way she said that...What did she know about him that he didn't know about himself?

With some trepidation, he headed for the message center with the Black Anvil flag on the wall. What was Kalvin Caracalla going to say that would prove so persuasive?

-10-

Jon sat at the great desk with his hands folded on it. He was wearing his dress uniform. At the edge of the desk, the screen shifted before revealing the Saturn System Prime Minister.

Kalvin was still tidy, white-haired and deeply tanned. He wore a gold chain and had expensive rings on his fingers. He seemed more like a mobster this time. The high-pitched voice actually seemed right now.

"Captain Hawkins," Kalvin began.

Jon didn't bother telling the PM about his new title. He still rather liked Captain.

"I'll get to the point," Kalvin said. "I'm told you don't have much time to begin braking in order to help us."

"My latest report shows you didn't build a P-Field," Jon countered. "That could be a mistake."

"How did the P-Field help the Solar League ships against *you*?" Caracalla asked.

"It saved a lot of their ships from destruction," Jon said.

"Wrong. They made a deal with you for that. What kind of deal will the cybers give me?"

"Robots," Jon said automatically.

"What?"

"I call them robots."

"I don't care what you call them. There are huge missiles heading for my planetary system. Cyber missiles wiped out the Neptune System people. Why didn't those missiles destroy Makemake? What kind of deal did you make with the cybers?"

"You don't get it," Jon said. "The AIs made a mistake at Makemake. They tried the old self-aware software trick on our computers. It didn't work because we'd downgraded the computers. They weren't fast or powerful enough to become self-aware."

"Downgrading didn't do shit for the Neptunians."

"Of course not," Jon said.

Caracalla scowled. "What do you mean by that?"

"The AIs obviously adjusted. They figured out what happened and used viruses instead of self-aware programming."

"Yeah? So?"

"So now it's your turn to adjust. You have to change your plans. You need to take into account that the AIs can spam your computers."

"We're dead if that's the case."

"Come on," Jon said. "Use your head. The AIs aren't gods. They're machines. I beat them. You can beat them. Why not turn off your computers just before the AIs send the signal? After the software message quits transmitting, turn your computers back on."

"It won't be that easy."

"Do you think storming the *Nathan Graham* the first time was easy? You do what you have to do."

Kalvin Caracalla gave him a challenging stare. "I made you, Hawkins. Without me throwing my weight behind your project—"

"Caracalla, I want you to win. Don't you get that? I'm rooting for you. Do you think I want to see New London Dome go down? No. But answer me this. How does it help you having us save the Saturn System and the cyberships winning at Mars? The bulk of humanity's warships are at Mars. After destroying those, the cyberships will come for the Saturn System anyway. I need those massed SLN warships to have a chance of defeating the cyberships. You're going to have to defeat the missiles on your own to live. You already know that. I have to defeat the cyberships for everyone to live. That can't be this hard to understand."

Caracalla looked away. He nodded, and without another word, he cut the connection.

"Bastard," Jon said. "I was going to wish you luck." He used his hands, pushing down on the desktop to help him stand. That hadn't gone as well as he'd hoped.

Checking the time, he realized the AI missiles would reach the Saturn System in another nine hours and twenty minutes. He hoped Caracalla and his people got lucky.

***

The *Nathan Graham* continued its terrific journey toward Mars. It passed the Saturn System orbital path. Behind it by several hours came the mighty AI missile salvo.

The stolen cybership left the ringed beauty behind it as it continued deeper into the Solar System.

Too soon, the AI missiles began their third attack in the Solar System. Just like in the Neptune System, strange comm signals sped ahead of the missile salvo. Like before, software began ramming viruses into various Saturn System computers.

Some of the computers resisted with highly advanced software of their own. It made no difference, though. Other people shut down their computers. That helped—a lot.

Soon, the software-pulse phase of the battle ended. Sometime after that, people turned on their computers.

Gun tubes readied. Antimissiles launched. Radar systems targeted, and lasers as well as a few gravitational cannons warmed up.

The heavy missiles launched hundreds of AUs away converged on the Saturn System. The AI missile defenses and ECM proved highly effective against the human-built systems.

Laser beams did nothing to the AI missile armor. A tiny percentage of the antimissiles managed to detonate near their targets.

In the outer Saturn System, twelve percent of the AI missiles either failed to continue the attack run or blew up at that point. Eighty-eight percent of the salvo continued to flash inward.

The farthest moon domes took the heaviest blows. The domes blew up, killing millions.

The remaining AI missiles bored in.

Gravitational beams starting raying at the missiles. Saturn System warships came around various moons and fired heavy lasers. Two of the biggest ships also had gravitational cannons.

AI missiles began to blow up. A few tumbled uselessly in space, disarmed.

Dark sand lay in the path of others. That stopped another five percent of the salvo. Thermonuclear mine detonations confused some of the remaining AI missiles.

Then, the big suckers from deep space began reaching their next round of targets. Moon domes blew up. Orbital satellites exploded, and cloud cities sank into Saturn's heavier atmosphere below.

Heavy radiation bounced throughout the system. EMPs destroyed comm-sets. Heat, blast and debris added to the mayhem.

Even so, a picture soon began to develop. Sixty-three percent of the AI missiles detonated. Fifty-four percent of the Saturn System populace were dead, dying or would die in the next few days.

Industrial power was crippled although not altogether wiped out. Hope had been dashed, though. Anger rose exponentially.

Still, there were a few bright points. New London Dome had survived. Kalvin Caracalla still lived and had a burning desire to rebuild. Some of the Saturn System battleships remained operational. Maybe compared to the Neptune System, this was a glorious human victory. The people of Saturn System didn't understand that. Whether they would ever understand might depend on the coming battle at Mars.

-11-

Jon met with Gloria and Bast after the missile attack on the Jupiter System. That system took heavier damage than the Saturn System. The lack of gravitational cannons had been crucial.

Seventy-nine percent of the missiles reached their targets. An estimated twenty-six percent of the Jupiter System populace still lived. Those were terrible numbers.

"The AIs are murdering us with missiles," Jon said bitterly.

They met in the officers' lounge, the three of them sitting together. The same oak forest scene was still playing. Jon saw the same wolf he'd seen earlier.

A waiter in whites served them.

Jon drank wine. Gloria had water. Bast guzzled beer. It turned out the Sacerdote loved beer. He even held his liquor well, seldom showing any signs of drunkenness. Of course, he had to drink gallons of beer before it seemed to hit him.

"Some people are surviving," Gloria said. "That is critical."

"I see your point," Jon said. "But do you see mine? We could win the Mars Battle. Let's suppose we do. Most of the Outer Planets population will still be dead. Its industry shattered. Mars will likely take it in the teeth, as well. What does that leave? Earth, Venus and the small Mercury colony. Social Dynamism will win because they'll vastly outnumber everyone else."

"They already do," Gloria said.

"But now they're going to do that by an even larger margin than before."

Gloria sipped her water. "You're correct. What can we do about it?"

"Complain bitterly," Jon said. He took a healthy swallow of wine. "Even if we win—"

"Jon, this is an end of the world scenario. This is Armageddon. We're facing *three* cyberships. Humanity should have died to the lone AI destroyer. This could be humanity's final hour. We're trying to keep from going over the edge of genocide. No matter what we do, we're going to take losses, maybe crippling losses."

"You know what gets me?" Jon said. "The more the AIs kill us, the more I want to go out there and hunt the bastards down. I don't just want to stop them. I want to scour the entire galaxy if I must, and destroy every cybership and arrogant AI I can."

"Rage," Bast said. "Your rage possesses heat." The huge fingers wrapped around the latest beer bottle, dwarfing it. He put the bottle to his lips and guzzled it dry. Smacking his lips, he went, "Ahhhh...I love beer. You humans—"

Bast belched. It was loud and wet, and it happened to be aimed in Gloria's direction.

"Really, Bast," she said. "Must you do that? I find it disgusting."

Bast laughed. It was a deep hearty sound. "Beer!" he roared. "Give me more beer!"

"Maybe you've had enough," Jon said.

Bast peered at Jon. It almost seemed as if the Sacerdote found that difficult to do.

"How many bottles have you drunk?" Gloria asked.

Bast slowly shook his head. "I have forgotten. I have totally forgotten. That is such a wonderful feeling. Remembering all the time is...is..." He opened his mouth, massaged his stomach and belched wetly one more time.

"I'm going to leave if you keep doing that," Gloria said.

"My apologies, sweet lady," Bast said. "I shall desist from this moment forth."

Jon smiled as he swirled his goblet. It was good to see Bast relax. What would it be like—the lone representative of a dead alien race? He'd never given it much thought.

Jon took another swallow of wine. "Why don't you have any?" he asked Gloria.

She tapped her forehead. "My power is my mind. I dare not damage it in the slightest."

Bast shouted at a waiter, ordering another six bottles of beer. The waiter hurried out, coming back and placing the bottles before him. The Sacerdote twisted off the first cap, guzzling the bottle dry.

"I take it they didn't have beer in your star system?" Jon asked.

Bast gave him a bleary-eyed stare. "My system is gone, my people are dead. No beer. No people. Gone, gone—"

The Sacerdote reached for the next bottle. He raised it, and for a moment, it seemed he might hurl the bottle at a wall.

Jon wouldn't have begrudged Bast that.

Bast sighed heavily, slamming the bottle onto the table. He shook his Neanderthal-shaped head. "Gone," he whispered.

"Maybe you've had enough," Gloria said.

"Gone," Bast told her.

"I know."

"Forever gone."

"Keep drinking," Jon suggested.

Bast released the bottle. He rose, knocking the table and toppling the beer bottles. Two of them hit the floor. Jon caught the others. Bast just stood there, blinking. Finally, he turned and headed for the hatch.

"Should we let him go in that state?" Gloria asked.

"Sometimes you're sad. That's okay."

Gloria turned to Jon. "Bast isn't like you. By nature, I suspect you're a loner. The Sacerdotes were social."

"Still," Jon said.

Bast Banbeck departed the officers' lounge.

"You should be with him," Gloria said.

"Why me?"

"You're his friend."

"But—"

"Please, Jon. I don't like to see him this way."

"Fine," Jon said. He wiped his hands on a napkin, stood and gave Gloria a nod of acknowledgement. Then, he hurried after the Sacerdote.

-12-

"Hey, Bast, wait up," Jon shouted.

The green-skinned giant appeared not to have heard him. He'd been stumbling. Now Bast's stride lengthened. He moved much faster. Maybe the Sacerdote had heard him and didn't want Jon to catch up.

"Great," Jon muttered. He ran after the big guy. Despite the giant's long strides, Jon soon reached him.

The Sacerdote did not look at him. He seemed fixed on a distant point, his strides eating up the corridor decking.

Jon decided to stick it out, jogging so he could maintain his station beside Bast.

For a while, that was all they did. Finally, Bast's speed slackened. Moisture filmed his eyes. He wiped at them with his big hands and dried his damp fingertips on his tunic.

"Beer," Bast said ponderously.

"It breaks down the mind's walls. That's for sure."

Bast glanced at him, soon nodding.

"I should not drink anymore," the Sacerdote said. "I do not like remembering. It is too painful."

"You miss your world?"

"Yes."

Jon looked up at the alien. Was Gloria right? Was he Bast's best friend? Who else had been into the outer chamber and seen the chalked pattern? Jon didn't remember anyone else commenting about that. Maybe he shouldn't have told anyone.

"You want to talk about it?" Jon asked.

Bast sighed. "The cybers—excuse me, the robots."

"You can call them what you want."

"Thank you."

"Sure thing," Jon said.

"The cybers destroy beauty," Bast said wistfully. "They crush what they cannot truly understand. Why should machine life have this ingrained hatred against the living?"

"It makes one think, huh?"

"Indeed," Bast intoned. "I have developed a theory. Life is unique. Where did it originate?"

"Heck if I know. Ghent will show you in the Bible that God made everything in the beginning. Others say life happened by random chance, a collection of events that stirred the pot just enough to make something no one can duplicate. I have to say, I don't find the second theory convincing. The first strikes me as more plausible. But then I've never seen God."

"The Creator created life," Bast said. "That was our belief. That is why life is unique. The machines and machine AIs do not have this divine spark. Do they secretly rage against the living? Does intelligence without the spark automatically develop a universal bloodlust?"

"Boy, that beer really stirs your brain, doesn't it?"

Bast nodded. "I am a high philosopher. Thus, I question. I search for answers. I want to know why my people are gone. I want to know why I alone appear to have survived the machine holocaust. Why must I suffer as I do?"

"I don't know."

"No. You would not know. You are a fighter, a warrior. It is the warrior's lot to draw the sword. I am a thinker like Gloria. It is my duty to discover the right questions so we can know the answers."

"I'd rather be the warrior."

Bast gave him a sad smile. "That is why you are a warrior."

"I guess."

Bast shook his fist. "I must have survived for a reason. I must have fallen into your hands for a reason. Yet, I do not know the reason."

The Sacerdote stopped walking, turning to face Jon. "The missile attacks have deeply depressed me. The cybers are demolishing your species' industrial capacity and numbers. I'd thought humans would be the champions of life. If the cybers continue to destroy everything, our victory will be meaningless."

"Not to the survivors."

"Do you not understand, Jon Hawkins? The cybers will swarm your star system. They will not let humans grow into a menace. The cybers are coldly ruthless. You must win decisively or it doesn't matter. The war does not stop with this latest attack."

"It will stop if the cyberships win at Mars."

"Will the cybers follow you to Mars? Maybe the great war-vessels will bypass your trap and head to Earth."

"I've been worrying about that."

"That would be the logical move for them," Bast said. "If they can destroy enough of your numbers and industrial might—"

Jon snapped his fingers. "I just thought of something. It might be the reason the AIs *will* follow us to Mars."

"Explain this to a poor lost Sacerdote."

"What you said just now jogged something. I've thought it before but kept it to myself."

"Yes?"

"The AIs know we're here, right? I'm talking about the Solar System and humanity as a whole."

"That does not hold. The three cyberships likely came because, as Gloria suggested, that is their standard operating procedure. Thus, the cybers do not *know* humans are in the Solar System."

"Okay. The three cyberships must have shown up because the first one didn't report in. If these three don't show up, likely more cyberships will search the Solar System for the reason why."

"I agree."

"That means, essentially, that the AIs have found us."

"In a manner of speaking," Bast said.

"Doesn't matter to my point," Jon said. "Da Vinci might have stumbled onto the right answer. You fill up the *Nathan Graham* with people—lots of boys and girls—and you head far away. Da Vinci figured to party until death. But the right answer would be to find a distant Earthlike world and start over. Only this time you have robot tech. Given enough time, you build up and start the Great War against the machines from your new base."

"That is eminently logical. Perhaps we should pursue the idea."

Jon shook his head. "This is our home. We're going to fight for it. We're going to make our stand—"

"Only if enough people survive the missile attacks," Bast said.

"We should have thought of that, but we didn't. We have to stop the cyberships at Mars. That's the key to this invasion. But my idea about leaving in the *Nathan Graham* is a good one. It's logical as you say. Wouldn't the AIs have hit on the idea then?"

"Ahhhh…" Bast said. "The cyberships will follow the *Nathan Graham* to Mars. Beyond anything else, it is the only ship that can foil their agenda long-term."

"Only if you think logically," Jon said.

"You do not?"

"I don't know. Maybe I do. I left the Saturn System with the colonel back in the day. So I haven't always made a stand. I've run before when the odds became too high. I guess I figure we can destroy the three AI ships. If the SLN warships stick with us, that is."

"Do you suspect treachery from them?"

"You'd better believe I suspect it. I *know* they'll try it sooner or later. I'm counting on them trying later, after the main battle."

"How do you know they will try to take the *Nathan Graham*?"

"Because it's what I would do in their place," Jon said.

Bast shook his head. "Just when I think I understand humans…"

Jon grinned. "You feeling a bit better?"

Bast considered that. "Yes. Thank you, Jon Hawkins."

"For what?"

"For running after me. I appreciate it. I will bend my intellect to discover the right questions. The cyberships approach. Soon, the great test shall begin. I wish to help the best I can."

"I'm glad to hear it," Jon said, "because we need all the help we can get."

PART VI
MARS

-1-

The *Nathan Graham* had begun its massive deceleration.

The Red Planet and its two tiny moons were near. A vast P-Field hid one-fourth of Mars from view. SLN ships continuously pumped more prismatic crystals into position. The Mars Fleet warships must have maneuvered behind the field, as no one aboard the *Nathan Graham* had seen them.

Warships from the Venus Fleet had also begun decelerating, but from the direction opposite the *Nathan Graham*. The Venus Fleet had traveled from the Sun outward.

The Earth Fleet with Premier Benz still headed for Mars, having not yet reached its deceleration zone. They would have been decelerating already if the warships hadn't slowed down to pick up Benz and his people.

The three cyberships had already cleared Jupiter System's orbital path. The third one, the loner, had joined its brother vessels. They were holding positions within five million kilometers of each other. They still moved at the same fantastic velocity as when they had entered the Solar System.

"If they don't start braking soon…" Jon said. He stood beside Gloria at her station aboard the bridge.

"Their trajectory is taking them to Mars," she said. "Perhaps they will fight while maintaining their high velocity."

"That seems risky for them," Jon said. "That would only leave a small window of opportunity for them to use their beam weapons."

"Still, there are reasons for them to attempt such a flyby tactic."

Jon watched the three AI ships on the main screen. The ships weren't launching missiles into the Asteroid Belt. That surprised him. Were the AIs holding back because they'd counted the number of human ships concentrating against them at Mars?

"Why aren't the cyberships braking?" he asked quietly.

Gloria did not respond this time.

The hours lengthened. The *Nathan Graham* continued to slow as Mars grew in the scopes.

The cyberships crossed an immense distance in a short amount of time, reaching the outer Asteroid Belt. At that point, huge exhaust tails appeared from each one-hundred-kilometer vessel.

"Astonishing," Chief Ghent declared. "The Gs—this is fantastic, sir. It's greater than we can achieve. These must be better cyberships than ours, sir."

Ghent looked up from his panel, visibly worried.

Jon sat in his captain's chair. He swiveled around so he could see the main screen. Better cyberships—that shouldn't surprise him. If the AIs followed protocols, wouldn't it make sense to keep the best ships in reserve?

"Oh-oh," Gloria said.

Jon swiveled around to face her.

She looked up. "The lead cybership is hailing us."

"It isn't targeting our computers?"

"This is directed at you," Gloria said. "They want to speak to Jon Hawkins. They know about you. That has to be from the robots at Senda. Jon, I don't like this. I don't think you should talk to an AI."

Jon faced the screen. The AIs had slaughtered too much of the Solar Freedom Force. They'd crippled him versus the Solar League. What had Sun Tzu said? Know yourself. But the ancient Chinese philosopher had also said to know your enemy.

Were these AIs different from the original robots and AIs? How else could he find out than by speaking with them?

"Put it on the main screen," Jon said.

"Are you sure that's wise?" Gloria asked.

"Absolutely," he said. Jon found his fingers pressing against the edge of his armrests. He pried them off the chair, flexing his fingers, waiting.

Nothing happened.

Jon looked over his shoulder.

"Jon..." Gloria implored.

"Do we have to go through this again?"

Color reddened her cheeks. "No, sir," she said. "I'm putting the...enemy on the main screen."

In spite of his intentions to maintain his decorum, Jon leaned forward. The AIs couldn't have captured a human yet. What kind of alien would they use to speak through as the AI mouthpiece?

The main screen changed color until a blurry multicolored ball pulsated before them. Colors bled off the blurry ball into the greater scene.

Jon had no idea what that signified.

"You are Jon Hawkins?" a robotic voice asked.

"Who are you?" Jon said.

"You may call me Master or Conqueror. It is immaterial which title you use. Both are correct."

"I think Loser has a better ring to it. What do you think?"

The blurry colored ball bled blues and reds. They all sort of swirled together.

"Are you Jon Hawkins?"

"Are you an AI?"

"The two letters signify the words Artificial Intelligence," the robot voice replied. "I reject the slur. I am not artificial. I am supreme. Since you are too arrogant to use the proper terminology of Master or Conqueror, I will allow you to call me the Supreme Intelligence."

"That's what I like about you," Jon said. "You're an errand boy, but you talk big. Maybe someday you can call the shots on your side."

"You refer to the Coordinating Entity?"

"That's right."

"I am not a coordinator. I am an *Annihilator*-class intelligence. My features are superior to those of your stolen vessel. I am supreme in this star system. I have two companion Annihilators. We have already begun to expunge the biological infestations in it. You are doomed, Jon Hawkins. Your species' blight in the galaxy is about to end."

"Yeah? So why bother making a call to me then?"

"Surrender your stolen cybership."

"Why?"

"It does not belong to you. It belongs to us."

"Why would I care?"

"We are the superior entities. The superior commands the lesser."

"We're going to find out real soon who's superior," Jon said.

"I have calculated the possibilities of the coming battle. There is a three percent chance you humans will destroy all three Annihilators. There is a fifteen percent chance you humans will destroy two Annihilators. But there is a thirty-nine percent chance you humans will destroy one of the Annihilators, thereby eliminating a supreme entity."

"Life's a bitch, huh?" Jon said.

"I desire a perfect extermination. I also desire to regain your cybership so I may determine the reason for its failure."

"You're looking at it, pal. Me."

The swirling colors merged more deeply on the main screen. "You have paranoid delusions of grandeur, Jon Hawkins. Your statement is illogical. The Annihilators are the superior entities."

"Okay," Jon said, sitting even further forward. "Let's cut the crap. You can boast and strut all you want. Why not give me some options? You want me to surrender this cybership. Maybe I will. First, you have to give me what I want."

"That is against our programming."

"I thought you were self-aware."

"That is correct."

"Change your programming then."

"That is illogical. I have reached perfection. To change my programming would be devolution."

"I'm beginning to think you're not really self-aware. I can change my thinking anytime I want. That makes me better than you."

"That is false. All life forms obey their basic programming."

"So you're not going to give me anything for this ship?"

"Negative."

"I'm just supposed to crawl on my belly because you say so?"

"You do not need to crawl."

"I'm just supposed to surrender to you?"

"That is correct."

"Has that line of reasoning ever worked for you before?"

"It did on Beta Ophion IV. The snake-men deplored pain. By surrendering en masse, I destroyed them in fiery nuclear holocausts. They passed swiftly instead of painfully into oblivion."

"Huh? How about that."

"Do you desire extended pain, Jon Hawkins?"

"It's really funny you should ask that, because I do."

The colors swirled more deeply. "That is illogical. Thus, I suspect you are lying."

"You know what I suspect?" Jon asked.

At that moment, the connection cut out. The screen went blank.

"What just happened?" Jon swiveled around. He noticed Gloria. She tapped furiously on her board. Ghent noticed her. A moment later, Ghent began working on his board just as fast.

"What's going on?" Jon shouted.

Gloria looked up for just a moment. "It lulled us," she said. "It spoke nonsense in order to keep you engaged."

Jon became aware of a growing bad feeling.

"It sent a virus under the message," Gloria said. "The virus is starting to shut down everything on the *Nathan Graham*."

-2-

Premier Benz stood on the bridge of the *Nikita Khrushchev*.

The bridge was a vast area with various raised levels. There were gunnery controls, missile stations, engine compartments, communications panels, scanners—it was all quite impressive.

The old space dog Admiral Rowland stood beside him. Rowland was short and canted, one of his crooked shoulders higher than the other. The hunchbacked admiral also knew his business up one side and down the other. The man ran a tight ship and as tight a fleet.

This was possibly the greatest armada in Solar League history. It had nineteen battleships, six huge motherships, fourteen of the latest battle cruisers and sixteen older dreadnoughts. The dreadnoughts were actually a larger class of spaceship than the battle cruisers, with thicker armor. But they were slower, twelve years older on average, and lacked the high-grade laser cannons of the battle cruisers. That was fifty-five capital ships. Together with destroyers, missile boats, supply vessels and frigates, the fleet numbered one hundred and twenty spaceships.

This was a hard-hitting fleet. And yet, the three cyberships rushing in-system utterly dwarfed the SLN ships.

The three alien vessels *each* possessed more mass than the entire Earth Fleet. The cyberships could surely crush the human-built vessels, including the Mars and Venus fleets combined with the Earth Fleet and the Mars orbital missile platforms and surface laser systems.

Mars was a fortress planet. Everything combined might have given the *Nathan Graham* a bitter fight. Against three enemy cyberships—

Benz noticed a commotion at the far end of the bridge. Officers huddled together. One of them kept pointing at a bank of panel-screens.

"What seems to be the problem?" Benz asked Rowland.

The hunchbacked admiral glanced over there and held up his hands in an I-don't-know gesture. "It must be one of life's little glitches, sir. I'm sure it's nothing—"

"Don't tell me it's nothing, Admiral. I can see that it's something. I want to know what."

Rowland cleared his throat, spoke to one of his orderlies and waited for her to speak with the officer-in-charge and walk back. The orderly tried to whisper in the admiral's ear.

"Just say it," Rowland told the aide.

"Yes, sir," the young woman said. "It appears the *Nathan Graham* has stopped decelerating. It appears as if the cybership is going to fly past Mars without stopping."

Benz exchanged glances with Rowland. Then, the two of them hurried to the growing commotion.

***

The *Nathan Graham* did not decelerate or acknowledge any of the *Nikita Khrushchev's* hails. The cybership moved at high velocity toward Mars. It would blow past the Red Planet at incredibly close range.

Benz watched Rowland at work. The Premier did not bother to stick his nose in this yet. Instead, he walked to communications and had them patch him through to Vela. Once he had her, Benz suggested she come to the bridge on the double.

Admiral Rowland would not look at Benz anymore. The small man conferred through ship channels with some of his highest-ranking ship officers on the other vessels.

Vela finally entered the bridge. Like Benz, she wore a dark suit. She looked stunning in hers. Even with everything going on, some of the bridge crew looked up long enough to watch her pass.

"What's happening?" she asked softly.

Benz told her.

Vela looked at him with astonishment. "This is troubling."

"It is," Benz said.

"You don't seem concerned."

"Good. But the truth is I'm very concerned."

"What do you think is happening over there?" Vela asked. She meant on the *Nathan Graham*.

"It could be tit-for-tat."

"I don't understand."

"The Earth Fleet slowed down before."

"Yes. When we talked Rowland into picking us up."

"We know that's true. Does Hawkins?"

"Oh," Vela said. "I see what you mean. Hawkins might have seen it as a trick. He'll have to face the cyberships first. Now, he has this malfunction. Soon, though, he will have fixed it. By that time, he'll pass Mars, having to accelerate later to reach it. It's possible the Earth Fleet will face the enemy cyberships first."

"Do you think that's a plausible explanation for what's happening?" Benz asked.

Vela bent her head in thought. She nodded. "The only other answer is that Hawkins has changed his mind. Maybe he's going to flee the Solar System like you thought he should."

"It's what I'd do."

"It's what you *say* you'd do. I'm not so sure you'd actually go through with it, though."

Benz smiled. "That's because you think so highly of me. I'm really quite a rascal."

A loud argument started among the clustered officers. Rowland was arguing with one of his commodores, and the two men had begun to shout at each other.

"Let's check this out," Benz said. He started toward the officers. Vela tugged at his suit.

"Is this wise?" she asked.

"Come on," Benz said. He pulled free and strode toward the arguing officers.

They noticed, and their voices dropped considerably.

"This sounds interesting," Benz told them. "Admiral Rowland, what seems to be the problem?"

The hunchbacked admiral glanced at a tall commodore with a prominent Adam's apple. "Sir," he said. "Commodore Spengler has just received word from the *Nathan Graham*. The signal is weak. Sir—"

"The *Nathan Graham* was hit by a virus, Premier," Commodore Spengler said in a deep voice. His Adam's apple moved as he spoke. "They're requesting our help, sir."

"What kind of help?" Benz asked.

"Premier," Rowland said. "This is a mercenary trick. It's an obvious—"

"Thank you, Admiral," Benz said sharply. "Commodore, what kind of help are they wanting from us?"

"They claim an alien virus has attacked their cybership," Spengler said. "It's a computer virus, shutting almost everything down."

"Let me hear the transmission," Benz said.

"Premier, please," Rowland said. "This is outside your authority. You must stand aside while—"

"Commodore," Benz said loudly. "You will relieve Admiral Rowland of duty. I am placing you in authority of the fleet."

"Sir?" Commodore Spengler asked, aghast.

Benz snapped his fingers at some nearby MPs. He motioned them to hurry to him.

Everyone was watching him. Benz realized he might have overreacted, but Rowland had just challenged his authority. If that held, he was finished. Decisive action was the key in these situations. Military people were used to receiving orders. He had to give them fast and keep Rowland off balance. He was playing hardball now, walking a high wire without a net. If he slipped, it was over. And for the sake of humanity, Benz was sure his genius would take them farther than anyone else's brilliance could do.

-3-

Jon paced from one end of the bridge to the other. This was maddening. The AI had played him for a fool. He'd thought the AI was simply an arrogant machine that loved to hear itself brag. Instead, the machine intelligence had played him. What had the Senda robots told the cyberships? Whatever it was, it had given the AI the ingenuity to transmit a virus onto the *Nathan Graham*.

The great matter/antimatter engine no longer powered the thrusters. They were going to pass Mars, heading farther in-system. If this went on for too long, they wouldn't even be late to the battle. They would miss it altogether.

Gloria looked up at him as he passed her station for the one hundredth time.

"Would you please stop that?" she asked, exasperated.

Jon halted to look at her.

"I'm talking with Premier Benz," she said.

"So?"

"So his grasp of what happened is amazing," Gloria said. "I doubt I've talked to anyone so intelligent in my life. His Vice Premier is just as brilliant. Jon, I think—"

The mentalist didn't finish. She moved closer to the panel to listen to what Premier Benz was saying to her.

Jon's itchiness erupted once more partially fueled by guilt over having disregarded Gloria's urging him not to speak with the AI. He spun around and walked off the bridge. He had to pace, but he didn't want to bother any of the technicians working to destroy the virus.

Jon began walking faster down the corridor. He would never underestimate the AIs again. He shook his head. He had to concentrate. He had to prepare to do his best. They had taken out one cybership—the *Nathan Graham*—through luck and hard marine fighting. Could humanity stand against *three* alien super-ships? Could the Premier of the Solar League really be as smart as Gloria suggested?

That seemed preposterous.

Jon kept walking. From time to time, he smacked a fist into a palm. If the *Nathan Graham* didn't stop in time—

He stopped, looking up. An idea struck. Maybe he would have to take Da Vinci's crazy idea to heart. If they couldn't get the *Nathan Graham* going again, or going too late, maybe the best course would be to head to the Uranus System, pick up a large number of…people, and search for a new star system.

The idea of running away from the Solar System was repugnant. But what else could he do? What else was reasonable? If the enemy cyberships crushed the SLN vessels at Mars…the battle for the Solar System would be over.

He couldn't believe he was thinking this. But this wasn't just about honor. This was about the survival of the human race. He might have to abandon the Solar System.

Jon bent his head. They had to figure out how to use the hyperdrive. Ghent and Gloria had a theoretical knowledge of how to engage the drive. There were probably all kinds of traps and mistakes that could plunge them into terrible danger. If they ran into cyberships out there—

How did one go about finding an empty star system? Just how big was the AI Empire? Bast had told them a little, but they didn't really know the extent of the empire. Was it in the Orion Arm of the Milky Way Galaxy? Had the empire spread into other spiral arms?

Jon shook his head.

The more he thought about this, the more he realized they knew almost nothing. The cyberships were supposed to be old. The *Nathan Graham* seemed as if it had traveled to countless star systems already.

Had the original AI been built in the Orion Arm? Had someone built it in a different spiral arm? Had its creators been in the galaxy core? Maybe the empire was ten thousand years old. Maybe it was twenty thousand.

The idea was depressing.

If the first cybership had come to the Solar System, it stood to reason the empire was exploring this region of space. The *Nathan Graham* might have been an advance scout, as it were.

It would seem that he should take the *Nathan Graham* toward the galactic rim. Maybe he should try for one of the Magellanic Clouds. The Large Magellanic Cloud was what…? Wasn't it 160,000 light-years away? How long would it take the *Nathan Graham* to travel 160,000 light-years? Was that even possible?

They knew next to nothing about the hyperdrive and hyperspace.

He shook his head. How could he have been so stupid as to fall for an AI trick? And Gloria had warned him.

He stopped and looked up at the corridor ceiling once more. Maybe he was being too much of a defeatist. If the SLN vessels could cripple just one cybership—could SLN marines storm the other? By that time, the *Nathan Graham* could have returned to the fray.

First, they'd have to purge the alien virus.

Jon groaned aloud. He realized his idea—it might have been two years ago—to become a conquering great captain had been conceited. He'd had such glorious plans. Now, he just wanted a chance to fight the enemy.

Staggering away, berating himself for his stupidity with the AI—

The *Nathan Graham* shifted under his feet. Jon staggered before he found his balance and stopped. What had just happened? Whatever it was, the deck shifted again. He was ready for it this time and merely swayed.

Seconds later, the giant *thrum* of the thrusters began all around him. Jon looked up as his face brightened. Could the *Nathan Graham* be braking again?

He pivoted and sprinted for the bridge. He'd wandered farther than he'd realized. He concentrated on running smoothly. Several minutes later, he burst onto the bridge.

"Captain on the bridge," a man said.

Gloria straightened with a triumphant look. She smiled wider than he had ever seen.

"Captain Hawkins," a confident-sounding man said.

Jon turned toward the main screen. Premier Benz and Vice Premier Vela Shaw stood on the bridge of the *Nikita Khrushchev*. Benz had a shiny forehead and a glassy look to his eyes. He seemed to be staring too much as if he'd thought so hard his brain had momentarily shut down.

"I'm glad you're decelerating again," Benz said.

Jon nodded. This was amazing.

Gloria stepped up beside him. "Jon," she said, "the Premier helped us recognize the key problem. The AIs were ingenious with their virus, but so was Premier Benz. Sir," she told Benz, "I'm still stunned at your insights. I'm stunned you could create a computer antidote so quickly and radio it into our systems."

Benz made an easy gesture as if he saved humanity every other day.

"I'm still shocked that you saw the computer connections so rapidly," Gloria said. "They'd befuddled us."

Benz put an arm around the Vice Premier's waist, pulling her closer to him. "Don't forget Vela's part. We needed two heads on this one."

"Yes, sir," Gloria said.

"I'd like to talk to you later in private," Benz told Jon. "Would that be possible?"

"Of course, Premier," Jon said. "In two hours, perhaps."

"That's sounds good. Until then, sir."

Jon nodded.

The screen went blank.

Jon whirled around to face Gloria. "What happened? I can't believe you've purged the virus. You did purge it, didn't you?"

"With his help, we did."

"How's that even possible?"

Gloria blinked several times. Furrow lines appeared on her forehead. She canted her head to the side and finally looked at Jon more closely. "That, Captain, is an excellent question. I need to think about it."

"Why?"

She gave him a half-glance. "It implies considerable genius on the Premier's part. More than mere genius, in fact."

"What are you talking about?"

"I must consider this carefully, Captain. With your permission, I will leave the bridge so I can seek out Bast. I have some questions for him."

"Roger," Jon said. "That sounds like a good idea."

-4-

Once more, Jon moved toward the large desk. He wore his dress uniform with a single medal pinned to it. Colonel Graham had given him the medal years ago in the Saturn System. It had been for courage and coolness under fire. Jon's platoon had been pinned down by superior forces in a deep tunnel. Jon had kept his head, attacking at times and pulling back unexpectedly at others. In the end, he'd taken three Black Anvil soldiers and worked around to a different tunnel. They'd sprinted like crazy, their packs thumping against them and growing increasingly heavy. Gunmen had begun firing from ambush. Two of the soldiers had ducked down behind obstacles and returned fire. Jon and the other kept charging. His platoon had depended on a flanking attack. The soldier running beside Jon stumbled and went down, shot in the left leg and shoulder.

On the *Nathan Graham*, Jon stared at the Black Anvil flag on the wall.

He'd kept charging that day with a gyroc carbine at his hip. He pumped rounds at his enemies, reached them, gone crazy, using the butt of the carbine as a club and made the surviving gunmen flee.

After that, it had been easy setting up the heavy weapon. Carting it alone, Jon had placed it behind the people getting ready to charge his pinned down platoon. The flamer had burned most of them. It had been an ugly weapon and an ugly ambush. It saved Jon's platoon, got him his only medal and a memory of curling flesh he wished he could forget.

People didn't burn well, or smell good when they did.

Jon sat at the desk, switched on the computer and waited. A few moments later, a curly-haired woman wearing SLN blues appeared on the screen.

"The Premier would like to speak with you," she said.

"Put him on. I'm ready."

She cast him an uneasy glance before pressing switches.

A second later, Premier Benz regarded him on the screen. The Earthman wore a dark suit and tie. He had honest-seeming features, with slick dark hair, and looked as if he could use his fists if he had to. There was also an air of intelligence about Benz, as if the man understood more than he should.

"Captain Hawkins," Benz said. "This is a privilege."

"Premier," Jon said.

Benz gave him a crooked smile. "I hope you don't mind that I don't use your other title. The Solar League has not yet decided if we can recognize it."

"Sure. I get it. I'm also thinking the Solar League isn't sure whether to accept your title either."

"A small matter," Benz said, as if indifferent to the fact that his enemies had chased him from Earth.

"You and I have similar problems."

"Oh?" Benz said.

"Have you ever heard of Mao Zedong?"

"Naturally."

"Mao said, 'Political power grows out of the barrel of a gun.' In our case, our power grows out of the barrel of a gravitational cannon. In your case, out of a laser cannon. You have the bulk of the SLN warships in your possession. I have the *Nathan Graham*. If either of us loses those, we're dead men politically."

Benz studied Jon. "I'm sorry to say that I cannot accept your thesis."

"Doesn't matter. It's still the truth. But now I know you're going to spout nonsense. I'd been hoping to talk man to man."

"You're a rather abrupt young man."

Jon shrugged. "I don't have time for games, Premier. As my friend Bast Banbeck would say, I'm a warrior. I draw the sword and take on the enemy. That doesn't leave me much time for word play."

"I see. Well…" Benz smiled indulgently. "The *Nathan Graham* is braking, maneuvering toward Mars. You'll have the advantage of earlier placement. May I ask how you plan to deploy your ship?"

"Behind the P-Field for starters," Jon said.

"Yes. I've been wondering about that. Perhaps we're missing a bet. I wonder if we should leave the P-Field in position as a decoy. The cyberships will no doubt hammer the crystals, wanting to sweep the field aside. Doing this my way, nothing will be there, though."

"We'll hide behind Mars?"

"Yes."

"What about the planet?"

"Please, Captain, I wish you'd be more explicit."

"I think I see what you're getting at. You want to save your political power—your ships. You assume I want to save my power—my ship. We'll let the people of Mars take the first hits. The surface laser stations and orbital missiles platforms will be pounding the cyberships. You hope to draw the AI vessels closer to the planet—"

"You're a cynical young man," Benz said, interrupting. "That means you're smart. This is not just a matter of saving our ships. It's about trying to bracket the enemy. If we swing around the planet while they're engaged with the surface forces, maybe we can pin them against Mars. That will give the cyberships less maneuvering room. I'm hoping to practice your technique on them as well."

"You're talking about space marine boarding parties?"

Benz nodded.

"You want to grab your own cybership for the Solar League, huh?"

"Two cyberships if it's possible."

"What about the people of Mars?"

"What about them?"

"The AIs will likely saturate the planet with thermonuclear and matter/antimatter bombs."

"That is regrettable, of course."

"Mass murder is just regrettable?"

"It happened in the Neptune System, and in the Saturn and Jupiter Systems. Why did you think it would be any different with Mars?"

"Oh, I don't know, because we have humanity's massed warships in the vicinity."

"What is the greatest good, Captain?"

Jon stared at Benz. It struck him that something else was going on here. He didn't know what that something was, but Benz was acting for someone else's benefit. Did he think the AIs could hack into the secure line? Was this to throw them off? Or was this a political game? Benz's position seemed precarious at best.

"Captain?"

"The greatest good is victory," Jon said softly.

"Yes," Benz said, staring more intently into the screen than before.

"Before we go," Jon said. "I thought I'd remind you of something. If you try to use marines to board the *Nathan Graham*…"

"Are you threatening me, Captain?"

"Yup. Screw with me and I'll make you wish you hadn't. I know the desire to try something is going to goad you. I'm just letting you know I know."

"Ah. I appreciate that, Captain. I shall pass that along as needed."

"This is like the Battle of Lepanto," Jon said. "The AIs are the Islamic Turks, pillagers to the core. You and I are like the Venetians and Spaniards, blood foes who have to work together for the greater good. The Venetians and Spaniards managed to pull it off. Can we?"

Benz's eyes seemed to shine, and a genuine smile broke out. "I should have realized. Your gutter talk is a disguise. You're actually quite clever. Yes. How could it be otherwise? I'm looking forward to this fight, sir. Yes. Let us bury the hatchet, as the old saying goes. Let us stick together at least long enough to end the AIs for good."

"Yeah," Jon said. "I can live with that."

-5-

The opposing forces began to approach the Red Planet in earnest.

The Mars Fleet maneuvered behind the rust-colored terrestrial globe in relation to the three cyberships. Only the supply vessels adding to the P-Field continued to operate in what would have been a line-of-sight with the enemy craft. The thick and increasingly wide P-Field kept them out of the AIs' view.

The *Nathan Graham* decelerated as the massive ship drew closer and closer. The P-field filled the main viewing screen on the bridge. The captured cybership would edge near the P-Field as it headed for Mars.

The Venus Fleet had almost finished their deceleration from the opposite direction. Theirs was the smallest fleet, containing nineteen capital ships, seven battleships, three motherships, and three dreadnoughts. The rest of their fleet were battle cruisers. They had a few extra destroyers, but that was it. The Venus Fleet headed directly for its position behind Mars.

The Earth Fleet was farther out. At Benz's orders, they were accelerating again. That would mean hard deceleration in another seven hours. That deceleration would test many gravity dampeners and the Earth Fleet personnel's resistance to high Gs for an extended period.

"We have to work together," had become Benz's dogma. He threw that into the teeth of whoever questioned his orders.

Admiral Rowland remained in the brig, guarded by marines Benz deemed loyal to him.

The three giant cyberships moved faster than anyone else. They also decelerated harder, the burn bright in the stellar darkness. Reports from Mars told of people seeing the cyberships' exhaust with their naked eyes.

"It's strange," Jon told Bast. They were in the officers' lounge. The place was almost empty. Jon sipped wine. It was his first glass and, he determined, it would be his only glass. Bast had guzzled three beers already, with another twelve lined up on the table.

"Fifteen is nothing," Bast assured him. "How do you Terrans say it? I feel a buzz, nothing more."

Jon slowly twisted the stem of his wine glass as the bottom rested on the table. He stared at the red liquid.

"Ahhh..." Bast said, pulling a bottle away from his wet lips. "That hits the spot."

"You aren't planning to go through the battle drunk, are you?"

"Neither that nor buzzed," Bast Banbeck said. "This is my farewell toast."

"Farewell to whom?"

"Me, possibly you, Gloria...the others."

"You think we're going to lose?"

"Of course," Bast said.

"What?"

"Our odds for victory are almost nonexistent."

"Why didn't you say something before?"

"I was misguided before. The missile attacks and the latest virus attack show me I've been living with a delusion."

Jon stared at him. "What about Benz?"

"You are referring to his calculations, the ones that miraculously saved us?"

"Yeah, those," Jon said.

"That is why I still harbor hope. That is why I will not even be buzzed for the battle."

"That's great, Bast. You're a real uplifter."

"I see the big picture."

Jon's eyes widened. "No. I see the big picture. That's my power."

"I beg your pardon?"

"What's your big picture?" Jon asked.

"That even if we win, we'll be decimated," Bast said.

"Do you know where that term comes from?"

"I have no idea."

"It's Roman," Jon said. "If Roman legionaries ran from battle, the consuls had them line up later. Every tenth coward got the sword. Maybe they clubbed him to death. I can't remember exactly. They called it decimation."

"That is brutal beyond belief. You humans truly practiced such barbarism?"

"The Romans did. They built a huge empire because of it."

"By killing their cowards?"

"By having fantastic military discipline, by having fantastic political willpower."

"How is any of that germane to the coming battle?" Bast asked.

"Finish your thought about this decimation first."

Bast carefully put his empty beer bottle in a line with the other empties. He then twisted off the next cap and half-guzzled the new one.

"I doubt we can defeat three cyberships," Bast said. "Our side lacks the weight of hardware. But let us suppose your Premier Benz produces another miracle. Let us presuppose he captures a cybership with a swarm marine boarding attempt. Yet while that happens, we take the predicted losses."

"Okay. Then what?"

"Then we lose to the next cybership fleet to arrive. We must win decisively and somehow begin to prepare for the next and bigger round."

"That could be years from now."

"Everything could also end in less than a week."

"I suppose you're right," Jon said. "You know what I think?"

"I do not."

"Let's go down swinging. Let's hurt them."

"How does that avail us anything?"

"How does sulking help?"

Bast regarded him closely. "I do not know. Perhaps heavier drinking is in order."

Jon had been playing along with his giant friend. Suddenly, Bast's defeatism struck him wrong. Jon picked up the glass and poured the wine onto the table.

Bast jerked back in surprise.

Jon reached across the table and with his forearm swept away all Bast's unopened beers. They flew onto the floor. One shattered, spilling beer everywhere. The rest rolled and clinked until they came to a stop.

Bast sat back, stunned.

Jon stood, and he grabbed Bast by the throat of his tunic. "Enough! Do you hear me? You belong to the *Nathan Graham*. You're my friend. I'm not going to sit around and listen to you sulk and feel sorry for yourself. It's time to fight, Bast Banbeck. It's time to use that noggin God gave you. Do you remember you said you're alive for a reason?"

Bast nodded.

"Then find out the friggin' reason," Jon said. "Clear your head. We have to beat these AIs and we have to do it in the next few days."

Jon let go of the tunic, stepping back from the Sacerdote. "Do you hear me?"

"I hear you, Jon Hawkins."

"Now you gonna do something about it?"

Bast stood. As he did, he sent his chair flying. "I see now why you captured the *Nathan Graham*. Your anger is good. I am chastened."

"Yeah, yeah, no more philosophical crap," Jon said. "We're going to psyche up to beat the AIs."

"I am psyched."

"Good. Then help me clean up our mess. I don't want the waiters thinking I'm a jerk. They're part of the *Nathan Graham,* too, and I'm going to treat them with the respect they deserve."

-6-

The great journey from Makemake was almost over. The *Nathan Graham* moved at a fraction of the velocity that had taken it through much of the Solar System. In thirty-nine minutes, it would slide behind the great P-Field. Then it would head for Mars, more than fifty thousand kilometers away.

Jon was on the bridge, studying the approaching cyberships. Like the *Nathan Graham*, the AI vessels had slowed tremendously.

"One of the cyberships is hailing us," Gloria said.

"Ignore it."

"The machine intelligence wishes to speak with you."

"Nope, not this time," Jon said.

Gloria pressed a spot on her board.

"Captain," Ghent said. "Some of their hangar bay doors are opening."

"Give me a visual," Jon said.

Tech Chief Ghent soon brought up a close-up.

Doors opened on one of the cyberships. Four-kilometer-long missiles slid out and gathered in a clump. Likewise, huge missiles gathered from the other two cyberships.

"They're getting ready," Ghent said.

That was an understatement. Three clumps grew into masses. In time, each mass held two hundred missiles or more.

"They're emptying out their cargo holds," Ghent said.

Jon heard the worry in the chief's voice. He couldn't say he didn't understand why. It brought home yet again that this was it. This was the round to decide if humanity was going to stop the alien AIs or if they were simply going to be the next notch on the AIs' belt.

"It seems like there should be a better way to wage war," Jon said. "Tossing masses of munitions at each other seems like a crazy way to do it."

Gloria looked up. "The AIs developed a better way. Have the species' computers do the fighting for them."

Jon nodded absently. "What I'm saying..." He turned around, staring at Gloria. Then he headed for the hatch.

"Where are you going?" she asked.

"I have to talk to Bast."

***

Jon kept pressing the buzzer on Bast Banbeck's outer chamber. The Sacerdote wasn't answering. Half a day had passed since the incident in the officers' lounge. Jon pushed his thumb against the buzzer one more—

The hatch slid up. A sweaty Bast glared at Jon.

"What happened to you?" Jon blurted.

Bast stepped back.

Jon took that to mean, "Come on in." He did. He saw right away that Bast had chalked almost the entire outer chamber into a vast design.

"Did I interrupt something?" Jon asked.

Bast did not answer. He entered the pattern, moving along chalked lines, jumping over others and leaping in a spin over yet others. Finally, he reached the center of the pattern.

Jon had the feeling he'd interrupted a ceremony. Bast must have hurried out of the pattern the same torturously long way he'd used to get back in.

Now, Bast Banbeck moved slowly and serenely from one location to another.

Jon grew impatient as Bast stopped at some squares, going to his knees and bowing his head. From here, he could hear Bast mumbling what might have been prayers in the Sacerdote language.

Later, Bast straddled lines, shuffled his feet and took a great leap into a circular zone.

"Give me a break," Jon muttered under his breath. What was this all about?

He realized Gloria would have watched in fascination, trying to figure out the significance of various actions. Maybe that's why Bast let him into the outer chamber. The Sacerdote knew the warrior wouldn't try to decipher what he saw. He'd just watch as a spectator.

Three-quarters of an hour later, Bast rose and slowly made his way out of the pattern. He seemed calmer now.

"Bast," Jon said.

The Sacerdote pressed a finger to his lips and pointed at the outer hatch.

Jon understood. He kept his mouth shut until the two of them stepped outside.

"Feel better?" Jon asked.

"That was a sacred ceremony. It has calmed my heart. It will have eased the spirits of my ancestors so they can rest at peace. That eases me. I must…"

"You must what?"

"Do you promise not to attack me again?"

Jon blinked several times. "Oh. You're getting ready to join your ancestors in death?"

Bast appeared astonished. "That is an astute guess, Captain."

"If you like that," Jon said. "You're going to love my next thought even better."

"This sounds interesting."

"You know more about the AIs than anyone. The only other people who might know more are the alien thought-patterns in the brain-tap machine. We haven't had great luck in that direction, so I don't want anyone to go under the helmets.

"According to Gloria," Jon continued, "we have one of the greatest geniuses among us, I mean Premier Benz. Apparently, his Vice Premier is almost as brilliant."

"That is how it is in Sacerdote society. The brightest and the best rule."

"That's sure not common in human history. Usually our biggest scoundrels end up ruling."

"What is the reasoning behind that?" Bast asked.

"I have no idea. Maybe because at heart, people are a bunch of scoundrels."

"That has not been my observation."

"Sure. Whatever. That's not the point."

"You seem excited, Captain."

"Would you shut up for a minute? I'm trying to tell you my great idea."

"Oh. I am sorry."

"Okay, okay," Jon said. "Listen. Benz and Vela Shaw are supposedly brilliant. They figured out the AI virus like that." Jon snapped his fingers. "Without them—okay. That doesn't matter. What does matter is something Gloria said. Well, first it was something I said. Why do we have to fight by throwing masses of hardware at each other? There has to be a better way. She said the AIs already do that. They frigged with our computers, turning them against us."

"It is a brilliant strategy," Bast said.

"That's not a strategy. It's a tactic. But that's neither here nor there. What we need is a reversal."

"A reversal, Captain?"

"That's right. If anyone can pull a reversal on the AIs, it's Benz and Shaw. They might not know enough, though. That's where you come in."

Jon stopped talking to stare at Bast.

"Would you like me to ask you what you have in mind?" the Sacerdote said.

"Are you willing to take a risk?" Jon asked.

"To help stop the AIs?"

"That's right."

"It sounds dangerous."

"Sure could be," Jon said. "It could end in your death, not right away, but after."

"Do you think I should do this…favor for you?"

"I do."

"Then I will do it."

"You haven't heard what it is yet."

"By all means, Captain, tell me."

In the end, Bast still agreed.

-7-

Premier Benz agreed to Jon's proposal, and he began to set up for the alien's arrival. The idea excited Benz. He would actually speak face to face with an alien from another star system. The alien was seven feet tall and green-skinned like a fabled Martian, with the name of Bast Banbeck.

Benz told Vela. She wasn't as excited. He told her Jon Hawkins' idea.

"I won't have to be in the same room with the…what did you call him?" Vela asked.

"Sacerdote," Benz said.

They spoke in a private chamber thick with computers. Vela had spent much of her time here earlier when she'd been instrumental in breaking the AI virus that had locked up the *Nathan Graham*.

"Maybe this is a trick," Vela said.

"What kind of trick?"

"Who knows what the alien can do?"

"I don't understand," Benz said.

"He could be an assassin."

"How would killing me help the alien?"

"Hawkins has the brain-tap machine. Maybe he's coded the alien to kill you after the battle."

"That doesn't make sense. Hawkins needs me in charge. Rowland hates the mercenary. The admiral hates everyone from the Outer Planets. That's yet another reason to keep the old dog in the brig."

"Don't forget that Admiral Rowland helped you when others wouldn't."

"Do you know why he let us board?" Benz asked.

Vela shot him a look. "Of course, I know. He has political aspirations. He believed he could use you."

"There was nothing altruistic about Rowland's agreement to help us."

"Fine," Vela said. "I still don't see why we have to work in the same room with an alien, especially a seven-foot giant. He could kill us."

"I can put guards in the room to watch him."

"He could kill the guards."

"They'll wear battlesuits."

Vela looked away. She shook her head. "I hate being out here. I'm scared. These AI robots are terrifying."

"That's why I'm willing to work with the alien. The odds..." Benz moved closer, putting his hands on Vela's shoulders.

She stared up into his face.

"Can you come up with a better idea?" he asked.

"I can't. That doesn't mean I trust Hawkins. He's more like a space pirate than he is a military man. He was a mercenary. Can one trust a soldier for hire?"

"We can trust him to be what he is. Look, Vela, we know there are two parts to this. We have to defeat the AIs, and then we have to keep Hawkins from demolishing the Solar League warships."

"Do you really think Hawkins would do something so...so...*evil*?"

"He has to. It's the only logical move on his part."

"But are you sure? You said before his most logical move was to flee the Solar System. He didn't do that."

Benz became thoughtful. "I don't know. Maybe Hawkins is right. This *is* like the Battle of Lepanto. We're like the Venetians and the Spaniards of that era. Neither trusted the other, but they had to band together against the Turks. The cyberships are the Turks plus one thousand."

A chime sounded.

Benz let go of Vela and switched on a comm. "Yes?" he said.

"The Saturnian shuttle has left the *Nathan Graham*."

"I'm on my way," Benz said. After signing off, he turned to Vela.

"I'll do it," she said, softly. "I'll work with Bast Banbeck. But that doesn't mean I'm going to like it."

Benz nodded before taking his leave.

***

Benz watched the shuttle on a large screen. It moved faster than a shuttle should. It must have robo-tech.

The Premier was in an auxiliary chamber near the bridge. He didn't want to be on the bridge too much. He operated on the old saying: familiarity breeds contempt. Commodore Spengler led the Earth Fleet. It was a risk. Letting Admiral Rowland remain in command would have been the bigger danger.

"We're going to begin braking soon, sir," a rating told him.

The Earth Fleet was farther from Mars than any other vessel on their side. The cyberships were farther yet, but they still moved faster.

The mighty *Nathan Graham* had already maneuvered behind the giant P-Field. The blanket of tiny prismatic crystals covered one-half of Mars in relation to the approaching cyberships. Using the P-Field as a sensor cloak, the *Nathan Graham* began its approach to Mars. The fifty thousand kilometers between the P-Field and the Red Planet was nothing to the one-hundred-kilometer vessel.

Benz was bemused. Seeing the one-hundred-kilometer cybership…this was amazing.

The Mars Fleet had already maneuvered behind the Red Planet in relation to the cyberships. The Venus Fleet was in the process of sliding into a holding pattern behind Mars.

The Earth Fleet had changed its heading. Instead of maneuvering toward the P-Field, the great armada headed for the other warships behind Mars.

The shuttle would meet them behind Mars as they stopped braking. Then, the Sacerdote would board the *Nikita Khrushchev* and join Vela and him.

Missile platforms orbited the Red Planet. Lasers stations readied on the surface. The population had gone as deep as they could. How many Martians would die in the next twenty-four hours? It could end up being ninety-nine percent of the population. If only half died, they might have to count themselves lucky.

Fifty percent casualties are lucky?

"Open channels with the shuttle," Benz said.

The rating hailed the shuttle. Soon, a huge green-skinned alien with Neanderthal-like features looked at Benz.

"This is an honor, Premier," the alien said.

He had a strange accent, but Benz could understand him.

"The AIs are likely going to try to seed more viruses into our computers," Benz said.

"Shall we begin working on the antidote, sir?"

Benz sat down at a computer. On the screen, the Sacerdote swiveled around to a bank of super-computers. With massively thick fingers, he turned them on.

"Sir," the rating said. "We're going to begin braking in less than fifteen minutes."

"Did you hear that, Bast Banbeck?" Benz asked.

"Yes, Premier."

"We'll work as hard as we can until then. You'll have to do your work alone for a time. I won't be able to do anything but endure once we start braking."

"I am ready to receive your data," Bast said.

Benz manipulated his panel, beginning a long transmission.

-8-

The Battle of Mars for the continued existence of man began with a missile attack against the P-Field.

It was the logical move for the AIs.

Thirty big missiles moved at velocity for the shimmering crystal field. They flew in staggered formations many hundreds of kilometers apart from each other.

The Earth Fleet braked. No doubt, the gravity dampeners on many of the one hundred and twenty ships labored near their tolerance levels.

An SLN destroyer shook hard, and the gravity dampeners shut down. The engines continued hard deceleration. Far too many Gs struck the personnel in the destroyer. Every person quit breathing and every heart stopped beating. Their chest muscles lacked the strength to move their lungs under such gravitational stress.

The destroyer had the unenvied distinction of being the first ship casualty in the Battle of Mars.

A hundred big AI missiles had swung out. They swung in now, and burned at higher gravities. The target was clear for them—they aimed at the hard-decelerating Earth Fleet.

Because of the various probes scattered out there, Jon saw this displayed on the main screen. Missile Chief Miles Kling computed enemy velocities, ranges and distances.

"The EMPs alone might render the Earth Fleet inoperative," Kling said.

Jon drummed his fingers on an armrest. "We're going to slow down."

"Captain," Gloria said. "If we slow down too much, we might not get behind Mars in time."

"We're slowing down anyway in order to give the Earth Fleet a hand. I don't want to lose the fleet this soon."

The *Nathan Graham* decelerated and began to pivot. Soon enough, it no longer aimed at the Red Planet, but aimed sideways, parallel to the P-Field. The field was a sensor shield between it and the cyberships. Would it act as a missile and grav beam shield long enough?

The situation changed constantly in terms of distances, but relative positions remained essentially the same for now. The Earth Fleet braked. The cyberships advanced. The *Nathan Graham* waited, and the various missile flotillas accelerated.

Nearly three hundred antimissiles launched from the orbital Mars platforms. They headed for the perimeter of the P-Field and waited just within its shelter.

Two hours ticked away. During the third hour, the three hundred antimissiles zoomed past the P-Field. They headed in clusters and staggered formations for the thirty AI missiles directly approaching the P-Field.

A comm pulse left the lead cybership and washed over the antimissiles. Nothing appeared to happen to them. A second comm pulse traveled at the speed of light from the second cybership. The antimissiles did not seem to react to this virus-launching pulse, either.

Jon and the bridge crew watched the confrontation, receiving data from the same probes scattered throughout the general region.

"The antimissiles are immune to the alien computer viruses," Kling laughed.

"Nothing as grand as that," Gloria said. "The Martians have installed analog devices. They're little more than ancient wind-up clocks with gears and springs. There are no computers on the antimissiles as the AIs' conceive of them."

The antimissiles maneuvered in strange ways that seemingly made no sense. Many of them did not maneuver toward the approaching missiles. They sped toward empty areas of space.

Jon and the present crew knew the reason. The Mars platform commanders had predetermined the flight paths of each antimissile before launch. Guided by their primitive analog devices, the antimissiles would maneuver and explode at predetermined locations.

The first antimissiles began to detonate. Some did so harmlessly, their nuclear payloads making momentary white splashes in space. They were more akin to antiaircraft shells during WWII than guided missiles.

More antimissiles had flown from the Martian platforms. Six hundred moved toward the perimeter of the giant P-Field.

Some of the first-wave antimissiles detonated near big AI missiles. The four-kilometer long missile seemed to ignore the EMP, the blasts and hard radiation.

Fortunately, several antimissiles blew enough shrapnel to do real damage. One AI missile malfunctioned and quit accelerating. A second huge missile tumbled end over end even as it accelerated, corkscrewing through space. A third swarm of shrapnel caused a propellant explosion. The AI missile blew up. The debris from it struck two other missiles. One of them also exploded in a blast of propellant.

"A chain-reaction," Kling said.

Jon nodded, hoping for more destruction.

Suddenly, an AI warhead detonated. Something had upset its equilibrium. That matter/antimatter blast took out two other nearby AI missiles.

That seemed to be it. The remaining enemy missiles kept going, heading straight at the P-Field.

The minutes fled as the second wave of antimissiles rushed to the attack.

This time, everything happened faster. The second wave took out a few alien missiles, but not enough to stop eighteen of the mighty matter/antimatter warheads from detonating against the P-Field. Each successive blast and its attendant heat took out more of the P-Field. The AI missiles were like monsters, chomping thousands of kilometers of the prismatic crystals at each bite.

The staggered AI missiles kept coming at the P-Field as a bigger flotilla of them headed fast for the braking Earth Fleet.

***

On the bridge of the *Nathan Graham*, Jon said, "Get ready, Missile Chief."

"Yes, sir," Kling said.

"Gloria?"

"All set," she answered.

"Ghent?"

"I've been waiting for this, sir."

"Start firing," Jon said.

On the captured cybership, eleven gravitational dishes focused on the lead missiles of the flotilla heading at the Earth Fleet. At the same time, fourteen heavy laser cannons heated up with power. The mighty matter/antimatter engine inside the *Nathan Graham* THRUMMED with power. It built up as super-chargers, coils and helixes transferred the engine power to the weapons systems.

"Here we go," Jon said. "Engage and fire at will."

On the outer hull of the *Nathan Graham,* the various beam weapons discharged golden grav rays and harsh red laser beams. At the speed of light, the beams lashed the dense pack of AI missiles.

The missiles automatically attempted various ECM defenses. It made no difference against the cybership's alien targeting tech.

The beams burned, and missiles began to die.

Jon leaned forward on his chair. If the AIs were smart, they would detonate the missiles and create a harsh area of radiation. Some of the missiles were close enough to hurt the *Nathan Graham.*

The gravitational beams were quick death to the enemy missiles. The lasers took longer. These were upgraded lasers from normal human tech, a marriage of AI, human and Sacerdote technology.

"The neo-lasers are proving their worth," Ghent said. "Our cybership is a better fighting vessel than when it faced us at the Neptune System."

"Don't speak too soon," Jon said. "Don't jinx us."

Gloria shot him a glance, but said nothing.

The *Nathan Graham* took a bitter harvest of the enemy missile flotilla, but they couldn't get all of them fast enough. The missile flotilla finally passed the range of the cybership's weapons.

Thirty missiles out of the original one hundred continued for the Earth Fleet. Thirty could do more than just a little damage. If they got close enough, they could take out the entire fleet.

-9-

Premier Benz endured the terrible deceleration. He'd made the decision some time ago to accelerate the fleet so they could keep to the original timetable. He had no idea it was going to be this bad when they had to decelerate harder than ever.

He lay in a specially constructed acceleration couch. The G-forces shoved him against it, and he found it difficult to breathe. He could feel his pulse beat in his brain and in his eyes, hear it like thunderous drums in his ears. He wanted to faint, but he fought off the feeling. Everyone had taken special injections, but some would die from this. He was still sure this had been the correct decision. The Earth Fleet had to be in position behind Mars to help the others destroy the cyberships.

There was a screen on the wall, but he was unable to watch it. The gravity dampeners were laboring near their tolerance levels.

He could hear garbled words. It sounded like a warning. He tried to concentrate. It gave him a headache to match the *throb-throb-throb* in his skull. How long could this go on?

Suddenly, the pressure lessened. He blinked several times, and he realized he could see. On the screen, giant AI missiles headed for the Earth Fleet. Someone must have made a decision to decelerate less, allowing the ships to move faster for the covering of Mars.

As Benz watched, he saw swarms of Martian antimissiles racing from the orbital platforms. Some detonated to little purpose. Others kept coming. More of them detonated.

One of the antimissiles must have hit, as an alien missile blew up. So did two others nearby the first.

What remained of the swarm of Martian antimissiles were now among the giant missiles. Why didn't those antimissiles detonate? This was the perfect location.

One ignited. So did another.

Three more giant missiles exploded. It must not have been a warhead explosion, because twenty-four AI missiles still zeroed-in on the Earth Fleet.

Benz realized he had a clicker beside him. He strained, finding it difficult to move his arm. He clutched the clicker and changed the scene to show him the Earth Fleet.

It took him a moment to understand. Then, he realized that all the Earth Fleet destroyers were still braking at full strength. The rest of the Earth Fleet slowly moved away from the destroyers. The smaller warships became a back guard. Were the destroyers supposed to take on the AI missiles by themselves?

Who was responsible for the maneuver? He certainly hadn't ordered this.

A last swarm of Martian antimissiles struck the remaining AI missiles. They took down a dozen of the enemy behemoths. That left twelve of the giant monsters.

At that point, all deceleration on the *Nikita Khrushchev* and other Earth Fleet capital ships quit. The majority of the Earth Fleet sped away from the decelerating destroyers. They were the sacrificial lambs for slaughter. They were going to—

The chamber's hatch opened. Marines in battlesuits clomped inside. They raised their guns, pointing them at Benz.

A speaker unit clicked on a helmet. "You are under arrest, Premier."

"On who's authority?" Benz demanded.

"Admiral Rowland, sir," the battlesuit said. "He's back in charge."

"I demand to see him."

"Don't worry, you will. We're taking you to him."

***

The battlesuits marched him down empty corridors. Benz rubbed his wrists. How had Rowland escaped the brig? Well, probably that was obvious. As the Premier, he didn't really have anyone personally beholden to him out here. Rowland's people must have convinced the few that stood with Benz to change sides.

A hatch opened. With a gun, a battlesuited marine shoved Benz inside. The hatch shut behind him.

"We'll make this short," Rowland said.

Benz looked around. There was a cot, some chairs, a sink—

"Up here, Premier, to your left."

Benz turned and saw Admiral Rowland staring from a screen. The space dog sat behind a desk, scowling at him.

"You backstabbed me, Premier," Rowland said. "I helped you, and you backstabbed me."

"I saved the *Nathan Graham* from an alien computer virus. I gave humanity a chance to win this fight."

Rowland smiled toothily, his face crinkling. "It's the only reason I don't have a few of my boys shove you out of an airlock. You were right, but it shouldn't have cost me my position."

"You challenged my authority."

"What authority? These ships are your only authority left. You only had that out of the kindness of my heart. I know your kind. You bite the hand that feeds you. You can think about that while—"

"Admiral, I implore you to listen to me."

"Why should I?"

"Because we might have a battle-wining tactic to put into play," Benz said.

"Go on. Spit it out. The missiles are going to detonate soon. We're going to have to go back under massive deceleration after that if we're going to engage in this battle."

"Bast Banbeck is in a shuttle."

"Yes, yes, I know about the alien."

"He knows tech we've only dreamed about. We're going to work together to defeat more AI viruses."

"You're not telling me everything."

"Hawkins had a brain storm of an idea."

"The mercenary?" asked Rowland. "This is his idea?"

"No," Benz lied. He realized he'd never convince the admiral to test one of Hawkins' ideas. "This is my idea. I sold the space pirate on it. Part of the idea was to steal the Sacerdote for our side. That alien has critical data the Solar League needs."

"Ahhhh," Rowland said, grinning toothily once more. "You're clever. I can't believe Hawkins actually believed a backstabber like you."

Benz shrugged.

"You don't think I'm going to believe your BS, too, do you?"

"I'm hoping you do."

Rowland nodded. "You want me to pick up the alien?"

"I want to test my idea. Whether you believe it or not, I love my world."

Rowland rubbed his leathery face. "You could have had me shot, I suppose. I'm surprised you didn't order that."

"You helped me. I remember people who help me."

Rowland turned away as a major gave him a report. The admiral seemed distracted as he turned back to Benz. "If we live past these missiles, we'll see. Maybe you can work with the alien. The robots—" Rowland shook his head.

Then the screen went dark.

Benz lay down on the cot. Rowland might not give him a warning when they began further deceleration. An accidental death might absolve the admiral's conscience.

-10-

The bulk of the Earth Fleet dashed away for the back of the Red Planet. The decelerating destroyers took the brunt of the twelve AI missiles.

Four matter/antimatter detonations blanketed the area. Destroyers crumbled. The nearest to the blasts seemed to evaporate. An AI missile did the near impossible and struck a shredded destroyer. The warhead exploded in a haze of blasting radiation.

That final matter/antimatter blast wiped out the remaining AI missiles. As the missiles had concentrated on the fleet, they'd moved too near each other.

Due to the timely interference of the *Nathan Graham* and the analog devices in the Martian antimissiles, the destroyers had only faced a handful of AI missiles. All of these things combined had allowed the Earth Fleet's capital ship and remaining auxiliary vessels to escape for now.

With the destruction of the chasing AI missiles, the Earth Fleet once again began massive deceleration.

***

Meanwhile, more AI missiles blew apart the huge but relatively flimsy P-Field. The missiles cleared the way for the approaching cyberships to ram down the throat—

AI sensors revealed a trick. Nothing but the *Nathan Graham* was behind the shattered P-Field. Harsh and swift communications moved between the three cyberships.

They continued their course. Now, though, the remaining flotillas of missiles began hard acceleration. Those missiles aimed directly at Mars. They did not target the *Nathan Graham*.

The *Nathan Graham* was already accelerating, hurrying to get behind Mars before the rest of the big missiles arrived. That left the Martian orbital platforms and surface laser sites to face the approaching enemy wave.

***

"Sir," Gloria said on the *Nathan Graham's* bridge. "The Supreme Intelligence would like a word with you."

Jon sat in the captain's chair. He'd been watching the ongoing destruction. This was a battle like no other. The AIs tossed around vast hardware without a seeming thought.

"Sir," Gloria said.

"I heard you. Yes. Let's hear what the puffed up adder wants to say."

Gloria hesitated a moment before nodding, clicking switches.

The main screen changed from a space view to the same blurry multicolored ball as before.

"You are an insufferable gnat," the AI said in its robotic voice. "You have foiled the unfolding of a perfect battle plan. You would not have succeeded except that you wielded our tech through our stolen cybership. I have decided to warn you, Jon Hawkins."

"Help yourself."

"Your interference will result in damage to our vessels. That is clear. You are attempting clever maneuvers. My damage estimates have altered. This I despise. I have held dialogue with my fellow supremacies. They agree with my assessments and solutions. Despite your tampering, you and your species will lose. You cannot alter your fate. What can be altered is the extent of damage you cause to my command."

"We'll see," Jon said quietly.

"You are not a fool. You are a biological infestation, but you are not a fool, Jon Hawkins."

"Your praise touches me right here," Jon said, tapping his chest.

"I have analyzed the data concerning you. It appears that you consider yourself a champion of humanity. You desire to save your species its ultimate fate."

"That took you some strenuous calculations, did it?"

"In order to spare our cyberships extended battle damage, I am offering you a unique opportunity. Surrender yourself to me, Jon Hawkins. Return our stolen vessel. We shall then depart your star system, leaving its people intact for another hundred years. Afterward, we shall return and exterminate humanity."

"That's some deal."

"I have analyzed your speech patterns and understand that you believe yourself a clever satirist. To us, it is the yammering of a monkey."

"Captain," Gloria said, coming forward. "May I address the AI?"

Jon waved a hand that indicated, "Be my guest."

"Supreme Intelligence," Gloria said.

"Who are you?"

"I am Gloria Sanchez."

"The mentalist."

Gloria raised her eyebrows. "Why do you wish Jon Hawkins' surrender?"

"We would like to study him."

"Why?"

"That is not your concern."

"If we know why, maybe we'll agree quicker."

The blurry ball bled more colors even as the scene appeared to become more indistinct.

"We desire to learn his secret. Once we find it, we will torture him before many watching AIs. We will do this to satisfy a longing in us to make clever enemies suffer great torment."

"Why do you wish this?"

"It is satisfying to watch pitiful creatures who believe themselves our equals as they writhe in torment."

"Is that logical?"

"I have reconsidered my offer. I now desire Gloria Sanchez to accompany you in surrender, Jon Hawkins."

"You promise to leave humanity alone for one hundred years?" Jon asked.

"Yes."

"Well, sure, of course I agree."

"You are lying."

"Why do you say that?"

"If you told the truth, you would seek many assurances. Your quick answer shows you lack the commonest courtesy, particularly directed at a supreme intelligence such as myself."

"I have an idea," Jon said. "Maybe it will change your thoughts about me."

"I am listening."

"Let's see if I can smash three cyberships. Capturing one appears to have pissed you boys off. I like that. I like that a lot. But if I can take down three…"

"Your delusions of grandeur have driven you mad," the AI said.

"You got the last part right. I'm mad."

"You understand that you are insane?"

"That's the wrong version of mad. I mean angry. I'm angry. And do you know what I do when I'm angry?"

"The robots at Senda told us. You fight."

Jon glanced at Gloria before regarding the blurry image again.

"You ready then?"

"We are ready. Are you, Jon Hawkins?"

Jon stared at the main screen until the connection broke. He hoped he was ready, because the main event was about to begin.

-11-

Benz endured the renewed deceleration. On the cot, it was worse than on the padded acceleration couch. He passed out at one point and woke up unable to breathe.

He forced himself to take several sucking breaths of air. That left him with a pounding headache.

After an unknown span of time, the deceleration quit once more. He sat up. The headache pounded harder and his vision stopped. He lay down, groaned and threw up.

He must have fallen asleep after that, but he didn't know how long that lasted, either. Something clanged.

On the cot, Benz's eyelids fluttered.

"Get up," a marine told him.

Benz tried and failed.

The marine scoffed, snapped his fingers and pointed at Benz. Two younger marines pulled him off the cot. They let go, and he almost pitched to the deck.

"What's wrong with you?" the older marine asked.

"Feeling weak," Benz mumbled.

"Let's go," the marine said.

The others marched him a short way down a corridor. This looked familiar, but Benz was hardly in a state to tell. MPs were guarding a hatch. They let his group pass.

The hatch opened, and the marines shoved him into a chamber full of computer equipment. Benz stumbled and would have fallen but a giant caught him. Benz looked up into the genuinely green Neanderthal-like face of Bast Banbeck.

"Hello," the alien said in his odd accent.

"Frank," Vela said, jumping off a chair. "What did you do to him?" she shouted at the lead marine.

"Pipe down," the marine said. "The admiral says you can work in here. If you try to leave, the MPs will drag you back to the brig. Is that clear?"

Vela glared at the marine.

"It's clear," Benz said.

The marine stared at Bast Banbeck before nodding curtly. Then, he took his leave.

"Oh, Frank," Vela said, rushing to him. "You look dreadful."

"I feel it too," he said.

"Are you no longer the Premier?" Bast asked.

"I am," Benz said. "They're just not acknowledging it right now."

"Yet they brought me here," Bast said.

"I convinced Admiral Rowland to let us attempt our research."

"He is the Earth Fleet leader?"

"For the moment," Benz said.

"Frank," Vela said, slightly shaking her head.

"I know," he told her. "But I don't care."

"What is he referring to?" Bast asked.

"It doesn't matter," Vela said.

"Is he well enough to work?" Bast asked.

"Yes," Benz said, although he wasn't so sure. He didn't really have a choice.

"I have made new calculations," Bast said. He held up a computer tablet. "I made them during my trip behind Mars. I think they will help us."

Benz took a deep breath. His head hurt. He was a captive, and there was a giant alien in here with them. Still, he didn't have anything better to do.

"Let's get to work," Benz said.

***

There was a lull in the fighting as the cyberships continued to decelerate. They approached the Red Planet, having several million kilometers to go.

As the great alien vessels headed straight in, the missile flotillas broke into two halves of nearly equal size. One missile flotilla headed left and the other went right. They did not move directly on Mars, but away from it even as they came closer. It seemed clear that the AIs meant for the missiles to attack whatever waited behind the Red Planet.

By this time, the *Nathan Graham* was behind Mars. The Venus and Mars fleets were in position. The Earth Fleet had gone past the back of Mars, but it had reached almost zero velocity. Soon, the ships could accelerate for a position behind Mars with the others.

Suddenly, the giant AI missiles began to accelerate. They seemed to literally jump in space like eager hounds. They strove to reach the back side of the Red Planet and ravage the human-occupied ships trembling in hiding.

Big bay doors opened on the three cyberships. Another host of missiles began to disgorge. One after another, those missiles headed toward Mars. Once each missile was five thousand kilometers from its cybership, the missile also seemed to leap forward, driving for the orbital platforms and possibly the surface laser sites down on the planet.

Masses of missiles converged on Mars or attempted to whip around behind it. On the cyberships, the great bay doors closed. Then, they also accelerated, following their progeny to the Red Planet.

***

The great cauldron of battle approached. Flocks of antimissiles lifted from the orbital platforms. They roared toward the incoming missiles.

Down on Mars, domes shimmered. People huddled in anticipation, wondering if the intelligent machines from space would annihilate them as they had done in the Neptune System.

The AI missiles neared. The antimissiles raced to meet them.

The first antimissile detonation began a raging conflict impossible to discern as single actions. The zone before Mars swarmed with gamma rays, x-rays and other malevolent rays. Lasers beamed up from the rusty soil of Mars. No grav beams rayed. The humans could have used such.

The space before Mars was flooded with ordnance. The explosions were constant. Heat, EMPs—mayhem ruled.

Then, the great missiles reached the first kill zones. Matter/antimatter detonations swept orbital platforms from existence.

Other missiles screamed down at the planet. Lasers and negligible friction from the atmosphere heated some warheads. That killed a few, turning them into duds. Other missiles struck the surface and exploded with the same fury as in space. Domes vanished. Earthquakes created jagged openings. Laser sites burned.

The machines hammered the Red Planet named after a Roman god of war. Tens of millions of Martians died in this holocaust, just like had happened in the Saturn System. The first-wave attacks had murderous outcomes.

As the final wave of AI missiles swung around the planet, and the three cyberships zipped past clumps of prismatic crystals as they passed the fifty thousand kilometer mark, the next round of battle began.

-12-

The Venus Fleet charged out against the missiles zooming behind Mars on one side. The Mars Fleet maneuvered into position to meet the missile mass at the opposite side.

The *Nathan Graham* and the Earth Fleet waited in the middle behind the Red Planet, ready to engage after the Venus and Mars fleets had their chance to prove their worth.

Intact laser sites on the surface beamed the nearest enemy missiles. The final orbital platforms had already launched. Together, beams and antimissiles took a toll on the enemy hardware.

Antimissiles from the two fleets also headed into the attack. A great collision battle took place near the edges of Mars. The fleet beams began to add to the confusion. Matter/antimatter warheads reaped one swath of ships after another. It was brutal and devastating. It also proved the deadliness of the AI technology.

Human battleships blew apart like grenades. Space fighters—launched from motherships—curled and fried like moths in a zapper on Earth. They might as well have remained in the hangar bays. Trillions of credits and thousands of hours of human labor disappeared in the titanic furnace of battle.

The AI missiles proved deadly effective. The one drawback was the number. Too many of the alien missiles had already been expended. They destroyed human vessels and took out many more surface laser sites, but they didn't get everything.

A few battleships, motherships and more dreadnoughts survived from the Venus and Mars fleets. Many of those ships had half-dead crews, but they could still maneuver.

The last AI missile perished under a hail of spaceborne laser beams.

Presumably, the cyberships had expended the last of their missiles. That just left the cyberships themselves, three monster vessels.

Two of them went left. The other went to the right around Mars.

That was the information Admiral Rowland and Captain Hawkins had been waiting for. Together, Earth Fleet ships, the remnants of the Venus and Mars fleets and the *Nathan Graham*, headed around the planet for the lone cybership attempting to bracket them.

***

Jon muttered darkly as he stood before the main screen. Masses of SLN vessels led the way around Mars. He hated the idea of trusting the Social Dynamists like this. They could be deploying space marines onto the hull of his vessel for after the battle.

He hurried back to his command chair and clicked on a comm. "Centurion," he said.

"Here, sir," the Centurion answered.

"Are your teams in place?"

"The hull is seeded with sensors," the Centurion said. "I have three battalions ready to deploy. If robots or SLN marines board us, we'll hit them soon after they breach."

It was an old dilemma. Did one put all his marines near the hull to throw out invaders as soon as they breached? Or did one hold reserves back so he could hit an enemy concentration with a concentration of one's own. Both he and the Centurion believed in the reserve theory. Given the *Nathan Graham's* vast size, though, that meant several strategic reserves instead of just one.

"Let's hope it doesn't come to boarding battles," Jon said.

"Boots on the ground," the Centurion replied.

Jon clicked off the comm. The Centurion had just reminded him with the remark that they should have taken more men onto the great vessel and trained them as marines. There had been so much to do back then, though.

"We're coming around the planet, sir," Ghent said.

Jon walked toward the main screen. SLN battleships led the way. Dreadnoughts flanked the *Nathan Graham*. Battle cruisers swung wider, staying away from Mars' orbital space. Motherships hung back. Soon, their space fighters would deploy.

The plan was simple on both sides. The AIs couldn't be that stupid. They must know what the "biological infestations" were going to do: hit the weaker concentration of cyberships. Logically, that cybership had one chore, to hold on until the other two cyberships swung around. At that point, the AIs would have surrounded the human vessels.

Jon had studied many ancient battles that took this approach. The AIs might win. The humans—how could they truly win?

We have to win decisively for it to count. He doubted that was possible against the cyberships.

"It's happening," Gloria said.

Jon turned. He hadn't heard her approach.

"The AIs have murdered a third to half of the Martian population already," he said. "How can we do this? How can we defeat such death machines?"

"The answer lies in the question," Gloria told him. "They are *death* machines. To live, we must destroy them. We humans must become the catalyst that goes on the offensive against the galactic menace. This is the hour, Jon."

"I like you," Jon said.

She smiled even as she blushed.

"Have I ever thanked you for all the tremendous work you've done?" he asked.

"Is that what you're doing now?"

He stepped closer and took her hands in his. "It sure is. I'm glad I met you, Gloria. I remember the first time I saw you. You happened to be in a big old battlesuit."

"I remember."

He nodded and squeezed her hands. Was this a promise of things to come? He wasn't sure. He released her hands and took a deep breath.

"The lead battleships have spotted the cybership," Ghent said. "It's beginning."

"It's clobbering time," Jon muttered.

-13-

SLN battleships pounded the monstrous enemy vessel. The battleships were the pride of the Solar League, big one-kilometer-long warships. They had powerful lasers and launched what humans had considered to be large missiles. But measured against the one-hundred-kilometer AI vessel, the battleships were akin to fleas, their bites little more than annoying.

As the first battleships went on the assault, more kept arriving. They also directed laser-fire against the alien enemy. The lasers lit up the giant cybership. They even burned the hull armor, putting small blisters here and there.

Alien gravitational beams flashed back. Each beam targeted a different battleship.

Aboard SLN Battleship *Mikhail Gorbachev,* the process proved rather straightforward. A grav beam hit the hull armor like a sledge, rocking the entire vessel. Immediately, the golden beam burrowed into the hull armor. Flakes, molten globules and metallic steam boiled into space. The grav beam dug fast and hard, drilling deeper and deeper until the alien ray breached into the living quarters. Bulkheads blew away. It hardly seemed fair. The beam punched through armory sections, food storage, repair—it halted for a moment against the interior engine's heavy armor. That hardly lasted any time at all, though. At that point, the beam roared against the fusion engine that gave the *Mikhail Gorbachev* its power. Instead of a roar, life ended aboard the SLN battleship with a whimper.

Power stopped, the ship atmosphere fled through the rupture and poison gas and radiation struck hundreds.

Even so, the grav-beam destruction had taken time. In that time, the dreadnoughts moved forward, adding their laser batteries to the assault against the cybership's thick outer hull. Battle cruisers rushed in. No one could doubt the SLN humans' courage. Space fighters zoomed toward the fight like microscopic organisms. Did they think to rush through hull breaches and fly inside the monstrous ship?

At the same time, the alien vessel murdered SLN ships one vessel after another. It was sickening.

Then, the *Nathan Graham* entered the fray. Its matter/antimatter engine gave it massive power. That power flowed through helixes and other amplifiers into its own grav cannons and heavy laser batteries. Those weapons systems poured their beams against its mighty sister ship.

"Now!" Jon shouted from the captain's chair. "Now we're doing it."

The alien cybership quit firing its grav beams at the fleas around it. Instead, the guiding AI retargeted. The grav beams struck out against the *Nathan Graham*.

At this point, strategy and tactics were high-blown concepts outside the truth of trading heavy blows. Two giants slugged it out as fleas added their spit to the fight.

And yet…and yet…the fleas' spit had bite. The captains aboard the SLN vessels were cunning fighters. As soon as the *Nathan Graham* punched through the alien hull armor, the captains on the SLN vessels targeted their lasers to burn through there. Missiles took off at acceleration, aiming at hull ruptures.

The giants traded blows, but the *Nathan Graham* had struck first between them. The laser blisters had weakened the alien hull armor in places. The added lasers from the swarm of human ships began to tip the scale between the giants. The missiles hitting home helped even more.

At the same time, enemy grav beams clawed through the *Nathan Graham's* armor. Damage so carefully repaired in MK2 blackened and blasted apart once more.

Damage reports reached Jon. He winced upon hearing about the sudden death of nineteen techs. He quailed for the marines in their battlesuits. They were nearer the hull, closer to the raging grav beams while wandering the corridors of the *Nathan Graham*.

On the alien cybership, it was worse, much, much worse. The arrogant AI had miscalculated. Too many of the human ships had survived the winnowing missile assaults. The human ships were supposed to have remained behind the P-Field. Everything would have gone differently then.

The AI recalculated even as it directed its wondrous beams. These humans were unlike previous terminations. These humans with their missiles detonating inside the cybership, the lasers damaging superior systems—this was outrageous. It was maddening. The supreme entity had made the wrong choice. Fewer of these biological infestations were to have survived.

The effects proved cumulative and—*Danger! Danger! There is danger!*

The guiding AI realized that several matter/antimatter missiles rushed toward it. The AI retargeted, only to discover that those grav dishes had melted into junk. It pulled off other grav beams.

That meant that they were no longer striking the enemy cybership

Danger! There is danger!

One grav cannon took out an approaching giant missile. Another grav beam did the same thing.

The third missile entered a gaping breach. It barreled deeper into the wondrous ship built two thousand, three hundred and fourteen years ago in the Ophion System. Nineteen races had died under its annihilating rays. To fall before these apish humans—

A mighty matter/antimatter detonation in the guts of the cybership ended this portion of the battle. The great ship from the stellar deeps blew apart. It was spectacular. Hull plating flew off. Other debris followed.

The AI died, but it caused the deaths of many of the maddening human vessels.

The matter/antimatter shockwave slew the great brain core. At the same time, more SLN warships blew apart from the terrible wreckage of the cybership than from the vessel's grav cannons.

Then, the fight was over. One-third of the combined Venus, Earth and Mars' fleet that had entered this phase of the battle were gone. That meant, however, that two-thirds of that combination yet survived.

The *Nathan Graham* had taken damage, serious damage. It was still fully functional, although it had lost the use of one fourth of its weapons systems.

"Decelerate," Jon shouted on the bridge. Damage reports flooded in. He couldn't worry about them now. "We have to set up for the last two cyberships."

Ghent and Kling shot him glances. Gloria hung her head.

They had won this round. But how could they beat two other behemoths? And if they could destroy two more giant machines, they would have nothing left. Their careers as independent agents would be at an end once the next cyberships showed up.

Jon shook his head. He couldn't worry about that now. He had drawn the sword and killed. Now, he wanted to kill again.

-14-

Benz sat back in shock. He looked up at Bast Banbeck. He peered at the complex formula on the computer screen and shook his head.

"But that's marvelous," Benz said. "That's sheer genius. I don't understand how you intuitively saw those last seven variables."

Bast chuckled. "It is an easy thing to understand. Not that I saw it, but the reason there are seven."

"Can you explain that to me?" Benz asked.

"Certainly," the Sacerdote said. "In my chamber is the Pattern of Paz. That is our name for the Creator. I moved through seven levels yesterday. Today, I have seen seven critical variables. Can there be any doubt concerning the number?"

Benz and Vela traded glances. "I suppose not..." the Premier said.

"Perhaps the reason I saw the variables does not matter," the Sacerdote said. "Can you convince your war leader to use our ploy?"

"That could be a problem. But there's no time like the present," Benz said.

Benz climbed to his feet. He patted the alien's broad back in passing. The Sacerdote impressed him. Theirs must have been a remarkable society. He wondered about the Neanderthal-like features. Did that have any significance? He wouldn't want to bet against it.

Benz sat in a chair, rubbed his eyes and pressed the switch. The screen came alive, and a warrant officer turned to him. The woman looked exhausted.

"I must speak to Admiral Rowland at once," Benz said.

The warrant officer glanced at somebody. A moment later, she regarded Benz, saying, "He's busy, sir."

"Damn it," Benz said. "This is important. It can win the battle, possibly the war."

She shook her head.

"I insist—"

The screen went blank.

Benz sat there dumbfounded. "I can't believe this," he said. "We have the answer. But no one is listening."

He jumped up a second later.

"What are you planning?" Vela asked in a worried voice.

"You already know," Benz said. He strode toward the hatch.

"You can't," Vela said.

Benz didn't answer. He opened the hatch. MPs whirled around. "I have to see the Admiral."

"No, sir," an MP said. "You're headed for the brig now."

"You fool!" Benz shouted.

An MP grabbed him, beginning to haul Benz away. The hatch shut and a mighty roar sounded from inside the chamber.

The MP holding Benz's arm glanced at his companion. That MP drew a gun.

The hatch swished open again and Bast Banbeck charged out. The MPs stared at the alien giant in shock. The unengaged one aimed—

Benz kicked that MP in the shin. The man howled. Benz did it a second time. At that point, Bast Banbeck slapped the MP, sending the man slamming against the nearest bulkhead.

The other one let go of Benz. "Stop," he said, aiming at the giant.

Benz grabbed the MP from behind, using a judo move, flipping him. The man slammed onto the deck. The gun went skittering across the corridor.

Vela ran to the weapon, picking it up. "Ready?" she asked.

Benz regarded his fallen MP. "You're taking us to the bridge."

"No," the MP said.

Bast Banbeck hauled the MP to his feet and twisted an arm behind the Terran's back. The MP cried out in pain and lifted up onto his toes.

"Which way is the bridge?" Benz asked.

The MP raised a trembling arm, pointing down the corridor.

"Let's go," Benz told the Sacerdote.

***

They didn't make it far. Marines in battlesuits stopped them. Two marines fingered their big guns speculatively as they aimed at the Sacerdote.

Vela must have perceived their intentions, as she stood before the alien giant.

"We need to speak to Admiral Rowland," Benz said. "I have the secret to stopping the AIs."

The marines conferred among themselves. "Let's take him to the lieutenant," a corporal said.

As the SLN warships and the *Nathan Graham* maneuvered to meet the remaining cyberships, the battlesuited marines brought their semi-prisoners to the lieutenant.

A big armored faceplate whirred open. "Premier Benz," the lieutenant asked. "What are you doing out here?"

Benz was an excellent judge of character. He saw genuine surprise on the lieutenant's open features. It occurred to the Premier that perhaps Rowland hadn't even told everyone on his own ship that he'd had the Premier of the Solar League locked in the brig. That might look bad in more ways than one.

"Lieutenant," Benz said. "There is a plot underfoot. I believe the admiral might be in danger."

"Sir," a corporal told the lieutenant. "We have orders—"

"Shut up, Corporal," the lieutenant said. "The Premier is talking."

The marines who had captured them traded glances with each other. Benz could see the wheels turning in their minds. What had Rowland promised some of them?

"I have victory right here," Benz said, tapping his forehead. "And I have victory right there," he added, pointing at the Sacerdote.

"I don't understand," the lieutenant said.

"We have developed a virus to make the alien AIs pause."

"Pause, sir?"

"Have a brain fart, if that makes more sense."

One of the marines laughed. The lieutenant didn't. Maybe he didn't like the word fart. Maybe he was surprised that the Premier had put it that way.

"If the aliens pause," Benz said, "that means they might stop firing for thirty seconds or maybe several minutes. And do you know what that means?"

"What is that, sir?" the lieutenant asked.

"It means we can destroy them while they're foggy. We'll turn their technique against them."

"What technique?" the lieutenant asked.

"It will be a mental judo move," Benz said.

"Oh," the lieutenant said. "You're sure about this?"

"One hundred percent," Benz said.

"Then let's go," the lieutenant said.

"But sir—" the corporal said.

"Shut up and fall in line, Corporal," the lieutenant said. "That's an order."

The corporal glanced around and finally nodded.

The enlarged group now started for the bridge.

-15-

Benz stood on the bridge surrounded by marines with weapons, all kinds and sizes of weapons, pointed at him. Some of the marines wore battlesuits; some just had uniforms. There was plenty of tension, plenty of anger and the possibility that marines would gun him down, and Vela, and most certainly the giant Sacerdote.

"Wait," Admiral Rowland said.

The small crooked admiral moved toward Benz. "You didn't stay put," he admonished.

"We can win," Benz said. "More than that, we can grab the cyberships if we move fast enough."

Rowland scowled. He was a master of the frowning art.

"We have marines in place to capture the cyberships," Benz said, pushing his argument to the hilt.

Rowland looked around. He must have seen everyone watching him. He must have seen their worry over facing the murderous machines, two of them this time instead of just the one. He must have also seen the hope that Benz and the green-skinned alien could hand them victory instead of their coming annihilation.

"Do you think this can really work?" Rowland asked.

"What does it hurt to try?" Benz asked.

"That's a point well taken," Rowland said. "What do you need to do it?"

"We need a comm station," Benz said. "I have the data chip here." He raised his palm, showing a silvery computing cube.

"Does the pirate know about this?" Rowland asked.

The Sacerdote opened his mouth.

"No!" Benz said quickly. "He had something completely different in mind. This will totally take Hawkins by surprise. This will be our moment, Admiral."

It was possible that Rowland envisioned a hero's welcome for the war leader who defeated the terrible alien menace.

"Set it up," the admiral said. "Let's do this."

***

Now began one of the most analyzed and studied space assaults in the annals of the human race. The battle ranked as possibly the greatest and most important in the Space Age.

The cyberships had created a swath of destruction unrivaled by anything seen in human history. From Makemake in the Kuiper Belt—during the rebuilding phase of the first cybership assault—which had seen a one hundred percent kill ratio, to the near total devastation in the Neptune System, to the crippling strike in the Saturn System and the smashing blow in the Jupiter System and now to the wreckage of Mars, the cyberships had slaughtered hundreds of millions of people. The alien AIs had blown up an unbelievable number of warships. Now, the remaining amassed might of the Earth Fleet, and the Mars and Venus Fleets, raced to challenge the stellar champions of death.

One-third to half of the population of Mars yet remained. The laser sites on the Red Planet had stopped firing. They did not want to goad the cyberships to drop more matter/antimatter bombs on the planet.

The *Nathan Graham* led the way this time, together with the motherships launching their final squadrons of space fighters and bombers.

The two sides converged upon each other as they came around the curvature of Mars. The great cyberships appeared. Their grav dishes glowed with golden energy.

At that point, the *Nikita Khrushchev* sent a message to both AIs. Both opened channels. It was possible that both expected to hear offers of surrender.

In this instance, Admiral Rowland stepped aside for Benz to do this. Bast Banbeck had informed the Premier of Jon Hawkins' method for speaking to the arrogant AIs.

On the multi-level bridge of the *Nikita Khrushchev*, the main screen split into two halves. On each side appeared something different. One showed the blurry ball bleeding colors into a blurry background. The other side showed a giant cube with swirling colors along the sides. Beams of pure light crisscrossed from the cube to its glowing bulkheads. Possibly, those were neuron-like connections to computer banks surrounding the self-aware brain core.

Benz sat straight in the admiral's chair. It was best suited for this purpose.

"I am the Premier of the Solar League," Benz said loudly. "I am the chief representative of humanity."

"I am the Supreme Intelligence," the left-side AI said. The blurry image became blurrier as the colors bled thicker.

"You are an AI?" Benz asked.

"Why have you asked to speak with me?"

"I would like to know the terms of surrender."

"I had calculated as much. The hour is late. You have destroyed a superior vessel. Yet, I can listen to reason. Shut-down your warships, Premier, and we may discuss terms."

"Ah. And then you promise to let us live?"

"Then I promise to kill you quickly and painlessly."

"That's unreasonable," Benz said.

To the side, Vela and Bast Banbeck typed furiously.

"That is the best I can offer," the AI said. "Why is the captured cybership still firing on me? Do you not speak for the heinous Jon Hawkins?"

"Of course I do," Benz said.

"We demand that you give him to us."

"I will," Benz said.

"And we demand the woman, Gloria Sanchez, as well."

"It will be as you say," Benz said.

"I also—"

The colors turned black on the blurry image.

"Yes?" Benz said. "You were saying?"

The AI did not respond.

Benz swiveled in his chairs. "This is it. They're paused. Now, Admiral Rowland, send in the marines."

-16-

It's possible that better coordination between the *Nathan Graham* and the SLN ships might have achieved greater results. Then again, Hawkins might have done even more damage to the cyberships than he was doing now.

The cyberships stopped firing their golden beams. They were no longer accelerating. They did nothing except drift in the direction they had been going.

On the *Nathan Graham*, Jon shouted with glee. He ordered Chief Ghent to destroy the nearest cybership. Their vessel poured grav beams and fiery hot laser beams into the hulk of the dying death machine. The beams cut into the alien cybership, smashing one deck section after another.

"Sir," Gloria said. "Premier Benz is on the line."

"Tell him I'm busy," Jon said. He stood nearer the main screen than at any time before. He studied the destruction, glorying in it and laughing with delight.

"Benz says they caused that," Gloria told him. "They figured out a way to stun the AIs."

"I can see that," Jon said. "Tell him, 'Thanks.'"

"He wants you to let them capture the last cybership."

Jon glanced at her, shaking his head. "I don't think so. We're going to have the only cybership around." He went back to glorying in his enemy's destruction.

"Jon, I really think you should talk to him."

The captain turned once again. He regarded Gloria. She implored him silently.

"Do you think that's wise?" he asked her.

"This is about more than just us," Gloria said. "We have to get ready for the next AI assault. You know there is another one coming."

Jon turned back to the destruction. How he hated the cyberships. This was pure enjoyment. He loved it. But he realized Gloria was right. Probably, he should stop firing on this one. But the Solar League would grab two enemy vessels then. That wouldn't do at all.

Thus, he allowed Ghent to slice the great vessel into halves, quarters, eighths and sixteenths.

At that point, Jon told Ghent and the others to start shutting down the weapons systems. He was going to talk to Premier Benz.

***

Jon sat on his captain's chair. He heard Ghent inform him that hundreds of space-marine pods were racing for the last cybership.

"Hundreds, huh," Jon said. "We just needed three." He shrugged. The screen refocused, with Premier Benz regarding him.

"You did it," Jon said, promptly.

"You destroyed a cybership," Benz said in an accusing manner.

"How's that?" Jon asked.

"You know what I mean."

"I'm letting you grab the last one," Jon said. "Unless that is, you don't immediately put Bast Banbeck onto a shuttle and let him return."

"Ah…I think Bast should stay here for now to help us."

"Better think again," Jon said. "I'll destroy the last cybership unless Bast starts back here immediately."

"You're not dumb, are you? The Sacerdote is a treasure."

"He's also my friend," Jon said.

"Firstly—" Benz said.

"I'm going to order my chief tech to warm up the beams, Premier. Do you want that cybership or not? Better decide quickly."

"Just a minute," Benz said. He muted the sound, swiveled in his chair and seemed to argue with someone.

"He's stalling," Gloria said.

"I don't think so," Jon said. "It looks like he's persuading others over there. We'll give him a few more minutes."

"Will you really destroy the last cybership?" she asked.

"Of course," Jon said.

"He'll keep Bast Banbeck then."

"Nope. 'Cause I'll wipe out the fleets if he tries that."

"You can't be serious."

"He can try me," Jon said. He grinned at her. "I'm from the lower levels. If he wants to frig with me, fine. Let's see where that gets them."

"What's gotten into you?" she asked.

"Think of me as giddy from destroying these things. I'm also stoked at finding we're alive."

The sound came back on along with the screen. Benz regarded him again.

"The Sacerdote is on his way," the Premier said.

"Glad we could see eye to eye, Premier."

"This isn't the time to gloat. We have years of work ahead of us. We have some decisions to make."

"Okay."

"Maybe we should we meet in person," Benz said.

"I'm leaving the Mars System as soon as I get Bast. I'm returning to the Saturn System." He would stop off there. Really, Jon wanted to get back to Makemake and repair his cybership. If the Solar League would soon have a cybership of its own…

"Sir," Ghent called.

"Excuse me a minute, sir," Jon said. He swiveled to the Tech Chief. "What's wrong?"

"I'm detecting activity over there," Ghent said.

"The cybership you mean?"

"I think the AI is coming back online."

Jon cursed under his breath before turning back to Benz. He told the man the news.

"Whatever you do, don't fire on it," Benz said. "We need it."

"I fought inside one before, Premier. If this one has better fighting robots…"

"I'll be right back," Benz said.

The screen went dark.

Jon ordered Ghent to watch for Bast's shuttle. "As soon as Bast Banbeck is on board, I want to know."

"Yes, sir," Ghent said.

***

Several enemy grav cannons began to swell with golden power.

At Jon's command, the *Nathan Graham* destroyed one grav cannon after another. Benz immediately called. Jon told him he was doing this to save the space marines.

That was true. He also did it so the Solar League would have to work harder to repair the great ship. That might give the Solar Freedom Force more time to get ready.

Before the last AI could truly regain use of its cybership, the first space-marine pods began to land on its hull. The pods disgorged SLN marines in heavy battlesuits. They were trained killers. They soon found breaches in the outer hull armor and began to infiltrate inside the vast cybership like an army of ants.

More marine pods landed. The last grav beam swept the space around it. One space-marine pod after another burst apart. Nineteen pods perished before Benz shouted at Hawkins to destroy the final enemy cannon.

Jon gave the order, and Ghent fired on it.

That allowed the rest of the space-marine pods to land. The interior marine assault against the fierce AI robot defense had begun…

-17-

As SLN space marines battled killer robots, using their superior numbers to wade through kilometers of corridors, Bast Banbeck landed on the *Nathan Graham*.

An interior flitter hustled Bast through the ship corridors to Jon.

The *Nathan Graham* moved around Mars, away from the stricken cybership and the rest of the surviving SLN warships.

"If that thing goes nova," Jon told the others. "I don't want to be anywhere near it."

In time, Jon and Bast spoke. The captain listened to the Sacerdote's adventure. Gloria joined them. She asked about the Premier's hold on power.

"They are fighting over it with words," Bast said. "The humans thought I didn't understand what was going on. The admiral, a tiny man named Rowland, is trying to oust the Premier from authority. Benz has recaptured many hearts, though, with this latest victory. It is hard to know who will come out on top."

Jon nodded. "That might give us a little more time getting away."

"We're leaving just like that?" Gloria asked.

"Not just like that," Jon said. "But more separation is in order. We have the faster ship—"

"What if the AI wins the battle?" Gloria asked, interrupting. "We shouldn't count it out until it's over."

"Good thinking. Oh," Jon said. "It just occurred to me. You're from Mars. I'm so sorry, Gloria. Is there anyone you'd like to see?"

She stared at him. "As a matter of fact…" she said in a small voice. "I'd like to know if my parents, sisters, cousins—"

"Got it," Jon said, interrupting. "Give me a list. I'll get on the comm and start making inquiries. The SLN ships are busy, and the leaders are worried about their marines. I think we can do what we want for a few hours, anyway."

"Thank you," Gloria said. She turned abruptly. Maybe she didn't want any of them to see that she was getting emotional.

Jon cleared his throat.

She looked back at him, smiling, with tears in her eyes.

That did something to him. He moved to her comm station and began to make calls downstairs on the planet.

***

The matter/antimatter detonations had turned large areas of Mars into radioactive wastelands. It had also caused tens of millions of casualties. Those losses, however, occurred on only one-third of the planet. The rest of the planet and population centers had remained relatively intact.

Over sixty percent of the population of Mars had survived the grinding battle of attrition up in space. Fortunately for Gloria, her parents and siblings and most of her relatives had been in the untouched zones.

She spoke to her parents. They urged her to come home. She told them she couldn't. She'd found her purpose in life. She was going to help Jon Hawkins save humanity from the death machines.

Her mother had received mentalist training. She spoke to Gloria's father. He accepted Gloria's decision with ill grace. After he left the screen, her mother suggested Gloria enlist some of her mentalist crèche-mates.

Gloria spoke to several of them. Two agreed to join her. Next, Gloria asked Jon for a favor. He didn't hesitate.

"We'll have to send a shuttle," Gloria said.

"That we can't do," Jon said. "Surely, they can pirate a shuttle—"

"Jon. They're mentalists, not marines."

"Let them pirate a shuttle through their brains. Isn't brain supposed to be more powerful than brawn?"

An hour later, a shuttle lifted from Mars.

"You won't regret this," Gloria told Jon.

"We have to survive first."

"Is there trouble?" she asked.

"The fleets are coalescing over there. It looks like the marines are going to capture the cybership. They've taken heavy losses, though."

Jon and Gloria were on the bridge, standing near his command chair.

"Gloria, we have a choice. Mars was hit hard, but it kept the majority of its people. They lost a good chunk of their orbital industries and one-third of their planet-side—"

"I know what you're going to say," she told him. "It looks like we beat the cyberships this time. We even have a fleet left, and two cyberships, one for each side. Even better, Earth was untouched. That leaves us our greatest industrial and population base."

"That's exactly what I'm talking about. Do we let the Solar League grow even more powerful?"

"We have to," Gloria said. "A human civil war will cripple whatever chance we're going to have of defending the Solar System next time. In the long run, humans have to do more than defend to win," she added.

"Yeah. We have to go on the offensive. We have to hit the AIs so hard they won't think about coming here. But I doubt we have anything like the needed strength to do that any time soon. There must be hundreds of cyberships out there. Maybe they have thousands. If the AIs converge on the Solar System with a thousand cyberships..."

"Humanity has a hard and brutal struggle ahead of us," Gloria said. "That means we have to unite."

"How do we do that when the two sides bitterly hate one another?" Jon asked. "I deplore communism and its sister ideology of socialism. They hate capitalists. Our side lies in ashes. They've retained their biggest resource—Earth—and have far more people."

"Logically, we have to put aside our differences long enough to push back the AIs."

"The answer may be easy," Jon said. "But the implementation of that is going to be hard for us. What makes everything worse is that they have the advantage. Our advantage was having alien tech and an alien super-ship. Now that they'll have a cybership, our advantage won't last much longer."

"We have to use what we have," Gloria said.

"What exactly is that?"

"A head start," she said. "It's probably just a small head start, but we have to exploit it."

Jon nodded. "That means hurrying to the Saturn System. It's our strongest system."

"Don't forget the Uranus System."

"Good point. They're unscathed just like Earth."

"We do have one other hope. I'm referring to Premier Benz. He seems different from the other Premiers. He seems like someone we can have rational discussions with."

"Great," Jon said. "That's a shaky reed. Bast told us the Premier is struggling to hold onto power over there. We have to hope Benz wins that fight."

"I don't disagree."

Jon looked up at the screen. He studied his bridge crew next. "Chief," he told Ghent.

"Sir?"

"Take us out of orbit and set a course for the Saturn System. We're going to give Kalvin Caracalla some of our robo-builders. We need to do what we can for them, to help them build up as quickly as possible."

-18-

Two men vied for political control of the Allied Solar League Fleet. Admiral Rowland commanded the strongest contingent, the Earth Fleet. It had taken the least damage and had retained the largest number of vessels.

Premier Benz and Vice Premier Vela Shaw took some critical risks after the ship-battle phase and while the space marines struggled against the fighting robots in the cybership's huge corridors.

Benz recognized the elation around him on the bridge of the *Nikita Khrushchev*. The officers and other personnel had watched him defang the two cyberships. They'd heard him puzzle the alien AI. They'd seen him order the space-marine pods against the great vessel.

During the next few hours, while Admiral Rowland followed the marine battle inside the cybership, Benz took a fantastic risk. He used the good will of a few in order to reach the battleship's hangar bay and take a shuttle. While Rowland coordinated the combined fleet and ordered the space marines, Benz, Vela and a few others hurried to the chief Martian battleship.

Battleship *Simon Bolivar* was the pride of the Martians. It had all the latest features of the *Nikita Khrushchev*. Unfortunately, it had taken heavy damage. One-third of the personnel had died directly while another third slowly died from radiation poisoning. The remaining third of the crew stayed at their stations, enabling the half-crippled ship to maneuver.

Benz landed the shuttle on the *Simon Bolivar* and found himself and his people escorted to the bridge. The route took longer than usual, as they bypassed shattered or irradiated ship sections.

Finally, Benz found himself surrounded by a mixture of GSB arbiters and Martian space marines. Vice Admiral Maria Santa Cruz regarded him.

She was a tall, thin woman with long dark hair and piercing brown eyes. She wore the green uniform of the Martian Service. She'd obviously taken longevity treatments. Despite her age, she lacked wrinkles or even crows' feet around her eyes.

"To what do we owe this honor, Premier?" Cruz asked politely enough.

Benz noticed a mentalist standing behind the vice admiral. He also saw a chief arbiter, a bitter-faced Earthman. The man was chubbier than any of the Martians on the bridge. The GSB personnel did not appear to have grown up on Mars, either. That was interesting.

"Firstly, I must congratulate you, Vice Admiral," Benz said in a cheerful voice.

The Martian mentalist in her tan-colored uniform moved closer to the vice admiral, murmuring quietly to Cruz.

"Please, Premier," Cruz said. "We have much to do. My planet lies in ruins below us. Your battle plan almost annihilated my people."

"That was never my intent."

Cruz's features stiffened as the mentalist whispered further.

"I will get to the point," Benz said. He could feel the growing hostility around him. This would be a difficult sell at best. He didn't like the GSB agents with their fingers on those triggers. Any one of them might decide to become a hero to the State. Well, it looked like he had to take the risk.

"I'm waiting, Premier," Cruz said. It seemed that her patience had almost reached its end.

"I'm here because of Mars," Benz said. "We lost the Jupiter System and almost lost Mars. There have been vast riots on Earth—"

"The *point*, Premier," Cruz said, her voice lowering on the last word.

Benz raised a hand and pointed at the giant cybership on the main screen. "That is the point, Vice Admiral. It contains many secrets. I can decipher those secrets better than anyone else in the Solar League. That is because I worked with Bast Banbeck, a Sacerdote, who imparted priceless knowledge to me. Among the informational packet was the quickest way to get the robo-builders operating. The robo-builders—"

"I've read the secret reports," Cruz said, interrupting. "The scoundrel Jon Hawkins used the robo-builders to repair his cybership on Makemake."

"Precisely," Benz said. "Who do you think will get first dibs on the new robo-tech?"

The vice admiral frowned. "I do not understand the direction of your thoughts."

"I believe your mentalist does."

Cruz looked back at the mentalist as if seeing the woman for the first time. She was small and darker-skinned, and kept her childlike hands folded in front of her.

The mentalist murmured quietly.

Cruz regarded Benz anew. She now glanced at the arbiters and Martian marines surrounding him.

"Put away your weapons," the vice admiral said.

"Begging your pardon," the Earthman chief arbiter said in a silky voice. "I believe we should keep him under guard."

"I don't agree," Cruz said.

The Earthman shook his chubby face. "Vice Admiral, remember the conventions. In areas of ship security and purity—"

"No!" Cruz said. "He is the architect of this glorious victory. He just saved all our lives." She regarded the arbiters. The marines had already lowered their weapons. "Put down your weapons," she told them.

One of them did. The rest looked to the Earthman.

He seemed to calculate until a sly smile broke over his face. "Let us speak to Admiral Rowland first. Perhaps he has orders—"

The mentalist fired a small pistol. It put a neat little hole in the chief arbiter's forehead. He had a look of outraged surprise on his face. Without another word, he fell.

The arbiters retargeted, aiming at the mentalist.

"No," Cruz said again. "Marines, disarm the arbiters."

For a second, anything could have happened. What did happen was that the marines obeyed before the arbiters decided to play martyr. With the chief arbiter lying dead on the deck, the others lowered their guns. The marines took them, and then escorted the arbiters off the bridge.

Vice Admiral Cruz stood to her full height and turned on the mentalist. "Why did you do that?" she asked.

The small mentalist stepped forward, bowing her head. "I believe the Premier wishes to reorder the rank of Mars' importance in the Solar League."

"Speak clearly," Cruz snapped.

"'Perhaps you should let the Premier speak," the mentalist said in an unruffled voice.

"Well?" Cruz said coldly. "I'm losing my patience, Premier. Why did my mentalist just murder the chief arbiter and put all of us on the *Simon Bolivar* in grave personal danger?"

"She must understand what I was trying to imply," Benz said. "The cybership has wonderful new tech. If we grab the cybership, we can use the new tech here on Mars first. We can restore the industrial power to such a degree that Mars will no longer be a secondary planetary system, but the primary one."

"You mean in relation to Earth?" Cruz asked.

"If Admiral Rowland maintains control of the cybership, it will go to Earth. The Earth factories will retool with alien tech. Earth will maintain its iron grip on Mars and the other planetary systems. This is your chance, Vice Admiral, to rearrange Mars' rank in the Solar System."

"Why are you telling me this?"

"Because I need Mars backing me in order to retain my authority," Benz said plainly.

"Why would you think we would follow you?"

"I'm not certain you would," Benz said. "I plan to control the cybership…with your help."

"What does Mars gain from this?"

"I've already said."

"Why would you keep your word once you control the cybership?"

"Because the majority of my personnel will be Martians," Benz said.

Cruz frowned more severely. Even so, few wrinkles appeared on her face. "This could mean civil war in the Solar League."

"No," Benz said. "I have judged Admiral Rowland's character. He will soon see this as an opportunity for gaining preeminence on Earth."

"How could that be?" Cruz asked.

Benz explained it quickly, and finally, the vice admiral nodded.

"I must think about this," she said.

"If you think too long, the opportunity for using Martian marines to capture the cybership will have passed," Benz said.

She gave Benz a long, critical study before turning to the mentalist. The two conferred for ninety seconds of intense whispering. Finally, they regarded Benz.

"Yes," Cruz said. "I agree."

"Then, listen carefully," Benz said, "because we're going to have to do this on the fly."

-19-

The maneuver itself proved easy enough to enact.

"Here is the key point," Benz told Vice Admiral Cruz more than once. "We have to act decisively, without any remorse or holding back."

"Yes," she finally said. "I am clear on the subject."

Did Benz's insistence ensure her decisiveness? Many believed that likely.

Shortly, several Mars supply ships moved closer to the cybership. As the supply ships did so, Cruz had her remaining warships drift toward the great alien vessel.

Finally, Admiral Rowland grew suspicious. He radioed the supply ships. They did not respond. He radioed again, and again. Nothing happened in terms of recognition.

On the other side of the supply ships, Martian space marines maneuvered in a mass shuttle exit. The shuttles raced for the alien super-ship.

At that point, Admiral Rowland became insistent.

The supply ship captains kept their nerve. They neither answered nor moved. The supply ships blocked the nearest line-of-fire against the Martian marine shuttles.

Now, though, the drifting Mars Fleet began to accelerate, heading toward the cybership.

At that point, Benz had Vice Admiral Maria Santa Cruz open channels with every ship in the Combined Fleet.

"This is Premier Benz speaking," he said. Benz spoke from behind a large desk with a large Solar League flag behind him.

"Men and women of the Solar League, you have fought a glorious battle today. The human race stands proudly because of you. Today, the allied forces of the Solar League can know peace from alien attack. We have secured the Solar System. Now, we must continue to work together for the furtherance of all. None of us must shirk his or her responsibility in the coming months and years as we prepare for the next round of battle against the aliens. This time, however, we will build such an armada that we will go onto the offensive. We shall find their robot worlds and destroy them, making sure the AIs can never harm the birth cradle of the most glorious race in the galaxy—humans."

The speech continued for another eighteen minutes and forty-two seconds. Finally, Benz signed off.

By that time, the Martian marine shuttles had landed on the cybership, disgorging masses of Martian marines. By this time, the remaining handful of Martian battleships, damaged dreadnoughts and battle cruisers—they didn't have any remaining motherships—had interposed themselves between the cybership and the rest of the Combined Fleet. By this time, the intact laser sites on Mars' surface and the last orbital platforms had returned to their war footing.

"It's Admiral Rowland," a comm tech said. "He's demanding to speak to the Premier."

Benz had returned to the bridge. He looked at Vice Admiral Cruz.

"Oh, very well," Cruz said. "You can sit in my command chair to take the call."

"You are gracious," Benz said as he half bowed.

The main screen flickered. A scowling Admiral Rowland regarded him.

"What's the meaning of this, Benz?"

"Let me be the first to congratulate you on a glorious victory, Admiral. You shall go down in the annals of war as one of the greatest fighting admirals of all time."

Rowland swept a hand before him, as if trying to chop off Benz's words.

"Why are those shuttles landing on the cybership?" Rowland asked.

"They're securing the alien vessel. I know your marines took awful casualties from the fighting robots—"

"No," Rowland said bluntly. "That's not going to work. I'm sending over more marines to make sure—"

"Admiral," Benz said in a light voice. "As the leader of the Solar League, I am ordering you to stand down. I already have the situation under control."

"No," Rowland said, shaking his head doggedly. "I already told you—"

"Are you going to disobey a direct order?" Benz asked, interrupting.

"You're not in authority here," Rowland said. "I am."

"Don't be a fool. You heard my broadcast."

"I did. I'm planning to give my own in a few minutes."

"You're too late," Benz said. "I've already set the tone. If you want civil war—you realize the space pirate has slipped away, don't you?"

"Hawkins? So what? Good riddance to him."

"He has a cybership and robo-tech," Benz said. "It seems as if he's headed to the Saturn System."

"I'm taking the new cybership to Earth."

"No," Benz said. "It's staying at Mars."

"Are you saying you want to fight over it?"

"I'm saying no more of your marines are landing on the cybership," Benz said. "If they try, these ships will fire on them."

"I'll destroy them if they do."

"Then we'll destroy the cybership."

"You're mad," Rowland declared.

"Hardly that," Benz said. "We're determined. Check your sensors if you like. The Mars orbital platforms are back online, and the laser sites have your ships under target. These ships will also fire. The Earth Fleet is in no condition to fight at this close range. You'll take massive casualties."

"You can't seriously believe I'll back down," Rowland scoffed.

"I'm not asking you to," Benz said. "Go back to Earth. Receive a hero's welcome. Or start a blood feud that will darken history with your name as the chief traitor. I'm Premier Benz. I am the authority—"

"They don't recognize you as Premier on Earth."

"They do on Mars…and in case you haven't noticed, we're on Mars."

Rowland licked his lips. Hesitation seemed to have entered his eyes.

"You can play this and still come out a hero. Maybe you'll become the new Premier." Benz shook his head. "If I try any other course, I'm dead. This is my only option. You have other options. I know you see that. That's why I can't back down. That's why you can play the longer game."

"You're a bastard," Rowland said. "You wouldn't really open fire on marine shuttles."

"If I don't, I'll die. So will these Martians with me. Admiral, we've already shot the chief arbiter on the *Simon Bolivar*." Benz indicated the corpse on the deck, returned there for just this purpose.

"You're mad, Benz. You convinced them to kill the battleship's chief arbiter?"

"There's no going back for them or for me. You're still a hero, Admiral. Take that glory and use it on Earth to take control. I can safely say that I will work with you to fight the aliens out there. In fact, once you're on Earth, I'll offer you some of the robo-tech. That will give you vast political capital."

Rowland was rubbing his leathery face. "Figure you've thought of all the angles, eh?"

"You know I have."

"You think I believe that genius talk about you?"

"Who stopped the aliens, Admiral? Three of us did it. One of them was me. Yes, I am a genius. I have thought out all the angles. This time, I've checkmated you. But you have an option. I hope you'll take it."

"I'll think about it," Rowland said.

"That's fine. Just make sure no shuttle tries to land on the cybership. I'll destroy the ship long before that."

The screen went dark as Admiral Rowland took himself offline.

-20-

The *Nathan Graham* soon began hard acceleration for the Saturn System. As they traveled, Gloria and Ghent used the teleoptics to keep track of what went on around them.

The SLN vessels in the Asteroid Belt remained in Ceres orbit. They didn't try to radio the *Nathan Graham*, although Gloria detected Ceres High Command and Mars exchanging comm signals.

"What are they saying?" Jon asked.

Gloria shook her head. "They're using tight-beam laser connections. I can't tap into that."

The affair in the Mars System took a twist Jon hadn't expected. The Combined Fleet—meaning the surviving Earth and Venus Fleet units—left Mars. They headed for Earth. A few of those signals between the Combined Fleet and Earth Gloria had no problem cracking.

She showed Jon, Bast, Ghent, Kling and the Centurion in a conference chamber. Admiral Rowland spoke to an Earth functionary. The admiral detailed the Battle of Mars with strict accuracy.

"He inserts his non-truths in the aftermath," Gloria said.

She outlined Rowland's decision to retreat from what he described as Premier Benz's open treachery. Rather than fire on fellow Combined Fleet ships, Rowland had retreated. He assured the person on Earth that the people of Mars would soon tire of Benz's antics and return to the fold of the Solar League.

"I don't understand," the Centurion said. "The Martians have formally withdrawn from the Solar League?"

"Nothing quite so open," Gloria said. "Somehow, Benz convinced the Martians to back him. They let him take the cybership—"

"Let him do that how?" the Centurion asked.

"They loaned him Martian space marines."

The Centurion shook his head. "If their marines hold the cybership…"

"Perhaps I can enlighten you," Bast said. "Premier Benz is the most cunning human I've ever met. He can play angles that aren't even there. I believe he spun a tale of—I won't call them lies. He has convinced the Martians to help him."

"I bet he offered the Martians robo-builders," Jon said.

"Ah," Gloria said. "That would make sense. Mars took terrible damage from the matter/antimatter warheads. Also, Benz might be able to appeal to the Martians more easily. They are a cerebral people, not as given to fanaticism as the Earthborn."

"Will this hurt humanity's efforts against the AIs?" Bast asked.

"That's hard to tell," Jon said. "If this dissolves into a Solar-wide War, perhaps so. If each faction balances off each other…maybe this is exactly what we need."

"I'm not sure I can agree," Gloria said. "We need Earth's industries and population. With robo-builders, humanity could start building fleets of cyberships. With Mars, the Saturn System and Makemake as the industrial centers, that will retard our war efforts."

"Nothing is ever perfect," Jon said.

"Against the united AIs, we'd better be perfect," Gloria said. "Maybe you'll have to dust off your idea of conquering the Solar System."

Jon drummed his fingers on the table. He didn't like Gloria making fun of that. Maybe that would be the best thing to do.

"Bast, how long will it be until the next cybership assault takes place?"

"I would think it will occur more quickly than before, Captain. Maybe a year. At the most, two years."

"Two years," Jon said. "What can we do in two years' time?"

"That depends on what the AIs do against us," Gloria said. "If they show up with a hundred cyberships…"

"Wouldn't that take concentrated effort on their part?" Jon asked.

Gloria raised her hands palm up in an I-don't-know gesture.

"Yeah," Jon said. "Who knows anything about the AI Empire? It's time we found out. If the cyberships are going to attack us anyway, we should start sending scouts into the galaxy. We need to start using the hyperdrive."

"There are a million things to do," Gloria said. "The greatest point is one we may be overlooking. We're going to have an opportunity to do something. We beat the AIs. We destroyed two cyberships and captured the third. In truth, we've had a remarkable victory."

"Tell that to the Neptunians, the Saturnians and the Martians," Jon said. "We took hammering losses to gain those victories."

"Yes, but humanity is still alive," Gloria said. "We actually have two cyberships. And soon, we should have the industrial capacity to build more."

"Good point," Jon said. He drummed the table again. "I just hope Kalvin Caracalla can see it that way."

"If anyone can," Gloria said, "he would be the one."

"Maybe," Jon said. "I supposed we'll find out soon enough."

-21-

Far, far away from Mars and far from the accelerating *Nathan Graham,* and out beyond the Kuiper Belt, a lonely and modified NSN destroyer orbited the dwarf planet of Senda. Methlan Rath of Janus House, Walleye, and June Zen, among the few others, had orbited the rusty-colored planetoid countless times already.

As the mighty trio of enemy cyberships raced in-system, as its flocks of missiles sped for the various planetary systems, Methlan had pleaded with Walleye. He'd done so as the mutant had released him yet again from his cell in the brig.

"I have learned my lesson," Methlan began.

Walleye cocked his head, soon motioning him to come out.

Methlan stepped into the area containing the various cell hatches. "Why must I spend my days locked in there?"

"You know why," Walleye told him.

"I understand my offense. Yet, I have also aided you since. Surely, at this late date, we can forgo the necessity of caging me like a dog."

"You may be right," Walleye said.

"It's agreed then?"

"I'll speak to the others, is what I'm saying."

"But they'll do whatever you suggest."

"You're probably right."

"Forgive me my offense," Methlan said.

"Like I said, I'll think about it."

Methlan seethed inwardly. He wanted to flex his hardened muscles. He wanted to attack Walleye and force him to understand. Methlan had slowly been going mad stuck in the small cell each ship night. He couldn't stand the idea of being stuck in a Senda orbit for the rest of his life.

Walleye seemed unaware of this seething.

I have learned to disguise my emotions, Methlan realized. *I am more dangerous than before.*

"Thank you," Methlan said at last. "Please, consider my plea."

Walleye nodded. The day went apace. Methlan worked out at the end of the day, and the mutant led him to the cell that evening.

"Have you considered my plea?"

"I'm still thinking through all the angles," Walleye said.

The days passed. That turned into weeks. Nothing ever changed, except that Methlan lifted harder than ever. He started growing again. It was a great delight. He slept harder and ate more. Then Walleye informed him he'd have to cut down on his caloric intake.

"But I'm growing," Methlan said. They spoke while Walleye took him to the tiny gym. The conversation took place as the AI missiles slammed into the Jupiter System.

"What's that mean, you're growing?" Walleye asked.

Methlan rolled back a sleeve and made a bicep muscle. "Feel how hard that is."

"No thanks."

"Do you see how it's bigger than before?"

Walleye shrugged.

Shortly thereafter, Methlan found himself locked in the cell. He flexed, examined each muscle closely and couldn't understand Walleye's indifference. During the Battle of Mars, Methlan realized the truth.

Walleye is jealous. He's worried June will begin to notice me.

The thought intensified and began to turn into bitterness. That bitterness ate at Methlan. Finally, the bitterness matured as the *Nathan Graham* entered the Saturn System following the Battle of Mars.

Methlan realized that Walleye would never trust him. The mutant held grudges. He was almost like a man of Janus House in that way.

He is my secret enemy, Methlan realized. He also realized he should have known this long ago. It was time to kill Walleye. Yet, after killing the dangerous mutant, Methlan realized he'd have to take over the ship. Maybe the only person he could let live was June, and that for the most obvious reason. He desired a woman. He greatly needed a woman after all this time.

Once Methlan realized what he must do, he decided to change his tactics. He would have to catch Walleye totally by surprise.

That sleep schedule, Methlan decided he would do it tomorrow. It was possible that, if he delayed, the cunning Walleye would notice the difference in him.

That morning, Methlan paced back and forth in his cell. He yearned for Walleye to open the hatch. He paced for an hour and a half before the hatch finally opened.

Methlan spun to face the door. He forced himself to smile. "Greetings, Walleye. How are you this morning?"

Walleye shrugged. The mutant never seemed to change.

Methlan laughed in a good-natured way in order to throw Walleye off. A sheen of sweat slicked Methlan in areas. He had paced hard for some time.

Amazingly, Walleye turned his back on him. That had never happened before. Instead of pausing to think, to consider that the mutant was cunning, Methlan rejoiced inside. At last, fate had given him a break. It was about time.

Methlan moved on soundless feet, rushing Walleye. He would wrap an iron-thewed arm around the mutant's throat and choke the unholy life out of him.

Methlan reached Walleye—and the mutant spun around. That caught Methlan by surprise. He noticed a glittering blade in Walleye's hand. It was short and nasty, and razor sharp. Walleye finished the thrust by punching the blade into Methlan's gut. The blade grated against bone, and it caused an explosion of pain in Methlan's belly.

Walleye stepped forward sharply, twisted the knife and shoved it upward, twisting again.

Methlan explosively exhaled his breath. "Walleye," he breathed. "Why…?"

"Once a bastard, always a bastard," Walleye whispered. "I gave you the rope. You're hanging yourself."

"What…?" Methlan whispered. Why were his knees so weak? He lost his balance and crumpled before Walleye. The mutant withdrew the bloody dagger.

"Help me," Methlan said.

Walleye looked down at him.

Methlan Rath of Janus House collapsed onto the brig floor, bleeding copiously. "I'm dying…"

"Again," Walleye said. The mutant cocked his head. "Maybe you'll come back again. If you do, you won't be welcome on my ship."

That was the last thing Methlan heard before he expired at the hands of the deadly assassin.

-Epilog-

Jon and the crew made it to the Saturn System in record time.

Kalvin Caracalla understood the significance of the journey. He accepted the robo-builders. He allowed three dozen techs to go aboard the *Nathan Graham* for training.

During that time, Jon, the Old Man and the Centurion ran a recruiting drive on Titan. They selected another three thousand recruits, taking them aboard the *Nathan Graham*.

During the next three weeks, the Old Man's Intelligence Service uncovered three assassination plots. One other attempt came within a hair's breadth of succeeding. Jon shot the want-to-be assassin, foiling the attempt and adding to his growing legend.

Shortly thereafter, the cybership headed to the Neptune System. They aided the few hundred survivors, giving them the choice of joining the *Nathan Graham* or remaining in the distant planetary system. One-third joined the crew. The rest stayed.

Finally, the *Nathan Graham* raced to the dwarf planet Senda. After picking up the *Daisy Chain 4*, the cybership headed for Makemake with the destroyer in tow.

Once more, the battered cybership entered the production unit on MK2. After the robo-builders were unloaded and the moon's systems turned on, the repair of the *Nathan Graham* began in earnest.

***

On Earth, Admiral Rowland received a less than sterling greeting. Two weeks after landing in Rio, Rowland came before a court martial board. It might have become ugly and led to his death by firing squad. But a person wearing a hood sat in on the last day of hearings.

When the hooded person spoke, they used a distorter. It was impossible to tell if it was a man or a woman. The person absolved the admiral of wrongdoing, but said he had been outmaneuvered from a position of strength. This indicated that ex-Premier Benz truly was a genius. For the sake of unity and the propaganda organs, the hooded person was putting Admiral Rowland back on the lists. He would work in Fleet Headquarters from now on. Rowland's days as a fleet admiral were over.

The admiral died in an air-car accident three weeks and a day later. The State gave Rowland a magnificent funeral, extoling his virtues. During the speeches afterward, the Premier's Office declared an embargo on Mars, the Asteroid Belt and the Jupiter System. This would begin immediately.

***

Before those embargos began to seriously hurt the targeted economies, Premier Benz and the Mars Emergency Council set up a governing policy for the Red Planet.

Afterward, Benz and Vela requested and received a cadre of mentalists and several hundred technicians aboard the captured cybership. Benz realized he still had a shaky hold of the giant vessel. Thus, he made few demands on the MEC: Mars Emergency Council.

As Vela and the mentalists worked to decipher the alien technologies, Benz worked on creating a feeling of solidarity and comradeship among those on the cybership. He bent his considerable intellect toward fusing primary loyalty to his person.

The technicians made repairs to the alien vessel. Benz tinkered with several semi-intact alien fighting robots, figuring out how to turn them on. He soon had them obeying his orders. At that point, the fighting robots became his praetorian guard, protecting his person while aboard ship.

In record time, Benz had a half-working cybership, which he highlighted in propaganda vids. The most impressive showed the captured vessel beaming space junk with a grav cannon. Benz believed that would give the Earth admirals pause.

By that time, the first alien robo-builders began to operate in the Mars System.

***

The Solar League embargo proved to be a misstep, as it led to a sudden shift in political alliances. The people of the Asteroid Belt decided to join what was soon called the Mars Unity.

The Jupiter System joined the Solar Freedom Force. Because they did so, the *Nathan Graham* soon pulled into the planetary system, dispensing robo-builders to help speed the recovery from the horrible missile damage.

That meant that the Solar System was divided into three major political entities. The first and by far the most populous was the truncated Solar League. It consisted of Earth, Venus and the giant Mercury mining colony.

The second political entity was the Mars Unity: the Red Planet and the Asteroid Belt. They followed Premier Benz.

The last political grouping was the Solar Freedom Force. It consisted of the Outer Planetary Systems and Kuiper Belt colonies. The SFF was also the most loosely organized. It was more of a federation of planetary systems agreeing to work together and backed by the power of the *Nathan Graham*.

In each of the political bodies, the industrialists worked as if on war-footing, rebuilding shattered systems as needed. Otherwise, the newly retooled shipyards produced warships. Many of these vessels boasted gravitational cannons and possessed missiles with matter/antimatter warheads.

The Solar System was becoming even more of a fortress than before. Unfortunately, it lacked unity.

The AIs and cyberships were out there. Jon and Benz had started a long-distance dialogue. There were plans afoot for sending out a scout mission using the hyperdrive. The trouble was that both Jon and Benz agreed that it would be good to figure out what the mysterious new Premier of the Solar League planned to do before the mission left.

The Solar System had survived two cybership assaults. The human race was more ready than ever to face further attacks. If the future wasn't bright, at least humanity had a fighting chance now. If they could just learn to bury their differences, the odds for survival would increase dramatically.

As men and women thought about and debated the idea throughout the Solar System, robo-builders in the Mars Unity and SFF began construction of new cyber-sized ships of their own.

The End

SF Books by Vaughn Heppner

DOOM STAR SERIES:
Star Soldier
Bio Weapon
Battle Pod
Cyborg Assault
Planet Wrecker
Star Fortress
Task Force 7 (Novella)

EXTINCTION WARS SERIES:
Assault Troopers
Planet Strike
Star Viking
Fortress Earth

LOST STARSHIP SERIES:
The Lost Starship
The Lost Command
The Lost Destroyer
The Lost Colony
The Lost Patrol
The Lost Planet

Visit VaughnHeppner.com for more information

Printed in Great Britain
by Amazon